FAMILY STORY

Alison Scott Skelton was born and grew up on the eastern seaboard of the United States, and now lives in Inverness-shire, Scotland. She is also the author under the name of her late husband C.L. Skelton of the bestsellers *Hardacre's Luck* and *Beloved Soldiers*.

ALISON SCOTT SKELTON

Family Story

HarperCollins*Publishers*

HarperCollins*Publishers*
77–85 Fulham Palace Road,
Hammersmith, London W6 8JB

This paperback edition 1996

1 3 5 7 9 8 6 4 2

First published in Great Britain by
HarperCollins*Publishers* 1996

First published in the USA by
A Wyatt Book for St Martin's Press 1995

Grateful acknowledgement is given for permission to quote from the
following works: 'The Death of the Hired Man' from *The Poetry of
Robert Service*, edited by Edward Connery Lathem, published in 1969
by Henry Holt and Company, Inc., New York; from *The Valley of the
Assassins*, by Freya Stark, published by John Murray Ltd., London;
from 'And Death Shall Have No Dominion' from *Poems of Dylan
Thomas*, published by David Higham Associates Ltd., London, and
New Directions Publishing Company, New York. Copyright 1943 by
New Directions Publishing Company. Reprinted by permission.

ISBN 0 00 649836 1

Set in Stempel Garamond

Printed and bound in Great Britain by
Caledonian International Book Manufacturing Ltd, Glasgow

For
Henry and Danny,
thank you

And for my dear Adirondack friends,
Anne and Rick Morse

Home is the place where, when you have to go there,
They have to take you in.

–ROBERT FROST

Family Story

Annie

A TALL, STOOPED white man with dirty hair and a dark plaid jacket got on the subway at Forty-second Street. He hooked his left arm around a pole as the train moved off, and held out his right, low down, the fingers clutched around a stained paper cup from Dunkin' Donuts. Annie reached in her coat pocket for the cache of quarters she kept for New York's street people, but he turned the other way, beginning his speech.

"I'm not any happier being here than you people are seeing me here." No one looked at him. Across from Annie, a Korean girl sat silently, a black art folder beside her, her face a mask. "I'm a Vietnam vet. I've served my country. I'm willing to work at anything." A heavy, middle-aged black woman on the seat beside Annie shifted a pile of law texts on her knee and reached for her purse. "I can't find a job. Maybe you have something, some food left over from lunch, a bit of fruit you didn't eat . . ." The speech was rehearsed and the voice faintly familiar, although Annie was sure he wasn't one of the regulars. "It may not seem like much to you, but I'll be glad of anything." Annie's fingers closed around the coins. She kept her eyes down on the tote bag, heavy with manuscripts, at her feet. "A quarter, even a dime. It's not a lot to you, maybe, but it's a lot to me." He held out the cup, his back still to Annie.

A pair of out-of-town teenagers scrabbled in their mountainous packs, opening clumsy, vulnerable wallets. Annie, feeling motherly, willed them to put them away and divest themselves of their Midwestern innocence before New York did it for them. The man accepted their dollar bills without acknowledgment.

The train slowed jerkily, rattling into Fiftieth Street, and Annie tucked her feet, in their Nike sneakers, closer around the tote bag. The Korean girl gathered her art folder and stood up. Two black teenagers in sequinned baseball caps clambered past her, pushing by Annie's knees. Annie lost sight of the beggar in the crush of departing and entering passengers. She leaned her head back and made a shopping list in her mind for the deli on Columbus. The doors closed and the train pulled out. A big, tired-looking man in denims slumped into the seat the Korean girl had left. Annie thought: pasta, milk, coffee, tomatoes, basil, endive, couscous. And what was that other thing Merrilee was craving yesterday. Avocado? No. That Greek thing. Hummus. Hummus and black olives. She smiled. Rather conventional as pregnant cravings go.

"Maybe a piece of fruit left over from lunch." Annie looked up, startled. The beggar was standing in front of her, facing the tired man in dungarees who looked past him with weary, unfocused eyes. The speech, the second time around, sounded lifeless. "A quarter, even a dime . . ." His plaid jacket was dark blue and green, a tear at the shoulder seam exposing a white triangle of lining. It had the dull griminess that came from the street. She took her fingers from her pocket, the cluster of quarters ready. He turned, "It may not seem much to you . . ." She extended them, as the cup swung around and the quarters whispered into the paper, a smooth urban ballet. She glanced up without thinking.

His eyes were blue, with strange crystalline irises, his cheekbones sharp, the cheeks gaunt, the stubble on them red-blond. The unwashed hair had grayed. So, of course, had hers, in ten years. Her hand shook and fumbled against the cup. Her eyes widened in involuntary shock. "Eric," she whispered.

Confusion crossed the dirty face, then curiosity, and then recognition. And last, before he turned away, horror. She clutched his sleeve. He jerked back, stumbled into a dark girl with a violin case, who cried out, hugely outraged. He dropped the cup with his small heap of coins, his two dollar bills, and pushed through the crowd. The train was stopping and Annie cried, "Eric!" aloud, half rising, tripping over her tote bag. Turning in confusion, she collided with the violin case.

"*Oh!*" the violin girl cried, assaulted again, in her voice the anguish of all the city.

"I have to. I'm sorry," Annie was muttering.

"Hey, your bag," the woman with the law books said, irritated but dutiful. The doors opened. The crowd surged out, the plaid jacket a dark patch in its midst. Annie fought toward the opening, but people were piling on, with plastic bags, sports equipment, briefcases, folders. The paper cup and Eric's money rolled, spilling, under the molded plastic seat. The doors hesitated, then shut tight, and the train whined and hurtled itself away.

Annie stumbled back to her seat and gathered her canvas bag and her purse and pushed her way to the door again, thinking frantically. She'd get off at the next stop, grab the next downtown train, and go back . . . no, she'd go up to the street and run the nine blocks. She clutched her bags, trying to slow her breathing. Sense quickly prevailed. It would take fifteen, twenty minutes. Even if the downtown train was waiting. Or if she was running in sweats and unburdened. But it was rush hour. And she had two heavy manuscripts in the tote bag, and a fashionably short, tight skirt, making a joke of the Nike sneakers. And Eric would hardly be waiting for her. The look of horror in his eyes came back, filling her own with tears.

She did not get out at Fifty-ninth Street or at Sixty-sixth, but stood stoically as people pushed by on either side, only blinking as the train pulled out again. At Seventy-second, her own stop, she got off calmly and climbed the stairs into a wet and windy fall night. The frenetic desperation slipped away as she walked quickly across town, replaced by a dull sense of shock and frustration. She had been close enough to Eric to touch him, and even now he was perhaps half a mile away. Quite likely, she would never see him again. The moment she had sought for a decade had come and gone and led to nothing. But then, of all the ways she had imagined it, none had remotely resembled this.

"What's happened to you?" she whispered into the dark, anonymous evening crowds. "What's happened to us all?" A brightly lit high school gym flashed into her mind, the bleachers crowded with teenagers in varsity sweaters, plaid skirts, corduroy pinafores. The tall, lanky boys in white shorts, sweating and serious, huddled with their old gray-haired coach on the polished wood of the basketball court. And herself in a blue cheerleader's dress—its short skirt slashed with triangles of gold-white socks, white sneakers, prancing and chanting with Marion and Sue, Polly and Dot,

> Eric, Eric, *he's* our man,
> If he can't do it, *no one* can!

Her heart leaped briefly with the leaping children of the past, and then sank into a middle-aged present. It was six o'clock on a cold October night. She had shopping to do, a meal to cook, Merrilee and David to console once again, Martin, strained and weary, coming home from work, and a stack of reading of her own. And Eric. Eric their star was out on the streets of New York, cadging quarters in the rain.

The latches clicked from within as she bundled her shopping out of the elevator, and Merrilee met her at the door of the apartment with a mug of chamomile tea in her hand. Merrilee was large and soft and placidly pregnant. She had a good way of being in the right place with the right idea, as she was now, with the tea. Annie accepted it gratefully, in one hand, dropping her bags with the other, and leaned to kiss her daughter-in-law's cheek. Merrilee nuzzled like a happy child.

"Mmm. Good day?" Annie shrugged her coat off, and her delicate mouth turned down wryly.

"Not exactly." She heard a small tremor in her voice.

"Mmm?" Merrilee, the emotional weather vane, turned to instant concern.

Each of her son David's previous girlfriends had been slim, high-energied replicas of Annie herself, all of them blue-eyed, one even with her own distinctive red-brown hair. And yet, despite the flattery of those mirror images, Annie had seen instantly in brown-eyed, blond, sumptuous Merrilee, the right choice. After that, she merely waited for David to see it too. And how fortunate, Annie felt now, to have this quiet girl, gentle as a cloud, drifting about the apartment, rather than some restless high achiever hassling poor David for success.

Annie looked into the trusting, optimistic young face. She hesitated. Eric seemed too big a burden to lay on such innocence.

But suddenly he was also too big a burden to carry alone. "I saw my brother," she said.

Merrilee blinked. Her mouth opened slightly, but she said nothing. Annie thought for a moment she would have to explain. Perhaps Merrilee didn't even remember. The convolutions of David's family could well have eluded her.

"The one whose daughter..." Merrilee whispered. Her lips were pale, and Annie remembered that awful emotional vulnerability of pregnancy.

"That's right," she said briskly. "My brother Eric." She almost added, "Molly's father," to make it clearer, but stopped, angry as always that Eric's personal identity was forever hijacked by the manner of his daughter's loss.

Merrilee was watching her, trying to read her, uncertain what response was expected. She said, "I thought he was in San Francisco."

"So did I," Annie said, turning her eyes away. Not that she did, really. The last contact had been San Francisco, but that was four years ago, and it wasn't even with Eric himself but from a friend looking for him. Apparently he owed some money, electric bills, and the rent. Martin had sent a check. They hadn't even told the rest of the family, Eric and Annie's parents in Florida, or their sister Joanna in Colorado. There was nothing worth knowing really; only that Eric had been somewhere, but wasn't any longer, and had left without settling his debts.

It had happened twice before. Once, after he'd been gone a year, he'd written to their parents for money. And a year or two later, he'd appeared out of the blue in Denver and accepted two hundred dollars from Joanna. Annie was angry about that, angry that he'd taken anything from Joanna who had so little and was so softhearted, and angry that he had not come to her and Martin, instead. But in ten years, that was all. Until this.

"Where is he?" Merrilee asked. Annie looked back into the big dark eyes. "You *saw* him..." Merrilee's voice softened in confusion. She looked around as if expecting Eric to be near.

"On the subway," Annie said. Her thin shoulders shook, and she began to cry. "He was begging. With a cup." The cup mattered, somehow, the damn cup. "With a paper cup." Merrilee wrapped her in her big, strong, girlish arms and pressed her up against her bulging stomach, the secret warmth of the grandchild between them.

———

LOOKING BACK, Annie felt she had just one easy year in her life. It was not a complaint, just a fact. It wasn't even a year she particularly yearned to have back, but it was the only year in which life could be called easy. David and Merrilee were newly married, living in their first proper apartment. Danya, Annie's daughter, was in her first year at Brown, and she and Martin had the family apartment on West Seventy-fifth to themselves.

When they first moved into the apartment, Danya and David were already eight and twelve. It was expensive, but Martin's practice was growing, she'd just been promoted to senior editor, and they felt they deserved it. They had both been working hard since they married, with Martin doing his residency and Annie in her first job after college. Even then they had managed on their own and never needed to call on their parents. Martin's dad did help him set up the practice, but his own father had done the same for him, out on the Island just after the War.

Then there were the child-raising, juggling years of nannies and nursery schools, of piano lessons and ballet, riding and tennis and skis. In the middle of it all, they bought the Connecticut place, weathering the resistance of both sets of parents, just as they'd fended off objections to their first move into the city years before. Somehow they still squeezed in enough visits to the old shared Adirondack camp to keep the peace. When Martin's mother muttered darkly about the money they spent, Martin reminded her, since she hadn't appeared to have noticed, that the Depression was over.

He was right enough, back then, anyhow. Finances were not the scarce commodity in their lives. They were both earning serious money. The deal over the new medical building had not yet revealed itself as the full-feathered turkey it was, and Martin's lead fingers in investment were still just a family joke. They had money; it was *time* that was brutally scarce. But Annie managed it all—work, play, vacations, parents, driving lessons, college applications, entertaining, travel.

Then suddenly, the kids were away. First David went to Ann Arbor, then Danya to Brown, and there they were, on their own, the apartment big and roomy after the years of crush and intimacy and noise. Annie's friends talked sadly about empty nests and menopause and loss, but Annie was loving it. Time to read, to study, to really concentrate on her career. Time to entertain, to stay out late, to grab weekends at the country place, take in doses of Caribbean sun, fly to Italy to stay with Martin's brother, Seth. It was wonderful. It was paradise. And if at the time a small snake had crept in, in the form of an ugly little malpractice suit against Martin's partner, Annie refused to let it upset her Eden. It wasn't *Martin's* failing, as she told him again and again, and it certainly wasn't hers.

And then, at the end of that year, Annie lost her job. Of course, she should have seen it coming. Like everybody else in the city, she should have seen the signs, read the warnings. In fact, she had seen them. She just never imagined they were meant for her. She had been in that job for eight years, having come to it with fanfare and applause in the heady days of the early eighties. She'd brought two sought-after authors with her and had discovered two more, one of whom had vaulted up the list with her first book. Annie was good at her job, well liked, and well respected, something she rather foolishly assumed would be obvious to the young high flier the accountants ushered in to deal with the slump in sales.

Annie liked younger people and expected them to like her back. She went into her new boss's office prepared to be the supportive older woman, ready to share her accumulated expertise with a new young colleague. Maureen did seem to like her and, therefore, to regret genuinely the words she was saying. Her good wishes for the future were fervent and real. But Annie was still out of a job. It was a hideous day, easily one of the worst in her life, but she survived it. After Molly, nothing, nothing in this world, could ever really drag her down. By the time she'd cleared her desk, she already had new options lined up in her mind.

She fully expected to have another position within the week.

She nearly did, but a hugely encouraging interview dissipated into a long wait for telephone calls and then a formal letter explaining exactly why another candidate had been chosen. After a month, she had her first doubts. After two, the doubts were many and large, but she kept them to herself.

She couldn't talk to Martin, in the same way, since the lawsuit. Never mind they'd won it, and it *was* his partner's alleged malpractice anyhow. The suit had dragged on, splashily and publicly, and the eventual conclusion was a Pyrrhic victory. Their insurance premiums went up, a scattering of long-term patients drifted away and were not easily replaced. The endless and expensive hassle with Mandelbaum's practice over the cost of the building repairs suddenly mattered a lot more.

But it was the suit itself that hurt Martin. Medicine was a tradition in his family. Both his father and grandfather had been doctors before him. He carried from them an inherited sense of honor regarding the profession, perhaps out of sync with the current world. The challenge to his competency, even at one remove, hurt. Legal vindication did not heal the wound. He lost confidence and grew depressed and anxious, doubting his judgment in the most trivial matters.

The children were baffled; his aging parents worried. His brother and sister, at first supportive, grew increasingly frustrated and impatient. Annie was left alone to shore up his self-esteem. Her own took, of necessity, a backseat. When the reader's job in the Adelman Agency was offered, she took it. It was grad student's work, a bottom-rung position. Annie didn't argue. These days there were a lot of people at least as qualified as she was without even a foot on the ladder.

But there was less money all around. Danya volunteered to transfer to Albany State, an offer vehemently rejected by her father, pained that she should even imagine such a failure in his support. Martin and Annie briefly considered putting the apartment on the market and looking for something smaller, but then David had *his* crisis.

David had studied history at Ann Arbor, but held a not-too-secret desire to be a writer. They hadn't discouraged him, either in his academic pursuit or in his private dream, clinging to a stubborn belief that such choices were honorable. His first job after graduation had been in publishing. It lasted eight months before he was turned out, albeit with glowing references, into a rapidly shrinking market for his skills. There followed a stint in a bookshop and then a brave few months writing a novel and working part-time in a bar. Merrilee, managing a SoHo gallery for an artists' cooperative, was the main breadwinner. The week the gallery folded, she found herself pregnant. David's novel went into a drawer, and he went back out looking for a full-time job. Ironically, it was only Merrilee, so far, who had found one. She worked in a Columbus Avenue gift shop, selling giraffes—painted giraffes, pottery giraffes, giraffe sweaters, stuffed giraffes. The store was called "Giraffe," and Merrilee assured Annie that there were indeed enough giraffophiles in New York to keep it afloat while publishing houses and art galleries sank beneath the waves.

Giraffe could not pay enough to cover the apartment lease. David and Merrilee, slightly stunned by the hand of fate, moved into David's old bedroom and camped there, like two embarrassed teenagers. For the first week or two it was awful, with everyone colliding at bathroom doors and Annie trying to cook for Martin and herself around Merrilee's separate preparations. Then sense and habit prevailed, she became Mother again, and the household functioned once more like a family.

Fortunately, Danya spent the summer in Italy with Seth. Annie and Martin had their weekends at the country place and retreated to the Adirondacks with his parents in August. When they returned, David and Merrilee were still there, but it felt almost normal now. The airy adult year of ease had faded into memory. Annie decided that struggle and chaos were probably her natural state.

Secretly, she liked having the four family places at the table filled again. They were all good talkers, and meals became lively debates. Merrilee filled Danya's role unconsciously, as if Annie's family must always have its innocent idealist. When they were kids, it was Joanna passionately defending stray puppies as an eight-year-old, and napalmed children at seventeen. Then her own Danya, berating her for paying Fatima to vacuum and load the dishwasher and dust. Now Merrilee, looking out of those big golden retriever eyes and saying so earnestly, "We have to find him. We can't just leave him out there."

"Merrilee," Martin said softly. "Merrilee." She turned cautiously to the mixed sounds of affection and reprimand. Merrilee had grown up without a father, and when Martin got fatherly with her she both yearned for and resented him, at once. "Merrilee, he ran away from Annie."

"So?"

"So maybe he doesn't want to be found?"

"Well of course he didn't. He was embarrassed. He was ashamed. But he shouldn't be. It's not his fault, is it? We'll just have to show him . . ."

"Merrilee, you can't do this to people," Martin said gravely. She stopped short, pulled up by the real seriousness of his voice.

"Do what?" She tossed her hair defiantly and looked across the table to David for support.

"Pressure them. Eric's fifty years old, sweetheart." Martin stopped speaking and closed his eyes a moment. Annie watched him kindly. He had been a handsome youth, with his thin, solemn face, vivid blue-gray eyes, and dark hair. But age and weight had softened the angular edge of his features. Pads of tired flesh beneath his eyes and at his jawline turned solemnity to sorrowfulness, a hangdog look that was normally deceptive. Yet at the moment, tired from the day's work and stunned by Annie's news, it spoke well for what he felt. He said, to Annie alone, "Christ. Fifty."

"Forty-nine," Annie said, comforting. Her mouth twitched in a tiny smile. "You're both forty-nine. I'm fifty." Annie, unlike Martin, liked getting older and found his age anxieties amusing.

"What are you saying, Dad?" David said, his voice quarrelsome with protectiveness, "What, this is some kind of free choice of Uncle Eric's and Merrilee's got to honor it? Is that it?"

"I'm saying," Martin said tiredly, spooning gravy over his potatoes, "that you can't force someone into being a happy human being."

"We have tried," Annie said quietly to Merrilee.

"But you have to keep trying," Merrilee said urgently. "You have to get through to him. Somehow. Just keep at it and at it until he sees that life really is worth living, and then he'll let you help maybe." Her voice trailed into silence and her eyes dropped away from Martin's dark stare. His graying brows drew together and his heavy jaw tightened.

"What am I going to say, then, Merrilee?" He spoke very softly. "Sure, Eric. Life's a rainbow. Never mind your marriage has broken up and you're all alone because your only child, your pretty little girl, was kidnapped and murdered and no one's ever even found what they left of her? Never mind trying to picture it, because whatever you picture, you'll never get it right, and there will always be something even worse that they did. And never mind wondering where, or when, or if it was maybe months after, or even years, and what they did with her before and how many of them did it and whether maybe they filmed it and some screwball bastard's watching it all on video even now and jerking off? Yeah, just forget that, because anything, anything you think of, some bastard's done even worse. And if you don't believe me, ask some of my colleagues who deal with abuse."

"Martin," Annie said.

"But I can always say: Sure, Eric, life's worth living, pal, because little Merrilee who's twenty-three years old and knee-deep in hormonal sentimentality says it is. And she can't be wrong."

"Dad. Come on. What's the shit . . ." David said.

Merrilee got up, a little awkwardly, but as politely as she could, and left the room. David ran after her, kicking his chair against the table and slamming his open hand against the door frame. Annie sat back in her chair, her head resting against the waxed pine.

"Oh, Martin," she said sadly, "why?"

"I'm sorry. I'm sorry."

"She's just a *kid*, Martin, trying to make things right."

"I know. I know. I'm sorry."

"You'd better go tell *her*."

"I will." He ducked his head, leaning his forehead against his fist. "I'm really ashamed."

"Go see her."

"I will. Give me a moment please, Annie."

"Martin?"

"It's been some day. A real fucker."

"Mine wasn't great either," Annie said, without malice. He reached his hand out across the table to her.

"I had this kid in today. Nice kid. Eleven. I've been seeing him, oh Christ, since he was two. Fell off his skateboard in the spring. Banged his knee. Nothing much. Lacerations. A bit of bruising. Nothing that needed treatment." He waved a dismissive hand, paused, and then started speaking slowly and carefully. "So when the kid started saying his knee was sore again, the mother hardly thought . . ." He broke off suddenly.

Annie leaned forward, puzzled, "Martin?"

"She's a single parent," Martin said then, his voice earnest in the woman's defense. "An attorney with a small firm. Went through law school after the husband left. She'd just qualified and she'd been with them about a year. Anyhow, she was the first to go when things got bad. And the insurance went too, of course. I mean, she wasn't stupid. She wasn't even irresponsible. Kids are always banging knees, playing rough. Except this time it's a sarcoma. And if she'd come to me maybe three months ago, we could have done . . . a lot. We could have done a lot. Now?" He shrugged hopelessly and then straightened in his chair. "I'd better go see Merrilee."

Annie squeezed his hand. "Martin?" He looked up. "How are we going to find him, anyhow?"

Joanna

"YOU GOT HOMEWORK?" Joanna heard herself yelling it before she even thought it, as if the latch of the trailer door switched her on, yammering like the TV on remote.

"Yes," Tess answered wearily. "I've got homework." Great start, Joanna thought. This was going to be their new routine. No nagging, no hassling, no bossing, on her side. No lying around useless, no ducking out of chores, and no smoking, on Tess's.

Joanna was in her bedroom, the bigger one, at the back end of the trailer, changing for her evening shift. She went on at five. Tess got out of school at three-thirty and always managed to parlay the twenty-minute bus ride and ten-minute walk into an hour's journey. That left just enough time for the two of them to get into a fight, and never enough time to make up.

"I thought we made a deal," Tess said. She slouched in the doorway, hips angled belligerently, giving an adult shape to her child's body, still skinny and straight in jeans and sweatshirt. The sweatshirt displayed a board rider with a baseball cap and dreadlocks and the words "Frozen Waves." Tess wore a cap like the rider, her pale blond hair pushed through the gap at the back. The peak shaded her eyes. Joanna resisted the desire to push it up. She stepped closer and caught a dreary tang of tobacco smoke.

"So did I," she said dryly. She made a pointed sniff at the shoulder of Tess's sweatshirt.

Tess pulled back and said sourly, "Is it my fault my friends smoke? All their clothes stink. Is it my fault it gets on mine?"

"You're the only one who smokes."

"Cathy smokes."

"Cathy's eighteen. And stupid. You're eleven. And smart. Or you're supposed to be."

"You smoke."

"I'm quitting."

"Oh, sure. You're always quitting."

Joanna faltered. She pushed back her heavy blond hair and said, "I'm pretty stressed right now."

"And I'm not?" Tess looked imperious, her eyes glinting under the cap's fuzzy peak. "You'll never quit," she said.

"Oh yeah? Yeah?" Joanna half raised her hand and then dropped it. "Stop treating me like some kind of a failure always," she said. "What do you know about stress?"

"What are you besides a failure?" said Tess.

Joanna turned her back and began coolly slipping silver and turquoise earrings into her lobes. Her eyes, on her own face in the gray-spotted mirror built into the shoddy dresser, still registered Tess, leaning on the door frame on the edge of the reflection. Once, in one of their occasional long telephone calls, she had asked her sister, Annie, what instinct led children to so perfectly pinpoint their parents' greatest vulnerabilities. (Annie having begun child rearing so long before her, Joanna regarded her as an expert.) Annie had said, "We tell them, of course. Words, gestures, looks. By the time they're five they know our nightmares, our guilty secrets, all our posturings. They save it all up for ammunition and start firing it back as soon as they hit their teens."

Tess had started early. When she was seven she could push all Joanna's buttons: smoking, money, men. Oh, she was an expert on men. She knew a mile off which ones mattered, the ones for whom she saved her special treatment. Sometimes Joanna thought her daughter knew before she knew herself, so that her own first inkling of falling in love was a splash of vitriol from Tess.

Tess hung there at the doorway like an unscratched itch. Joanna unfastened the top buttons of her plaid shirt and reached in with her roll-on, dabbing hastily under her arms.

"That's disgusting," Tess said. "Pink over stink. You'd yell at me if I did it."

"So your mother's a slob," Joanna said, grinning at her reflection, hitching up her jeans and stuffing in the shirttail. She left the two buttons undone. The guys at work liked her a little decorative. It helped with the tips.

"You should wear a bra," Tess said. "You're too old for that."

"Get liberated, kid. I haven't worn a bra for twenty years. I don't own a bra."

"You're saggy."

"I'm not, you little shit." Joanna whirled around and, too late, caught the glimmer of devilish satisfaction in the shaded blue-green eyes.

"Maybe if you'd worn a bra, you wouldn't be," Tess said, practically, "but you are." Joanna straightened her backbone, thrusting her tits out. They weren't bad. They weren't bad at all for forty-six.

"If I am it isn't for not wearing a bra. It's for having you and nursing you for months, you little lamprey."

"Oh, yuck, spare me," Tess winced.

"Then you spare me, thank you," Joanna said stiffly. She turned back to the mirror and grabbed her hairbrush and stroked vigorously through her thick, honey-colored hair until it frizzed up all around her shoulders in the dry, electric air. When she had finished she turned defiantly to face her daughter. Tess slipped three fingers in each of her jeans' pockets, hooking thumbs through belt loops.

"You look like a hippie," she said, with a final triumphant smirk.

Joanna leaned back against the dresser, her eyes slitty, about to answer. Then she thought better of it, grabbed her shoulder bag, stuffing her hairbrush and cigarettes inside, and strode across the little room.

"I gotta work," she said. She'd intended to sweep by Tess, but the narrow trailer doorway meant she collided with her instead. It was a good metaphor of their lives, she thought, with the cramped, half-size, tinny surroundings of the house trailer standing in for the skimpy confines of their impoverished single-parent family. There was never any room in their lives to get things settled between them. The trailer wasn't even theirs, but rented from the owner of the ski-wear store facing the highway, in whose dirt backyard it sat. And behind it, where once had been nothing but silent pines, was now a construction site, with the half-built frames of three ski cabins for the city people who came to the valley to play.

The trailer itself was belligerently claustrophobic, its two bedrooms, kitchen, bathroom and shower crammed into a space as pinched and skinny as a railroad car. Joanna wormed past her daughter.

"There's milk in the refrigerator, and chocolate donuts."

"I'm on a diet, Mom." Tess followed her into the kitchen and opened the refrigerator. She poked at its contents and came out with a Diet Pepsi.

"And a chicken dinner in the microwave. All you have to do is switch it on."

"I know."

"I'll be back at eleven." Tess said nothing. Joanna laid her fingers on the book bag Tess had dropped on the folding kitchen table. "If you get this done early you can maybe watch a video. Or play a computer game," she added grudgingly.

"You don't have to feel guilty," Tess said solemnly. "I know you have to work." She looked up, and Joanna could just see her eyes under the cap's peak, wet and glistening. She stopped at the doorway and turned, trying to slow herself down, to make her attentiveness visible.

"What's wrong, sweetheart?" she said.

"Bobby dumped me."

"Dumped you?"

"Yeah," Tess said. She pulled off the cap. It snagged messily in her long hair and she tugged it free.

"Your friend Bobby? What do you mean? He won't play with you?"

"He says I'm a lousy lover. So he dumped me." She sounded weary.

"Tess, for crying out loud. You're eleven. He's eleven. What have lovers got to do with it?"

Tess shrugged, "I don't know. He just said it."

"But what . . . but why . . . what were you doing?" Joanna stared.

Tess shrugged again expansively, "Nothing much."

"Like what?" Joanna glanced quickly at her watch. It was five past five. Tess saw the glance.

"I don't want to talk about it." Her eyes went expressionless. She put the cap back on, scrunched down over her tousled hair, and drank quickly from the soda bottle.

"Tess, I think . . ." The door rattled. Tess froze, the Pepsi at her lips. Joanna turned to the flimsy glass door as it swung open. Mike Hewitt stepped up into the trailer. He was a short, well-built, dark-bearded man, in denim jeans and jacket. He grinned, his eyes, large and blue, lighting up happily. "Well, how's the two prettiest ladies in Colorado?"

Tess slammed her Pepsi bottle down on the table and ran up the little corridor. The back door opened with its unused, unoiled screech and crashed shut behind her, shaking the glass. From the metal-framed window, Joanna saw her running, long-legged and clumsy as a colt, through the broken red ground of the construction site, up to the ridge of pines beyond.

"Oh shit," she said sadly.

"I say something wrong?" The man blinked, bewildered, his big hands hanging awkwardly. Joanna shook her head. "Do you want me to go?" he asked.

"I have to go, Mike. I'm five minutes late already and John will sure let me know it." She picked up her shoulder bag, looking sadly at Tess's discarded Pepsi. "Come on, walk me over, okay?"

Mike Hewitt wasn't exactly her lover, though everyone in town thought he was. In the past they had occasionally been lovers and even now had their sexual moments, but before any of that, he was her friend, and he remained her friend still. She'd met him the last year of the dude ranch, after Sean Kelly had walked out and left the whole mess for her. She'd hired Mike to patch up the stable roof after the snow had brought part of it down. He was invaluable that winter. Joanna was a tall, tough woman, but still some of the heavy work around the place was beyond her.

When Mike was finished working, he'd sit in the battered, low-ceilinged kitchen of the ranch house, his big hands around a coffee mug, listening thoughtfully while Joanna talked. Even Tess had liked him from the start, maybe sensing that her mother would never be in love with him. She talked to him, too, and let him help her with her homework, though, semiliterate at best, he wasn't a lot of help. Sometimes she'd even sit on his knee as if he were her daddy. He had three kids of his own, and a wife, in a big, new log A-frame he'd built up the valley. He was making a lot of money. The ski resort had expanded, and there were new condos and Swiss chalets cropping up all over, though for ordinary people like her it was hard to find a place to live.

That had been a rough winter for Joanna. The dude ranch business, always a struggle, had collapsed finally under the pressure of the recession. She spent half her time arguing with the bank, and the rest of it arguing with her daughter. Tess, who had resented Sean Kelly as she had resented all Joanna's lovers, and had fought furiously against his moving in, then fought with Joanna about his moving out. Mike listened. He was kind but not indulgent, sympathetic but not maudlin. He'd cut her off when she got bitter or began to moan. He did her a lot of good.

Then one day, when she was washing dishes, he came and stood beside her, to help dry them. And then he was behind her, arms around her, gentle, unhurried, stroking her breasts, leaning to kiss them through her flannel shirt. And she stood there while his big, compassionate hands explored, still in no hurry at all. When his fingers touched the bare skin of her stomach she was practically crying for him, wanting to turn and embrace him. But he held her like that, stroking her until she was quivering and shaking and then melting into the best orgasm she'd had in months, leaning against him, her legs slack with pleasure, in her own kitchen.

After that it happened from time to time, always when her guard was down, her hormones up. He could read her like a book. A few times they had real sex, in her bed upstairs, and once even, later, in the unprivate trailer. But there was always the fear of Tess's coming home early from school or waking suddenly in the night. And Joanna couldn't get used to there being a wife a mile up the valley—and those three kids. Mike didn't argue and he never pressured her. He seemed to get as much pleasure out of those surreptitious orgasms of hers as any of his own.

Lately, she had pulled back. There was talk around, and though she couldn't stop that, she could handle it better if she knew it wasn't true. Every now and then, she'd lose her resolve and find herself once again braced deliciously against the trailer wall, blissfully riding Mike's tough, sensuous hand. But, mostly, they were simply friends.

He followed her out onto the rough wood deck and down the three wooden steps. At the bottom he stood looking worriedly up the hill. "I'm sorry I upset the kid," he said.

Joanna glanced briefly at the tall pines where Tess had disappeared and looked away. "She's okay, Mike. She'll come down as soon as we've gone."

"I guess I should've knocked."

"It's not you, Mike." Joanna paused. "She likes you." She shrugged, settling the strap of her bag on her shoulder. "It's me. And it's her. She's all hung up about some boy. Already. Shit, Mike, she's eleven years old. She's worrying about not being a good lover. Whatever that's supposed to mean at eleven."

He laughed, "Not what it means at our age, you can bet. They pick up the language, Jo. From TV and music and the older ones. That's all."

"When I was eleven I was playing Cowboys and Indians." She stopped for a moment at the end of the dirt alley that led from her trailer up between the ski store on the left and the Slalom Bar and Grill on the right. In front of her was the broad blacktop highway and across from it the big new shopping center, behind which was the Edelweiss Cafe where she worked. Beyond, the land sloped upward, greenly pine clad, now shadowy with evening. Above, floating golden pink against the clear, pale sky, the bare rock summits of the mountain ridge pulsed with light. "Will you look at that," she said softly. Sean Kelly had called it the alpenglow, but Joanna wasn't sure whether that was the real name for it, or something European he'd borrowed to show everyone he'd skied everywhere, not just at home in the Colorado Rockies.

"Pretty," said Mike. "Real pretty."

"All we had when I was a kid was a couple of acres on Long Island. I made mountains and valleys and ranches out of that. She has all this, and she lies on her bed with the curtains shut all day."

"I bet it wasn't all you played," Mike said.

"What wasn't?"

"Cowboys and Indians. I bet you got up to other things."

Joanna smiled to herself, waiting for a big trailer rig to thunder past before she crossed the highway. It threw up a cloud of dry red dust. "I wish the snow would come," she said.

"So does everybody. Excepting me. I got foundations to pour."

"Yeah, we got up to other things," Joanna said softly. She smiled again. "You forget, don't you?" She strode out across the road with Mike beside her, but at a proper public distance. Once, climbing a mountain, all alone, she'd reached to take his hand, and he'd pulled his away. There was no one in sight, just the two of them and a hill full of pine trees. It taught her a lesson, about where she stood with him, and let her know she wasn't cut out for affairs with married men. Joanna had no taste for secrets.

"That's the trouble with adults," he said, as if he wasn't one himself. "They forget." He reached his hand across the space between them and clapped her on the shoulder. "See you around, Joanna. Don't take any wooden nickels."

She watched him walk off toward his red Dodge pickup that was parked in front of the 7-Eleven. She felt itchy and lonely and irritated with him for being so confidently married, while she couldn't even keep a ski-bum like Sean Kelly for more than a handful of years.

The Edelweiss Cafe was a single medium-sized room, its white-painted walls rimmed with dark wood booths and a handful of wooden tables scattered around a central wood burner. Pictures of mountain scenes hung on the walls, some of them local but most of Austria and Switzerland. A pair of old wooden skis were fixed to the wall above the kitchen door, and a set of bentwood snowshoes dangled from the ceiling by their leather binding straps. The Edelweiss was owned and run by a big ex-logger from Oregon called John Bowes, who did most of the cooking, much of it mundane grills and fries, but with the occasional Wiener-schnitzel and sauerbraten thrown in to keep up the image. In the daytime and off-season, it served local construction workers and passing truckers. After six, during the season, white cloths and candles in wine bottles went on the tables and Gluhwein and Viennese coffee appeared for the après-ski set. The ski business carried the burden of the slack season successfully enough to keep on a small year-round staff of whom, for the past year, Joanna Carlson had been one.

The cafe smelled of wood smoke from the freshly lit kindling in the stove, and garlic and grilling meat. Joanna slipped in quietly and went quickly through to the kitchen. She put her bag away and lifted her white linen apron down from its peg. John stood at the big griddle with his back to her.

"Five-ten, Joanna," he said, without turning. He cracked three eggs and dropped them with a staccato sizzle on the griddle. "Bonnie's running her ass off out there alone."

"Sorry, John." Joanna ducked her head, taking up her pad and pen.

"Yeah, you're sorry." John said morosely. "Everyone's always sorry. How about on time for a change instead of sorry?" Joanna tied her apron with a smart snap of the cloth and said nothing. It wasn't fair. She had been late maybe twice in the past three months. John had a memory like an elephant and a sense of self-aggrievedness to match, but it didn't matter. He was the boss and she needed this job more than she liked to think. Those scary days, after the dude ranch went bust and before she found the Edelweiss, hung around the back of her mind and made sure she never answered back or showed John just what she thought of his tyrannical moods. His other moods, the amorous ones, were easier to handle, though, Christ, she could show Anita Hill a thing or two about harassment.

Sometimes, when she was really fed up, she thought about moving on again. But it wasn't so easy anymore. Tess was settled at school, if you could call it that. And it had taken long enough, after the move up from Denver. Tess hadn't so much liked Denver or their rented house or her school, as she disliked change, any change. She'd resisted in turn each new stage of their lives, the antique store in Denver, the dude ranch after that. She resented the house trailer and Joanna's low-rent job most of all, but she'd still cling on in desperation if Joanna tried to leave.

Besides, the real question was, where would they go? Not back to Denver. Joanna hadn't liked it much herself, and with no capital now and no skills, she'd end up in a bigger, noisier version of the Edelweiss. If she was going to work at a ski-bum job, she'd just as well have the mountains and the snow to go with it. She could go farther, back to San Francisco even, but there was nothing there for her any longer. Her friends were long gone, most of them married and with families and scattered around the country living ordinary middle-aged lives, except for the few who got lost along the way to drugs, or accidents, or AIDS. And the city itself was so changed from the days when she'd come to the Haight in her beads and her Indian muslin, with half a college education and a stack of books on Zen.

She thought about Oregon, or Washington State, maybe somewhere on Puget Sound. Or Alaska even. But when she mentioned those places to Tess, she'd screw up her face and say, "What's wrong with here? Why do you always have to change everything?" And she could never find a good answer, any more than she could when Tess asked why Sean Kelly wasn't staying with them any longer, or, before that, Ben Murgatroyd. Or even Larry McLeod, who was the man she'd been living with when Tess was born, though not her father.

Sometimes she thought of going back East. When her best friend, Sara Levine, wrote that she'd come back to Long Island to look after her parents, Joanna felt a tug of nostalgia for home. But there wasn't really any home to go to. Her own parents were in Florida now, and the old family house was full of strangers. Her sister, Annie, had lived in New York since she married Sara's brother Martin. They led busy city lives, and Joanna could not imagine herself and Tess in their world. The family seemed so scattered. They hadn't really been together since her brother, Eric, left them. Thinking of how they used to be filled her with homesickness, as if Eric had taken home away with him when he went.

There were three of her regulars at table four. She picked up the glass coffeepot and a hand span of white mugs and walked across the room, giving them a big grin.

"Hey, Joanna."

"There she is."

"Thought we weren't going to see you. Almost ruined my day."

"Yeah, yeah, George. I'm sure it did." Joanna set the mugs down in an easy ring and sloshed coffee into them one after the other.

"Go on, fill it right up. Right up, sweetheart."

"I'm filling it, George," Joanna said, still grinning.

"Right to the top. You know how I like it. All hot and steamy. Like I like my women."

Joanna kept the grin on. The other guys laughed and one punched George's shoulder. She thought of saying, "The line's 'hot and black, like I like my women,' George," but imagined he'd fall backwards off his chair and onto his thick red neck, if she did. Just as he might if she actually showed any sign of taking up the invitation he was always so enthusiastically extending. But she said nothing and set the metal jug of milk and the sugar bowl down between them. "What can I get you boys?" she asked, trying to make it sound neutral, her eyes focused on her order pad.

"*Well*. Now you've asked."

"Oh, shut up, George, and order." That was Rick. He was big and quiet and liked his food. He couldn't be bothered waiting through George's routine to get his steak. George shut up, embarrassed. He was a fat, nervous man, an electrician, who for years had lived with his mother in a trailer up a dirt road. Joanna liked him. He wasn't a bad guy. He just didn't have any other language with which to talk to women. Joanna liked them all. They were her friends, more than were their wives, several of whom she knew. She had more in common with the men because she lived on her own, raising Tess alone, being the mainstay, the sole breadwinner of the family.

When they talked work, she knew the references. They were small businessmen: George, the electrician; Rick, who ran a ski supply store in the winter and rented mountain bikes in the summer; and Dan, who had a little store selling leather goods and boots and Western souvenirs and supplemented it by driving a shuttle bus around the resort during the season. When she was running the dude ranch (even with Sean Kelly there to help with the horses, it was always Joanna who ran it), they were her cronies. Now that she'd fallen on hard times, they, who were threatened always with the same fate, were the first to understand. She knew they were glad she'd stayed on and stuck it out when things turned bad. They were proud of her, in their way.

Joanna took their orders back to the kitchen, the usual—Rick's steak, George's burger and fries, and chili for Dan. Sometimes they switched it around or threw in a pizza, but generally she could write the order before she reached the table. They liked the comfortable regularity and her knowing their choices before they made them. She liked it too. Waitressing, a job she'd been driven to by desperation, was surprisingly pleasing, providing her a niche in the town, a role she filled with verve, like a rough and ready Western geisha, smoothing the cares of men's lives. Joanna liked men. They were her weakness. She knew herself well enough to acknowledge that much, though not well enough to avoid the pitfalls.

Sooner or later she'd fall for another Sean Kelly. The place was a lodestone for his kind. They arrived each fall with the first whitening of the mountaintops, as regular as the wild geese over-head. They found a room or a trailer, picked up a job in a bar or on the mountain, worked, drank, and skied. They were all good looking and rarely short of women.

But they were young. Each year they were younger. Joanna felt she had just been marking time since Tess was born, while a whole new generation had grown up around her. Sean Kelly was a decade her junior. It was fun and it was undoubtedly flattering. But something had changed in the years with Sean. She wanted more than flattery from a man now. And she wanted more than a season or two of vigorous sex and then a lighthearted glad-to-know-you and good-bye. She knew without asking that she wasn't going to find what she was looking for here.

She came back out of the kitchen and stopped with her pad at the table for two occupied by Peter and Gordon, the refugee Californians. They had taken over the Dreamcatcher Arts and Crafts and sold romantic Western prints and Native American jewelry. They fussed over the menu and asked searching questions about the cooking as if they were really in Breckenridge or Vail. She answered kindly, suppressing a grin.

"*Joanna.*" John Bowes's big, bearded head appeared around

the kitchen door, his broad, stained apron filling the entry-way. He stood there, glowering. "*Telephone*," he announced for the whole room to hear and added, hugely aggrieved, "for you."

"Oh. Oh sure, John." She stepped away from the table. "Sorry. Bonnie will take your order, okay?" She caught the other waitress's eye, nodded, and hurried to the kitchen. "Who is it— Tess?" she said to John. He had his back to her again and was glowering at his griddle.

"*I* don't know," he said, and then added, "Some woman. Long distance. *Some*body you gave this number to, anyhow."

"I don't give this number out," Joanna said sharply, wiping her hands on her apron and reaching for the wall phone he'd left dangling from its cord.

"Well, she's got it," he said. Joanna lifted the phone to her left ear, pushing her earring aside, and shielded her other ear from the noise of sizzling meat and clattering pans.

"Hello? This is Joanna Carlson."

"Oh, Joanna, Tess said you were at work. I'm sorry but I had to talk."

The voice was urgent, clipped, very New York.

"Annie." Joanna glanced quickly to where John stood turning a line of burgers, his head cocked sideways, listening. She bent over the phone, making a shell of privacy. "Annie, what is it? Mom and Dad? Is something wrong?"

"No. They're fine." Annie's voice was drawn out, hesitant. "Joanna, it's Eric."

"Oh, Christ." She put her forehead against her hand, covering her eyes, shutting out the noisy kitchen. She didn't want to hear this here, in this ugly, public place. Her voice went scratchy and she whispered, "Annie, is he dead?"

"No! Oh no!" Annie's voice, vigorous, compassionate, flooded her with such relief she half-laughed, drawing in a sudden shaky breath. John shifted his weight, glancing at her.

"Oh God, I was so scared. So what is it? Have you heard from him?" She was excited now, almost happy. With the darkest possibility vanquished, all others looked bright.

"You're not going to like hearing this, Jo," her sister said.

—

SHE WORKED THE REST of her shift with her mind half a continent away. George gave up dropping innuendos, when it was obvious she wasn't listening. Peter and Gordon had one of their showy public arguments for which she was meant to be the audience, but failed to attract her attention. Even John, dimly perceptive, left her alone and asked at the end of the night if something was wrong.

"No, nothing," she said briskly, folding her used apron and dropping it in the laundry hamper.

"You sound down," he said lamely.

"Oh, just a family thing," she said. She made a small deprecating smile.

"Families," said John. "Full of shit. If you ask me."

"I'm sure you're right." She grinned and walked out into the crisp, frozen night.

—

TESS WAS ASLEEP, sprawled on a red and blue beanbag in front of the flickering TV. A new half-finished Diet Pepsi sat beside her with the rind of a sandwich. The chicken dinner was still in the microwave. Joanna woke her gently, shaking her shoulder. "C'mon, sweetheart, time to go to bed." Tess curled inward from her mother's hand, like a troubled snail, and then woke, muzzily, looking around.

"Is the movie over?"

"Looks like it."

"I missed the end."

"You can see it again. C'mon, sweetheart. School tomorrow."

"I'm not going."

"Okay. But bed anyhow." Tess blinked wearily, saw Joanna would not engage in combat, and capitulated. She got up and staggered sleepily to her room, then stopped and reached her arms out for a goodnight kiss. Joanna grabbed her quickly and kissed her tangled hair. "Good kid."

"You know what I think?" Tess said. Joanna shook her head. "I think Bobby's a piece of dogshit." She grinned suddenly.

"That's what I think." Grimly cheerful, she padded softly in her white sport socks across the small living room and into her bedroom at the end of the trailer.

Joanna turned the TV off, put the Pepsi bottle on the kitchen table and the sandwich crusts into the garbage. She took the chicken dinner out of the microwave and put it back in the refrigerator. Then she picked up the Pepsi again, swigged its flat contents, and carried it with her into the bathroom. She set it on the edge of the bath while she brushed her teeth and washed her face. In the blue fluorescent light above the mirror the skin around her eyes looked tired and old.

Picking up the Pepsi again, she went into her bedroom, leaving the light switched off to save drawing the curtains over the high, awkward windows. Instead, she undressed in the dark, kicking off her boots, leaving her jeans and flannel shirt on the floor and pulling the old T-shirt she slept in out from under her pillow. She slipped it on, took a final swig from the soda bottle, and set it down on the floor. Then she climbed in and sprawled girlishly across the width of the bed, looking up at the window and its rectangle of black night and crystalline, perfect stars.

Outside, beyond the highway and behind the shopping center, where the Rio Grande railroad line ran along the piney hillside, a long, lonely whistle was leading a hundred-car freight through the town. Joanna lay listening as the slow rhythm filled the darkness with memories. They'd grown up in a house near a railroad, she, Annie, and Eric. And across two fields, Sara, Martin, and Seth. Every night of her childhood she'd gone to sleep to that restless, comforting sound, whether in her bedroom or in Sara's; it hardly made any difference, since they all moved in and out of each other's houses as if they were both their own.

When she and Sara were seven and Seth a tagalong six-year-old, Eric and Martin and Annie decided to formalize their ersatz family into a secret society, a blood brotherhood. They'd gathered in a secret room they had discovered in the Levine attic, in reality no more than a chimney sweep's passage, but in Eric and Martin's ten-year-old minds, a chamber of mystery unknown to any adult. She could smell it still, a dry smell of dust and heat and plaster, and feel the thick, webby blackness when Annie shut the flashlight off to frighten them into promises of secrecy. Seth cried, as he often did, and refused to extend his finger for Eric's penknife. She and Sara were scared and stoical but desperate to please Eric, squeezing out bright red drops onto the gray wood floor. Annie organized it all and wheedled Seth, with closed eyes, into a tiny pinprick. Then they were together in the flashlight beam, six forefingers extended, bloody pads pressed together.

"Brothers forever," Eric and Martin said.

"Brothers forever," said Annie. And Joanna and Sara and Seth muttered it after them, awed. "One for all and all for one," Annie whispered heroically.

"Till death do us part," said Martin. Joanna never took her eyes off Eric. Blond and handsome in the beam of light, he held up his bloody finger.

"Till death do us part."

Outside, echoing loud beneath the bare, uninsulated roof, the train whistled and rumbled steadily by.

⸻

FROST FEATHERED THE WINDOW when Joanna awoke. The trailer was icy cold. She reached out and turned off her alarm before it could ring and lay on her back, making her decision. Then she got up out of the warm comfort of blankets and crumpled sheets and dressed quickly in the shivery dawn. When Tess awoke an hour later and came stumbling out of her room, Joanna was sitting at the kitchen table, her bank statements and checkbook spread out before her.

"Mom! I'm late. You didn't wake me. I'm late for school."

"You said you weren't going," Joanna said, smiling slightly. She sipped from a coffee mug, not looking up.

"*Mom!*" Tess cried, outraged.

"You can go in the afternoon," Joanna said lightly. Tess drew closer, her head tilted.

"Mom? Is something wrong or something?"

"How'd you like to go on a trip?" Joanna said. She looked up and gave Tess her biggest, most encouraging smile.

Seth

A PLUME OF DUST on the hillside marked the slow progress of a vehicle up from the village. The soft greens of pine and cork oak screened the road itself from sight, and Seth could not tell if it was Alessandro's ancient taxi or a shiny new rental car, but he knew its passenger would be the British woman. With some regret, he folded his copy of *La Repubblica*, laid his reading glasses down on top of it, and sat back awaiting her arrival.

It was warm for October. So warm that he had chosen to sit beneath the dappled shadow of the grape arbor rather than out in the full sun among the leggy red geraniums at the front of the terrace. Even from here he could see everything, so well situated was the old stone villa. Before him were spread the steep green hillsides, the red tile roofs of the village below, the square, buff campanile of the eleventh-century church, and, far away where it touched and blended into the sky, a blue wedge of Mediterranean, as pure and dreamy as when Ulysses sailed. Seth had spent three years in careful search of the Riviera looking for this place. Like most of the good things in his life, its casual perfection was the result of serious work.

Work was not what he felt like at the moment. He'd only been home a week. He was still on his malaria drugs, which always affected him badly. It was unfortunate, considering how much time he spent taking them. That was one of the prices of a life of exotic travel. Others, such as loneliness and a gradual alienation from the culture that had bred him, were more subtle. The rewards were all around him, as he sat basking in the Ligurian sun.

When the woman from the London newspaper telephoned for an interview, he was tempted to refuse, but with the Ladakh book scheduled for publication next week, it was a temptation that the businessman in him resisted. He had even volunteered to meet her in Genova, but she hadn't wanted that. Like the rest, she had to make the trek up here and root him out, the writer in his sanctuary. Always that obsession with the place, the setting. It was not just the villa, but the workroom, his actual desk. As if understanding the surroundings would go some way to making the esoteric trade of writing understandable too.

The dust cloud was at the second to last switchback by Bernardo's farmhouse, and he pictured the intrepid Londoner clinging white-knuckled to the wheel or, worse yet, trembling in the back of the taxi as Alessandro hurled it at the hairpin bends. He smiled to himself, wryly, and imagined this feature, like most, would begin with a description of the road, expand to a lyrical evocation of the village, and culminate in a paean to the villa: real Peter Mayle stuff. With luck she'd get around to the book title by paragraph four.

The roar of the engine reached him, and the whine of aggressively changing gears.

He decided it had to be Alessandro. But then a bright red Peugeot rounded the final bend and nipped through his stone-pillared entrance, flashing by the open wrought iron gates. It pulled up beneath a peach tree and a woman got out, carrying a black leather case on a shoulder strap, incongruously locked the door, and began walking quickly toward the terrace. Seth stood up, watching her. She was tall and fair, chin-length blond hair held back with a black headband, a slender, quick-moving body dressed in a mustard-colored linen suit. She saw him, slowed, and lifted off her sunglasses. "Mr. Levine?" Seth smiled and walked down the terrace steps to meet her. What had been a duty looked to hold at least the potential of a pleasure.

"Ms. Wedderburn?"

"Caroline."

"Seth."

She smiled. It was a pretty smile. She was tough-looking and rangy, almost his own height—the way he liked his women. He wondered how she liked her men. Probably tall, blond, and British like herself, he thought ruefully, as he followed her up the crumbling stone steps, amidst orange and yellow nasturtiums trailing in autumn disarray.

"What a stunning place," she said, turning and taking in the view. "How do you ever get any work done?" He grinned. Good. At least he wasn't going to get the "inspiration" bit.

"With difficulty."

"You must have a million houseguests, for a start."

"How did you know?"

"It's the 'pretty house in the country' syndrome, isn't it? Only on rather a grander scale." He laughed.

"Exactly," he said, and then relaxing his voice back into its original accent, " 'Hey Seth, we're just swinging by Milan on this little tour of ours and we've been looking at the map . . . ' " She nodded, grinning. "Or," he changed his voice again, making it British, " 'I say, Seth, haven't seen you for donkeys' years . . . just saying to Evelyn, isn't it ages since we've seen Seth? How's London? Oh, a bit drear this time of year . . . ' "

"How about," she said, tossing her blond hair, " 'Let's do a story on that travel writer, Seth What's-his-name. I'd love a few days on the Italian Riviera.' "

"Oh, please," he said, offering her one of the old wooden chairs under the arbor, "you're crushing my ego. You're supposed to say, 'I've read your books for years and I can't believe I'm meeting you at last.' " He sat across from her, the green painted wooden table between them, a taut, muscular man with very black hair and sharp brown eyes.

"Actually," she took a tape recorder and a notebook out from the small black leather case, "I read three last week and one on the plane."

"Did you like them?"

She paused, too long and too coolly for comfort. "You're perceptive for an American," she said.

Seth tilted his head back, warily. "Do I thank you for that on behalf of myself or get offended on behalf of my country?"

She made a small smile, and he became suspicious that she was teasing him. "Up to yourself." She paused. "I suppose it depends on how patriotic you are." Before he could answer she laid the notebook down and said, "Are you patriotic, Seth?"

"That's a funny question," he said slowly.

"Not at all. It's an obvious question when a man chooses to live abroad." He leaned back in his chair, studying her smooth, tanned face. Thirty, thirty-two. Sporty. Probably rides. Undoubtedly skis. Keeps fit. Aerobics. Maybe even pumps a bit of iron.

"What do you think?" he said. She looked up briskly from her notebook.

"Oh yes, probably. Most expats are. Do you mind if I switch this on?" She patted the little recorder she'd laid on the table. He shook his head.

"Why is it," he said, as the machine hummed, "that when other nationals go abroad to live they're emigrants, but Americans are always expatriates?"

"Because nobody in their right head leaves America for good. Everyone knows that, Seth." Her voice was flawlessly assured. He laughed quietly.

"No wonder the Europeans hate you people," he said. "You're so fucking arrogant."

"Not half as much as they hate you," she said with her cool British smile. Seth sat up stiffly in his chair. His eyes fell on the little machine humming on his table.

"Shall we talk about the book?" he said.

"Yes, I'd love some coffee," said Caroline.

Maria-Luisa brought them cappuccino, made properly with last evening's espresso and fresh foaming milk, and one of his local pottery dishes piled with *farinata*.

"Oh, gorgeous," Caroline said, nibbling one of the small corn cakes with a sudden schoolgirlish enthusiasm. Seth softened to her again. Over her cake she followed Maria-Luisa's departure with an equally schoolgirlish curiosity. He sipped his coffee, watching with amusement. Maria-Luisa, like most young Italian women, dressed and moved with a natural elegance that denied ready assumptions about her role. She had more than once been taken for his mistress by those, like Caroline Wedderburn, unaware of her position as housekeeper or of her husband working with his father-in-law on their small holding below.

"It could be lonely here, I imagine," the journalist said suddenly.

"It could." Seth sipped his coffee again and decided to give her no clues. She picked up his recalcitrance at once and became professional.

"If we could just recap a little, Seth." She lifted her notebook. He wondered, considering the machine, why she used it. Habit? Image? Something to do with her hands? "You were born 2 June 1947 in Long Island, New York. Youngest of three brothers."

"A sister and a brother. My older brother, Martin. My sister, Sara." She made the correction in her notes.

"Your father is a doctor." She looked up, "I believe your brother is a doctor too."

Seth nodded, "So was my grandfather."

"What was their reaction to your becoming a writer?"

"Sheer delight." She looked puzzled. "Do you know what med school in America costs? Even back in the sixties?" She looked confused and he said, placating, "My sister's a dancer. So I'm not the only screwball, if that's any help." She didn't look as if it were.

"But you did attend university." She flipped a page back.

"Bard College. Upstate New York," he filled in. "For a while."

"Until you were arrested for possession of cannabis and asked to leave."

"If you know it all, why ask?"

"Accuracy. We don't want any libel suits, do we?"

"You're hardly going to get one from me," he laughed. "Particularly not over that."

"Don't you care what I write?"

He smiled, his eyes narrow in the strengthening sunlight. "Not a lot. As long as you mention the title of the book. Often."

"A bit of a cynic, are we, Seth?"

"A man with his living to earn, like everybody else."

She smiled. "You seem to be doing all right."

He shrugged. "Appearances can be deceptive."

She looked unimpressed. "Has success come easily, Seth?"

"I haven't always been successful."

She smiled again wryly and looked at her notes. "*Hotel Tibet* came out when?"

"In the seventies. That's a long time ago."

"It's still selling," she said.

"Very well." Seth met her eyes. His own were disarmingly honest. "It bought most of this." He made a quick proprietary gesture with one hand. Then he leaned back in his chair and studied her thoughtfully. "I was lucky," he said. "It struck a chord. When that happens it's usually because someone has been in the right place at the right time."

"You're modest," Caroline said.

"No, I'm not modest. It's a good book, well researched and very well written. I'm good at my job, Caroline." He paused and then said quietly, "But I've written other books since, some of them as good and some of them better, and none have struck the chord."

She thought for a moment, checking her notes, and then looked up and said, "They haven't, have they?" She smiled brightly. "They are all a bit grim, though, Seth, aren't they?"

"Grim?" His eyes narrowed warily. He was well aware how an admission of weakness invited attack.

"Well, you know. Mosquitoes and ghastly food. Do you never go anywhere nice?"

"Mosquitoes and lousy food are the fate of most of the human race."

"Well, quite," she said briskly. "But it's still not jolly holiday reading, is it?" He shrugged and looked away. She watched him carefully and then glanced down at her notes. "This drugs charge . . ."

He threw up his hands. "It was the sixties, for Christ's sake. I had half an ounce of hash I brought up from the city to share with a couple of friends. It was my turn that week. Me and half the college-age population of the state, by the way."

"You were asked to leave."

"It was suggested I leave before the case went to court. It was also suggested I reapply later. They weren't *all* hypocritical idiots."

"But you went to India instead."

"Once again, with half the college-age population of America. You don't remember the sixties, do you?" She looked offended that he even considered she might. "Of course you don't," he said gallantly. Ruffled, she stroked her blond hair, and a wave of compassion swept over him, partly at the terrible vulnerability of beautiful women, hostages always to the whisperings of time, and partly because she reminded him, quite suddenly, of someone else.

"Half the college-age population of America didn't stay on there, in a Buddhist monastery for over a decade."

"No," Seth said slowly. "I suppose not." Nor had they lost the girl they loved to their older brother either, thought Seth. But he didn't say anything, because they had reached the part of his life he didn't want to talk about and he needed all his wits to distract this pretty terrier and set her on a different trail.

"Did you find enlightenment in the East?" He recognized that arch mannered voice the British used when they were being serious about something that embarrassed them.

"No. I found enlightenment at home on Long Island listening to John Lennon, like everybody else." She raised her head and slipped her sunglasses off.

"Sorry, Seth, am I out of bounds?" He shrugged. "Only you do write what I have to call 'spiritual' books." She sounded pained.

"You mean I don't tell people about wonderful little unspoiled finds that of course will be spoiled when they get there? I'm sorry," he said coolly, "I'm not into that kind of one-upmanship."

"Then what do you tell people about?" she said instantly. He realized he had opened another gap of potential vulnerability and sat back, reluctant to answer. She waited in polished silence, her smile serene.

Eventually he said, "I tell people about themselves, seen in the mirror of the world."

She grinned gleefully, "Oh, ho. Big stuff."

"You asked." He looked at her sourly. "I travel," he said, "I *think* when I travel. It's an old tradition, actually, a *British* tradition. Have you read Freya Stark?"

"Of course," she said, surprising him.

" 'An unwilling horse, a dragging child, and a woman who insists on explaining her motives . . .' "

" 'The three most wearying objects in creation,' " she replied, further surprising him. "I always thought she had an American woman in mind."

He grinned slowly. "You know, Caroline," he said, shifting his legs lazily under the table, "I think you're something of a bitch."

"Whatever it takes to get the work done."

"Whatever?"

She looked up and put the sunglasses back on. "Mostly whatever." She picked up the notebook again, abruptly. "Of course, India was a nice place to avoid Vietnam. Once you'd lost your student deferment."

"I didn't need a student deferment. I was one-Y."

"What?" she said. The curve of subtly darkened lashes flicked up behind the shaded lenses. "What's that?"

"Marginally medically unfit." She looked incredulous. "I had a bad knee." She guffawed, crudely, upper-class coarse.

"You've walked across half of Asia."

"Not carrying a full army pack," he said reasonably. Then suddenly he got irritated. "Look, don't trust me. Go check with my draft board. Ask the guy who did my medical."

"All right, Seth. Don't get angry. I believe you." She smiled sweetly. "So otherwise, am I to understand, you would have valiantly served your country?"

"No. But the issue didn't arise."

"Convenient."

"Those were difficult times. It's easy to be glib about them now. It wasn't easy then. It tore families apart. Divided friends. Everyone forgets." He moved his coffee cup aside and stared off across the green Mediterranean hillside. He was thinking of Eric Carlson and of what Martin had told him when they talked last week, just after his return.

"Did you lose friends?" the woman asked.

"Not in the way you mean," he said. He shifted in his chair, looked distracted. She rearranged her notebook and pen on her knee and adjusted the little cassette recorder, thinking quickly of how to regain the momentum of the interview.

"Your first book, *Hotel Tibet,* came out of the India experience of course . . ." she began. Suddenly a door banged open, and two small children ran, shouting, onto the terrace. Caroline Wedderburn looked up, startled and slightly annoyed, as the boy and girl, brown-skinned and dark-eyed and, like most Italian children, noisy, ran toward the table.

"*Bambini!*" Seth Levine shouted, and she looked back to see him suddenly transformed. The glum distraction had vanished, and also that intellectual reserve that she had found attractive. In its place was all the disconcerting enthusiasm of the child-mad parent.

"Antonio, Lucia," he had the little boy hooked under one arm and the little girl, on the opposite side of his chair, under the other, "This is Ms. Wedderburn. Say hello." They giggled and squirmed and he looked mock severe until each, still giggling, had said, "*Buon giorno*" and solemnly shaken her hand. Seth watched while Caroline accepted each small, damp hand. Then he released the children and they scattered away, like leaves in the wind, still shouting in Italian. Caroline turned to Seth.

"Yours?" she said, astounded. He laughed, imagining she was dying to cross-check her notes. The door opened again and Maria-Luisa appeared, shouting also, while the children shouted back and only eventually went back inside. Caroline winced. Smiling broadly, Seth stretched his legs out again.

"Hers."

"And she . . ."

"My housekeeper."

She absorbed that slowly. "You don't mind that she brings her children to work?"

He shrugged. "What else is she supposed to do with them?"

Caroline looked irritated. "Oh, come on. There must be someone she can leave them with."

"Italian parents don't like leaving their children."

"I've *noticed* that," she said, suddenly conspiratorial, one outsider to another. "In the hotels. Restaurants. Everywhere. And all hours, too. Don't they ever go to bed?"

"When their parents go to bed."

"Ridiculous. You wonder what they imagine is going to happen to the little darlings if they let them out of their sight for once."

"No," Seth said, "I don't wonder at all."

He looked stunningly bleak. She didn't know what to say. After a long, uncomfortable silence she said, "You have no children of your own?"

"No."

"You've never married."

"No."

"Why is that?"

"Has this anything at all to do with my book on Ladakh?"

She was coolly collected. "It might," she said, "but you obviously don't want to answer it, so we'll talk about something else." She smiled, the pretty, disarming, schoolgirl smile, and he felt his crustiness soften.

"Let's have lunch," he said.

Lunch was at the trattoria in the village. They drove down the hill in her rental car. She drove it slickly and well, arousing his respect. They sat outside, at a table by the roadside, and ate bread and salami and a seafood salad. Seth ordered a bottle of the local red wine. She paid for the meal with her newspaper's lira. He got a little drunk in the warm sunlight and said, "You remind me of someone."

"What a line."

"I mean it. You do."

"Someone good?" He paused long enough that she said with mock distress, "Someone bad?" He smiled distantly.

"It's a compliment," he said.

Over lunch they talked about his work. After all the initial personal prying, she proved a good, astute interviewer. She'd read everything and asked intelligent questions. As they finished their espresso, they became involved in a serious debate on the impact of travel on vulnerable cultures. They were still discussing it vigorously when they returned to the villa, and instead of simply dropping him off, she got out and, talking intently, walked with him around the overgrown gardens.

"Do you like it like this?" she asked suddenly.

"Like what?"

"I don't know. Sort of decadent." She waved her hand to a

rosebush tumbling, long unpruned, over a half-obscured stone bench.

He laughed, "A garden should feel soft. Sensual. Like you could lie down in it anywhere and make love." He looked up quickly. Their eyes met. Hers were clear blue-green and younger than her confident face. He liked that mix of brisk panache and vulnerability. English boarding school. I bet she played hockey. I bet she was captain of the team.

"Your writing has been described as 'flagrantly seductive,' Seth. Would you agree?" she said with a smile. He tilted his head and gave a small shrug, looking sideways at her from under a displaced lock of black hair.

"What can I say?"

THE VILLA WAS COOL and dark and silent within. Maria-Luisa had taken her children home and would not return until tomorrow morning. She had made his bed and turned back the sheets and closed the shutters against the afternoon heat. Their bare feet sounded soft and intimate on the terra-cotta floor. Caroline thought the sparring, the lunch, the flirtation on his part, had all been just for this, but she'd been in enough beds for enough years not to care. She had her needs and she serviced them at her own discretion.

The truth was quite opposite. He was enjoying her company, and sex was an easy way to retain it. Whatever he'd told her, or let her think, his life was lonely, peripheral to the country in which he lived, and peripheral to other people's lives. He did not merely tolerate Maria-Luisa and her children. He yearned for them, looking too eagerly for their arrival each morning, missing them all on Sundays when they did not come, and too readily accepting invitations to the farmhouse for Sunday lunch. It was worse since the summer, when Martin and Annie's daughter, Danya, had filled the house with adolescent argument, tuneless music, and swarthy boys who rode up on scooters from the coast. Everyone had offered sympathy at the intrusion, but it was the best summer since he'd been here, the best summer in years.

—

THE BEDSIDE TELEPHONE woke them both. He had meant to unplug it but had forgotten. Reaching over Caroline, he answered it on the second ring. The cord trailed over the bed, skimming the white linen sheet draped over the curve of her hip. She snuggled down, with that smug, nesting look women got after good sex. Seth said softly, "Hello?"

"Is that Seth Levine?" The voice was female, American and tentative.

"Yes," he said, straightening up in the bed. "This is Seth Levine."

"Seth, it's me. Joanna."

"Joanna!" The woman beside him stirred, and he glanced instinctively. The smug, cuddly look had gone, replaced by an arched eyebrow, a whimsically questioning mouth.

"Shall I leave?" she whispered briskly and with the bouncy girlish smile. He touched her arm under the sheet and shook his head, but his mind was on the voice on the phone.

"Where are you calling from?"

"Home. Colorado."

"Joanna, it's been ages . . . how nice to hear from you."

"I know, Seth. Time gets by."

"How's Tess?"

"She's fine. Seth, I can't talk very long . . ." She sounded nervous.

He said quickly, "I know. Give me your number there. I'll ring you back."

"No, it's all right."

"Come on, Jo, money's not an issue between us."

"I know. It's only . . . Seth, have you talked to Martin?"

He came brutally awake, realizing at once why she'd called. He sighed quietly then and said, "Yeah, Jo. I rang him when I got back last week. I always do." He paused. "He told me about Eric, Jo." He shifted his weight in the bed, feeling awkward and uncomfortable beside the pretty British stranger. "I'm sorry," he said.

"Seth, what are we going to do?" He was silent. The feeling

of discomfort grew, and he wished now he'd accepted Caroline's offer of privacy. But he couldn't. It would be too unkind.

"Jo, I can't see that we can do anything." He heard her sigh.

After a silence she said wearily, "That's what Martin said." He realized she had expected more of him and hated himself.

"Jo . . ."

"Seth, we can't just leave him out there. He's ours. He's one of us. He's our family."

After another silence, he said measuredly, "Joanna, every other poor bastard dozing on every other street, in New York, or LA, or London, or Delhi, is, or was, someone's family."

"I don't care about that," Joanna said, her voice fierce over the distant line. "Maybe they didn't have families like ours. But we did, and we don't leave my brother begging in the street. No way." He could hear she was crying.

"Jo," he said softly.

"I always thought, Seth, that you and I were, you know, simpatico. The same."

"Oh, we are. We are." He heard the sudden burst of passion in his voice. Caroline Wedderburn heard it too. She sat up in the bed, holding the sheets over her breasts. She drew up her knees and wrapped her arms around them. Her head dropped onto her arms, her face turned away. He knew he should say something quick and final and impersonal to Joanna and get off the phone, but he couldn't make himself do it.

"I thought you still believed in him too."

"I want to, Jo," was all he could say.

"I'm going to New York."

"You are?"

"Me and Tess. I'm going to find him, Seth."

"To what end, Joanna?" he asked solemnly. Her voice was controlled when she answered, and cool.

"You're just like Martin," she said.

"I'm not. You know me better than that."

"I knew you. I don't know you anymore."

"Whose fault is that?"

She sighed again, "I can't get into this, Seth. It's costing me a fortune."

"*Let me call you back,*" he said, frustrated. "Or let me pay for the call. I'll send a check. I'll pay your whole bill, for God's sake."

"I don't want your money, Seth Levine. I want your help. And it looks like I'm not going to get it."

"Now wait a minute, Jo."

"Good-bye, Seth. I'm sorry I bothered you."

"You didn't bother me. Jo. Jo, wait." He heard the phone go down, not instantly, as in anger, but after a long empty silence, as in despair. He banged his receiver down and put his head against his fist.

"Oh shit," he said. "Shit."

Caroline still sat with her face turned away. After a careful interval she raised her head on its slender neck and turned toward him. She looked thinner and older than when he'd made love to her.

"Old friend?" she said calmly.

"Yeah," he said, his voice husky and distracted, "a very old friend." He stared straight ahead and said "Shit" once more and wrenched his mind off Joanna, struggling to regain his decency. "I'm sorry," he said. "I wouldn't have talked so long, but I honestly haven't heard from her in years. Years. We . . . we grew up together and her sister married my brother."

"Oh, I see," Caroline said politely.

"Something's come up. A family problem. She needed to talk."

"Of course," Caroline said. Her voice was distant. "Look, Seth," she glanced at her wristwatch, "I really must be going."

He made all the graceful gestures of persuasion, as convincingly as his distracted mind allowed. She only shook her head and gave her schoolgirl smile. They shared a last glass of wine, and then she drove away in her red Peugeot, down the dusty road. He went inside, and sitting on the rumpled bed in the shuttered dim light, dialed his travel agent and booked a first-class flight to New York.

TESS

"THERE'S NOTHING TO DO," Tess said. She curled her long, skinny legs up on the train seat and picked at the hole in the knee of her jeans.

"Look out the window," Joanna said, turning a page of her magazine.

"I've looked out of it. I've looked out of it for two whole days. It's all the same."

"No, it isn't." Joanna looked up with strained patience. "Look, this isn't anything like home, all those hardwoods and the houses with the porches and the coal mines. Look, you can see the coal there in the ground. That's fascinating."

"Oh, great. Coal," Tess said. She stared out the window bleakly and then returned to the frayed denim of her knee. "I'm missing school," she said. "I'll get behind. What's the use of doing my homework all the time and then you decide to take me out of school?" Joanna sighed and closed her magazine.

"This is educational. You saw the prairie and the Mississippi and the Missouri, and the tallest building in the world in Chicago."

"We didn't go up it."

"But you saw it," Joanna said harshly, thinking, Six dollars to ride an elevator. They should have done it maybe, but she had so little money and so far to make it spread, and this trip was already costing more than she dared think. "Seeing it was educational. All of it. It'll help your geography."

"No, it won't. We've *done* America already. Now we're doing Europe. So it won't help at all."

Joanna closed her eyes wearily. "Fine. It won't help at all," she said.

Tess kicked at the seat in front of her with the toe of her sneaker.

"Don't do that; it's annoying," Joanna said without opening her eyes.

"When Sonia went to Disney World, her parents flew," Tess said.

"They have more money than us."

"Everybody has more money than us."

"No, they don't," Joanna said tiredly. "That's not true."

"Name someone who hasn't," Tess said instantly. "Go on. I dare you." Joanna said nothing. Tess kicked at the seat once more with her toe and then curled her legs up again and unraveled a nest of blue threads from her knee. She rolled them in a knot and laid them on her armrest and looked out the window at the highway beside the train.

She imagined herself and her mother in a big old-fashioned convertible, wearing head scarves and sunglasses like Thelma and Louise. That would have been exciting at least. She thought about it a while, picturing herself all dusty and with the wind blowing her hair over her shoulders. But this was Pennsylvania, not Utah or Arizona. She gave up imagining and picked at her knee again.

"If I had a Game Boy I wouldn't be bored now."

"If you had a Game Boy I'd never see your face. The only reason I'm seeing it now is because I've at last got you separated from that damn computer. And the reason you're bored is you've forgotten how to think without your electronic umbilical cord attached."

"I haven't forgotten how to think," Tess said. She flopped over and pressed her chin onto the narrow strip frame of the train window. Outside, gray leafless trees rolled by. They were different trees, not cottonwoods and pines and aspens, but she didn't care what they were. They were just trees.

The trouble was not that she couldn't think, but that she couldn't stop thinking. She closed her eyes, rocking gently with the train's movement, and ached for the feel of the control pad in her hand, the firing button under her finger, and Prince Valiant or Spiderman on the screen. Then everything was simple, and what happened and what didn't was all up to her. There was never anything to worry about.

Books weren't as good. She tried getting really far into books, and sometimes it worked. She'd read a real good Stephen King between Omaha and Chicago. But she read too fast and finished it, and the book from the Sweet Valley High series she tried after that was too stupid and she started to think in the middle and the words disappeared off the page. Then everything started circling: her mom and Sean Kelly and the ranch they used to have, and losing it, and the trailer they had now that she hated. And Mike Hewitt, whom she liked and didn't like at the same time, half wishing he'd come and live with them and half wishing he'd leave them alone. And even dumb dogshit Bobby, who'd said she ought to know how to screw already because her mom was sure good at it. As if that dumb thing he always wanted to do, lying on top of her in all his clothes and everything and bouncing up and down, was *screwing*. She sighed, scornful and lonesome for him at the same time.

"Tess, read a book."

"I've read them all."

"Look at that beautiful barn with the big silo."

"What of it?" Tess raised her head wearily. The train slipped through farmland, rolling fields, stands of woodland. It passed some small houses, painted yellow, with white porches. On each of the porches were plastic leaf sacks colored orange and black to look like pumpkins. Real pumpkins sat beside one of them, and someone had made a ghost out of a sheet stuffed with cloth and hung it to a tree.

"Oh, look at that, Tess."

"It's not very scary."

"It would scare you at night." Tess looked back at it critically as the train rolled past.

"It might," she said. "Are we going to have Halloween in New York?"

"I don't know. Maybe."

"Oh, great. Can I trick or treat?"

"I thought you were too old for that. You said you weren't doing it this year."

"But in New York. Think of all the candy you'd get. All those big buildings."

"Yeah, sure," Joanna said. "I can just see it. Maybe we'll go to a movie or something."

"Oh, great," Tess said, raising her eyebrows wearily. More houses passed.

A trailer park made Tess think of home. Then there was another highway running beside the train. The cars looked different, sleek city people's cars, not pickups and four-wheel drives. They looked free and exciting, and she thought of being in one and turning up one of the side roads and maybe parking in front of one of the neat, small houses of the town they were passing through. They'd get out of the car, carrying big bags of groceries, and other kids would come out to meet them, and then a man who would say, "Hi, honey," to her mom, and then they'd all go inside and sit around a big table, in a big yellow kitchen with a dog lying on the floor, and everybody would talk and laugh and make lots of noise. She closed her eyes, concentrating on the picture. When she opened them, the houses were far behind and they were following the highway through the boring part of the town that had old factories with broken windows and a river crossed by a dark iron bridge.

"Oh, look," she said, prodding her mother, "a Burger King." Joanna was reading her magazine again, but she looked up.

"Oh, real exciting."

"If we were in a car we could stop."

"You hungry? I'll give you some money. You can go to the lounge car."

"I want a burger."

"They have burgers."

"I want a Burger King burger."

"Tess, stop being such a turd."

"I do. I want one. Why didn't we take the car?"

"Because that old Buick would fall apart by Denver and you know that, and because it's too far for me to drive all alone."

"Well, why didn't you get someone to come with us?"

"Like who, for God's sake?"

Tess shrugged, "Like Mike? Mike would like to go to New York. And we could have driven in his pickup. I could've ridden in the back, out in the open."

"All the way to New York."

"Yeah. It would be great."

"I thought you said you didn't like Mike."

"I do like Mike. Only not all the time."

"Well, anyhow, Mike wouldn't be able to come." She paused and then said, "He's got a job."

"*You* have a job."

"Yeah. Well, that was a problem for me too."

"You're not going to lose your job, are you?" Tess curled her fingers around the edge of the armrest, picking at it, studying it carefully.

Her mother shrugged quickly and said only, "It wouldn't matter. I can get another job."

Tess said nothing. She looked down at her fingers and felt an ache in her stomach. She reached into the top pocket of her pack, which she had jammed between her footrest and the back of the next seat, and pulled out her Walkman, clamping the headphones onto her ears, and listened to Michael Jackson while Pennsylvania went on and on outside the window. She thought about Mike some more. She saw why he really couldn't have come with them, at the same time as she could see him actually doing it. Two pictures blended together like a double-exposed photograph. She knew he was married, because there were three Hewitts in the school, Dawn Hewitt, Stevie Hewitt, and Mike Hewitt junior. In spite of them, she sometimes imagined Mike living in the trailer with her and her mom, and her mom not having to work at all.

Mike had offered to buy her the Game Boy she wanted, but her mom wouldn't let him. She still half wished he had, especially right now, but in another way she was glad she didn't owe him anything. Sean Kelly had bought her Nintendo, three years ago when he was still living with them at the dude ranch and still always grinning and sweet-talking with her mom. She knew the computer was to make her like having him there, or at least make her *act* like she liked having him there. She should have refused it, but she wanted it so bad, and she knew her mother would never have enough money to get her one, so she gave in and thanked him for it. Even then, he spent as much time playing on it as she did, and often he'd hog it so much she didn't get to use it at all before he was sending her off to bed. Real early too; he had real strict ideas about kids. But he was smart, and he could get round her too easily. Like promising to teach her snowboarding and then putting it off again and again so she waited hopefully all winter. And when he finally did take her out, they spent half an hour on the boards, and then some friends of his came and she ended up teaching herself outside the lodge while he sat inside and drank beer. Sean Kelly was always making promises and not keeping them. And yet she cried and cried the day he left, though even now she wasn't quite sure why.

When the tape ended, she got up to go to the bathroom, still wearing her headphones, the cassette player stuffed into the pocket of her sweatpants. She climbed over her mom and the magazine she was reading and stood in the aisle stuffing her feet into unlaced sneakers, balancing on one leg and then the other as the train rocked around a bend. Two little black kids were playing in the aisle. On the seat across from Joanna and Tess, their mother sat holding their baby brother. She smiled at Tess, because this morning they had had breakfast together in the lounge car and Tess had played with the baby.

She felt like she had known everybody on the train forever; the old man who snored all night, the Australian who kept stopping to talk to her mom, the Chinese women at the end of the car who carried their babies on their backs. They'd even been on the first train, the one from Colorado. She almost felt that in spite of being bored, she'd rather stay with them here than get off in New York, where she wouldn't know anyone at all.

The bathrooms were beyond a door at the end of the car. There was a girl in a long dress standing in the corridor outside the one marked for women. She was about Tess's age, tall and thin, with pale skin and pale brown hair. The hair was drawn back very tightly, and over it she wore a little white hat of thin, stiff cloth. The dress was dark maroon and very plain. She looked like somebody in a television show, and Tess stared at her for a long while. The girl looked back, calmly. Her eyes were pale blue and, without blinking, they looked straight at Tess. Tess pretended to adjust her headphones. Then she opened the door to the women's bathroom and ducked inside.

When she came out again, the girl was still there, but she had been joined by three boys in black suits, holding black, wide-brimmed hats, and a tall man with a long beard. He nodded to Tess and smiled, a quiet, peaceful smile that made her smile back without thinking. Then they walked away toward the next car in a long black line, the girl in her maroon dress following last.

When Tess got back to her seat, her mother was talking to the Australian. She squeezed by them and settled herself, making a nest out of her dark blue sleeping bag and the pillow the steward had given her last night. After a while the Australian went away, and Joanna picked up her magazine again to read.

"You know those people in that movie we saw about the kid who sees a murder? They wear old-fashioned clothes," Tess said.

"You mean *Witness?*"

"Yeah. Those people."

"Amish."

Tess nodded urgently, "There's some on the train."

"I know," Joanna said. "I saw them." She was still looking at her magazine.

"Are they real?" Tess asked.

Joanna looked up. "Of course they're real."

"But why do they do that?" Tess asked.

"What, the clothes?"

Tess nodded, her face troubled.

"It's their religion."

"I know that. But why? What's religion got to do with wearing old-fashioned clothes?"

Joanna sat silent a moment and lowered her magazine, laying it flat on her jeans-clad knees. "It's about rejecting the present, I think," she said slowly. "Some people think the past was a better time. Simpler. No cars or television or computers." She grinned, tossing her ponytail of blond hair. "Just your scene, Tess. Why don't you turn Amish?"

Tess ignored the teasing grin. "Do you think they're right?" she asked. Her narrow forehead was lined with concentration.

Joanna laughed, "Do you?"

"I asked what you think."

Joanna sighed and then answered honestly, "I think you can't go back to the past. You can't unimagine things. You have to live with them."

"They look real happy," Tess said. Joanna, startled, turned to her daughter.

"I know," she said. "It beats me how."

"You don't have any religion, do you?" Tess said. Her eyes were narrow.

Joanna laughed again, louder, "How do you know? Because I don't wear a black dress and a muslin bonnet?"

"You don't do anything. You don't go to a church, or read the Bible or anything."

Joanna rested her head back against the seat, feeling the humming vibration of the wheels rising through it. She kept her voice light. "I can have my own religion, Tess. I don't have to go to a church to have one."

"Yeah," Tess said impatiently. "But it's not a real religion, is it?"

"Who says?"

"Nothing in our lives is real. We haven't got a real house. You haven't got a real husband. I haven't even got a real father. Everything's always been fake."

Joanna snapped the magazine shut. "Look, Tess, get off my case. We've been over this ground a few times, and you know as well as me it doesn't get us anywhere."

"All right. Don't bug me about it."

"You're bugging me, Tess." Tess said nothing. Joanna drew two slow breaths and asked reasonably, "Now would you like to tell me what's eating you?" Tess shrugged and squirmed around in her seat.

"Nothing."

"Nothing."

Tess looked out the window. "What are we doing this for, anyway?"

"Doing? Doing what?"

"This. This dumb-ass trip." Joanna leaned back in her seat and stretched her legs out on the leg rest, looking wearily at the back of the seat in front of her with its folded airline-style tray.

"We've been through this, Tess."

"Yeah, but *why?*"

"I told you. I want to help my brother."

Tess closed her mouth tightly, her slightly crooked top teeth nibbling her bottom lip. "What's *wrong* with him that he needs help? Is he sick, or what?"

Joanna thought carefully before saying, "He's unhappy . . . he lost his job and he hasn't got any money."

"We haven't got any money, either," Tess said.

"We have some."

"You're not going to give him our money, are you?" Tess's voice wavered between disgust and alarm.

Joanna shook her head angrily. "Stop *worrying*, Tess. Christ, you've never starved, have you?" She shook her head again and stood up. "It isn't about money, anyhow."

"Where are you going?" Tess said.

"There's no point talking to you when you're like this." Joanna dropped the magazine on her seat and picked up her shoulder bag.

"Where are you going?" Tess said again.

"To the lounge car."

"You're going to smoke."

"Yes, Mother Teresa."

"God, you're weak. How long did you quit for this time? Three whole days?"

"Piss off," Joanna said in a mouthed whisper, so the woman with the baby wouldn't hear. She stalked off down the train, and Tess flopped gloomily into her seat, turned her tape over, closed her eyes, and sank into the music once again. In a little while she felt the seat sway as her mother got back into her own. There was a click as the tray in front of her was lowered. She couldn't resist looking, but she kept her lids together so her mother wouldn't notice. Through a furry fringe she saw a big paper container full of popcorn and a Diet Pepsi. She opened her eyes.

"Hey," Joanna said. Tess scooped a handful of popcorn into her mouth.

"Is that what you were really doing?" she asked.

"That's what I was doing," Joanna said.

"Hey, thanks." Tess stuffed another handful of popcorn into her mouth and looked out the window. "I hate Pennsylvania," she said cheerfully.

———

ANNIE HEARD MARTIN put the phone down and waited. There was a shuffling of feet on the thick bedroom carpet and the sound of drawers opened and shut, the squeak of the closet door hinge, a rattle of hangers. The noise built to the crescendo she had anticipated, crowned with a querulous, "Annie? Annie? Where's my gray striped shirt?"

Annie carefully applied mascara to the lashes of her left eye, raising her little reading glasses to do so and dropping them back to assess the effect. She took the glasses off and called, from behind the closed bathroom door, "In the ironing basket. Wear something else." Martin's heavy feet clumped across the bedroom, and the door opened. Martin glared at her.

"What's it doing in the ironing basket? I need it."

"Fatima didn't get to it. Wear the blue one."

"Goddamn it, Annie, why hasn't Fatima done my shirts? What does she do, anyhow?" His voice was childish and peeved.

Annie said mildly, "She does enough," adding, "she had to leave early. Her sister had a doctor's appointment and couldn't look after the baby." She stepped past him and walked through the bedroom and out into the hall. Glowering, Martin followed.

"So I don't get my shirt done." He spoke more quietly, as he entered the kitchen, because Merrilee and David were there. He poked about in the laundry basket in the utility alcove beside the back door of the apartment. Annie looked over Merrilee's shoulder at the chili she was stirring on the stove.

"Hmm, good," she said. She edged by Merrilee's widened hips to the refrigerator.

"You could iron your own shirt," she said with a little smile.

Martin stared at the wrinkled sleeve he was holding. "I haven't time."

"Sure you do. The train'll be late anyhow. They're always hours late. I don't know why she didn't fly."

"Because flying costs money, Annie," Martin said stiffly. He dropped the shirt. Annie took out a bottle of spring water and set it on the green-tiled counter. She looked unimpressed.

"I'd have sent her some. I said so." She opened the bottle and then set it down again and said impatiently, "I don't know what's with her."

Merrilee turned around from the stove. "Maybe pride?" she said softly.

Annie shrugged, "It's only money. Who cares anyhow?"

David looked up from the Arts section of the the *Times*, "People who don't have it care," he said.

Annie stopped midway through pouring her glass of spring water. She turned to her son and waved the bottle at him. "I don't need a lecture from you, Dave. I've been broke, too. Dad and I were broke for years. I know what it's like."

Martin stared at the laundry basket and then said slowly, "We were young, Annie. We knew it wasn't going to be forever. It's different for Jo."

David smiled, a worn smile, bringing out the new adult lines at the corners of his mouth. He said, "I'm young now, Dad, and I don't know that." Merrilee spun about from the stove, a tablespoon still in her hand.

"Yes, you do, David," she said urgently. "Of course you do." She was glowing with confidence, her face pink-cheeked from the heat of the stove. "You're just bummed out at the moment. You've got everything going for you." Martin studied his son and daughter-in-law quizzically, seeing the quick smiles that passed between them. He looked at Annie and turned away, walking heavily out of the room.

When Annie followed him, she found him in the bedroom, putting on the blue shirt and frowning at himself in the mirror of their antique oak dresser. She leaned against the doorjamb and watched him.

"You're just going to meet my sister, you know." She gave

him her wise look. He avoided her eyes. He opened a drawer and peered into it. "What did Seth have to say?" Annie asked mildly.

"Nothing much. Where's my . . . oh, here it is." He drew out a gray and blue silk tie. "He was being mysterious."

"Mysterious?"

"I think he called to find out about Joanna."

"What about Joanna?" Annie straightened up.

"When she was coming."

"Why should it matter to Seth?"

Martin shrugged, his fingers fumbling the tie knot. "Who knows? Maybe he wants to call when she's here. Maybe he wants to talk to her." He looked vague and turned away, slipping his heavy shoulders into his jacket. "He has a new book out in England. There was a big review in one of the London papers. He's faxing a clipping to my office."

"A good review?"

"Would he be sending it if it wasn't?" Martin asked dryly.

"He might," Annie answered. "Seth's funny with you, sometimes. He's almost too self-deprecating, if anything."

"He can make it look that way," Martin said.

Annie stepped away from the door. She folded her arms. "You're jealous of your brother," she said.

"I'm not."

"I can always tell when you've been talking to him. You get all restless and grumpy and start picking arguments."

Martin sighed. He sat down on the edge of their bed, his shoulders slumped, and slipped on his shoes. He looked down at them and said, "Seth always did exactly what he wanted, while I worked my butt off. Now he's living on the Italian Riviera and I'm still working my butt off." He looked up and grinned boyishly. "I'd be crazy if I *wasn't* jealous."

Annie didn't return the grin. She said, "You always make a joke out of it, but you don't really think it's funny." Martin straightened his back and sat with his hands on his knees, studying her tiredly. Annie never seemed to change. She looked exactly the way she looked at college, slim and vibrant, in tight jeans and an open-necked white shirt, thin gold chains across the delicate skin of her throat. He knew there were lines there, but you certainly had to look for them. He had a sudden image of her standing like that, hand on hip, big violet-blue eyes challenging, a *high school* memory, not even college. She was wearing that mustard seed necklace that for some reason all the "in" girls wore, and that challenging look, and she'd just caught him up in his bedroom, fooling around with Joanna. That was the day he learned he couldn't lie to Annie Carlson.

"I resent Seth," he said, looking straight into her eyes.

"Why?" she returned unbudgingly. "Because he's successful? You're successful too." He sighed again and got up. He scooped his change off the dresser and slipped his wallet into his pocket.

"I'd better go. I'll be late." He stepped past her, out of the door.

"You have time," she said. He heard her following him down the corridor.

He stopped in the living room and found the car keys among the piles of bills on his desk in the corner. David and Merrilee were watching CNN news with eager young intent. He gave it a quick wry glance and turned to Annie. "I don't resent his success, Annie. I resent his irresponsibility. And the fact that his irresponsibility has contributed quite largely to his success. It may be petty of me, but I find it awfully unfair somehow."

Annie smiled, "*Karma*, as Seth would say . . ."

"Yes," Martin said angrily. "I bet he would. Karma." He shoved the keys into his pocket. "He's never pulled his weight in this family."

Annie cocked her head sideways and gave him the forthright look. "Have we? Look at Sara looking after both your parents all by herself. That can't be a whole lot of fun these days." Martin glared at her, looked around in frustration, and then slammed his hand down on the desk.

"What do you want me to do? Move them in here too? We're having enough trouble putting up Joanna and her kid for a visit." He stopped short, seeing Annie shaking her head, a quick, almost imperceptible gesture. Out of the corner of his eye he saw Merrilee look away. David got up from his seat on the couch beside her and turned his back to the television.

"Look, Dad," he said. "If you want us to move out, just say

so, okay?" His lips were tight. Martin shook his head, clumsily apologetic. "Only don't hint about it."

"He doesn't want you to move out," Annie said, her rich voice smooth and placating. "He's just grumpy. Ignore him."

"*Annie . . .*" Martin protested.

"Go on. Meet Jo's train." She ushered him out into the hall.

"Thanks a lot, Annie. That was real supportive. 'Just ignore Martin, everybody.' How am I supposed to have any standing in this family if you treat me like some glorified Fred Flintstone?"

Annie was laughing, "Oh, grow up. You don't need support. They do. Come on, where's your sense of humor?" She straightened his tie. "You look great," she said kindly, undoing three locks and letting him out the door.

Getting out of the apartment felt too good. He didn't want to admit to himself what a liberation the ride down in the elevator had become, how welcome the cold Hudson river wind outside the building. He loved his son. He loved his daughter-in-law, truly like another daughter. He loved his wife. But the three of them, all the time, all so close and trying so hard and usually excruciatingly thoughtful . . . and then there was all that stuff at work. His new receptionist screwing up on the computer all the time, and his partner's seemingly permanent divorce wrangle that went on and on, until Martin was tempted to suggest he drop medicine entirely and take up law as a more realistic use of his time. And on the subject of law, another letter from Mandelbaum's attorneys over some ridiculous detail of the new security system. To top it off, there was always the fine art of medicine, though sometimes it seemed he was the only person in the damned building who remembered their purpose for being there.

But he did remember, and so today he had that immaculately dressed woman in, once more, with her immaculately dressed little girl; those bruises again, and yet another cock-and-bull story about falling off a swing. But no proof. No proof.

He put it out of his mind and thought of Seth and the pictures of the place in Italy that Danya had shown them so eagerly. "Uncle Seth says you must go out this winter." Danya burbling on with that lovely innocence that comes only when someone else is still responsible for making life work. Christ. Italy. He and Annie were killing themselves just trying to get away for a couple of days in Connecticut. They hadn't been to Seth's place in two years.

He found the car where he'd left it across the street, with windows intact, radio inside, and was cheerfully surprised. He got in and pulled out into the traffic, turned left on Columbus and headed downtown, savoring the time alone in his metal cocoon, the sound system soothing him with Mozart, the anonymous lights of the city a brilliant background to his thoughts. He was early, as Annie had kept telling him, but he wanted to be early, to find a place to park, to find the right gate, and to sit and draw out the pleasure of anticipation.

In the main concourse of Penn Station he bought a bagel and coffee and a copy of *Newsweek* and sat down on a plastic seat to wait. He pulled the tab in the top of the coffee container, sipped it once, then set it on the seat beside him, and holding the bagel in his right hand, flipped open the magazine with his left. He glanced at the lead story and then picked up his coffee again and sat, looking blankly out at the crowd of waiting travelers. He thought of Jo.

Ten years. Eleven. Tess was eleven. He couldn't believe it. His last image of them was yet so vivid; Jo, flustered and heavy breasted, hair in disarray, huddled over her baby with that animal new-mother protectiveness that still thrilled him whenever he saw it. Tess was two months old and Joanna had brought her home to show the family. Looking back, he saw that visit as a brief golden moment in an increasingly black year. But at the time it seemed a redemptive reunion, a time of healing old wounds.

It was fall of the second year since Molly Carlson had vanished from their Adirondack camp. The police search had been scaled down to tired formalities. The story had faded from the papers. One by one, members of the family moved on with their own lives. He and Annie threw themselves into their careers. His children, stunned yet by the loss of their cousin, stepped cautiously into adolescence. Sara resumed touring with her dance company, and Seth went back to Europe. Time was passing for everyone. Except, he realized now, for Eric.

He could not today understand how he had failed to recognize Eric's growing instability. The signs were all there: his obsessive pursuit of meaningless leads, his refusal to accept the decisions of the police, his fierce resistance to a memorial service for his daughter. Martin kept assuring himself that time would fix all that when, in reality, time was just making it worse.

When Dina and Eric separated that spring, it had saddened everyone and surprised no one. She had relinquished their child to death, and he relentlessly sought her in life. They had no common ground on which to grieve. And yet, Martin somehow convinced himself the break was temporary. He had, he realized, simply chosen to ignore it, because he couldn't face what it signified. He was still telling himself that Eric was doing no more than exhausting every logical avenue. And he was so logical, so disciplined, so rational in his essential irrationality, that it was hard to conceive that he might also be insane.

And then in the midst of everything, Joanna did that wild, stupid thing and came back from the West all golden-haired and beautiful with her golden-haired fatherless child . . . as if with one enormous gesture she could mend their world. They had a big family gathering, both sets of parents, everybody except Seth, and, of course, Dina. They held it up at the camp. Martin's father had set that up, and Eric hadn't resisted.

It was a warm, cathartic time. They all felt so close, aware they were making their peace with the past, consciously closing the door. Eric seemed so normal—with his parents, with Martin's own kids, with everybody. Martin could still see him so clearly, sitting with his feet up by the woodstove, Joanna's tiny baby sleeping on his shoulder while they talked and played cards.

When Joanna flew back to Denver, Martin and Eric had taken her to the plane. Annie was tied up with work, so it was the two of them who hauled Joanna's bags of soft toys and diapers and the changing mat printed with teddy bears to the gate at La-Guardia. How funny to see his free spirit Jo laden down with the paraphernalia of parenthood. How funny and how sad.

Eric carried Tess through the airport and handed her back to his sister at the gate. Jo stood there in her jeans and cowboy boots, clutching her baby and saying a tearful good-bye. Martin still liked to think that a few of the tears might have been for him.

After she had gone, he and Eric drove back into Manhattan,

to the apartment on York Avenue Eric had taken after the sepa-
ration. They had a couple of beers and talked about football, and
then Eric told him that he and Dina were getting a divorce. Martin
argued about it for hours, dragging out all the old clichés about
grief and time passing and not making quick decisions. Eric didn't
say much. He didn't really seem interested. And then quite suddenly he announced he had a good new lead and was going to
California to look for Molly.

Martin could still feel the sick jolt the words gave him. He
hadn't argued. He hadn't said anything. He'd slipped into professional calm and sat nodding silently. He could think of nothing
to do, and so he did nothing. He never even told Annie. He
simply shut it out, and a few weeks later Eric left them, abruptly,
without warning or good-bye. It was the biggest failure of Martin's
life, the one he would never forget.

He had not seen Joanna since that day. Somehow the years
just seemed to go by. Joanna never had any money, or else she
was tied down by a business—the store, and after that, the ranch.
Annie made the trip out West three or four times and brought
back pictures. Martin tried not to let his eyes stray always from
the daughter to the mother. Somehow, between their social and
family and working schedules, there was never the time for him
to go too. Nor the excuse. She was his wife's sister, not his.

How odd that a person who had once centered his world could
become, in time, a Christmas and birthday correspondent, her
love a scrawled afterthought on the back of a card. He sipped the
coffee. His hand was trembling. He felt foolish and old and
thought suddenly of Annie, imagining her wise, knowing smile.
Annie knew him too well. It was the best thing about their relationship, and the worst.

He wondered whether it was her being that one year older.
That had mattered a lot when they were kids. It shouldn't matter
now, surely, and yet she had retained that small emotional edge
over him, and in some ways being married to her was like being
married to an older sister who'd seen it all before. He could never
impress Annie.

Her support of him was rock solid, but it was strangely unsat-
isfying. It was too reasonable, too rational, took too much account

of his failings. It was mature and right and all he should ask, and yet something inside him cried out for that impassioned, unreasoned faith that Merrilee had in David, a faith grounded only in love. But that Annie had never had. Only Joanna had felt that for him. Until, of course, he had let her down, once, and so badly that nothing could ever be the same again.

The thought of that time brought its own familiar weight of remorse and regret. Brooding on it, he sipped again from the coffee and munched glumly at the bagel, ate half, and rose to throw the rest away. He turned around, looking for the nearest receptacle, and brushed roughly against a man who loomed up suddenly beside him, catching him in his moment of flagrant waste.

"You got any change?" The man was tall, thin, and beneath a layer of grime and a checked scarf wrapped around his head, fair-haired. Martin's heart thudded. *Eric.* He drew back with a jerk and saw that of course it was not Eric, but a younger stranger who really did not even resemble him. "Look, man, I haven't eaten in two days," the beggar said bluntly. The voice and the eyes were uncomfortably belligerent. Martin held his scrap of bagel awkwardly at his side and stared blankly. His beggar policy was more complicated than Annie's: sometimes he gave, sometimes he didn't. Mood, the attitude of the mendicant, weather, even the clothes he was wearing and the relative ease, or otherwise, of getting at the change in his pocket, affected his decision. The primary factor was speed. If he could get the whole act over with minimal human contact, he gave. What he shrank from was situations like this, when, obliged to wait on in his present locale, he might become the target of further approaches, of abuse by a crazy, or of the loquacity of a drunk. But somewhere among this anonymous band of reject humanity was the man who had been for thirty years his closest friend, the knowledge of which imbued the stranger before him with awful resonance.

"Okay," Martin mumbled. He juggled his coffee cup and the half-eaten bagel into one hand and, catching the magazine under his arm, slipped his other hand beneath his overcoat and into his trouser pocket. He had no special supply reserved for beggars, and what came out was largely nickels and dimes. He thrust a handful into the outstretched hand and started to push past. To his horror the man stood and counted it, spreading the coins out on his gray palm and sorting them with the forefinger of his other hand, as if the transaction had been not charity, but a legitimate purchase.

"I can't get anything for that," he said. Anger rose in Martin and was submerged by embarrassment. The food in his hand made him vulnerable, culpable, and physically awkward.

"What do you need?" he asked stupidly.

"Dollar and a quarter. Dollar fifty." The stranger looked almost contemptuous, as if Martin should know better than to ask. He reached for his wallet, but knew he couldn't maneuver it open with his hands full, couldn't put down his burdens without further awkwardness. The whole thing was taking far too long. He jammed his big hand back into his pocket, brought out the rest of his coins, and pushed them into the beggar's hand.

"That's all I've got." The man took it, looked at it sourly, and turned and walked away. Flustered, Martin scrambled out of the row of seats and piles of suitcases to the wastebasket and thrust his uneaten bagel and the half-filled coffee cup inside. A flow of people with luggage was pouring from the escalator. Involved with the beggar, he had missed the announcement of Joanna's train.

He hurried toward the crowd, scanning the laden passengers, turning to look behind him in case he had missed them and they had already gone past. He was nervous, sweating, annoyed with himself, annoyed with the beggar, and in a sudden violent reversal of emotion, annoyed with Joanna, whom a few minutes before he had awaited with such eagerness.

Why did she always do this to him? Why did she get him into these situations, these moral dilemmas that demanded more of him than he had to give? Somehow the beggar had become her creation, another challenge thrust into his world when all he wanted was peace. In a perceptive instant he saw Joanna's pursuit of Eric for what it was: another of her great crusades, holy and hopeless. How often had he been over this ground before? The sick birds of childhood, squeaking and crapping in their cardboard boxes. The black puppy that died of distemper. That poor brain-damaged girl in junior high, whom Joanna alone had befriended, ignoring her awkward walk, her clumsy speech, and drawing her into their circle. He could still feel the excruciating mix of right-eousness and humiliation as he sat at her lonely lunch table under Joanna's fierce, determined eyes, while his friends snickered behind his back.

Then it was college and Vietnam, and her moral ferocity was turned against everything his fifties childhood had taught him to believe. She made him think and question. She shook the simple convictions he and Eric had shared all their lives. She bullied him into protests and politics. She berated Eric savagely for accepting the draft rather than jail. But then it was Joanna who wrote to Eric so steadfastly, every faithful week of his tour.

Now Eric himself was her cause. Martin felt exhausted and yearned to run away, back home to Annie and the apartment and everything quiet and normal and sane. Then he looked up and saw her walking toward him across Pennsylvania Station, tall and strong and suntanned, and lightly tousled as if she still carried the Colorado wind in her hair. And beside her, lanky and awkward and staring around in amazement, was Molly Carlson's ghost.

Grown-Ups

"I LOVE THIS," Joanna said. "It feels just like home." She tipped her chair back from the big square butcher-block table, balancing it on its back legs and stretching her arms over her head.

Annie tilted her wineglass and said with a brisk smile, "I hope so, Jo. It *is* home."

"Like Mom and Dad's," Joanna said quickly. "I meant it felt like Mom and Dad's."

Annie turned the wineglass around in her hands and set it down. She shrugged and said without conviction, "Well, there's a lot of their stuff around, all right. They left a lot of things with me when they went to Florida." She stopped abruptly and then said, hastily, "You can have any of it you want, Jo. Maybe I should have said so before. Only, at the time, I didn't think you'd have room. You'd just left the ranch . . ." Her voice trailed off awkwardly.

Joanna said at once, "No, no. You were right. Where would I put *any* of it? I didn't mean that anyway, Annie. Not the stuff. The feel. The way we're sitting here around the table, the way we used to, at home." Annie nodded, understanding, and relaxed with a smile. Martin, watching her, relaxed too in a warm glow of contentment. He loved having them both in one room. It made him feel complete, whole, as if in all the rest of his life something was missing.

"I love seeing you together," he said. They looked up, startled. He grinned and shook his head, his hands held up, lightly deprecating, before his face. "It's nothing. It just feels good."

"We'd spend more time together if we could," Annie said

levelly. "It's just circumstances keeping us apart. There isn't any problem."

"I didn't say there was," Martin said. The room went quiet. They were sitting in the kitchen, the remnants of Merrilee's chili before them, a second bottle of wine refilling their glasses. It was a big, luxuriant kitchen; although the apartment also had a small dining room, they had taken to using that as an office for Annie since so much of her work in her new job was done at home. Annie liked them all in the kitchen anyhow, close to her, so that she didn't miss the conversation. "It's just nice," Martin repeated lamely. He avoided Annie's eyes.

"I'll just check on Tess," Joanna said, standing up. Martin dropped his big hands to the table and sat looking at them, disconsolate. He felt suddenly awkward and out of place, sharply aware of his verbal clumsiness, his inability to get things right. Joanna's jeans-clad thighs brushed by him as she left the table. He looked up as she stopped briefly by her sister's chair.

"See if she wants anything. Maybe another Dr Pepper," Annie said. Joanna said, "Sure." She lingered a moment and they exchanged a smile. Martin, watching, felt shut out and bewildered. Their emotional closeness always startled him, just as he was forever surprised by their physical differences.

They had never resembled each other. Joanna, like Eric, had their father's Scandinavian coloring and build, his loose-limbed, athletic walk. Annie was small-boned and delicate like their mother. By the time Joanna was ten, she had overtaken Annie in height and people were mistaking her for the older sister—a burden of unfair expectation that did her no good at all. Molly had been like that too: that bony child-woman look, the narrow hips, the firm little rear . . . like Tess. The comparison chilled him and he wondered suddenly, if Molly had been chubby and childish, would she be alive today? The thought stirred the deep core of anger that had burned in him for thirteen years. He sighed, wearied as always by that intractable grief. Annie looked up, but then Joanna came back into the room. "Okay?" Annie said.

"Oh, she's fine," Joanna said lightly. She straightened her back, tucked her shirt into her jeans, unconsciously thrusting her breasts forward. They were good firm breasts, still; Martin noticed and felt guilty. "They're watching some Woody Allen movie that looks too old for her, but what the hell." She sat easily. Martin, unaccustomed to seeing her as a mother, was struck by the casual confidence of her parenting. He wasn't sure he approved of the way she and Tess teased and insulted each other through supper like a pair of sisters. But the child seemed bright and honest, talking assuredly with Merrilee about school and her friends, asking David about the plot of the book he was writing.

He supposed it was natural that they'd all gone off together immediately after the meal, settling in front of the television like a bunch of kids. They were the younger generation, happy among themselves. But he knew also that David was avoiding him. Merrilee was wounded and struggling not to let it show. He hadn't meant to hurt them. He never did. But now that he'd done it he didn't know how to fix it. Words always failed him. He hated words.

"Do you think she wants to go to bed?" Annie said. She looked at her watch. "It's eleven-thirty."

"I think she needs to settle down first, if it's okay. She's still pretty wired from the trip."

"Fine with me, Jo. There were never a lot of rules around here with my kids."

Joanna laughed heartily. "Well, there sure aren't any with Tess." She paused, lifting her wineglass thoughtfully, and added, a little puzzled, "Kids today aren't like we were at all. She says things to me all the time that would have got my mouth washed out with soap from Mom and Dad."

"Do you mind?" Martin said suddenly.

Joanna shrugged, "I'm not sure," she said honestly. Then she shook her head, brushing the loose blond hair over her shoulder. Martin saw suddenly that some of the long strands were actually gray, and felt a pang of loss. "Anyhow," Joanna said, "whether I mind or not doesn't seem to matter. It's like the whole world has changed and it can't be any other way. When I start telling her about the way we were, I hear myself sounding like the Moral Majority so I shut up." Martin leaned forward, urgently, his deep blue eyes intent.

"Do you think we did this?" he said.

"We?" Joanna said, looking confused, "did what?"

"Us. You know, the sixties generation. Did we make this happen by being so liberal?"

Annie laughed so loudly that he turned to her, looking hurt. Still laughing, she said mildly, "Being so liberal is never something I'd have accused *you* of, Martin." She sipped her wine and giggled. "When it comes to responsibility for the moral decline of the nation, I think you're off the hook."

Joanna said seriously, "Compared to our parents, Annie, every one of us was."

"That's what I mean," Martin said eagerly. "And are we now paying the price?"

Joanna looked uncertain, but Annie responded instantly, "And if we are, and if the price is confident, strong-willed little girls, aware of the world and its dangers, then I'll pay it, Martin. Happily."

Their eyes met, and on a slow intake of breath, he said, "Of course." He glanced quickly at Joanna, but she was looking at Annie, nodding gently in affirmation and gratitude.

Martin watched them and then, after a pause, said cautiously, "You know, of course, Joanna, the first thing I saw when I saw the two of you in the station?" Joanna turned to face him, glanced quickly at Annie, and looked back.

"She looks so much like Molly?"

"Christ, Jo, she's the image of her."

Joanna nodded, "I know." She tilted her head, listening briefly. Tess was in the living room, talking to Merrilee against the sound of the TV. She sighed softly. "The funny thing is, when I had her I wanted her to be *exactly* like Molly. And I knew she would be. I was so absolutely certain I was carrying a girl, for a start, I didn't even bother to ask the results of the tests." She paused. "I had this crazy idea of sort of sharing her with Eric. I mean, Dina wasn't going to give him another child, and . . ." her voice dropped. "I think I was still a bit off the wall." She looked down at her suntanned, ringless hands. "As she's grown up," she said, "I've wanted it less and less. Now I don't want her to be like her at all, but she is, more and more all the time. It's pretty ironic." She sounded very sad.

Annie said gently, "Is she even a little like her father, Jo?" Out of the corner of her eye she saw Martin blink quickly.

Joanna grinned cheerfully. "Do you want the honest truth? I can't remember what he looked like except that he was a hunk. I chose him for his genes. I counted on her getting her brains from our side."

Annie laughed richly, though Martin was visibly shocked. "Well? Did it work?" she said. "I'd be worried, you know. She's sure got our looks, yours and Eric's and Dad's anyway."

"And the brains of a ski-bum? God help her." Joanna grinned again. Then she said, "I think she's bright enough. Whenever she works at it, she gets A's at school. And she knows everything about every computer on the market," she added a little sourly.

Annie waved one hand, lightly dismissive. "Oh, David went through that computer thing too. They grow out of it."

"I remember." Joanna laughed suddenly. "I can't get used to your son as a father-to-be. It just seems incredible. The last time I saw him he was this little chubby kid."

"You're not the only one finding it a bit of a shock," Martin said dryly. "David was catatonic."

"He wasn't," Annie said. "He was not."

"*Annie.* He was floored. He's rising to the challenge, but he was pretty shaken. It was the last thing he needed."

Annie set her wineglass down firmly. "Well, it was maybe not the best thing for Merrilee either."

"I'm not blaming Merrilee."

"You sound like it."

"For Christ's sake, Annie, I'm not blaming anybody. I'm just saying it was a mistake." Joanna reached across the table, lifted the half-empty wine bottle and filled all their glasses.

"Oh, so what," she said easily. "They'd have wanted a family eventually."

"Eventually," Martin said stiffly. "Eventually isn't now. Eventually is when you have a career, a home, a base."

"Security?" Joanna said with a faint edge to her voice.

"Yes. Security."

Joanna leaned back in her chair and studied him coolly. "Nothing ever changes," she said at last.

Martin shifted his heavy body in his chair and looked to Annie, who looked away. He raised his eyes to Joanna's defiantly, but dropped them almost at once. "Well, what's wrong with security?" he said querulously. "Stability. Children need stability. You don't know. I do. I work with children all the time."

"I do know," Joanna said solemnly.

"I didn't mean that," Martin said quickly. "I didn't mean you."

"But you don't approve." Joanna tipped her chair back, her eyes cool.

"I think you've done very well. Tess seems a very nice child."

"Don't patronize me, Martin."

Annie leaned forward, her forearms on the table, and shook her head. "Come on, you two," she said. "Don't start in."

"It's okay, Annie," Joanna said. "We understand each other."

"Jo, I wasn't criticizing."

"Oh no."

"I've a lot of respect for what you've done."

"I'm sure you do. Founding member of the Dan Quayle Support Group for single mothers, aren't you?"

"Will you two stop," Annie said, her voice ragged, "both of you? Come on, I'm tired." Martin and Joanna glared at each other. "God," said Annie, "it's just like old times."

Joanna looked away. With her eyes averted, she caught Annie's hand in her left hand, Martin's in her right, and held them both. When she spoke again, her voice was softened. "Speaking of old times," she said, "have you had any luck, Annie?"

Annie picked up the change in tone at once and said, "With Eric?" Joanna nodded. Annie shook her head. "No."

"Not for lack of trying," Martin said quickly, still holding Joanna's hand. He looked across the table at his wife. "We're not going to find him, Jo."

"Oh, don't say that," Annie said, anguished.

"Unless," Martin went on without pause, "he wants to be found. And it's obvious he doesn't."

"It's not obvious," Annie said. Her lips were set in a tight, frustrated line.

Martin leaned closer to her. "Look, Annie. You've tried everything. You've tried the hostels. You've tried the church groups . . ."

"Have you contacted any of his old friends?" Joanna said. "He may have gone to one of them . . ."

"I called Pete Fricke. And Gerry Connors. Pete's up in Westchester now. Neither of them had heard anything from Eric in years. And that's all that's left. People scatter. You know how it is." He paused. "Pete was real funny. Distant. The trouble with this kind of thing is it carries a sort of taint. People are afraid . . . like maybe it will rub off on them. Pete's settled down with a family of his own. He just didn't want to know."

"What about places he might be working?" Joanna said persistently.

"Well, he wasn't working, obviously," Annie put in, puzzled.

"No, but he might have tried to get work."

"Where do you suggest we look?" Martin interrupted. "*What* work? He moved around so much. He had about four different careers after he came back from Vietnam. And then he did that computer course."

"He did very well at that," Joanna said. "I remember."

"He did very well at everything," Martin answered. "That's not the point. The point is he never stuck to anything. He could never settle. And that was before Molly, don't forget." Martin laid his palms flat on the table and took a deep breath. "Look," he said. "If we're really honest about it, Eric was never stable."

"That's not fair," Annie said. "He'd been in a filthy, unpopular war. He'd lost friends. He'd . . . he'd seen awful things. It took time to get over that. And as soon as he was finding his feet again, he lost Molly. How could he be stable?"

Martin opened his mouth to argue, but Joanna interrupted again. "What about the police?"

"The police weren't interested," Annie said flatly. "They couldn't care less."

"Of course they weren't." Martin slid his wineglass in a laborious circle, leaving an untidy smear. "Eric isn't even a missing person, Annie. He just doesn't want to know us anymore. It's time you realized that. It happens to thousands of families. People just drift apart. Look," he said, leaning forward, turning one hand palm upward, for emphasis, "we're in the phone book. Same address, same number. All he has to do is pick up a phone and call. He doesn't want us, Annie. None of us. I know it's hard to accept, but it's true."

"Then why did he come back to New York?" Annie said stubbornly. Her eyes were wet, and she brushed them with the back of her wrist. Martin looked away and shrugged.

"Who knows. Familiarity?"

"He's following a lead," Joanna said. She looked straight ahead, her eyes unfocused. "The only thing that would have brought him back here is Molly. She's the only reason he does anything. He's following a lead, just like that time he came to Denver."

"I thought he came for money," Annie said.

Joanna shook her head impatiently. "I gave him money because he needed it. He didn't ask for it and he didn't come for it. He came for Molly."

Martin's heavy eyebrows rose in painful disbelief. "What could make him imagine Molly would be in Denver?"

"Eric lives in a different world, Martin," Joanna answered quietly. "It's like an alternative universe. Things work differently there."

"You mean he's crazy."

"No." Joanna dragged the word out slowly, as she looked calmly back at Martin. "No. He's got every reason to be. But I don't think he's crazy. He's obviously obsessed, but who wouldn't be?"

Martin joined his fingertips. He closed his eyes, sorting his words. He pressed the tented fingers together, making prayerful palms. "Jo," he said, eyes still half closed. "In my work I get to know a lot of parents who lose children. Sadly enough. The grief is terrible. Nobody would deny that. But they don't all end up like Eric."

"There's no comparison," Annie said at once. "A child dying in a hospital bed is an irrefutable reality. Eric has no reality."

"I agree," Joanna said.

Martin leaned forward intently, "Denial is not confined by

logic, Annie. When I was doing my student obstetrics, I had a second-stage laboring mother denying she was pregnant. I've also had parents of a child riddled with metastasized bone cancer insisting to the end that he was getting better." Joanna reached forward and laid her sun-browned fingers on his forearm. He turned to her, uncertain, but boyishly pleased.

"Martin. You're missing the point. This isn't about grief. Eric isn't grieving. Eric hasn't *lost* Molly."

"Of course he has."

"No. No, he hasn't." Her fingers lingered on his arm gently, and the warm glow of affection in him deepened and slipped toward passion. "Do you remember," she said thoughtfully, "what it was like that first week? That first day even? When she hadn't come back and we were all looking for her? We were angry she was causing all that trouble, and then when it started to get dark we were real scared?"

"Oh, Christ, Jo, I don't need reminding." Martin stared bleakly across the table.

"When did it end for you?" Joanna asked.

Annie said, "When did what end?"

"Hope. When did you realize she wasn't coming back? We weren't going to find her?"

"Within an hour," Annie said flatly.

"No," Martin whispered, turning to look at her.

"I knew," Annie said. She shivered, chilled by her own memory. "I just knew."

Joanna nodded. "It was the next morning for me," she said. "When I woke up and it was all still real."

"Christ, I hung on for days," Martin said. "I kept thinking up logical explanations . . . wilder and wilder explanations."

"That's it," Joanna said. "That's where Eric is. He's never passed that time. He's still able to make logical arguments that prove she's alive. Within that context, everything he does makes perfect sense."

"That's what insanity *is*, Jo," Martin said, "making logical sense in an illogical situation."

Annie shook her head abruptly, shutting her eyes, shutting her mind. She turned away from Martin, facing Joanna. "You talked to him last, Jo," she said, deliberately calming her voice, distancing herself from Martin. "What was he like?"

Joanna answered slowly and thoughtfully. "Very controlled. Methodical. He had a real organized plan. The whole country mapped out. A gridwork. The most likely places highlighted. You know, he'd read a lot. Stuff about missing children. Porn rackets. Kidnappers." She paused. "He had clues. That car with the California plates the police had looked for. That's what took him to San Francisco. The first time, anyway. And there was that talk about a couple with Midwestern accents. He was going to follow that up. And the city people who left one of the cabins in a hurry. He'd made a real science of it. He had her picture printed on little cards to hand to people wherever he went. Of course, he did realize the picture was out of date already, even then. He explained that . . . Annie, he was so coolheaded. He had an answer for everything. One night he explained to me how he realized he'd probably find her working as a prostitute . . ." She swallowed hard. "She would have been fourteen then. And he accepted that. He said he knew it wouldn't be easy. He'd have to rehabilitate her. She might resist. He'd probably need professional help." She looked across the table to her brother-in-law. "He's rational, Martin."

Martin studied her carefully and then said, "Except on one key point, Jo. He's not going to find her and rehabilitate her because Molly is dead."

"I know that, Martin," Joanna said. She sipped sadly at her wine, finishing the glass. Martin refilled them all with the dregs of the bottle, setting it to one side. He looked morosely at the three half-filled glasses and realized, surprised, that he was a little drunk.

Annie shook her head tiredly. She stood up, leaving her unfinished glass on the table. "I'm sorry. I've got to go to bed. I'm wiped out."

Joanna jumped up, but Martin said quickly, "Relax. I'm going to have some decaf while I load the dishwasher. Have one with me." Annie stood with her hand on her hip beside her chair. She raised one eyebrow and gave Martin her small, wise smile. Then she kissed her sister good night and left the room.

"I'd better check on Tess," Joanna said. Martin finished filling the coffeemaker and flicked on the switch. He stacked the plates on the counter above the dishwasher and then followed Joanna into the living room. The room was empty, except for Tess asleep on the sofa in front of the television.

"Where's David and Merrilee?" he asked Joanna.

She leaned over and switched off the television. "They must have gone to bed." She looked at him, puzzled.

He shrugged. "They didn't say good night to me," he said, and then realizing it sounded stupid, he added, "I guess they didn't want to bother us." He crossed the room as Joanna gently shook Tess's shoulder. "I'll take her," he said.

She didn't wake, but curled tighter when he lifted her, making a bony, awkward shape that reminded him of David. His own two children were so different from each other. From the earliest days he could categorize them by the texture of their embraces: Danya, soft and placid as the big old Persian cat they had the year she was born, and David, all shoulder blades and elbows and bony knees. One sought his arms, the other resisted, and yet it was from that resisting son he felt the most powerful need. He had treasured moments like this when David was little, that tense, turbulent body briefly acquiescent to his love.

"Well done," Joanna whispered when he'd finished tucking her daughter into Danya's old bed. "I can never manage that. She always wakes up and wants to argue until three in the morning."

"That was David," he said as he shut the bedroom door behind them. "Out like a light one moment, then wide awake and into mega-kvetch the next." He laughed softly as they returned to the kitchen. The coffee was ready and he poured two cups. "You know," he said suddenly, "I miss it all so much."

"You miss that?" Joanna said. She stopped midway through setting a dinner plate in the rack of the dishwasher.

"I do. It was so much simpler then, in spite of everything."

Joanna jammed the plate in and faced him, exasperated. "Oh, don't you tell me this is the easy part now. I want to climb the walls when people say that."

He leaned against the refrigerator, his coffee mug smothered by his two big hands. "No, not easy exactly." He paused. "It's redeemable still, though. When they're really little it's the most redeemable of all. You know, 'Daddy I hate you and I hope you die,' and then two seconds later, the kisses and the arms around you, 'I love you, I love you forever, Daddy.'"

"Tess is past 'I love you forever,'" Joanna said dryly.

He answered, "I know. I can see that; she's growing up. But she's still within your reach. In a little while, once she's really grown-up . . ." He paused and said softly, "they slip out of your grasp." He bent his head and sipped the coffee. Joanna finished loading the machine, shut the door, and switched it on.

"You're tired, Martin," she said.

He answered, "I think I'm getting old." She smiled and made a small, easy shake of her head, but he continued, "You know what puzzles me? I used to think that when I got here, where I am, this stage of life, at least I'd understand things, but I don't."

"What things?" Joanna asked. "Understand what?"

"I'm still waiting," he said, frustrated. "I'm still waiting to turn into my father." He set the mug on the counter and paced two strides across the kitchen, stopped and turned to Joanna again, "I guess in a way I have. I see him in the mirror every morning, but where's all the confidence and certainty I remember? That way he had of always being in control . . ."

Joanna said, "Maybe it just seemed that way."

"I don't know."

"Our parents were so much more remote. We never saw their flaws."

"You know what I think's the biggest surprise about growing up?" Martin asked. She shook her head. "You don't," he said. "It doesn't happen. You're fifty years old and it's still the first day of school, with your new notebook all stiff and unopened, and the floor smelling of polish, and the blackboard scrubbed clean, and the new crayons with none of their tips broken, and all the kids looking bigger and smarter than you, and you still don't know. You still don't know." His head slipped downward, heavily, a little drunkenly. Joanna stepped closer. He smelled the sweet, soft musk of her hair. She put her hands on his shoulders, and when he looked up his eyes were on a level with her own. He had only to move a fraction forward for their lips to meet. He hesitated and she slipped away, serenely out of his reach.

⸺

THE ROOM WAS DARK. Tess woke up because she'd heard a sound, but then couldn't hear the sound any longer and couldn't remember where she was. She thought of the train first, because of the way she would wake up whenever it stopped at a station, but the train wasn't this dark and, besides, she was lying flat in a bed with blankets, not curled on a seat in a sleeping bag. Then she thought of the trailer and tried to form the shape of her room around her, but the bed had the wall on the wrong side and the little light there was, coming through closed blinds, came from a different place. She waited until her eyes worked better in the light. There was another bed, beside her, in the middle of the room, and a humped shape under blankets. The shape moved and she knew it was her mother. Then she remembered she was in New York, in an apartment building, six floors up from the ground. She lay very still, thinking about it.

Sounds came from everywhere. She heard people walking, above her and below her, water running somewhere, and a sound like a train going by, inside the building, and police sirens outside, down on the street. She put out a hand and laid it against the wall and thought about the airy space just beyond her hand and pictured her bed, perched up on a man-made cliff. She pulled her hand back and then heard someone crying, and knew that was the sound that had woken her.

"Mom?" she whispered. But it wasn't her mother crying, but someone else, outside the room. For a moment she got real scared thinking about the girl who had died, whose picture sat on a table in the living room, and wondering if she was hearing a ghost. Stories with dead children in them always had ghosts, and the ghosts appeared to other children. But this wasn't a story; this was real life. She got up out of her bed and groped across the room to the thin crack of light under the closed door. The door squeaked when she opened it. Her mother turned around in her bed and half sat up.

"I'm just going to the bathroom," Tess said.

"You know where it is?"

"Sure." Her mom mumbled "Okay" and flopped down again into her blankets. Tess went out and closed the door. She stood for a moment in the short, dim corridor, looking down at her feet in grubby white socks. She was still wearing her tracksuit. She couldn't remember going to bed and realized, embarrassed, that her mother, or somebody, had picked her up from where she'd fallen asleep and carried her to bed like a baby.

THE NOISE CAME AGAIN, louder, of someone sobbing, and then voices talking. She crept down the corridor, trailing a hand along the wall. She passed a closed bedroom door and an open one, and the door to the family bathroom with its small, friendly night-light. The living room was dark, but she made her way through it by the glow from the kitchen beyond.

David and Merrilee were in the kitchen, David with his back to her, wearing his jeans and no shirt, his feet bare. Merrilee was facing him, but she didn't see Tess because she was crying and wiping her eyes first with the back of her hand, then with the heel of her palm. Her face was blotchy, her eyes puffy and red. She was wearing a big striped T-shirt, stretched tight over her round, pregnant stomach. Tess could see Merrilee's belly button sticking out, making a little lump through the T-shirt. She ducked down out of sight and heard David say, "Look, if he's making you feel this bad, we'll just move out."

"Where?" Merrilee's voice was high and squeaky.

"Somewhere. We'll find somewhere. We're not staying here. It's just not worth it."

"I don't think he meant to say it. He was just feeling hassled."

"I don't care. He *did* say it."

"He blames me. He thinks I've ruined your future."

"Well, fuck him."

"We shouldn't have had this baby."

"Yes, we should."

"No. He's right. We should have been more careful."

"We *were* careful. Is it our fault a screwing condom burst?"

Tess heard a giggle and was so surprised that she got up from her crouch and peered through the door. It was Merrilee giggling. She was holding David's hand.

"I think your mom's on our side."

"Oh yeah. It's just Dad being a tight-ass about it."

"Not really. He's just disappointed." David got up from his chair, and Tess squeezed farther back into the dark. But he didn't look at her, only stood behind Merrilee, his hands on her shoulders, the fingers of one caught in a few strands of her hair. "Are you?" Merrilee said.

"Me?" David's voice was suddenly loud. "Of course not." Merrilee put her hands up, feeling for his, tangling her fingers with his own.

"I think I am," she said.

"Merr?"

"Oh, not really." She gave a big, soft shrug. "Only, you know tonight, when we were watching TV, and Tess was there, all sprawled out on the couch, swinging her feet, so free, you know, not a care in the world, and all of a sudden I was so jealous. I just wanted to be her. Just to be a skinny kid again and not all fat and pregnant." She squeezed her eyes shut. "I don't think I want to be a grown-up yet."

"Of course you do," David said soothingly. "Of course you do." He looked up then and saw Tess watching. Their eyes met, and then Tess jumped back quickly and turned around and ran soft-footed through the dark living room and down the bedroom corridor. She found the bathroom with its night-light and slipped inside, pulling the door closed and pushing the button to lock it. She listened by the door until she was sure David had not followed her. Then she pulled down her tracksuit bottoms and underpants and sat on the toilet. She looked down at the small indentation of her navel, then pulled up her top and studied her flat chest. She thought of being round and soft and heavy, like Merrilee, and felt a thrill of excitement and, at the same time, a lonely anguish for her future lost self. She squeezed out a small trickle of pee so she could flush the toilet for her mother to hear. Then she got up and went out and stumbled back through the dark room to her bed.

Eric

ERIC AWOKE, immediately alert, slipped his hand under the flat gray pillow, checked for the wallet and the folder, and sat up. It was early. The long room was charcoal gray, the figures in the beds sleeping humps. Dawn was always the quietest time. The coughers and snorers at last were quiescent, the shouters and mutterers subdued. It was the best time for sleep, but he was an early waker, earlier and earlier it seemed. Perhaps it was the quiet itself that woke him. He was so accustomed to sleeping amidst the ugly, intimate noises of strangers.

He stood up and dressed quickly in his jeans and plaid wool jacket and his worn sneakers, still damp from yesterday's rain. He took the folder and the wallet from under the pillow, slipped the folder into the inner pocket of his jacket, and thrust the wallet into a front pocket of his jeans. Apart from a handful of dollar bills, the wallet held his driver's license, a sealed letter to his parents, and an American Express Gold Card, a decade out of date. The last he kept out of pure sentimentality, the last physical link with his past.

He unlocked the small metal locker beside the bed, with the key he'd hung on a string around his neck, and took out a gaudy sports bag, its corners fraying and grimy with age. In it he kept a single change of clothes and a plastic bag with a toothbrush, soap, a razor, a towel. When he was using the hostel, he kept the bag in one of the lockers, by a bed, or in the storeroom downstairs. But the locks were faulty, the keys often interchangeable, and he never trusted the wallet or the folder to their fragile security. On the street it was simpler. The sports bag became his pillow at night, and he wore most of the clothes to keep warm. He took out the toothbrush, towel, soap, and razor, returned the bag to the locker, locked it again, and walked between the rows of sleeping men to the washroom.

Windows of opaque nubbly glass let diffuse gray light into the room, dimly revealing the rows of urinals, the doorless toilet compartments, the line of chipped and cracked ceramic sinks. Eric flicked on the light switch for the cheerier yellow glow of the high, bare bulb. The floor, green linoleum worn down in places to its shredded brown backing, was puddled with water near the sinks, with urine elsewhere. He held his head high against the stinging ammonia stench, as if he could rise above both the stinking floor and the reality of his circumstances. Detached, peaceful, he washed, shaved, brushed his teeth. He looked hard at his reflection as he brushed his graying red-blond hair with short, stiff strokes, until there was only himself in the room, and the reflection, a middle-aged man with weathered good looks and glittering crystalline blue eyes, studying himself with morning appraisal, as men did in their bathrooms all over the city.

The highest panes of the tall, narrow windows were clear glass, and he stepped closer to one and craned his neck to gain a glimpse of the sky. The small slice that appeared beneath the peeling paint of the upper frame was opaque and white, too remote for him to tell a clear early dawn from cloud. The nubbly glass felt cold to his hand, and it rattled slightly in the wind that blew down the shadowy airshaft behind the building. All the hostel windows, dormitory as well as washroom, opened onto the same airshaft, consciously turning away from the outside world.

Still, it was a good hostel, and he was lucky to have found its almost invisible entrance, tucked away between a convenience store and a place selling army surplus, on Forty-eighth, west of Ninth Avenue. With a stand of aging tourist maps in its seedy little lobby, it had pretensions to being something other than a flophouse, which was why, among its clientele of drunks and crazies, addicts and down-and-outs, was a sprinkling of slightly bewildered European teenagers with guidebooks and knapsacks. Eric had discovered it at the end of August, when he was still sleeping rough, and marked it out in case he would need it in the winter days ahead. At the moment he used it intermittently; the October nights, though getting chilly, were still bearable, and there was more freedom, and indeed more privacy, on the street.

Eric had learned a lot in the four months he'd been back in New York. Of all the places he'd been, the hardest was New York where, ironically enough, he was virtually home. He'd hit the city at about the time his fortunes were touching their lowest point. Things had been gradually getting harder. Part of it was the recession biting in, wiping out the casual jobs he'd relied on in the first years. Part of it was himself. He was older, less fit, less presentable, less employable. He didn't like to admit it, but there had been a cruel downward slide in the last few years, and it was hard to imagine now that when he first began he was staying in motels and eating in restaurants and, actually, at the very beginning, using the American Express card.

Even so, he'd come to New York innocent in some respects. Apart from a balmy night or two on a California beach, he had never yet slept rough. His own innocence rather charmed him, looking back. His street ignorance had been monumental. That first time, huddled under his jacket beneath a tree in Central Park, lying awake half the night waiting to be mugged, he didn't even know what the poorest, most pathetic crackhead knew, about cardboard and newspaper and where to find it, and which churches let you sleep on their steps and fed you breakfast in the morning. In the surprisingly cold July dawn, how childishly proud he'd felt that he'd survived the night, like when he and Martin and Annie had slept out in the shadowy mosquito-ridden reeds by the creek when he was nine years old.

He knew a lot more now; New York was a city in which you learned fast. He knew about the shelters with their violent crazies, the private inviolate territories of the crack dealers, the public toilets where staying too long to wash and clean up risked a knifing or rape. And he knew the good things too. There were charities, churches, places that gave away food. There were good locations, where on a nice day when people felt kind, or on a bad one, when their consciences tugged, you could fill a paper cup with enough money to buy food and shelter in half a day and win yourself a half-day free. On the street, like everywhere else, money bought time. Time was what Eric needed most.

In New York he had begun to beg. It was a clear, logical choice, but not one he was happy with. Begging offended his integrity, not in itself so much as that it necessitated a lie. It was not true that he could not find work. He was certain he would find a job if he tried. But there was no job, no matter how tolerant the employer, that would allow him the time he needed. No one understood. Whether he worked as dishwasher, bartender, window washer, dog-walker, house painter, short-order cook, builder's laborer, gardener, or even, briefly, child minder for a crazy Chicago artist, the inevitable clash came. A lead would arise that he could not pass by, and he'd be forced to call in sick, lie, make excuses, until patience ran out and he was fired.

Precious time was slipping by. He acknowledged his return to New York as a watershed. Behind lay the conventional life he had always lived; here, a venturing into alien territory. It frightened him, but he would not relent. He would not step back into that safe, familiar world of work again until Molly was home. He comforted himself with the conviction that at least now it would not be long. So powerful was the conviction that he was at last approaching the end of his search that he allowed himself brief emotional respites, reassuring windows into the future that lay beyond. He began to think of practicalities, where they would live, what kind of work he would take up, what he would do about Molly's rehabilitation, her health, her education. How quickly, or how slowly, he should reintroduce her to family and friends.

He was aware in these last days of a kind of ferocious eagerness about him that made him harsh and intolerant of others, single-minded and self-absorbed, unlike his true self at all. The begging was an expression of his new urgency, and he had formed a vague idea about "paying back" those strangers who had helped him, once he'd found Molly. He would support a kid in Africa, or on an Indian reservation. Once he was earning regularly again, he'd make big contributions to AIDS research, or to charities for the homeless.

Maybe he'd even put one of those anonymous ads in a newspaper, a big one, telling about finding Molly and thanking everyone who gave. He wasn't sure, though, about the last. It smacked of crankiness, like people who thanked their favorite saints in the small ads, or who published personal pleas for World Peace. Eric wasn't a crank.

But that was all ahead. His present reality was a cold fall day and five dollars and fifty-seven cents in his pocket, out of which he must find breakfast and a subway token, the price of a short-cycle wash in the Korean laundromat at the corner and, with luck, something toward a room and a shower tonight.

Keeping clean was the hardest thing, and that drove him into the hostel almost more than the growing cold, so that once or twice a week at least he could shower and wash his hair. Keeping clean was expensive in the hostel, but on the street it was impossible. A splash of ketchup, a clumsy slurp of coffee, someone's soda spilled on a bench, and suddenly everything else must be put aside in a quest for a men's room with hot water, with soap, with paper towels. He needed somewhere and some way to clean up. Once a kid on a subway car had vomited all down his pants, leaving him sour and stinking and struggling to maintain his composure during the mother's profuse and useless apologies. Dealing with that had cost him an entire day.

He couldn't afford that. He had a job to do. He had to look halfway decent to get anyone even to talk to him. Even the small-time private investigator that people took him for would keep his clothes clean. Columbo wore a grubby raincoat, but he didn't smell of puke.

Eric wrung out his washcloth and put it, with his soap and razor and toothbrush, back in the plastic bag. He put his plastic hairbrush into his pocket, seeing suddenly, as he did, the two maple-and-silver-handled military brushes that had lain on his bureau at home. He wondered where they were. Did Dina still have them? Or had she thrown them out, or given them back to his parents as people gave back the possessions of the dead? He shut the thought away. Thinking of his parents was hardest of all. The misery it caused, like the misery now of knowing that Annie knew he was out here, was bearable only if he could cloak it in the temporal. Knowing he would return, triumphant, his daughter at his side, healed all hurts.

He wished he could talk to Annie. He'd even thought of calling her up—he had gone as far as to stand under the canopy of a public phone, staring at her number—but he knew he couldn't. All he wanted was to make sure she understood, that she clearly knew the truth: that he wasn't actually part of this. This wasn't his real life. The trouble was, he knew how it looked from the outside. He knew that, extraordinary as it seemed, an outsider might actually see no difference between him and, say, Ernie with his meths bottle, or Big King who thought the CIA was stalking him on the Seventh Avenue line, or even that poor kid with AIDS whom he'd seen lying on the steps of Penn Station last night. His unique situation, the overriding fact that he was only passing through this world, not part of it at all, and *that* only because of the urgency of the thing he had to do, was not, he had to recognize, visible. That's all he would have called Annie about, but in the end, he didn't dare. The risks were too great.

The lights were on in the men's dormitory when he returned, and people were stirring. A tall black-haired New Zealander who had come in late last night was dressing and studying the place curiously, adding another slice of America to his store of student memories. The gentle-voiced black Southerner in the bed beside Eric's was still sleeping, the dirty beige blanket pulled up around his ears, eyes squeezed shut, like a kid grabbing the last minutes before school. Eric moved quietly around the bed so as not to wake him.

He folded the blanket and left it neatly on the foot of the bed and straightened the undersheet. He shook the pillow into shape and replaced it. Then he took the bag with his clothes from the locker and walked out of the room. Whether or not he was back that night depended on the fortunes of the day.

He had breakfast at a place on Forty-ninth, a glass-fronted hole-in-the-wall that offered a special of bagel and fried egg and coffee for a dollar. There were no tables, but a line of stools along a narrow shelf, where a heavy man in gray dungarees was sitting reading the *News*. Eric bought the special and sat down on the farthest empty stool to eat. He took the folder out of his inner jacket pocket. It was a small, blue, plastic-cased book with several clear vinyl interior pockets, the kind traveling brush salesmen used to display pictures of their products. He laid it on the counter beside his paper plate.

He sipped from his coffee and ate the fried egg on the toasted half bagel and carefully wiped buttery fingers before he picked up the blue folder again. He opened it, reverently, to the first page. Her face looked out at him from a photograph he had studied so many times that he had to play little tricks on his eyes and mind to actually see it afresh, not just as a mass of light and shade, but a picture of a girl. It was the best likeness he had of her, her last school picture. In her fifth-grade portrait she was wearing the white blouse the girls were always told to wear, and her hair was still in braids. By the summer, the hair had been cut, chin length, the face matured from childhood to preadolescence. He always explained the differences whenever he showed the photograph, so there was no confusion.

On the second page he had a small collection of lesser photographs, snapshots, mostly taken at the camp that summer, some of them developed just after it happened. Those were the ones the police had used. Tucked into a third vinyl pocket, folded with brown, cracked edges, was a copy of the missing child poster they had used, with the name Molly Carlson and a badly lit close-up of Molly in front of the glassy waters of the lake. Beneath it, her height, weight, and age were listed with the clothes she wore that day: blue denim shorts, white T-shirt with yellow Garfield motif, white socks, white, green, and black Adidas sneakers. He had bought the sneakers for her in Glens Falls, on the way north. They hadn't had purple, her favorite color, in her size, and so she had settled, good-naturedly, for the green. He later thought of that, how if they'd had her size, the printed litany he knew so intimately would have been different.

But then, maybe *everything* would have been different. Maybe they would have gone fishing that morning, as she'd asked. Maybe Dina wouldn't have gone down to Lake George with Annie and David and Danya, leaving them alone. Or maybe Molly would have chosen to go with them. Maybe life just would have gone on as it did for families everywhere, another ordinary day of talking, playing, arguing, eating, washing, going to bed, and getting up to a day as ordinary as the one before. In all the last thirteen years, the only thing he would have asked of life was to be, again and forever, ordinary.

The picture on the next page was Eric's greatest treasure. It was not a photograph, but a drawing, and not, like all his others, over a decade old. It had been done a year and a half ago, in Phoenix, by a Native American artist he had met in the bar where he was working. It was a pencil and crayon sketch, and it showed not a ten-year-old child, but a grown woman of nearly twenty-three: Molly today. The artist had been a wonderful find. She worked freelance for police forensic units, but she did the sketch for free, employing computer graphics, her extensive knowledge of anatomy, Eric's descriptions of his sisters and mother and father, and her own intuitive mind, to extrapolate an image of the adult Molly would have become. When Eric saw the sketch it hit him like a hammer, as if Molly herself had stepped into the room.

He had expensive photocopies made on stiff, bordered cards. Those, along with similar copies of Molly's school picture, were packed neatly into the exterior pocket of the sports bag. He had forty left, of the original hundred of each he had made. He had distributed them all across the country for a whole year, and last June, in Seattle, they had finally brought him his wonderful lead. The bouncer at a club identified the sketch as the lead singer of a grunge band that had performed there the month before. In an instant, from among all the twenty-three-year-old women in America, Eric was focused on an individual. She had a name, a profession, an address.

Her name was Megan Carmichael. The initial "M" pleased him secretly, although he knew in reality the name meant nothing. She could have taken any name by now: a lover's, a friend's, a movie star's. Even her kidnapper's. He knew about the hostage bond between abductor and victim. He had even steeled himself for the possibility that he would find his daughter the now-willing companion of the man who had taken her from him.

The address was of little significance, only a run-down wood frame house, broken up into apartments, sheltering a fluid, transient society of young drifters. It did not surprise him to find no Megan Carmichael there. But what he had, as well as a name to go by, was a profession, and it didn't take very long to find that the grunge band calling itself Lilith's Daughter had left Seattle for New York. That was June. By July, hitching, riding buses, driving a van for a stranger carrying God-knew-what, Eric also reached New York.

The first few days after his arrival he was so elated, so convinced of the imminence of success, that he almost called Martin and Annie. Fortunately, sense prevailed. Things didn't work out so easily. First, there was the hard time he had finding somewhere to stay and then the difficulty with money. Day after day was wasted in just keeping alive. Then, the sheer scope of the city, with myriad clubs, whereas Seattle had had a handful, a huge world of musicians and hangers-on and would be's, all drawn to the same Big Apple magic. If anyone *had* heard of a band called Lilith's Daughter or a singer named Megan Carmichael, they'd forgotten before Eric found them. He scoured the Village and SoHo for posters. He checked out the new hangouts, where the college kids clustered on the Upper East Side. But he could only work at it when he had money. There were cover charges. He had to buy a drink to sit at a bar and ask questions. And he had to stay clean and get better clothes before he'd even get in.

At least now that he'd found the hostel, he was able to order his life into something of a routine. Now, like other men all over the city, he sat at breakfast, planning his day. It was a Saturday, and on Saturdays he had been accustomed to riding the Seventh Avenue line down to the Battery and working the crowds waiting to take the boat ride out to the Statue of Liberty. Then maybe he'd walk across to South Street where the packs of European and Japanese kids gathered at the Seaport Museum, and then in the afternoon, ride the subway back up as far as Columbus Circle, making what he could out of the ride, and finishing his day there. If things had been good, he could be done by four. And if they were bad, he could probably find Dan Grossman and ask for help. Though he hoped he wouldn't have to. He'd rather just talk to Dan if he met him, as if they were ordinary friends. The worst thing about being on the street was having no one to talk to, no friends.

It was easy to become overwhelmed by loneliness or worn down by sorrow. Not his own; when he thought of the plight of the homeless, his own part was automatically deleted, because he was not truly one of them. This was temporary. He was going back to the real world. But he identified with their sufferings, if not with them. And yet it had not made him despairing, only puzzled. He had seen also so much kindness on the street. It was not just from the city's unsung philanthropists, like Dan Grossman, who adopted a community of the homeless as their own, but from ordinary, plain, unremarkable people. Earnest-eyed kids, black or white, handing him dollars from their first lean paychecks. Sometimes they were so young and so poor looking, he wanted to hand their money back, but could not for fear of demeaning them. He remembered an old woman running after him because he had, while shuffling his possessions into a better order, inadvertently left his wallet on a bench in Bryant Park. So much kindness, so many big individual hearts. And yet so many people with nowhere to sleep.

The thought of Columbus Circle and the chance to talk to someone drew him powerfully, but in the end he abandoned it. No. He'd go over to Port Authority for the morning and then ride the shuttle to Grand Central. The shuttle was good, packed with innocently generous out-of-towners. And it was probably safer for him. He was wary of the Seventh Avenue line, since that day he met Annie. He was wary too of Columbus Circle, too close for comfort to Seventy-fifth Street.

The city was huge, but it was not infinite, as he'd felt it as a child. Nor was it the anonymous, amorphous mass of humanity people imagined. It was composed of myriad intersecting circles, social units where people constantly formed relationships and neighborhoods. Even the society of the homeless had a community of sorts. Men and women being habitual creatures, people lived in strict routines and patterns, including people like himself. Even the crazies harangued in a habitual format.

From his places in stations or in doorways, he saw, as the days passed, the same faces going by, until more and more were familiar. He had not seen Annie again, but he knew, inevitably, he would if he allowed his invisible neighborhood to again intersect with hers. It was not easy to hide, even here.

Then too, he was uncertain that if he saw her again, he'd have the strength to resist. For so many years he had fought this battle, a constant struggle against the desire to surrender and return, knowing to do so would mean abandoning his search, abandoning Molly. At the very beginning he had almost done that. He had felt himself drawn in by their terrible persuasive logic. He still remembered the insidious awful moments when the people he loved, the people he trusted, began to talk of his daughter in the morbid past tense, burying her alive in a mausoleum of words. Just in time he had recognized the danger and fled. He had tried to explain it to his parents in a letter, to Joanna that time in Denver, but he doubted any of them had ever understood. And so he discovered it was safest, and essential, to stay away. Yet the willpower required was at times formidable, with family and friendship at the end of a ten-minute subway ride.

———

HE WAS ABOUT to close the folder but he had a quarter of a cup of carefully rationed coffee left, so he turned it again to the fourth page, to the drawing of Molly. He rested his eyes on the sweet young lines of her face.

"I seen her, Eric." A hand jostled his arm as the voice, coarse and rough with tobacco smoke, whispered in his ear. Eric swung about on the stool, holding the folder to his chest, closely and defensively. The man was leaning over him, breathing in his face, holding a cigarette stub in one hand, trying to grasp the folder with the nicotine-yellow fingers of the other. "Gimme it a second, Eric," he said plaintively.

Eric held back. "Where?" he said cautiously. "Tell me where first."

"Jeez, if you'll just let me look to make sure."

"You've seen the folder, Artie," Eric said evenly, his voice artificially calm. "And the last time you saw it, remember, in the hostel, you tried to run away with it, didn't you, Artie?"

Artie shrugged, kiddishly, "That was a joke. Can't you take a joke?" He sat down heavily on the empty stool beside Eric's, flopping an elbow down on the counter. He was a big, oddly shaped man, with heavy female thighs, a weak upper body, a long, close-cropped head. His face, crisscrossed with the papery lines of the lifetime smoker, looked old, but he was fifty-three, hardly older than Eric. They had met during Eric's first night in the hostel, when, hungry for conversation, he had made the mistake of telling Artie his story. Since then, the man had plagued him with his shabby intimacy, making himself an unwanted accomplice in Eric's search, regaling him with a fund of eerie stories, most of them about little girls. Eric suspected he made them up to get attention, just as he was likely making this up too.

"Where'd you see her, then, Artie?" he asked again, patiently. The man turned away.

"You don't want to know."

"Yes, I do, Artie."

"Then show me the picture." Eric carefully held the folder up, back from Artie's reach, and opened it to the drawing. Artie looked hungrily. Then he wiped his lips and said, "Show me the other pictures." Eric closed the folder.

"You don't need to see them, Artie. Not to tell me where you saw her."

Artie looked angry, but as Eric turned away, he caught his sleeve, "At the hostel."

"The hostel?" Eric looked back, startled.

"Sure." Artie grinned, pleased at the effect. "And she was looking for you." A peculiar wave of emotion fluttered through Eric, part excitement, part fear, part simple wariness.

"For me. She was looking for me." Artie nodded. "How did you know?" Eric leaned forward, his intense blue eyes hard on the lined, saggy face. "Did she ask for me? My name?"

"She had pictures," Artie said. Eric narrowed his eyes. His voice was hard.

"Pictures? Pictures of me?"

Artie shrugged nervously. "Yeah. What of it?"

"You're making this up."

"No. I'm not."

"Yes, you are. You thought of the pictures because I had pictures. That's all."

"I'm not," Artie whined indignantly. "I'm not. I seen them. And something else." He got coy, dropping his eyes. Eric noted distractedly that the man had quite beautiful long eyelashes, totally in contrast to his damaged, unhealthy face.

"What else?"

"They were *both there*."

"Both? Who?"

"The woman and the girl," Artie said plainly. "Like both your pictures. Both of them were there."

Eric drew back, disappointed and repelled, "That's impossible," he said coldly. "They're one person, Artie. I told you. The woman *is* the girl, grown-up." Artie shrugged with unbudging confidence.

"Well, it beats me how, then, but I seen them both."

"You couldn't have," Eric said. He got up from the stool, turning to leave. Artie tugged at his sleeve and he pulled away angrily.

"What you mad about?" Artie asked querulously.

"I don't like when you make things up, Artie," Eric said. His voice was cool but still patient. "It upsets me." Artie rubbed his broad nose with the back of his hand. He sniffed noisily.

"Not my fault," he said. "You asked me to tell you and I'm telling you. I seen them." He shouted the last and then dropped his voice. "I'm the one you should listen to," he said conspiratorially. "I understand. You and me, we got a lot in common."

"Are you sure the woman looked like my picture?" Eric said slowly. He was thinking suddenly that it just might be true, that a woman came looking for him, even that she had pictures of him might be true. Only the woman would be Annie.

"Just like her," Artie said.

"You sure she wasn't maybe darker."

"Beautiful blond hair," Artie said. He closed his eyes. "I was so close, I could touch it almost. And the kid, she had it too." He sighed. "Beautiful blond hair." Eric reached out and touched Artie's arm.

Artie looked up happily. "You believe me?"

"Yes. I believe you. But are you sure about there being two of them? And the blond hair, maybe it just looked blond in the light . . ."

"I told you I seen it," Artie said. "Look, you think I'm blind or something? Jesus!"

A revolutionary thought was forming in the deep quietness of Eric's private mind. She looking for him? Molly looking for him?

She'd heard. She'd maybe seen one of the pictures. She'd traced him. A slow, wondering smile softened his tense mouth, and Artie, watching, grinned back. Wouldn't that be amazing? Molly finding him. He wanted to shout, to laugh . . . but the kid. The child, also. Molly with a child? A flood of excitement overwhelmed him. He'd never imagined . . .

"You see," Artie said, "I'm the one. I know about you. You and me, we're two of a kind. That scum in the hostel," he curled his lip, making a wet snarl, "waste of fucking space. All of them. But you, you got a family. You got that pretty little girl."

Of course. It was possible. Not just possible. Likely. Living that kind of life. He met kids all the time, thirteen, fourteen, with kids of their own.

"Me, I like kids. I've got two of my own, out in Mineola." He nudged Eric. Eric felt the nudge somewhere outside the sphere of his racing mind.

Molly's twenty-three. She could have a kid, eight years old, nine even. A kid the age she was . . . He laughed softly, stunned.

"Didn't know that, did you?" Artie nudged him again, warming to the effect he was making. "Surprised you, huh? People make assumptions. They see you on the street, think you've always been on the street. You're some kind of junkie or something. And, hey, most of 'em are. Lot of scum. But not me. No, I got a family. Kids. Oh yeah, I like kids. Some guys don't, you know. But I like kids. Sally, my wife, my ex-wife, some bitch, tries to turn them against me, puts them up to saying those things. Load of horseshit. Believe me. Load of horseshit." He turned to Eric, "You hear? Load of horseshit."

"Yes, yes," Eric said. His Molly a mother. Bringing her kid to him, maybe a little afraid, but oh no, he'd be so happy, so happy . . . it would be like having her back twice . . .

"Made a big stink, but what's in it, hey?" Artie said. "And I tell you, I'll get them off her. I'm not always going to be like this. This is just temporary. Just while I get myself sorted out. Get some answers to all those lies she made up. I'll show her. I mean, a guy's got kids, daughters, running around the way kids dress, you're not going to tell me he doesn't sometime . . ."

A grandfather. She's made me a grandfather, and I've never

known. His eyes filled with tears. He wanted suddenly to embrace the babbling, sordid man who had brought him this wonderful news.

"I mean," Artie said, "we're *men* aren't we?"

Eric looked up, his eyes refocusing, and nodded vaguely, "What did you say?"

"It's only normal, is what I say." Artie nudged him and made a sly communal grin. "We're all the same. Underneath it all, we're all the same."

Old Friends

THE PHONE RANG AGAIN. Annie put her finger on her place in the script, struggling to hold her concentration, and lifted the receiver without looking at it. "Hello, can I help you?"

"Hello." The voice was male, unfamiliar. "Is that you, Joanna?"

"This is Annie Carlson," Annie said briskly. "Do you wish to speak to Joanna?"

"Yeah, fine, ma'am. That'd be great." Annie recognized the western accent and a certain rough ease and knew she was talking to one of Joanna's men. An ill-defined irritation sharpened her voice.

"I'll get her for you." She laid the receiver down on her interrupted work, got up from her chair, and stepped away from the desk. The room was small and crowded. The dining room table was pushed up against a wall at one side and stacked with boxes of manuscripts and piles of letters. She had to edge round it to reach the door, which increased her irritation. The phone had rung all morning. The last call was Merrilee for David, the one before, Sara Levine for Joanna. Frustrated, she walked quickly through the old-fashioned pantry, now their laundry alcove, to the kitchen. Fatima, the maid, was loading the washing machine, her thick head of shiny black curls tied back with an orange scarf.

"Mrs. Carlson, I take tomorrow off and work Wednesday, okay?" she said as Annie passed.

"Fine," Annie said, holding her thoughts delicately remote.

"Because, you see, my nephew's school . . ."

"It's *all right*, Fatima," Annie said sharply, and then, ashamed, added softly, "it's fine," with the best smile she could muster. The script slipped from her mind. She clutched at it, but it was gone. Wearily, she opened the kitchen door.

David, Joanna, and Tess were sitting together around the kitchen table, the faded old family Monopoly board spread out between them. Piles of pink, yellow, orange, and green money were stacked at each of their places, along with handfuls of green wooden houses and red wooden hotels. Tess had her houses and hotels arranged in a minature courtyard, beside a glass of Diet Pepsi. Another half-finished glass sat on the counter behind her. The child seemed to live on the stuff. Annie wondered if Joanna ever thought about her teeth.

"That's the telephone, for you again, Jo," Annie said. She put more emphasis on the "again" than she'd intended. Joanna jumped up, too quickly.

"I'm sorry," she said, lifting the phone off its bracket on the wall. "I was afraid it would be for you. Business," she said awkwardly. She held the phone to her ear and said, "Hello," her eyes still on Annie.

"It hasn't been for me all morning," Annie said dryly. Joanna nodded unhappily, listening in two directions.

"Oh, hi, Mike, how're you?" She paused nervously, "Oh, fine, fine." Annie had turned away and was looking down at the Monopoly board. Joanna nodded twice quickly and grimaced. "Oh, shit," she said. Tess looked up, instantly alert.

"I mean, that's too bad, Mike," Joanna said evenly. Her voice turned cheerfully practical. "Yes, well, everything's okay here. I haven't had much luck, but I've only been here a couple of weeks."

Annie stood watching carefully. The grimace returned. Joanna said, "Don't worry about it, Mike. It's not your problem. I'll handle John. He's all bluster anyhow." She laughed suddenly. "He can advertise all he wants, Mike. There can't be too many people around dumb enough to want his damn job." She smiled wryly and said, "Thanks, Mike. It was real good of you." She smiled again, more gently. "Yeah, sure. I'll tell her. Of course she wants to hear it. Bye, Mike. Thanks for calling." She put the phone back in its cradle.

"Who was that?" Tess said at once.

"Just Mike," Joanna said easily. "He says 'hi' to you."

"What was wrong?"

"Nothing, Tess. Nothing was wrong."

"You said 'shit.' "

"Did I?" Joanna said vaguely.

"Did John fire you?"

"No. Of course not." She turned away.

"Who's Mike?" Annie asked.

"Oh, just an old friend." Joanna met Annie's eyes steadily, "Really."

"Nice of him to call," Annie said.

"Yes. Yes it was." She paused. "Look Annie, I'm sorry about all the interruptions . . ."

"It doesn't matter." Annie, having let the work go, felt softened and repentant.

"It does matter. You're trying to work and there's all this disruption."

"I don't mind, Jo, really."

"Anyhow, we'll be going out in a few minutes. I just promised Tess this game . . ."

"A couple of minutes—but we've just started. And I've almost got enough for a hotel on Park Place," Tess said.

"Hey, you," David said good-naturedly. "I thought you thought Monopoly was boring." Tess shrugged. He stretched a lanky arm out and caught her shoulders, giving her a big brotherly squeeze. She turned red and giggled.

"It is boring."

"Well, you're sure determined to get that hotel on boring old Park Place."

"Compared to Super Mario it's boring," Tess said. "But it's better than nothing." She giggled and looked at David and then glanced quickly at her mother. "And it's better than the Great Magical Disappearing Brother Hunt anyhow."

"You don't have to come," Joanna said sharply.

"Oh, I'll come." Tess shrugged with dramatic flourish.

"You can stay here," Annie said. "I have to work, but you can watch something, or read." Tess looked up at her mother from under lowered lashes. "I didn't say I didn't want to come. I just said it was boring."

"Suit yourself," Joanna said.

Tess prodded her small purple player's piece and sent it sliding across the board into her row of houses on Park Place. "I was going to get the skyscraper," she said.

"Skyscraper?" said Annie. Joanna laughed softly and fished around in the inverted lid of the game. She drew out a small wooden block, laboriously decorated with ballpoint pen windows.

"Remember?" she said, holding it up. "Eric made it. It was one of those long, long games up at the camp that went on for days, and in the middle of it, Martin and Eric rewrote the rules and made the skyscraper." Annie smiled, taking it from Joanna. She turned it in her slender fingers, studying the neat rows of windows.

"I'd forgotten all about that. You could pile all your money into it and totally wipe out anybody who landed on it." She turned to David. "Daddy and Uncle Eric were the Donald Trumps of the fifties. Just a bit before their time."

"Whenever I've used it," David said, "I've gone broke waiting for someone to land on it."

"Yeah," Joanna said, "that always happened. The theory was great but it never worked. God, those games. I can think about it for half a minute, and I can see the whole place, the cabin and that big round table with the oilcloth on it. Do you remember how Seth always used to lose first and go off to the woods in a huff? Jeez," she laughed, "I swear I can smell the kerosene lamp and the pine . . ."

"The table's still there," David said, eager suddenly to be joined to that older memory. "We all played on it too."

"I know," Joanna said quietly.

"Well, look," Annie was suddenly brisk again, "what do you say we take the whole game to the coffee table in the living room, and then you can finish it tonight. Okay?"

They got up together, carrying the board between their four pairs of hands like a holy object. When the game was safely in place, Annie said, to Joanna, "When's Sara coming?"

"She's not. I mean she's not coming here. She sent her apologies, but she's shopping for tutus and then she's got to get back. She doesn't like leaving them too long. I'm meeting her in the Village."

"She's shopping for what?" said Tess.

"Tutus. Little frilly skirts. You know. For ballet dancers."

"Jeez," said Tess.

"She runs a ballet school," Joanna said sharply.

"What a thrill."

"Yeah. I think so."

"I don't."

"Look, are you going to be a pain in the ass all day?"

"Me? Me? You're going to drag me around New York talking to all those drunk old men sitting on the sidewalk, and then we're going to a restaurant and eat some weird foreign food probably, and you and Sara are going to talk about tutus."

"She's my best friend, Tess, and I'd just like to see her if you don't mind." Joanna said icily. "And we're not going to talk about tutus."

"No," Tess said instantly. "No, you're going to talk about Eric. Great. Wonderful. Just what we've been doing for two whole weeks. While I'm missing school and my friends and . . ."

"So stay home."

"No."

"Shit, Tess . . ."

"Tess." David's voice was soft and reasoned. Like Martin's, Joanna thought suddenly. No. Like Annie's. Annie the peacemaker. "Tess, tell you what. Go out in the morning with your mom and then, if it's okay with her," he glanced at Joanna, "I'll take you to the Natural History Museum to see the dinosaurs." Tess hunched her shoulders. She looked at him sideways.

"I'm too old for dinosaurs," she said.

"Well, I'm not." David grinned. Tess's shoulders softened.

"Well . . ."

"Great. I'll meet you there. Okay, Aunt Jo?" Joanna smiled and nodded gratefully.

Going down in the elevator, Tess said, "Do you mind, Mom?"

"About what?"

"Do you mind me not coming?" Tess's pale forehead was scrunched into two thin lines.

Bemused, Joanna shook her head and smiled, "I said you didn't have to, Tess. Now, why are you worrying about it?" Tess shrugged.

Out in the street, Tess said, "Aren't you scared ever?"

"Of what?"

"I don't know. Those places and those men."

"They're just poor lost people with nowhere to live, Tess."

"Some of them are scary."

"Not really."

"Some of them are, Mom." Tess looked worldly and aware, and Joanna now shrugged.

"I avoid those," she said lamely. Then she added, "But you needn't worry today. All I'm doing after we meet David is going downtown to have lunch and talk with Sara." She paused. "And if I do go anywhere scary anytime, I'll make sure I have you with me, okay?"

"Promise?"

"Promise."

Tess cheered up then. She walked good-naturedly beside Joanna down Amsterdam, and waited, aloof but patiently, while her mother crouched down by a vacant-eyed black man sitting on the sidewalk at Sherman Square with a cardboard sign that said "Homeless and Hungry" in blue crayon. Joanna took a dollar from her pocket and put it in the flat woolen hat lying on the pavement and then opened her shoulder bag and slipped out one of the photocopied snapshots of Eric that she carried everywhere. She held it in front of the man. He gave no reaction.

"Have you seen this person?" she asked gently. There was still no response.

"He's blind, Mom," Tess said.

"No, he's not." Joanna leaned closer. The man's eyes seemed without focus, and yet she was sure he was seeing. He did not move when she took the photograph away.

As she stood up, he said in a low voice, resonant with distrust, "Don't know nobody. Nobody."

"Come on, Mom," Tess said, stepping from one sneakered foot to the other. "He doesn't know."

"All right," Joanna said evenly. "I'm coming."

Tess walked on a few steps and waited nervously by the awning of a restaurant. People were sitting beneath the awning at little sidewalk tables, enjoying the last-of-the-summer sun. Tess watched them watching her mother putting her photograph away. When they started down Broadway, she walked apart from Joanna, a space of empty sidewalk between them. Across the space, she said, "Do you have to, Mom?"

"Yes."

"They don't know him. Any of them. They're all drunk or crazy."

"One of them might know him."

Tess was silent, separate. As they neared the graceful facades of Lincoln Center, she said in a small voice, "Mom?"

"Hmm?"

"Is he going to be like that?"

"Is who?"

"Your brother, Eric." Tess spoke so quietly, Joanna had to step closer to hear. "Is that what we're looking for? Some old smelly man in the street?" Fear and revulsion were equally balanced in her voice. Joanna stopped walking. She turned abruptly and Tess shrank back, but all Joanna did was put her hands on her daughter's shoulders.

"No," she said. "I don't think so. I hope not anyway. But I want you to remember, even if that's what we find, he's my brother. He's your uncle. He's our family."

"I want to go home," said Tess.

Joanna left her sitting on the edge of a fountain in front of Avery Fisher Hall while she showed her picture to a long-haired boy with a Western accent who was making the rounds of the tourists with a paper cup. She showed it to a man selling ice cream, a black kid with a tray of silver and gold watches, and a woman in a gypsy costume who talked loudly to herself.

Then Joanna gave up, collected her daughter, and trekked resolutely down Broadway.

Columbus Circle, where Broadway crossed Eighth Avenue and Central Park West, hunkered at the edge of the park, its rush of traffic, its subway entrances and convenience stores and cheap cafes just brushing the chic grandeur of midtown. The street people clustered there begging, sleeping, talking—a tiny, lonely city within the city. Since she had arrived in New York, Joanna had canvassed their small community often enough that people were beginning to recognize her, and as she crouched down by the railing of the park to talk to one of the residents, she had a wry vision of becoming a familiar local herself—a crazy blond woman with pictures and a quest. Tess, standing ten feet away and brutally impervious, apparently shared the same vision.

As always, the only positive response Joanna got was from the natural con men. She had one now, a likeable, wiry black man with drink-bleary eyes. He sat beside her on a bench, while she nervously watched Tess scuffing a sneaker against the sidewalk, making sure she was never more than three paces out of reach.

"Eric. Eric. Yeah, that's him. Seen him down around Grand Central, a week ago. Told me all about that pretty blond wife of his. Needin' some money just to get himself together. Tell you what, you give me a few bucks for him, let him know you still care, I'll talk to him. He'll be back, sure thing. What do you say?"

"My sister's in publishing," Joanna said grinning. "I'll put you in touch." She handed him a dollar and got up from the bench.

Tess, arms folded, head down, was watching a pigeon's iridescent back. "What stupid birds," she said.

"Pretty smart birds," Joanna corrected, "staying alive in the middle of all this."

"I still think they're stupid. Can we go now?"

"In a minute." Joanna turned away, looking for other possibilities. Tess tugged her sleeve wearily. "In a minute," she said again.

Tess said, "Why don't you at least talk to him?"

"Who?" She turned back.

"Him," Tess said again. She pointed across the broad sidewalk, past a hot dog vendor's yellow umbrella. "He knows them all. And at least he isn't crazy." Joanna followed her daughter's pointing finger and saw a middle-aged man in an immaculate three-piece suit, a briefcase at his side, engaged in cheerful conversation with a shambling, pathetic figure in rags. The sight was extraordinary, bizarre.

"How do you know he knows them all?" she asked Tess quietly.

"Because I've been watching," Tess said and added, "while you've been crawling around on the ground with your friends."

"Don't get fresh," Joanna said absently, watching the two men.

"Well, talk to him. So then we can go. We told David twelve-thirty," she added pointedly. Joanna put her hand on Tess's shoulder to quiet her, while she continued to watch. The two figures were separated by an expanse of sidewalk, on which last night's rain had left a large gray puddle, and were conversing across the minature lake.

"Aw, what's happened?" the man in the suit called warmly. The ragged man was agitated, his voice high and querulous, like that of an upset child relaying an injustice, his words tumbling out in an incoherent muddle. The man in the suit stood smiling, his head inclined, one hand gently upraised to slow the torrent of complaint. The homeless man started to cross the distance between them, oblivious of the water splashing his shabby mismatched shoes. "Now, now, wait a minute." The man in the suit held up both hands. His voice was big, easy, a heavy New York accent. "Now don't get your feet wet." He picked up his briefcase and walked quickly around the puddle until the two were side by side. In close proximity they were even more incongruous. Joanna watched them as they talked, one telling a story, the other listening. She saw the well-dressed man take out his wallet, draw out several bills, fold them, and hand them to his companion, all the time listening, nodding, his attention to the other's words never distracted. Eventually they separated, the homeless man shambling off in the direction of the park, his benefactor picking up his briefcase and leisurely walking north.

Joanna caught Tess's hand and dragged her quickly along after the man. She came abreast of him on the sidewalk and matched their strides, glancing across. The man was looking straight ahead, absorbed in thought as he walked. He was balding and dark, with a prominent nose, brown eyes, and gold-rimmed glasses. He looked like a lawyer.

"Mister . . ." Joanna said, her voice softened by unease. He stopped at once, and she realized he had been aware of her all along.

"Can I help you?" he asked, and she saw the same intent concentration she had observed before now focused on herself. She held up her picture, fumbling it slightly in her haste.

"Do you know this man?" she said. He stopped, glanced down at Tess, who was watching them both, and took the picture carefully from Joanna. He adjusted his glasses and then removed them entirely.

"I should have bifocals," he confided. "But do you know? I'm vain." He studied the picture then, the glasses held aloft by one earpiece.

"Have you seen him?" Joanna asked.

"This man?" He slipped the glasses on and shook his head. "No. I'm sorry." He handed her the picture without further comment and with a brief, polite nod, walked away.

Joanna stood by the railing of the park in the leafy shadows, watching him go. Slowly she put away her picture and, with a small sigh, slung her bag back over her shoulder and turned to Tess. She brightened her face into a smile and said, "Well, how about David and those dinosaurs?"

"He knew him," Tess said. Joanna looked down curiously.

"No, he didn't," she said. Tess's face was screwed up with confusion. "It doesn't matter, sweetheart," Joanna added comfortingly. "It was worth a try. It was a good idea."

"Mom, I'm not saying it because it was my idea. I really mean it. He knew Uncle Eric. I could tell from his face when he saw the picture."

"Tess, I was watching too. He took his glasses off and he looked very carefully. He didn't know him."

"Before he took his glasses off. He did that thing people do when they see something they aren't meant to, or like when they hear someone say their name behind their back. That sort of little blink."

"He couldn't see the picture with his glasses on, Tess."

"That's what he said."

"Tess, this is crazy. Why would he lie?" Tess shrugged and looked exasperated.

"I don't know. I'm not psychic. All I'm saying is he knew him." She flung her hands up. "Sorry I mentioned it," she said.

Joanna sighed, "Okay. He was lying. It doesn't make any difference. He's not going to be any help." She took Tess's hand. "Come on, we're late." Tess pulled the hand away.

"Mom." She shied away until she had her quota of unadulterated space again, and they walked in parallel up Central Park West.

"You going to meet Sara now?" Tess asked, when they stopped outside the Museum Cafe on Columbus Avenue where they'd agreed to meet David. Joanna fished in her bag for money.

"After I've left you with David."

"Is she really your best friend?"

Joanna had her wallet out and was quickly counting the bills and wondering if she'd better stop at a machine. "Yes. She was. She is." She took out a ten and a five and gave them to Tess. "That's for your lunch and getting in. I wouldn't mind if there was some change."

"Mom?"

"Put it away carefully."

Tess wadded the bills and stuffed them into her jeans pocket, "What about Mike?"

"What about him?"

"I thought Mike was your best friend."

Joanna paused in putting her wallet away. "Mike's a man."

"My best friend is a boy."

"I thought he was a piece of dogshit."

"Sometimes. Sometimes he's my best friend." She grinned and raised her hands palms upward.

"I'd want to be sure which," Joanna said. She opened the cafe door and ushered Tess through. David sat alone at a table with a cup of coffee and a paperback book. He looked touchingly young to Joanna, in his red-and-black plaid shirt, black turtleneck, and jeans. Like a student with nothing but a student's negotiable academic cares. She felt sorry for him, weighted so early with family concerns.

He stood up, and she waved from the doorway as Tess bounced confidently across the tiled floor to join him. Watching her, Joanna had a quick vision of rooms she would enter in years to come and men who would rise like that to greet her. They would be grown men, then, not boys, and no longer family, but strangers. Lovers. Sunlight through the cafe windows caught her bright hair, glowed pink on her hooded sweatshirt, made a soft halo around her skinny child-woman shape. Joanna turned quickly and fled out the door.

JOANNA CROSSED THE STREET from the subway exit at Sheridan Square and saw Sara Levine sitting at an outdoor table at the Riviera Cafe. Joanna recognized her at once, even from behind, by her upright dancer's back, the fine balance of her head on its long, slender neck (that neck she had envied so as a child, and of which she had made cruel fun, in consequence). Sara was wearing jeans and a chunky Irish sweater against the crisp chill of the fall day. Her long dark hair was piled up in a glossy knot, and she sat in the sunshine, alone with a cup of cappuccino and a book, oblivious of the traffic rumbling by on Seventh Avenue. The hair, the book, the swinging silver earrings, seemed all unchanged since they were college girls together, out for adventure in these same streets. Joanna made her way inside the little fence that corralled the tables in their sidewalk paddock. Sara was so involved in her paperback that she did not notice until Joanna was standing before her table. "Good book?"

Sara answered automatically, still staring at the page, "Yeah, great. Oh!" She dropped her book and jumped up. "Jo!" They embraced amidst the confusion of plastic bags clustered around Sara's chair. Sara hastily stuffed them under the table as Joanna sat across from her.

"Tutus?" Joanna asked.

Sara grinned, holding up one hand and ticking off purchases on her fingers. "Tutus, leotards, tights, ballet shoes, ribbons . . ."

"Do you supply all that stuff?"

"God forbid. I'd go bankrupt. The parents pay for it. I'm just the bag lady." She paused. "If I let them choose their own stuff, I get some pretty amazing sights. So I lay down the rules, you know, 'Miss Levine says . . . ' "

"Miss Levine," Joanna cried, laughing. "I can't believe it. Somehow you don't look like a ballet mistress."

"I'm working up to the gray bun and the French accent and the big silver-handled cane to thump the floor."

"I'm still having a little trouble picturing it," Joanna said. Staring at Sara, she sat with her chin on one hand.

"I know," Sara said with a quick, wry smile. "Maybe it's because what I *do* look like is closer to reality: one more failed dancer out in the suburbs teaching the kids."

"Oh no, Sara," Joanna said, surprised to hear cynicism from Sara, once the bright optimist.

Sara shrugged it off and laughed, "Come on, let's have some lunch. It's so good to see you, Jo. You really haven't changed a bit. Somehow I thought, after Tess . . ."

Joanna laughed happily. "What, I'd get big and fat?" she said cheerfully.

But Sara stayed serious. "No, no. That doesn't happen anymore. Middle-aged women don't balloon. Everyone's too body conscious. If anything, they go skinny. But I thought you'd, I don't know, get more like your mom."

"You mean wear skirts and pantyhose and city shoes."

"Maybe. I guess it's like being a ballet mistress. There's a look we expect from parents." She paused and smiled slightly. "An all-grown-up look." She smiled again. "Annie and Martin have it. Sort of, anyhow."

Joanna laughed. "They've been parents longer than me. And they haven't got Tess. If I came on strong for family values and apple pie, she'd flip."

"Where is she?" Sara said, looking up from the menu. "I thought she'd come."

"I left her uptown with David and the dinosaurs. They're doing the museum."

"Oh, nice," Sara said. "Is she having fun in New York? It must be a big thrill."

Joanna put her finger on her choice on the menu, squinting in the bright sun. She said, "Insomuch as anything that's not on a screen thrills Tess, yeah. I think she's enjoying it. To be fair, it's not exactly a vacation, following me around the seedier corners of town, talking to drunks and junkies. Tess is probably the only eleven-year-old on the block who's had a guided tour of Manhattan flophouses."

Sara was very quiet. She said, finally, "You're really doing it."

"Oh yeah, I'm doing it."

"Are you having any luck?"

"Not yet."

Sara smiled sadly. "You're very brave," she said. "I wish I could help."

"You've got enough to do."

"It's not so much doing things. It's being there. They've come to rely on my being there."

Joanna nodded. She said, "Anyhow, I think maybe you can help me."

"How?" Sara said eagerly.

"I want to talk to Dina."

"Oh." Sara's voice went flat. Her wide, sensual mouth tightened and firmed. "She won't be any help, Joanna. She hasn't seen Eric since the divorce. And even if she could help, she wouldn't. You've no idea how bitter she's become."

A girl in jeans and T-shirt and a thick white apron arrived to take their order. She filled their glasses with ice water as she listened, then wrote their choices and gave a big, friendly smile. Joanna admired her cheerful expertise. She sat back until the girl was gone and then said, "Isn't it at least *possible* he'd have contacted her again?"

"All I can say is, I hope not. For his sake, I mean." She looked away across the avenue. Her big silver earrings flashed in the sun. Joanna was struck again by the creamy perfection of her dark skin and how little she'd changed. Just that spidering of gray hairs in her thick brown knot, and a few crow's-foot lines beside her dark, attractive eyes. She felt she herself had aged more, and waited, resignedly, for the old jealousy to arise. To her surprise, she felt none. "You know she's remarried, do you, Jo?"

"Annie told me at the time. I'm not amazed, Sara. It's been a lot of years. What's he like?"

"Oh, I hardly know. I don't see them anymore." Sara paused as the waitress returned with coffee and chef's salads for them both. "I suppose I could, if I tried harder. They're over in Stony Brook. He teaches at the university. He's a nice enough man. Obviously, he sees the whole thing through Dina's eyes, but that's not his fault. They have a little boy now."

"I heard that. I'm glad. For Dina, I mean."

"Yes. Well, I hope it was a good idea." Joanna looked up, questioning. Sara said, "She's very protective."

"Can you blame her?"

"She's not going to send him to school."

"At all?"

"She's going to teach him herself. At home. She's qualified, of course. She did teacher's ed after we left college." She paused. "The child sees no one. Okay, he's still only three maybe, but *no one?*"

"A bit weird."

"Very weird." Sara speared a black olive and ate it thoughtfully. "You know she blames Eric now entirely."

"Over Molly?" Joanna said sadly. "Really?"

Sara nodded. "As far as she, and now her husband too, of course, are concerned, it only happened because of Eric's incompetence as a parent. And 'incompetence' is putting a nice light on it. Sometimes, when you'd hear her, it sounded a lot more like outright neglect."

"Oh, that's so sad," Joanna said. "I can't believe it. They seemed so close. During the search. Dealing with the police. They seemed so supportive of each other . . ."

"At first," Sara said. "She changed later. She started to say that he simply couldn't understand. A father couldn't feel what a mother felt." She shook her head, briefly closing her eyes. "I know I should forgive her. What she went through . . . I can't even begin to imagine, but still, Eric went through it too. She could never see that. She made her grief an armor against him. I think it began when she first really acknowledged that Molly was dead. When she'd lost all hope. And, of course, there was Eric refusing to accept she was gone. I remember once Dina said to me, 'He's stolen her. Now he has her all to himself and I'm not even allowed to grieve.' "

"How awful."

"She was very angry. It's part of the grief, I understand. And somewhere in there, the anger turned around against Eric, and she began to say things. Little things. Like how she could never trust him to keep an eye on her when Molly was a baby. How he was too casual. How he'd never discipline her, was always letting her do what she pleased so he could look like the nice guy. Then it just sort of metamorphosed into a full-blown thing. Eric had let it happen. It was Eric's fault. It was just so sad. They could have helped each other so much. Instead, they ended up at each other's throats."

Joanna lifted her thick, white coffee mug in two hands. She sipped from it and stared through the steam at Sara across the table. Her mind kept flashing back to their young, foolish, funny, innocent selves, sitting at tables identical to this, carefully mimicking the worldly awareness that had come, now, relentless and unbidden with the simple passage of years. She said, "It's funny, in the movies or on TV when something awful happens to a family, the parents always learn they really love each other, even if they were all set to get divorced."

" 'Grief unites people.' It's like 'illness ennobles' and 'old age makes us wise.' Bullshit. In my experience grief isolates, illness diminishes, and old age . . . my parents were brave, clever, generous people, who climbed mountains and fought for civil rights. Now, sometimes all they seem to think of are their bowel movements. Breakfast conversation is scintillating, as you might imagine."

"Oh, Sara."

"I'm not complaining. I love them. But sometimes I want to cry, seeing what's become of them. They've grown so afraid."

Joanna put down her fork and leaned her chin on her hand. "I can't imagine your dad afraid of anything. I remember that time he took us all up Mount Marcy, scrambling around on rock ledges with Eric and Martin."

Sara smiled, "He always thought you were wonderful, of course."

"Me? Why?"

"Because you were never afraid of anything either."

"I was."

"Not that I ever noticed. Or Dad. He was always saying to me, 'Well, look, Joanna's doing it,' to egg me on."

"But he used to say that to *me*," Joanna interrupted. "He'd send you off first, and say, 'Well, kid, what about it. Sara's done it.'"

"Did he?" Sara asked, a cautious smile forming.

"Of course he did. I only did half the things I did because of you."

Sara's smile expanded into an easy, happy laugh, "I don't believe it. The old stinker." She sat smiling and thinking, and then the smile faded. "And now he's scared to climb the stairs. They sleep downstairs, you know, in that big room where we used to watch TV."

"I want to see them," Joanna said.

"You sure?" Sara asked. "It's not very exciting."

"Of course, I'm sure."

Sara's smile returned, a sudden flash of white teeth against her dark tan. "Oh, they'll love that. They really will. You were always their heroine, going off like you did. You were always so adventurous."

"Me? What about you, tramping around Europe, dancing at street festivals in Italy and France?"

Sara laughed softly, shaking her head. "I don't know. They were never so impressed by that. Maybe because I was with the company. I wasn't all alone like you." She gathered a small heap of lettuce with her fork and ate it. "God, that seems a long time ago. Another life."

"Sara, do you see any of them anymore?" Joanna asked curiously.

"I see Ralph and Toby." Sara drank from her coffee cup and set it down. "They have a dancewear shop in East Hampton. I send my older kids out there for shoes. Frankly, if they weren't so expensive I'd use them more. But you remember Ralph. 'Mustn't compromise, my dear. Art must never compromise.'" Joanna giggled gleefully. "Annette's with a company in Seattle," Sara continued. "Mara's married with a couple of kids up in New Hampshire. I haven't seen her, but Josh told me about her. She came down to see him." She paused. "He's dead now. He died in March."

Joanna closed her eyes. "Oh, I'm sorry, Sara," she said quietly. "I didn't know."

"That was somehow the end of it. Josh dying. When Josh first got ill . . . I mean when he first told us, that was the beginning of the end for the company. I knew we wouldn't go on without Josh. He was our spiritual core." She stopped talking and looked into Joanna's eyes. "I know that sounds phony, but he was."

"Do you miss dancing?" Joanna asked.

Sara tilted her head thoughtfully, an old familiar gesture. "Not really. Not anymore. I miss dreaming. But I'd stopped dreaming long before the dancing ended."

"Dreaming?"

"You know. Dreaming. Of being a great dancer. Of creating a great dance." Her large, expressive eyes were full of wistful self-mockery. "For a while," she said, suddenly animated, "when I first started teaching, I dreamed of making a great dancer. I had one kid, a boy actually, who I thought . . . but he dropped out when the kids at school teased him. I can't seem to find anything to dream about anymore."

"I know what you mean."

"Do you?" Sara looked up, hopeful.

"I think it's what's really meant by middle age. Too old to dream. Too young to just sit around and reminisce. I find myself jealous of my parents and my kid at the same time. She's got the whole future and they've got their past. I'm in the middle, and sometimes I don't seem to have anything except work and worrying about money."

Sara laughed ruefully. "When I was a real little kid, I always was begging my mother to come out and play with me. The sun would be shining and she was in that dark house working. I guess she had a lot to do, between her job and us. Anyhow, she was always too busy. Now she and Dad sit out in the sun with the newspapers, and they're always asking me to come and sit and join them. And now I'm in that same big, dark house and I haven't got time. Isn't life funny?" She twisted one of her earrings and then let it go. "Let's have dessert. This is too nice sitting here with that great blue sky. I don't want to leave."

Over chocolate cheesecake, Sara said, "What about men?"

"What about them?"

"Things to dream about?" Sara prompted.

Joanna grinned easily, "Well, Sara," she said. "It's like what you said about the dancing. There may still be men from time to time, but the dreaming ended long ago." She grinned again. "What about you?"

"Oh, there's nobody," Sara said, resigned.

"Nobody? Sure."

"Well," Sara said, holding up a hand with long fingers delicately spread, and ticking one off, "there's Simon, who's rich and kind and sweet and wants to marry me desperately and who's boring beyond belief." She ticked off a second finger. "There's Pete, who's into mountain climbing and cross-country skiing and has the most wonderful blue eyes and a wife that he's been going to leave next month for five years. And," another finger went down, "let's not forget smooth, cool, streetwise Ed who's got a Manhattan duplex, a BMW, in fact, every possible accoutrement of an eighties yuppie, including a purely recreational taste for coke."

"I'm getting the point," Joanna said.

"Have I told you about Dave? The nine-foot-square bed with the mirror on the ceiling and the parrot?"

"Be serious," Joanna said, laughing.

"This doesn't sound serious?" Sara made a flamboyant shrug. She said, "The real *fun* thing about being a nineties woman is you can have a choice of all the foibles of the eighties, the seventies, and even the dear old sixties, all wrapped up in the same wonderful man. And my mother wonders why I'm not married."

"Does she?" Joanna asked softly.

Sara looked away. She reached up with both hands and thoughtfully tucked loose, blowing dark hairs into her smooth bun. She said, eyes still averted, "My mother is an educated, sophisticated woman who knows there's more in life for a woman than marriage. But she is also a product of her culture. All six thousand years of it. As she gets older, it gets stronger." She dropped her hands and looked up at Joanna, "I've never been able to tell her about Josh."

"You mean she didn't know he was gay?"

"Oh, of course she knew he was gay. What she didn't know was that I was in love with him." She paused. "I think he was the only man I was ever *really* in love with, Jo. Except Eric, of course, and that didn't count. I was just a kid. He was my knight in shining armor. My perfect man." She shrugged again expressively, "God, Jo, what's brought us all here?"

"Life?"

"Yeah." Sara tilted her head again, whimsically. "Life. It didn't work out quite the way we planned."

"We didn't plan it," Joanna reminded her.

Sara said thoughtfully, "Then maybe we should have planned it. Maybe that's what's wrong." She crumbled the crust of her cheesecake moodily with her fork. The waitress came, with her bright smile, to refill their coffee cups. Nobody seemed in any hurry for them to move. Large white clouds sailed above the roofs across the avenue. A pigeon landed on the sidewalk and walked, head bobbing, up to the little wooden fence. Joanna studied its wind-ruffled feathers. The air was getting colder, winter creeping in from the river, but the sun was warm and comforting.

She said to Sara, "I keep remembering us all down here. Those summer evenings when we were seniors and Eric and Martin and Annie were all at college. The way we'd take the train in and wander around in all those crowds on Eighth Street."

Sara laughed. "My mother used to say, 'The Village is spoiled now.' She and Dad were old Village hands. And I felt guilty because I knew we were what was spoiling it."

"It always seemed there was this mysterious, wonderful excitement, always in the next street. So we'd go from place to place, and all there ever was was other kids like us, but still we were sure it was there. We were so sure of everything."

"I remember Seth was furious because we wouldn't let him

come half the time," Sara said. "We were real stinkers to Seth. He was just a year younger, but we sure lorded it over him."

"I suppose we had to lord it over someone. Annie and Eric and Martin did enough of that to us." Joanna looked up again at the sailing white clouds. "How is Seth?" she asked, her voice studiously mild. Sara looked startled.

"Oh, fine, fine." She dragged the words out oddly, as if she were thinking of something else, or lying.

"Something wrong?" Joanna asked.

"Oh no," Sara flashed a bright smile. "Seth's fine." She paused and said, "He's successful, anyhow."

"So I gather. Martin seems a little itchy about it."

"Oh, Martin always thinks Seth has things too easy. He was like that when we were kids. He's got a martyr complex." She laughed abruptly. "He's convinced Mom and Dad favor Seth. That they're somehow disappointed in him, by contrast. I try to convince him, from the viewpoint of the one person they definitely *are* disappointed in, that it's not so, but he won't listen."

"Oh, Sara, they're not."

"Yes, they are. It's Martin the doctor and Seth the writer and Sara the second-rate dancer running a third-rate school. A tape deck and a tinkling piano and all those little girls needing something to fill up their afternoons. Sometimes their mothers call up and ask if I can 'keep' Tamsin or Kelly for another hour because they're in a meeting and it's running late. I'm a baby-sitter."

"One of those Tamsins or Kellys might also have dreams," Joanna said gently.

"Yes," Sara answered. "And what am I doing encouraging them? Maybe I should be saying, look at me for God's sake, and then forget this crap and get yourself an education and a good steady job."

Joanna smiled sadly, "Do we want to raise a generation with no dreams?"

"I think I want to raise a generation whose dreams and reality don't end up so far apart. I'm a long way from Lincoln Center these days."

Joanna smiled again. She sat thoughtfully and then said suddenly, "Do you know, Sara, I think that's what was wrong with my life. I never had a Lincoln Center. I never had any dreams of that sort. I messed about at college with one subject and another and then I dropped out and went off and just followed the flow. I never seemed to be aiming anywhere. Things happened and I floated along, like a bit of driftwood on the river until I ended up beached in a diner in Colorado with a grumpy gorilla for a boss. The only definite, deliberate thing I ever did was having Tess, and that's the one thing my parents still think was an accident."

"Dreamers and drifters," Sara said. "That's our generation. It was a luxury, Jo. We grew up in the richest country in the world, in its richest time ever. We were the last. It won't happen again."

Joanna nodded and then sat, elbow on the small rickety table, her chin on her hand, and grinned, "Speaking of riches, I guess it's time to pay for this meal. It's three-thirty."

"Oh, gosh," Sara looked at her watch. "I have to run. I want to get the 4:19. I promised them I'd be back before six."

"You go on. I'll get the waitress and pay."

"Oh no. No. I was taking you to lunch, Jo. I'll pay. Where is she?" She looked around quickly, then stopped, distracted, her eyes settling on a point over Joanna's shoulder.

"We're both broke, Sara. Let's at least split it."

"No, that's all right . . ." Sara's voice trailed off, her attention elsewhere. Joanna looked up from her shoulder bag, in which she was rummaging for her wallet.

"What is it?"

She started to turn to where Sara was looking and heard a male voice, distantly familiar, say, "I've got a great idea. Why don't I pay?"

Joanna twisted quickly in her chair, looking over her shoulder. A man was leaning against a lamppost, just outside the fence behind her chair. He wore jeans and an expensive-looking tweed jacket and a blue turtleneck that looked like cashmere. The sun glinted on very black hair. His face, screened by gold-rimmed sunglasses, was darkly tanned. He lifted the glasses and smiled at Joanna.

"Seth!" she said, wondering. "Seth Levine." She stared at him as his white smile broadened and his eyes, dark like his sister's but sharper and more intense, crinkled at the corners. "I don't believe it." Joanna swung back to Sara. "*Sara?*"

Sara smiled nervously. She stood up, gathering her plastic bags of dancewear. "I gotta run," she said, as Seth stepped easily over the little sidewalk fence and slipped neatly into his sister's chair.

"What *is* this?" Joanna protested. "A setup?" She was laughing, rather delighted in spite of herself.

"Another coffee?" Seth said. "Before we go?"

Columbus Circle

ERIC STAYED IN the gay bookstore on lower Sixth Avenue for an hour. He read Jeanette Winterson and then switched to Andrea Dworkin. He worked his way though a shelf of books on AIDS and bereavement. The store was busy. People moved around him in the polite, apologetic manner of bookstore browsers. He retreated into corners, pressed himself against walls, head bowed over his reading, as unobtrusive as possible. Outside, the clear white sunshine and patches of blue between the yellow leaves of a sidewalk tree belied the cutting wind. He'd been on the street all night, and the cold had worked through to his bones.

Yet, when he did leave, it was not because the cropped-haired girl at the cash register told him to, but because he was aware of how long he had been there, borrowing shelter and warmth. The girl hardly looked up when he handed over the check slip and asked for his bag back from behind her desk. He thanked her and went to the door, clutching his plaid jacket across his chest in anticipation of the wind, now rippling the rainbow flags outside the window.

He stopped in the narrow doorway to wrap his scarf around his chin and, in doing so, saw the poster. It was crudely drawn and cheaply printed. A witch in a peaked hat, an earring through her nose, proclaimed a New Age Pagan Halloween celebration at a Hudson Street address. Music by Lilith's Daughter. The fuzzy picture below showed five young women in aggressive masculine clothes. The one in the center, with blond hair brushed stiffly upward from a fine-angled face, he knew at once was Megan Carmichael. His hands were shaking with excitement and cold as he stood in the doorway, scribbling down the address.

People brushed by him, tolerantly allowing him room as he wrote. Then there was a lull, and quite suddenly he was alone, unobserved in the doorway, with the poster before him. He reached out tentatively and touched it with his cold, trembling fingers, caressing the sullen printed cheek. He could not fully absorb the momentous nature of what he was doing. At his fingertips was an actual photograph, a real, vivid, adult photograph, the closest link in thirteen years. His outstretched arm was bridging time right back to that final moment, now haloed with such intensive concentration of memory as to be scarcely real: He stands in the low-ceilinged kitchen of the cabin, the air sweet with balsam fir. Molly in shorts and her Garfield T-shirt stands beside him. The refrigerator door is open. She is holding a carton of milk, a bowl of Cheerios in the other hand, and smiling. "Hi, Daddy." She reaches up and kisses him. He touches her shoulder, reaches past her into the refrigerator, takes something (he can no longer remember what it is—one of the sad little blank spots in his memory), and goes out of the room, back to his desk by the bookshelves in the living room. It is a moment of absolutely no significance, except that it is the last time he touches her. The last time ever, until now, his fingers hovering over the image of her adult face.

He could not bear to leave the photograph. There arose an anarchic, desperate desire to steal it, to take it down and make it his own. His fingers drifted to the top of the poster and strayed to a loose corner. He drew back. He couldn't do it. He had never stolen anything in his life. Even the clearly abandoned T-shirt he'd scavenged in Central Park tugged at his conscience. In poverty, even in hunger, it had never occurred to him to simply take what was not his. He stared longingly at the photograph and then turned away, comforting himself with the thought that it was here and he could return to it whenever he chose.

As he left the bookstore, a new determination filled him, pointless but invigorating. He could see the club. He could go there now and look at the place to which she would come, the place where her name was known, and where perhaps her voice had been heard over a phone line, where she might indeed already have been. She would not be there now. The performance date was days away. But he could still see it; the place where his thirteen-year odyssey would end, the place where they would meet. He hurried through the streets of the Village with the urgency of a lover, oblivious now of the sharp north wind.

The building itself was a disappointment, a faceless brick warehouse without even the romance of a cast-iron frontage. It had been converted to some sort of club, strictly nocturnal in its activities. A blank metal roll-down door, bolted securely to the sidewalk, sealed the entranceway. Before its blind gray eye a family of South American Indians had spread heaps of ethnic sweaters and shawls and were squatting on the pavement beside their wares. Behind their enclave a montage of Lilith's Daughter posters was plastered on the brick wall, a dozen of them, pasted end to end, top to bottom. Her face looked over the shining black heads of the vendors, multiplied like a Warhol painting. Eric knew suddenly and unarguably, that he could not leave there without one.

He stepped in behind the shawls and the sweaters, the Indian children and their woven baskets. He carefully peeled one poster free, rolled it neatly, and tucked it inside his jacket. Nobody watched and nobody cared. At the age of forty-nine he had committed his first criminal act. He walked away with the poster and its picture of Megan Carmichael like a warm jewel pressed against his heart.

Boyish-young elation filled him in a way he had not felt within remembered time. He decided to take the rest of the day off. He would have a holiday, a celebration. He made his way unhurried across the Village, following a catty-cornered route, crossing Seventh Avenue, turning off on Bleecker, wandering back to Sixth, looking in the windows of expensive galleries, admiring unpriced pottery and jewelry. He turned up Sixth, as far as West Fourth, and then crossed to Washington Square.

He sat for a while on a bench in the sun, watching two young mothers playing with their children in the park. They all looked like children to him. As he sat there, a slow transformation took place. Normality began to seep back into him like the strengthening sun soaking into his bones. He felt himself drift softly across an invisible line, the boundary between the underworld he inhabited and the other world, the big, real world of careers and homes and families.

He stood up and walked out of the park, past the arch where two roller-bladers cut swaths of clear pavement through clusters of pigeons. The feeling increased as he made his leisurely, measured way up Fifth Avenue. He began to associate it with the rolled poster that rustled inside his jacket against his shirt. With each thoughtful step he seemed to draw farther away from the streets, the hostel, the paper cup. He thought of Artie, his flabby body, his shaved head and petulant, hungry eyes; the image was remote, as of a half-remembered acquaintance he had not seen in years. He passed a blind man sitting with a bony German shepherd at his feet in front of a boarded-up storefront. With consummate assurance, Eric slipped two coins from his pocket and dropped them into the blind man's cup.

He began to look around, seeing as if his own eyes too had been blind and were now opened again. The streets were vibrant with busy, active, pressing people, working, shopping, going to meetings, going to meals, moving, moving. Faces glowed with intent and purpose. Conversations flitted by, arguments, gossip, deals, seductions. He was part of it now, an ordinary man, going uptown to meet a friend. He walked more quickly, absorbed into the hustle, waiting impatiently at each block for the lights to change, worming around turning traffic, slapping a proprietory hand on the flank of an indignant yellow cab. This was his city. He was home. Among the high, gray towers of midtown he walked proudly, a traveler returned.

He felt warm and fit when he reached Columbus Circle. The long walk had gotten his blood flowing, eased the stiffness in his knees caused by sleeping curled against the cold. Dan Grossman wasn't there, but buoyed by the day's good fortune, he decided to wait. Dan came most days. He would probably come today. Eric wandered to the edge of the sidewalk, bought a hot pretzel from a vendor, and stood watching the flow of bike riders, joggers, and skaters in and out of the park. The pretzel cost a dollar twenty-five, more than his whole breakfast, but he didn't care. It was a treat, a luxury feast in honor of Megan Carmichael. He ate it slowly, savoring it. He carefully picked the last crumbs and salt crystals from the paper, which he crumpled dutifully and dropped into a trash basket when he was done. The wind had risen, and, in spite of the pretzel, the warmth of the walk had begun to fade. It seemed cold for October, as he thought back to balmier autumns, hazy Indian summers, and wondered if it was his memories of the past failing him, or his frailer, older body, in the present. He stood shivering, with the sweat of exertion cooling on his skin, wrapping himself physically and mentally around the rolled stolen poster.

At four o'clock a man came from the far side of Central Park West, wearing a beige raincoat open over a three-piece suit. He wore glasses and carried a briefcase, and, as Eric watched, he made slow but deliberate progress toward the corner where he waited. He knew from experience that the man had seen him already, though he made no indication until he was within six feet of where Eric stood. He stopped then and said, "Ah," as if arriving at a meeting long planned. He shifted the briefcase to his left hand and held out his right. He and Eric shook hands.

"So how's it going, Eric?"

"Okay, not bad, Dan. Pretty good, actually."

"Good? That's nice to hear." He nodded, still shaking Eric's hand, and said again, "That's nice to hear." He let go Eric's hand and looked around thoughtfully. Then he said, "Tell you what, I could go for a cup of coffee. How about you?" His big, warm voice rolled over the sound of traffic and footsteps, and Eric savored it hungrily.

He waited a moment to answer, as if a free cup of coffee was an everyday, unimportant thing, and then said, "Yeah, sounds pretty good."

"Right. You wait here." Dan went off and came back after a leisurely few minutes with two lidded paper cups in a brown paper bag. "Regular, two sugars, that's you, right?" Eric nodded, taking the cup. "I threw in a couple of donuts. Coconut. You like coconut?"

"Yeah, great." Eric carried the coffee cups. Dan carried his briefcase and the paper bag with the donuts. They walked into the park and found a bench and sat down side by side. Dan took the lid off his coffee and handed Eric the open paper bag. Eric took out one donut and ate it quickly. He drank from the coffee cup, in quick gulps, burning his mouth and feeling the warmth flow down his throat. He wrapped his arms around himself, one hand clutching his jacket sleeve, the other the cup. The poster rustled beneath his jacket. He let his mind leave it, momentarily, and move out into the world. "Why do you do this?" he asked.

"What?" Dan looked amused. "What am I doing? Having a cup of coffee."

"Why, Dan?"

Dan shrugged. "Because I want to. Some people feed pigeons."

Eric laughed softly. "I really want to know."

"Ah, you don't need to know."

"No. I don't need to know, but I want to know."

Dan sipped his coffee and watched a pretty teenage roller-blader in pink lycra shorts. "This is a good place to sit. You see good things." He smiled slowly. "Your trouble is you're too smart, Eric. You'd do better if you were stupider."

He watched the roller-blader until she was out of sight. "Okay," he said. "My father loved America, Eric. He came from the old country penniless and built up a business. He had a ladies' garment store on the Lower East Side. Couple of years into the Depression, he went bust. He got a job then, cutting cloth. Lost that. Got a job in a dry cleaner's. Lost that. Got another job after that, wouldn't say what it was. He was selling apples on the street. Every day he'd get dressed in his suit to go sell apples. Then he pawned the suit jacket. It was winter, Eric. He was selling apples in his shirtsleeves. One day, some guy comes along, takes his coat off, puts it on my father." He sighed and sipped the coffee. "There was a blessing in that coat. Somehow, things got better after that. He got a job. We started to eat again. Then Roosevelt came in." Dan took the second donut out of the paper bag and bit into it. "My father would have gone to hell and back for Roosevelt."

He paused thoughtfully, "Once when I was six or seven I walked with my father along Riverside Drive at night. I remember looking down into Riverside Park, and the darkness was full of flickering lights. Campfires. There was a shantytown down there in the park. I remember my father saying Roosevelt was going to take care of all that. He always said that after Roosevelt it could never happen again. That was real comforting, growing up knowing it could never happen again."

Dan finished his coffee. "Sometimes I feel like Peter Pan. You know, when Tinkerbell's dying and he gets all the kids to shout, 'I believe in fairies.'" He leaned forward and cupped his hands around his mouth. "This is me shouting," he whispered, "I believe in America. I believe in America."

Eric laughed gently. Dan dropped his hands onto his knees. "Eric, there's someone looking for you," he said.

Eric sat up straight. His right hand came free from his upper arm. The coffee cup shook in his left. He stared, wondering, at his companion. "You've seen her," he whispered.

Dan stayed hunched over on the bench, an elbow on the knee of his trousers, his chin resting on his fist. "I've seen somebody, Eric," he said carefully.

"The woman . . ." Eric said.

"A woman. Yes."

"With the child. The woman with the child."

Dan sat up straighter and faced Eric. He said, with only a small surprise in his voice, "Yes. There was a child."

"It's her." Eric's voice shook with excitement. "She came to the hostel looking for me. She has a child."

"The hostel. Your hostel? On Forty-eighth?"

"Someone saw her. She's looking for me. She is looking for me." He smiled joyously. "Now you've seen her too . . ."

"I've seen someone, Eric," Dan said again. Eric shook his head, impatient with the other's caution. He opened the top button of his jacket and pulled out the poster. The round tube was flattened slightly and crumpled at the ends. He unrolled it, smoothing it carefully, and held it up to his companion.

"In the center," he said, "The girl in the center." He could not keep the note of triumph from his voice. Dan looked with interest. He held out his hands to the poster. Eric surrendered it reluctantly. Dan took it up with great care and peered at it for a long while. Then he removed his gold-rimmed glasses, rubbed his eyes and put the glasses back to peer once again. Eric's impatience swelled. "Don't you see?" he said. "It's her."

"It's who, Eric. Molly?" Dan's voice was clear and gentle.

"You've seen my picture of her. The drawing."

"Yes, Eric."

"Well? Isn't it just like her?"

"It's like her." Dan paused and then said slowly. "It's not really a very good photograph, Eric, is it? It's very shadowy and the reproduction is poor."

"But you can still see."

"Yes."

"Well?"

"What, Eric?" Dan's deep brown eyes were watery behind the glinting lenses.

"This is the woman you saw, Dan, the woman with the child."

Dan stared at the poster a little longer and then rolled it carefully and handed it back to Eric. He said slowly, "Eric, she had a photograph of you."

"She had?" Eric's eyes widened with amazement, and then, to Dan's surprise, a slow smile spread wonderingly across his face. "My photograph?"

"I think it was a photocopy. It was definitely you. You looked younger."

Eric was still smiling. He gripped Dan's sleeve. "That's wonderful."

"Is it, Eric?"

"*Of course.* She's really looking for me. This is *fantastic.*"

Dan finished his donut and rolled up the paper bag. He said gently, "Eric, how would Molly have your photograph? Have you thought about that?" His broad-lipped smile was sad. "You see," he said, "we have to be logical. It's very important to be logical."

"A newspaper," Eric said without hesitation. Dan blinked, baffled. Eric leaned forward, gesturing with his long, bony left hand. "Everywhere I went, San Francisco, Phoenix, Denver, Seattle, small towns too, the first thing I did was contact the features editors of every paper I could find." He smiled wryly. "I'm just the kind of story features editors love." He looked down at the rolled poster on his knees. "Half the time I could tell they thought I was crazy, but they liked the story anyhow and I didn't care, as long as it got my name and my picture in print. Every time it happened, I'd get people writing in, people who thought they'd seen her. I followed up every one. Most of them were just mistakes. Some were weird. Women with crystals and pendulums. Hoaxers wanting money." His eyes followed a bicyclist in tight yellow shorts and a purple helmet. "This is her, Dan. It has to be. It's just too much of a coincidence otherwise."

Dan said evenly, "She looked too old."

Eric said, "She's had a hard life."

Dan took off his glasses and rubbed them on his coat sleeve. He said, "All right, Eric, what do you want me to do?"

Eric looked up cautiously. "Can you find her?" he asked, wonderingly.

Dan shrugged. "I've seen her three times. We're creatures of habit." Before Eric could speak, he said quickly, "You have to remember, I'm not saying it's Molly. Maybe it's someone you don't want to see." He tilted his head wisely. "Think carefully now, Eric. I don't want to get you into trouble or anything."

"It's Molly," Eric said certainly. He smiled confidently. "But it doesn't matter, Dan. I've got this." He stroked the rolled poster. "I'll find her anyhow."

⌐

TESS CARRIED HER NEW roller blades reverently over her left shoulder. She wore her knee pads and elbow pads over her jeans and pink hooded top. Her hair, in a cluster of minute beaded braids fashioned by Merrilee the night before, was pulled back under her new baseball cap. The cap said "New York" on a badge at the front, over a picture of a red apple. Merrilee had bought it for her. David had bought her the roller blades. She stroked their stiff blue plastic, still amazed they were really hers. She hadn't asked for them. She'd just looked at them in the window and the next thing she knew, they were in the store trying them on. Tess had said "No" a lot, because she knew David didn't have much money, but he bought them anyway. The only bad thing had been getting them past her mom, who wouldn't believe that Tess had said "No" even once. She was really afraid that she'd have to take them back, but in the end her mother had given in, though she was still grumpy about them even this morning.

Tess walked slowly, several feet behind her mom and Seth. She didn't want to get to the park too quickly. It was nice savoring the first stage of possession, before her imaginings of spinning arcs on the roller blades were confronted with the reality of learning. She still remembered the snowboard and her afternoon of sore knees and aching butt while Sean drank with his friends.

She had really wanted to wait to try the skates when David could go with her, but David had a job interview and she knew it would be rude not to use them on the first day. So it had to be Seth and her mom even though she was angry with both of them.

She looked ahead to where they walked side by side, talking, her mom's chin raised with a happy, flirtatious tilt. Tess was bewildered and also hurt. The best thing about being in New York was being away from men, and that was suddenly gone. Only, Seth was supposed to be a sort of uncle, like Martin, so she wasn't supposed to notice or care.

Seth wasn't anything like Martin. She was just eleven years old, but she could see that. Martin was slow and worried and busy, like kids' fathers at school. You said "Hi" to them, and then they went away to do whatever they did. Even Mike Hewitt was sort of like that. Seth was like Sean Kelly. Tess lagged farther behind. They didn't notice. So all that shit about staying near her mother on the big, ferocious streets of New York was all forgotten. She scuffed her sneakers on the sidewalk and swung the roller blades petulantly. They were almost out of sight behind a crowd of people when she saw them turn into the park. They were still talking. She suddenly got scared and ran after them, the skates banging on her chest and back. In a moment she stumbled into them. They were standing waiting for her after all, but talking to each other just the same.

Everything had changed since Seth's arrival. When he came to the apartment for dinner, her aunt cooked special meals and they all had wine, though Seth poured Tess's half-and-half with water. They'd been out to dinner twice, in restaurants that served

Chinese or Mexican food at tables in glassed-in rooms on the sidewalk. Seth always paid, signing credit card slips with his big scribbly name while Annie and Martin argued. Seth was rich. Until he came, Tess had thought Annie and Martin were rich because they had three televisions (including one in Danya's closet) and Fatima to clean the apartment. But now she knew different. It was Seth, with his dark suntan and his glasses with gold rims and his beautiful soft sweaters, who was *really* rich.

That part wasn't bad. She liked the dinners and the excitement and the intense, serious look David had when he talked with Seth about books. She even liked the brittle atmosphere of argument that hung over the apartment. The adults were all different with Seth around. Her aunt was braver and said sharp things to Martin. Martin argued with Seth, long arguments that went around and around and got nowhere. Merrilee giggled and looked prettier. And her mom seemed different too, more like the way she was when she ran the ranch and showed Sean Kelly what to do—cooler, and stronger, and sure. When Tess acted up, she was slapped down quickly.

But other things had changed too. Now it was Seth who went out with her mom, looking for her brother Eric. Tess was left at home with David or Annie or Merrilee. She'd made such a fuss about it before, there was no way she could say now that she wanted to go with her mom, but that was the truth. She wanted it back the way it was, with the two of them together, all alone in the city, again.

They kept walking, with Tess following behind through the park, for so long that she began to wonder if they had forgotten that the whole reason for going to the park had been for her to try out her new skates. She got angrier and felt the anger settle deeper and deeper until everything about Seth, even things she had liked, like the shine on his black hair and the quick, certain way his hands moved, annoyed her. She was glaring at him when he turned suddenly and smiled. His smile was sweet, and she felt confused.

"How's this?" Joanna said. They'd come to a place with a pond and an open paved area. There was a fountain with a storybook statue of Alice in Wonderland sitting on a big toadstool.

"Fine," Tess said as flatly as she could.

"What's wrong?"

"Nothing. I said it was fine."

Her mother shrugged. "I'm going to get us some coffee," Joanna gestured to a cafe with small white tables set out in the sun. "Do you want anything?"

"I want to skate."

"You can skate. We're just going to have a cup of coffee while we watch."

"You won't see from over there," Tess said stubbornly.

"Of course we will." There wasn't anything Tess could do, because it was true enough. They could see, but she knew already they wouldn't watch. They would talk and look at each other instead.

"Can I help you with those?" Seth asked quietly, as Tess sat on a bench to put the skates on.

"I can do them." Tess said it sharply, and he didn't offer again. She took off her sneakers and set them beside her on the bench. She pulled up her white socks and pushed her feet into the skates, tying the blue laces and fastening the two Velcro tabs. She sat on the bench uncertainly, running the wheels back and forth on the tarred ground. Seth offered to hold her shoes, and she shrugged an affirmation. Tess stood up carefully, her hand on the arm of the bench. Her feet rolled smoothly away from her and she sat down hard on the ground. Seth reached to help her up, but she shrugged away from his hand.

"Come on," Joanna called to him, "she never lets anyone help her do anything." Tess wanted to shout, "I'd let *you*," but didn't. Her mother and Seth moved away and sat at a table, leaving her alone. Tess braced herself on the bench and stood up. She shuffled warily out into the open, by the pond, and made her way, pushing with her left foot and making short scooter glides with her right to the safety of a wire mesh trash basket. Concentrating, she hung onto its rim. Her feet felt treacherous, leaping out from under her at the slightest chance. She pushed off from the trash basket and was halfway to a green railing around some red-leaved bushes by the fountain, when two black boys on blue skates like hers came whirling from behind the statue. They wore Halloween masks and spun in circles and leaped off a step, landing in graceful curves and rushing by. Tess lost her balance as the first brushed her, and landed on her behind in front of the second. She shouted in outrage, "Hey!"

"Hey, what?" The first boy skated over and looked at her. Tess saw deep, alien black eyes behind the Freddy Krueger mask. The second boy lifted his green and yellow skull face and looked down at Tess too. Like the first boy, he was younger than she, and his eyes were sharp and aware, like the eyes of all the city kids she saw.

He smiled and said, "Leave her alone, she's just learning." Then he dropped the mask down and whirled away. They were gone in moments. Tess sat, humiliated, pretending to adjust her knee pad, feeling her mother and Seth watching her and thinking she'd kill them if they approached. She hated her mother suddenly, not just for talking to Seth, but for everything, most of all for living out in a dumb place like Colorado where it was impossible to learn anything that mattered, so that she ended up eleven years old and still a baby in everybody's eyes.

Seth watched as Tess tugged unhappily at her knee pads. "She's having a rough time," he said to Joanna. "Shouldn't we help?"

"Just leave her," Joanna said. "She has to do it herself." Her voice was matter-of-fact, but Seth thought her face was troubled as she watched Tess. He studied the fine lines on her forehead and the weathered crow's-feet at the corners of her eyes—white furrows in her tan from squinting in the high mountain sun. She reminded him of her father, the way he looked when they were kids, and Seth liked both the memory and the new, wise look the lines gave Joanna.

He looked back again to Tess, who had picked herself up after the little black boy had knocked her over. She was standing, coltishly awkward, her long, skinny arms outstretched for balance: the girl Joanna had been. Seth sat between the past and the present, remembering the awe in which his ten-year-old self had held that girl, wondering now how such charming innocence could once have appeared so daunting.

"It was ridiculous, David getting her those things," Joanna

said. "He really can't afford it. I'm still furious with her for letting him."

Seth touched her arm gently. "Come on. She's a kid. You can't expect her to turn down a gift like that."

"I can and I do. She's not a baby. She knows his situation. And it's not just that. When they came back from the museum she had this huge, yellow, furry dinosaur. Apparently the exhibit was being renovated and this was David's 'apology.' It must have cost a fortune. It's absolutely gigantic. The funny thing is, if *I'd* bought her anything as young as that, she would have been glacial. '*Baby toys.*' "

"Baby toys become love toys when they come from a young man."

"She's not in love with him, Seth," Joanna laughed, puzzled.

"Of course she is. Good for her. He's nice, safe, and conveniently out of reach. What could be better?"

"Seth, she's *eleven.*"

"I was in love when I was five." He smiled fondly, his hand tightening on her elbow. "He's trying to prove he's a man."

"Oh, Tess believes that, all right."

"It's not Tess he needs to convince. It's himself. And his father. Don't worry, Jo, I'll slip him something."

"He won't let you," Joanna said.

"I'll handle that." Seth leaned back in his chair, watching her daughter. She found herself believing him about David, about everything. He had an easy confidence that felt solid underneath. Having him at her side as she searched the streets these last few days, she found the whole city changed, a less frightening, more accessible place.

"I don't know what I would have done yesterday without you," she said with sudden honesty. "That shelter was a scary scene."

Seth looked up. He said evenly, "I would hope, Joanna, that you wouldn't have gone in to that scuzzbag shelter without me. Surely you've got more sense."

She shrugged uneasily. "I don't know, Seth. If I felt I had any chance at all of finding Eric there, I think I would."

He was silent for a while and then said slowly, "Joanna, however important finding Eric is, you've still got to keep some perspective."

"Like what?" she asked, her wide mouth tightening.

"Like the fact that you're a single mother with a dependent daughter. If someone gets sacrificed in all this, it can't be her." He paused, "I'm terribly sorry for Eric, but he's still an adult. In the end, he's responsible for himself."

"So we sacrifice Eric."

"I didn't say that."

"That's what Martin thinks too."

"He doesn't and neither do I. But," he looked away quickly, "I think Martin and I probably have more realistic assessments of Eric's future."

"You've given up on him."

"I didn't say that."

"You both have. You men. Sara hasn't. Annie hasn't. I haven't. But you two have. Fine. Eric doesn't make a heroic, brave recovery, put it all behind him and pick up the pieces, so you write him off. You can't deal with it. All those messy, untidy emotions, so you just close the door." She turned away and watched her daughter's clumsy, earnest progress on her skates. The dark waters of the pond reflected the brilliant yellows and reds of the fall trees and the deep blue of the sky. Remotely above the trees, the city towers floated.

Seth said, "Whoever took Molly took the soul of this family."

"That's a bit dramatic," Joanna said.

"Warranted. The circumstances are dramatic. We've all been changed by them." He paused, his dark eyes challenging. "You'd never have had Tess if it weren't for what happened." Joanna shifted in her chair, reassessing him. She was surprised he understood that. Seth continued, "It's made Martin a zealot. He thinks no one understands the evil in the world but himself." He paused again, then said, "And the kids. David and Danya. I was stunned last summer, seeing how it's still affecting Danya. She still sleeps with the light on. Always. She's terrified of being in the dark. One night, while she was staying at the villa, we had a thunderstorm and we lost the power. She woke up screaming hysterically. Just screaming and screaming. I ran in to her, took her back to my room. I've got candle sconces on the wall." Joanna had a sudden picture of a bachelor bedroom arranged for romance. "I lit the candles and kept them burning all night. She cried and cried and I was terrified they'd burn down . . . I couldn't find a flashlight or anything and the place is inky at night, up in the mountains. Eventually she climbed into my bed with me." He stopped suddenly. "I mean, on top of the covers. Like a little kid." He stopped again, looking at Joanna, and said hastily, "It was one hundred per cent innocent. And yet, you know, afterward, I realized I couldn't tell Martin. There was no way I could tell Martin. All I did was comfort the kid, but I couldn't tell my brother." He looked bewildered.

He glanced up, his eyes following Tess's cautious progress from pond to fountain. He said, still watching, "I think it's been hardest of all on Danya. She was younger, but they were very close. And the same sex. She realizes it could just as well have been her. Only it wasn't. She survived and Molly didn't. She feels she's carrying everyone's expectations. It's too heavy. That's part of why she came to Italy last summer. It wasn't just a vacation. It was an escape. She finds the family oppressive."

"You don't seem to think much of Martin and Annie's parenting," Joanna said. "To hear it from you, both their kids are pretty screwed up."

"They're wonderful parents," Seth said instantly. "That's not the point." Joanna looked uncertain, and he added quickly, "All kids need some other adult sometimes. It's part of growing up." He paused, smiling at her. "We were lucky, you know. I had your parents and you had mine. From as far back as I can remember, all I had to do was go over those couple of fields and up your back steps, and there was your mom in the kitchen, or out on the screened porch, reading. I remember those stacks of library books around her chair. *God*, she read."

"She still does, I gather," Joanna said fondly.

"But she'd always put them down and talk to me. Sometimes I went home to your house first after school, rather than mine." He smiled again, and his eyes crinkled. "It had the added attraction that I might be lucky and run into you."

Joanna half returned the smile, uncertain of his sincerity. She said, looking away, "What about you? How did losing Molly affect you, then?" Seth sat quietly. He stroked the slight stubble on his chin with the back of his hand and studied the paper cups on the table between them.

He said slowly, "I'm not sure. I'm forty-five and not married, but that's hardly unique." He thought again and said, "I think for a while it kept me away from America. It became my private symbol for what was wrong with the country. Hardly fair; these things happen all over the world. And other things, equally awful. Child beggars mutilated at birth in India. Eight-year-old prostitutes in Thailand; little AIDS-free virgins used up like disposable gloves. Oh, if Martin wants, I can match him atrocity for atrocity." He stared bleakly down at the table.

Joanna said, after a while, "You're funny about each other, you and Martin. You've both got chips on your shoulders."

"I have reason."

"He thinks *he* does."

"He hasn't. I never took anything from him. It's not my fault that I made the lucky choices. I mean about money, Jo," he added, his eyes meeting hers. "Any other way you look at it, he's got the better life."

"He's got a lovely family," Joanna said. "That's something, anyhow."

"That's everything, Jo. The rest of it's just trimming."

Joanna laughed. "Hardly what you expect from the 'captivatingly single Seth Levine,'" she said, laughing again.

"You read that English piece?"

"I found it on Martin's desk. You seemed to have scored quite a hit."

Seth smiled. "There were extenuating circumstances."

"Even so," Joanna said slowly, "it sounded like a pretty glamorous bachelor scene. The last thing you'd expect reading it is to find you yearning for family life."

"The lady saw what she wanted to see," Seth said, adding, "it's a common human flaw." He looked away from her at the brilliant trees and said slowly, "I'll never understand Martin. Or you, either. I'll never understand what went on between the two of you."

Joanna sighed. She shifted in her chair, felt a craving for a cigarette and thought about the pack of Marlboro Lights she always carried for security at the bottom of her bag. She pushed the craving away and said softly, "It was complicated." She drew back from him physically, her voice growing remote as she continued, "I was in love with Martin since I was fifteen. Ever since I realized there wasn't much future in being in love with my brother Eric. I used to fight Martin for Eric's attention, and then quite suddenly I had all Martin's attention and it was Eric who was left out."

"And me," said Seth.

Joanna laughed, "You were a little kid."

"I was one year younger, Joanna," Seth said good-naturedly. "One year."

Joanna tilted her head whimsically, considering. "You were a boy though. A fourteen-year-old *boy* is a little kid."

"Not in his heart," said Seth. He looked directly at her and said, with disarming honesty, "Oh, Jo. I was so much in love with you." She drew back, unnerved, but oddly pleased.

"Were you, Seth?" she said wonderingly. "You never really *showed* that, you know."

"How could I show it? You were always my brother's girl." He leaned back, laughing softly, lifted off his sunglasses, and rubbed the bridge of his prominent nose. He squinted into the white sun, thick black lashes meshing. "When I went out to India, you were inseparable. The next thing I know, he's marrying Annie. I read the letter twice. I thought my parents had gotten the name wrong."

Joanna laughed and said lightly, "I think you missed a few letters in between."

Seth put his glasses back on and leaned forward suddenly, "Why did you leave him?" he said. Joanna was silent and thoughtful. She waved to Tess, and Tess, standing still on her skates, holding the green railing, waved back halfheartedly.

Joanna said, "I'd better go see her."

"Answer me first, please," Seth said with great care.

Joanna turned from her daughter. She said slowly, "Sometimes, Seth, you live with someone for years before you realize you're incompatible because your souls are incompatible. Sometimes, if you're lucky, or unlucky, you have a moment of truth. We had a moment of truth."

"Such as?"

"Just that, Seth. That's all I'm going to say." Seth stared at her. She could see the glint of frustration in the eyes behind the smoky lenses. She shrugged, without conviction.

"You know," he said, "you *both* still treat me like the nosy kid brother in everybody's way. I'm forty-five years old. When is this family going to let me into the inner sanctum?" Joanna looked at him sadly but said nothing. She stood and picked up her paper cup and walked with it to the trash basket where her daughter clung, dejectedly swinging herself back and forth on her blue plastic wheels.

"How're you doing, sweetheart?" Joanna asked. Tess hooked her arms over the basket, leaning over it. She pushed her butt out and swung the skates back and forth, scraping the sides of the wheels against the tar.

"I'm no good at this," she said.

"Hey, sure you are," Joanna said. "You're great."

"I'm lousy," Tess said clearly, caught in one of her increasingly common bursts of adult realism. And then, having depressed herself with her own honesty, she turned angry, "How would you know, anyway? You weren't even watching."

"I was watching, Tess."

"Every time I looked at you, you were talking to him." She jabbed an elbow toward Seth. Joanna narrowed her eyes.

"Not him. Seth. And I wasn't. I was watching you lots when you weren't watching me."

"Sure you were."

Seth stepped forward then, extending his free hand. "Come have a Coke, Tess," he said gently, "You must be thirsty after all that."

"I didn't come here to have Cokes," Tess said angrily, "I came to learn to skate."

"Right," Joanna said, "and now we're going home."

"Mom . . ."

"I've had enough, Tess. The world doesn't turn around you,

young lady, whatever you think." Seth stood back. Joanna took
the shoes from him and directed her daughter to a bench. Tess
flopped down dramatically and indulged in a flamboyant unlacing
of her roller blades. Joanna could see her considering flinging the
skates from her, but resisting, too fond of David and his present
to commit the sacrilege. She pushed her feet into her sneakers and
stood up.

"Tie them."

"They're fine."

"You're not walking through Central Park with your laces undone. Tie them."

Tess flung herself back on the bench. "Who cares?" she said,
jerking the laces into a knot. "Half the people here have their
brains undone. Who gives a shit about my laces?"

Joanna ignored her, and when the second shoe was fastened,
she nodded to Seth and turned and walked away. He followed,
reluctantly, looking back at Tess as he did.

"She'll come," Joanna said, looking straight ahead. He walked
on, and after a few steps more glanced back again. Tess was walking sulkily behind, head down, eyes hidden under the peak of her
baseball cap, the roller blades swinging by their laces from a tightly
balled fist.

"We haven't been fair to her," he said quietly to Joanna.

"We've been fair."

"No. I haven't. She must be used to having you a lot more
to herself. I've been hogging your company since I got here."
Joanna turned to look at him.

"That's very thoughtful of you, Seth," she said. She gave him
an open, appreciative smile. "But the truth is she really gets plenty
of attention. Annie and Martin have gone out of their way. David
and Merrilee fall all over themselves for her. And until a couple
of days ago she wanted less of me rather than more. Unfortu-
nately, you've had the bad luck to hit her trigger."

"What? What have I done?"

"It's nothing you've done, Seth. It's because you're male, that's
all."

"Because I'm *male?* But so's Martin. So's David."

"Because you're male and she thinks I find you attractive," Joanna said, and then was suddenly embarrassed, feeling her face redden. "Don't take that wrong," she said.

"How could I?" Seth was grinning happily. "I'm flattered as hell. At least one woman in this family thinks I'm worth a second look. Even if she is only eleven." Joanna giggled and gave him a friendly shove. They walked companionably through the park, the shoulder of Seth's Italian raincoat brushing the sleeve of her denim jacket. At the Columbus Circle exit of the park, Joanna turned and waited until the pink of her daughter's sweatshirt emerged from behind a cluster of bike riders in their tight thigh-length shorts. She was still slouching along, but Joanna suddenly didn't give a damn. Defiantly, she took Seth's arm as they turned up Central Park West.

She could not have explained to Seth what made her turn around. They had gone a hundred yards farther, and she had been conscious of Seth twice making quick, secretive glances back, having less faith in her daughter's street sense than she did. Then, suddenly, she felt a prickling awareness down the back of her neck. She stopped and then turned.

"What is it?" Seth asked.

"Tess."

"She's right there, I saw her a moment ago."

"Where?" Joanna's voice was thin and delicately poised between reason and fear.

"Right back there." He raised a hand to point, and then lowered it. "I swear, I just saw her." He lifted his sunglasses.

"Tess?" Joanna called. "Tess?" she shouted. A bus changing gears drowned the sound. She flung her bag farther over her shoulder and began walking swiftly back toward the park. Seth caught up. Joanna began to run. "*Tess!*"

Quite suddenly there were crowds of people everywhere: people walking, people bicycling, roller-blading, jogging. Involved with the pleasure of a Sunday afternoon, they moved oblivious of her, blocked her vision, stood in her way. Joanna shouted Tess's name again and again. Seth ran on ahead, reached the park entrance, and scouted quickly back and forth. A hot-dog vendor watched without curiousity. Two homeless men looked up from their paper-bag-wrapped bottle.

———

"WHO ARE YOU LOOKING FOR?" Joanna turned. A heavy, well-dressed woman in jewel-framed glasses was tugging at her sleeve.

"Who? A girl, a little girl. My daughter."

"A little girl. In a pink top?" The woman spoke slowly, pedantically.

"Yes. Yes."

"Blond hair?"

"*Yes.* Have you seen her?" Joanna's eyes were searching the crowds of Columbus Circle above the woman's head.

"She was talking to a man."

"Oh, my God."

"Over there." The woman pointed to an empty space of sidewalk. "He's gone now."

"Oh, God. Seth! Seth!"

"They're both gone."

"Seth, she was with a man." Joanna's voice cracked, shaking with panic. Seth was at her side.

"Okay, okay. They can't be far. I'll go back into the park. You go over there," he pointed to the subway entrance, "and phone the police."

"Oh, God, Seth, this can't be happening." She looked to him desperately. Then, over his shoulder, she saw Tess. She was just standing behind a bench, her back to the wall bordering the park, holding her skates in front of her with two hands, and looking around intently, slightly bewildered but quite calm. The sight of her, blossoming from the emptiness that had, moments before, engulfed them, swallowed Joanna's words. She stood shaking and tugging at Seth's sleeve until she could whisper, "She's there. She's there."

"Tess." Seth ran to the child, grabbed her shoulders and then hugged her passionately. She stood still, confused but uncomplaining, as he released her. Joanna reached them and crouched down, gripping Tess's arms with tightening white fingers. Tess winced.

"Where were you?"

"I was here. Where were you?" Tess blinked cautiously. "What's the matter?"

"We couldn't find you," Joanna whispered. "Some woman said she saw you talking to a man, and then we couldn't find you." Joanna started to cry. Tess drew back, embarrassed.

"Jesus, Mom. How stupid do you think I am? I wasn't going to go anywhere with him."

"With who?" Seth said sharply.

"The man," Tess looked at him, exasperated.

"What man?" Joanna cried.

"The man." Tess flung her arms out, the skates clunking against the bench. "Will you stop treating me like such a baby? There's kids my age, kids littler than me, walking all around the city by themselves."

"You know not to talk to people."

"So what's going to happen right here with a million people watching? I knew what I was doing. I'm not going to get kidnapped or anything." She paused, her eyes bright with tears of outrage. "I'm not little Molly," she said scathingly.

Seth said, "Your mom's right, Tess. I know you're not a baby, but even a girl your age should never talk to strangers."

"He wasn't a stranger," said Tess.

"Then what . . . ?" Seth said. Tess turned to her mother. "He was that man we talked to. The one I said did know Uncle Eric."

"What man?" Joanna was wiping her eyes with her long, tanned fingers. "What are you talking about?"

"The one with the *glasses*." Tess shrugged, "So what was wrong with me talking to him? You talked to him before. He wasn't a stranger." Joanna crouched down again, taking Tess's elbows once more in her hands. Tess winced again in expectation, but this time Joanna was calm, her fingers light.

"Tess, just because I spoke to him doesn't make him any less a stranger. You had no business talking to him again."

"Well, what was I supposed to do? He spoke to me. What do I do, ignore him?"

"Yes, Tess," Seth said smoothly, "And if he was sensible he'd know why."

"He was sensible. He was nice." Tess glared at her mother. "Not like some of the scuzzbags you talk to. Why's it all right for you then?"

"I'm an adult," Joanna said instantly. "When you're with me, it's all right. You rely on my adult judgment. When you're alone, you talk to nobody. Nobody. Understand?"

"Your adult judgment?" Tess pulled back and flipped her mass of blond braids contemptuously. "If you had any adult judgment we wouldn't be in the mess we're always in, would we?" She turned her glare suddenly to Seth. "How am *I* supposed to know who I can trust? You're always making friends with men and telling me they're wonderful. You think he's wonderful," she raised an insolent shoulder at Seth. "I don't even know him."

"He's your Uncle Martin's brother, as you very well know."

"I don't care. I don't know him and I don't like him."

"Tess." Joanna reached for her, but Seth's hand, gentle on her sleeve, held her back. Tess wriggled out from behind the bench.

"You think all men are wonderful. You thought Sean was wonderful. And Mike."

"Tess, shut up!"

Tess jumped up on the seat of the bench, tauntingly. "Remember that one you brought home once who used to hang around the ranch house until we had to have the locks changed?"

"You little bitch." Joanna wrenched herself away from Seth and lunged at Tess, but Seth moved faster and put himself between them. Joanna stepped back against the park railing, still glaring at Tess. Seth sat on the backrest of the bench, smiling good-naturedly. Tess, her mouth screwed up from shouting at her mother, slipped down off the bench and stood looking at him. Her face slowly relaxed.

Seth said casually, "What did he talk to you about, Tess?"

She looked at him uncertainly, brushed the peak of her cap up and looked at her mother. Joanna was standing, one hand on her hip, looking at the ground. When she said nothing Tess looked back at Seth. "About Uncle Eric," she said.

Joanna raised her head, her eyes widening. "What about Uncle Eric?" Seth said in the same calm voice.

"He's going to meet us."

"Eric is?" Joanna whispered. "He said Eric is?"

"Where?" Seth asked. Tess looked uncomfortable, uncertain now of her judgment.

"I said in the park. I thought if he came to the apartment and he wasn't *really* Uncle Eric, he might steal things or something. So I said in the park." She paused. "I said by the statue of Alice in Wonderland. I couldn't think of anywhere else. The man said four o'clock tomorrow. Is that okay?" Seth and Joanna were staring at each other.

Seth said finally, "Is this real, Joanna? Who is this man?"

She shook her head, rattled. "I don't know. He was just this guy we saw hanging around Columbus Circle talking to homeless people. I showed him Eric's picture. I don't know who he is." She paused. "He said he didn't know Eric," she added.

"But he did," Tess said with a tiny smile of triumph, "I told you he did."

Lilith's Daughter

BRIAN, WHO MANNED the desk in the lobby of the hostel, smirked when Eric came in to ask for his mail. He smirked because there never was any mail (with one sole exception) and because, like the European kids who treated Brian like a servant, Eric broke the rules. He expected mail as though he was staying in the fucking Plaza. Brian amused himself thinking up new ways of saying no. Yesterday, he'd tried "I'll send up room service when it comes." He'd liked it enough to repeat it, but then this afternoon a Chinese kid came in and actually delivered a smooth white envelope with Eric Carlson's name typed on the front. Brian presented it to Eric laid flat on a plastic Budweiser tray, as if he were a butler in an English mansion.

"Your mail, sir," he said with a larger than usual smirk.

Eric was as surprised by the letter as Brian. Although he checked every day, because his name and this address were written on the back of each of Molly's pictures, he did so as a hollow ritual. In two months there had been exactly one response, from a crazy woman who wanted to "heal him with the gift of her body." He went to the far side of the dark lobby to open the envelope and take out the single sheet. It was nubby, expensive writing paper with "From the desk of Daniel M. Grossman" printed in black at the top. The letter was written by hand in black ink.

I have arranged a meeting for four o'clock tomorrow afternoon, at the Delacorte Fountain in Central Park. Attend only if you wish.

Dan.

Eric folded the letter back into its envelope and slipped it into his inside pocket. He went back to the desk and paid Brian for a bed. He had a shower and scrubbed himself meticulously amidst the scummy foam and mats of pubic hair. He went to bed early. Unable to sleep, he got up at four. By five he was walking the dawn streets of midtown, waiting for the sun to light the high peaks of the city and warm the empty canyons. He walked until six, bought a donut and coffee for breakfast, and walked some more. It was only when he was moving that he could cope with the excitement.

He began to worry about his appearance, stopping to stare into store windows, going twice into men's rooms, looking for mirrors. He saw the changes, the lines, the gauntness, the way the hollowing gave his eyes a glittering stare. He accepted that she might not know him. What he could not bear was that she might turn away from him in fear.

The day grew warm and golden. Street vendors, caught unawares by a return of summer, slouched around their tables of woolen scarves and gloves. He thought about the street vendors as he walked north up Fifth, wondering how they knew to change their stock, where the stock came from, how they could appear in a sudden summer shower with umbrellas, or in a power blackout with flashlights and candles, like those ephemeral water creatures that hatched in puddles in a day. There must be a network, a society, an underground. He became aware of the city tied together by millions of such networks, tremulous as spider-webs, and himself and his daughter suddenly drawn together by the vibrations of one fragile silken thread. He felt the thread go taut as he crossed Grand Army Plaza and entered Central Park.

When he reached the pond and the fountain he knew he was too early, and he struggled with indecision. Should he sit on a bench or at a table at the cafe? But might she miss him there? Should he stand in clear view? But would that be too bold, too threatening? Should he leave, walk around, return nearer the time? But what if she was just arriving and saw him go? Would she feel herself abandoned and leave as well? The choices were unbearable, fraying his exhausted, strung-out nerves.

And then, as he stood bewildered, absorbed by uncertainty,

he looked up. There she was, sprung in an instant out of the crowd, a dozen feet from him, a gangly girl on bright blue skates, before the statue of Alice in Wonderland. Long-legged and skinny, fair and lovely, child and woman, Molly, his Molly. Past and present, dream and reality, fused exquisitely, and Eric grasped his perfect picture.

But at once, blocks of illogic appeared in it, broke free, and tumbled out. How could she have those skates? Those skates didn't even exist. How can she be here, ten years old? She is not ten years old. She made an awkward stumbling pirouette and clutched the park railing. Eric clung to his happiness for a last trembling moment. The daughter, Molly's daughter. He summoned the image, so vivid and clear when he sat at breakfast with Artie, but it faltered now, pale and weak beside the flesh and blood of reality. The girl tripped on her skates and landed heavily, with a little grunt, her knee pads and bare hands slapping the pavement. She looked up, angry and stubborn, her palms white and marked with grains of dirt.

He felt another blind man's veil lift from his eyes. With weary realism he saw the subtle, true, particular resemblances beneath the general resemblance of wider family. Molly and her phantom daughter faded, the taut silk thread strained impossibly and broke. He stood, defeated, watching a real, unremarkable, and sullen child. Then he raised his eyes, looking calmly through the crowd until he saw Joanna, standing at a distance, watching him. The only surprise was Seth Levine, older and solemnly mature, standing at her side.

—

TESS STRUGGLED UP onto one foot and one knee, felt the wheels slip as she tried to stand, and flopped back. She sat on the pavement and stuck her legs out wearily in front of her, staring at the blue toes of her skates. She wished she had a pad for her rear end as well as her elbows and knees, and the thought made her grin in spite of herself. The grin brought its own flash of good humor, something else that had begun to happen lately, like her bursts of sudden honesty. This time she didn't feel mad at her mother or anybody. It wasn't anyone's *fault* that skating was hard. She looked up, still grinning, and saw the man looking down at her. He was tall and really good looking in a Clint Eastwoody way, craggy, with bright blue eyes. He smiled at her, and she was about to smile back out of habit, but then she remembered she was in New York. She pushed her lips together and ducked her head.

The man said, "Hello Tess." She looked up, astounded.

"Huh?"

"Tess Carlson?"

"Yeah." Tess's mouth fell open, and then she remembered yesterday. "I can't talk to you," she said. The man started to speak, but Tess saw a flurry of movement as her mother ran past her, straight at him. Tess thought she was going to hit him for talking to her, but then he opened his arms wide and her mother flung herself into his embrace. Tess sat staring while her mom and the man hugged and kissed and laughed and Seth, laughing happily, joined them. She remembered the warm feeling she had had when Seth had found her yesterday by the bench and hugged her just as he was now hugging the stranger in the park. She felt lonely sitting by herself and wanted to be part of their adult joy, but the skates and something else equally slippery and unmanageable kept her separate.

Her mother seemed to notice, because she slipped out of the tall man's arms and turned toward her, yet holding his hand. She said, her eyes brimming with happiness, "Come here, Tess, and meet your Uncle Eric."

"That's Eric?" said Tess. Her jaw went slack. "But he's not scuzzy at all." She clapped her hand over her mouth. Some of the happiness left her mother's eyes, but Eric laughed, tipping his head back, his hand still holding her mother's.

Then he let the hand go, stepped toward Tess, and squatted down beside her on the ground. He tapped one of her skates, "God, Tess, I tried those once in San Francisco and spent four hours on my behind. How do you do it?"

She smiled and shook her head, "I don't. I spend all my time on my behind." She looked at her mother and at Seth. Then she said, "How did you know my name?"

He leaned back on his heels and put one hand down to steady

himself. "I'm going to say one of those things kids hate, Tess. I knew you once when you were a little tiny baby." Tess grinned and reddened, but she didn't feel like hating him.

"But I've grown up. I'm pretty different now," she said uncertainly. There was a silence. Eric looked down at the blue wheels of her skate. He spun one gently with his finger, and when he looked up his glittering eyes were sad, but he said only, "You look just like your mom." He laughed softly, "I guess that's another thing kids hate." Tess shook her head and made a small smile. He watched her steadily. "I'm not what you expected, am I?" She shook her head again. "Better or worse?"

"Oh, better. Lots better." He smiled again and stood up.

"Good." He reached down one hand, and she took it and stood up cautiously, balancing precariously against his arm. "We're going to sit and talk. Would you like to come or would you rather skate?" Tess considered and smiled.

"I've skated enough," she said happily.

They went back to the same table where Joanna and Seth had sat the day before. Eric walked beside Tess, balancing her. He did it just right so that her feet got neither ahead of her nor behind. When they got to the table, he pulled out a metal chair for her and she sat down, her knees to one side and the skates tucked neatly beneath her.

"Let me get us some coffee," Eric said.

"No, no, we will." Joanna stepped to brush past him, but he put a hand on her shoulder. She looked slender and small beside him.

Seth said, "I'll do it; you two sit down," but Eric put a hand on his shoulder as well.

He turned to Tess, "What can I get you?" he asked. Tess looked quickly at her mother.

"I'm fine. I don't need anything," she blurted worriedly.

"Sure you do," Eric smiled. She shook her head vigorously. He smiled again and went off to the service counter.

Joanna looked at Seth, but Seth just raised a hand slightly and said, "Let it be." They sat at the table.

Tess leaned forward and whispered angrily, "Why did you let him do that? He hasn't got any money." Joanna shook her head.

She seemed confused. "Seth?" Tess demanded. "You should stop him."

"Let it be, Tess," Seth said. He looked as though he wasn't listening, and Tess got angrier. When Eric came back he'd brought her a drink anyhow. He'd brought a Seven-Up, which she hated, but she thanked him and looked hard at her mother in case she said anything.

"I'll finish it if you can't, Tess," Joanna said in a low voice, as Eric handed Seth his coffee.

"It's fine. It's nice," Tess said firmly. She smiled at Eric.

"Oh, this is nice," Eric said. He leaned back in his chair and stretched his long legs. The sun glistened on the silvered, red-blond waves of his hair. "You look beautiful, Jo," he said, his smile broadening. "I've never seen you look so good. Doesn't she, Seth?"

Seth nodded and said, "She's always beautiful."

"God, it's been a long time. Years. When was it that I saw you in Denver, 'eighty-four? 'Eighty-five? And you, Seth. I can't remember when. Are you back in this country now?"

"Just for a while." Seth paused, "I live in Italy. Near Genoa."

"Oh, right. God, that must be lovely. I've wanted to go to Italy since I did Art History my first semester at college."

Seth raised his hands and tilted his head in a quick expressive shrug, "So come."

Eric laughed quietly. "I just might, Seth. I just might."

Tess stared, first at him and then, in turn, at her mother and at Seth. She couldn't believe the things they were saying. She wanted to say, "Come on. Let's talk about what matters." But she dared not open her mouth. They all seemed queer and remote, as if they were suddenly actors in a scene in a movie. She had a feeling that if she spoke they wouldn't hear her.

"And you, Jo? I didn't know you were back in New York."

"I'm not," Jo said and added stiffly, "just a visit."

She opened her mouth to speak again, but Eric overran her words, "So you're still out in Denver then?"

"I moved out of the city. Up into the mountains."

"Oh," he said, "A lot nicer for Tess, I bet."

Joanna laughed suddenly and the stiffness left her voice. "Actually, she hates it."

"No, I don't, Mom," Tess said seriously. "I don't hate it."

Joanna looked at her as if just then aware of her presence. She said, "Well, you've sure fooled me."

"I don't hate it," Tess repeated.

Eric studied her kindly, and then, still looking at Tess, said, "Still in antiques, Jo?"

Joanna sighed. "No. No, actually, I had to give that up. Ben, you remember, the guy I was living with?" Eric nodded. "Well, we split up and I had to sell the business to give him back his half." She paused and said, "I bought a little horse ranch in Grand County."

"Did you, Jo?" Eric sipped at his coffee, his bright blue eyes steady on her face, "That's terrific."

"We lost that too," Tess said cheerfully. "We're real business geniuses." She cocked her head toward her mother and grinned. There was something loyal and companionable in the grin, and Jo was pleased to have some help with her litany of failures.

"Yeah, I guess we are." She smiled bravely at Eric. "I'm a waitress in a greasy spoon," she said. Eric nodded.

"I've done worse," he said.

"So have I," said Seth. Eric turned from Joanna to look more carefully at Seth.

"Not recently, I think," he said. Seth looked uncomfortable, as if suddenly aware of his expensively casual dress, but then Eric said, "I've read everything but the last. I couldn't get ahold of the last."

"Have you?" Seth looked up and removed his sunglasses. "Have you really? I didn't think you would even have heard of my stuff."

"Of course I have," Eric said.

Seth grinned. He said eagerly, "I spent eight months in Saigon four years ago, researching the Southeast Asia book. I thought of you all the time. Every time I came to some place you'd named in your letters, I got this amazing thrill." Eric nodded. His eyes looked out over Seth's head, over Joanna's, to the top of the bright-colored trees.

"It feels so long ago," he said.

"Eric," Joanna said, reaching a hand out and laying it on his, "Are you ready to come home?"

"Home?" Eric said. He straightened his back, slipping his hand from beneath hers, and drew in his legs.

"Home," Joanna said. "To us. To me. Or Mom and Dad. Or Annie and Martin." He sighed. He drew his hands in, resting them in his lap, studying his fingernails.

"It's Annie behind this, isn't it?" he said.

"Behind what?" Seth asked. He was staring intently at Eric.

"I thought maybe it was your own idea."

"It was my idea," Joanna said.

"Yes, but it was because of Annie." He looked up abruptly. "It wasn't the way it looked, Jo. I knew she wouldn't understand." Joanna nodded, tilted her head, tugged at wisps of her blond hair.

She said, "She would have understood a lot better if you'd talked to her."

"I couldn't," Eric said. He shook his head impatiently, "I wasn't . . . ready." Seth and Joanna looked up questioningly. Eric said, "You've got to understand. I've been so busy since I came back to New York. I haven't had time to look for a job. Of course, I will have to, soon, but I've been getting by. I had a bit put aside from Seattle. That's where I came from last." He stopped. Joanna and Seth were still looking at him. "What Annie saw wasn't typical. I'd needed some cash in a hurry. It was just that day . . ." He stopped and looked away. "She shouldn't have told you."

"Of course she should," Joanna said.

"You came back East because of it, didn't you?"

Joanna smiled encouragingly, "It was a chance to see everybody, Eric." Tess stared. She looked from Joanna to Seth and back to Joanna.

"Mom?" she said, "What are you lying for? The whole reason we came was to find Uncle Eric. Why are you pretending it wasn't?"

Joanna didn't look at her. With her eyes still on Eric, she said, "Tess, be quiet please."

Eric hunched his shoulders in his plaid jacket. He looked at Joanna coolly and said, "She's right, Jo. Let's be level. Okay?"

Joanna blinked, rebuffed. She sat silent for a moment and then leaned across the table to her brother and said fiercely, "Eric, what are you doing? Why are you hiding from us? Why did you run away from us? I know it was hardest for you, but it was hard for us too. Why did we have to lose you as well?" Her lip trembled and she wiped her eyes.

Eric reached gently to touch her shoulder. "Jo?" he said. His hand was strong and hard. The fingers brushed the hair beside her ear. "You all right, Jo?" She wiped her eyes again and said nothing. "You weren't going to lose me," he said soothingly. "I was always coming back someday."

"When, Eric?"

"You know when." Joanna turned away, the curled fingers of her right hand pressed against her upper lip. She closed her eyes and began to cry.

Seth squeezed her upper arm gently. He leaned across the table and said, "When, Eric? When you've found Molly?" Eric didn't answer. "Eric, it's been thirteen years." There was silence. "Eric?"

"I heard you."

"How many years can you go on?"

Eric looked away, then down at the table, and said, "I think forever if I had to." He paused and said distantly, "You can't understand, Seth. You haven't any children."

"I still have a heart." Seth leaned forward again and put his hands on Eric's upper arms. "Look at me."

Eric raised his head reluctantly. He looked directly into Seth's eyes and said, "You're just like Dina. Both of you." He paused. "All of you."

"No, we're not," Joanna said fiercely. "We're nothing like Dina. We would have supported you and helped you, but you left. You left."

"I had to. You were taking her away from me."

"We were what?" Joanna whispered.

Seth laid his hand on her arm again. He said quietly, "What do you mean, Eric?"

"You never believed she was alive."

Seth said, "Does what I believe matter, Eric? I can't change the truth."

"She is alive, Seth."

Seth looked tired and sad. "I hope so, Eric," he said.

Eric studied him and Joanna and Tess for a long while, leaning back in his chair, his fingers toying with his empty coffee cup. He said eventually, "I'm going to have to tell you everything."

He looked resigned, and Joanna, expecting at last a confession of his circumstances, said gently, "Tell us, Eric. We're your family. You can tell us anything."

"I've found her," Eric said.

"You've found her?" Joanna's eyes were narrow and startlingly bright. "Eric?"

"I was going to tell you all, soon. I was going to show you." Still reluctantly, he unbuttoned his jacket and drew the folder from his inner pocket. The poster of Lilith's Daughter was now incorporated in his collection, folded carefully with just the faces of the five young performers showing through the clear vinyl envelope. He had placed it after the Arizona artist's drawing. When he handed the folder to Seth and Joanna, he held it open at the sketch. "This," he said, "is Molly."

Joanna stared at the drawing, tracing its eerie, familiar lines with her finger. Seth, leaning over her shoulder, said, "When was this done?"

"Last year."

Joanna's head came up. Her eyes sparkled with excitement. "Last year? Where? Who did it? How did you get it?" Eric laid his big hand over hers.

"It's not from life, Jo. It's a projection. An artist's interpretation, from my description and Molly's old pictures."

"But it's so real. It's . . . it's the way Molly would have . . ." Eric took the folder from her and turned the page.

"Here's Molly now," he said. He laid the photograph of Lilith's Daughter on the table between them. Joanna studied it, turned back the page to the sketch, and returned to the folded poster. "She's a singer in a rock band. She calls herself Megan

Carmichael now. I got a positive identification from the doorman at the Seattle club where she played in June. He knew her right off." Joanna shook her head, amazed, looking back and forth between the two pictures.

Seth asked, "From your sketch?"

"Of course." Seth lifted the folder and studied it at length, then solemnly handed it back.

"Where is she now, Eric?" he asked, "Have you any idea?"

"No."

Joanna sighed. Eric allowed himself a slow, triumphant smile then, and said, "But she's playing down in the West Village next week."

"Eric," Joanna whispered, "this is unreal." She began to smile and looked up, wonderingly, to Seth. He met her eyes but did not smile back.

Eric smiled more broadly, "Next week, Seth. Next week. Do you see why I waited now?" He laughed, stretching luxuriantly. "You can tell Annie not to worry, anyhow. Next week, we're coming home."

Joanna laughed too, a cautious but happy laugh that expanded into delight. "Eric, I can't believe this."

"Neither can I," he said. He leaned closer to her, his voice intimate and confidential, "After all the years and all the places, to come back and find her here. I followed her from Seattle, you know. Over the years, I had a feeling I was getting closer, and then I met that guy in Seattle, and I felt I was right there, you know?" Joanna nodded again, eagerly. "Just an inch away." Eric held up his finger and thumb, a tiny bit apart. "I could feel it. To think, I might have brushed by her already on some street out there. Or even here. Even here. The city's funny. You do meet people. Look how I met Annie." The words tumbled out in a relaxed, happy flow. He was holding Joanna's hand.

Seth said suddenly, "How are you going to get through?"

"Through?"

"To meet her. Through their security."

Eric stopped smiling and turned to Seth. "You think they'll have . . . they're not a really big name or anything."

"Big or not, they're performers. An all-woman band. You bet they'll have security." Eric's expression changed from puzzlement to concern. "You might not even get near them," Seth said.

"Oh, Seth," Joanna said, "why tell him that?"

"I'm just warning him, Jo," Seth's voice was clipped. "Better than letting him go there and finding out then." Eric looked uncertain.

"I'll just tell them," he said. "I'll just tell them who I am. I'll tell them the truth."

"Eric," Seth said gently. "They're not going to believe it any better because it's the truth. They've heard it all, these guys. 'I'm her sister, her brother, her auntie from Baltimore.' I mean, people don't usually say, 'I'm an obsessed psychopathic axe-murderer,' do they?" Eric actually smiled. Seth smiled back. "I could help, Eric," he said.

"You?" Eric's expression struggled between relief and doubt. "How could you?"

"I'm a journalist, Eric. Journalists get in everywhere. Particularly," he paused and smiled slyly, "if they can promise a big feature in *Vox* or *Prima.*"

"Can you?" Eric said wonderingly.

"Sure," Seth grinned. "I can promise it. Keeping the promise is another thing, but all that matters to you is getting through the door. Right?"

Eric looked disturbed. "It doesn't seem fair," he said.

Seth watched him sadly and said, "And if she is Molly, Eric, do you think she'll care?"

———

ON THE NIGHT he'd agreed to meet Eric again, Seth had dinner with Martin's family at West Seventy-fifth Street. It was the Thursday before Halloween, and Lilith's Daughter was performing in the Village at ten o'clock. Seth drove in from the Island. He had taken Sara and his parents out to a lavish lunch as apology for his many absences. He was supposed to be staying with them. Up to now he'd spent most of his days in New York with Joanna, his nights at the Mayflower.

Lunch wasn't a success. His parents' favorite restaurant was under new management, and his mother didn't like the changes. Sara was harassed, in the middle of rehearsals for her dancers' Halloween show. His father ate a few bites of each course and fidgeted. Seth took them home and dropped them off and turned his rental car toward the expressway with guilty relief.

At the apartment, Merrilee had cooked one of her big meals. Seth, who had already had a big meal, tried valiantly to eat it. They were all edgy. David had failed another job interview, and Annie was behind in her reading. Martin argued with Seth all through dinner about Europe and why Seth chose to live there, and about the older things, America and loyalty and patriotism, on which they had always disagreed. Fascinated, Tess watched them, but Merrilee reddened and looked upset as she always did when people argued.

To divert them, Annie got Seth to tell again how he'd posed as an Italian journalist to convince the manager of the Hudson Street club to allow him an interview with Lilith's Daughter. Tess giggled at his adopted Italian accent and he exaggerated it to amuse her. Joanna laughed too, and Merrilee and David joined in.

Martin watched gloomily and then said, "It's hardly funny. This is hardly a funny situation."

Tess went quiet. Merrilee said quickly, "It's just Seth we're laughing at."

"You've made it all a joke," Martin said to Seth. "We're talking about a tragedy. Eric's going to be devastated by your little game."

"It's not my game, Martin," Seth said. "It's his."

"So why help him to delude himself?"

"I'm trying to protect him."

"The best protection I can think of is to tell him right out he's deluded. This Mary or Megan or whatever isn't his Molly . . . we all know that. Why are we colluding in this?" He glared at Seth with a surge of pent-up anger.

Annie said abruptly, "Leave Seth alone."

"Let him answer my question."

"That's not what you're fighting about," Annie said. She sounded weary and her face looked fragile and old. She looked around her table, at her son, her daughter-in-law, her tall blond sister, and then back at Martin. "You know what's eating you. Now leave Seth alone." The room went uncomfortably quiet.

"More lasagna anyone?" Merrilee said brightly. Her face was red again and there were little beads of moisture on her nose. David accepted the dish she was offering. He and Tess grinned at each other and divided its contents.

Joanna said cautiously, "Shouldn't we even entertain the possibility that we're wrong?"

"Wrong how?" David asked.

"About Megan Carmichael. That Eric's right. And we're wrong."

Martin sighed heavily and said, "Jo, this is just crazy scab-picking. The child died thirteen years ago. She's dead. Dead." His big soft lip began to tremble, and his deep moody eyes were wet. "This is cutting me up," he said suddenly. Annie reached a hand out and caught his as he fumbled with his napkin on the table. Seth watched and then turned to Joanna.

"Jo, Eric is building all this on the basis of a sketch by someone who never saw Molly, guessing what Molly might have grown up to look like, and the word of a probably bored and possibly strung-out nightclub bouncer, who maybe saw a resemblance to somebody in that sketch. It's not just a house built on sand. It's a sand castle built on sand."

"You don't believe Megan Carmichael could possibly be Molly."

"I know she's not Molly. You know she's not Molly." He shook his head, flicking back misplaced hair with a quick hand. "Don't slide *in*to this, Jo."

"Then why are you going with him?" Joanna said in a small voice.

Seth looked up. The whole family was watching him. He took a deep breath and said evenly, "Because I'm scared Eric won't believe the truth even when she tells him she's not Molly."

"He'll have to," Annie said.

Seth turned to her. "Don't underestimate people like this. He's got the excuses built in already." He looked back at Joanna, "You heard him: 'she may resist, may deny...'"

"What do you mean," Joanna said sharply, " 'people like this'?"

Seth kept his even tone, "Obsessional people."

"He's not crazy, Seth. We talked to him for more than an hour. He's sane."

Seth met her eyes. "Jo, I'm not interested in labels. He may be sane. His behavior at the moment is not. That's why I have to go with him. That's why I made up all that shit about security."

"You mean that was a lie?" Tess asked suddenly.

Seth looked at her honestly. "Oh, it might be true," he said. "Who knows? Anyway, it worked."

"That was pretty smart," she said. He grinned.

"Thanks," he said. He cocked his head toward the rest of the company. "A vote of confidence. At last." Seth stood up and left the room. He came back wearing a denim jacket over his jeans and black turtleneck. He looked at his watch and said, "Sorry, Annie, but I've got to run." Annie stood up. Martin remained seated.

"Where are you going to meet him?" Annie said.

"Penn Station. The ticket windows on the upper level."

"Why there?" Annie looked bemused.

"It's anonymous." She nodded.

Joanna said, "Do you think he really will meet you?"

Seth shrugged, holding up a hand and tilting it quickly, "Fifty-fifty. It's all the chance we had, Jo. We couldn't take him prisoner." Joanna looked sad. Tess, watching her, remembered how she'd felt in the park when Eric had walked away from them and disappeared into the crowd. She had wanted to ask him to come home with them, but she hadn't done it, and afterward she'd felt guilty, as if her saying it might have made the difference. She leaned up against her mother at the table and remembered suddenly that it was Seth she'd leaned against as Eric left them in the park. The way she felt about Seth confused her.

"I wish you'd found where he was staying," Annie said.

"It wouldn't make any difference," Seth answered, "He says he moves around. Anyhow, I'm glad. If he did tell me and lost his nerve, he'd end up having to leave. He might lose a good place."

"To leave?" Annie said, "Why?"

"To get away from us. To feel safe again."

Annie's face paled. "Oh, Seth," she whispered, "he can't think like that."

Seth looked pitying and said gently, "But he does, Annie. And he's right to. We would try to dissuade him, wouldn't we?"

Martin raised his head slowly, "And aren't we? Once you've finished tonight's little charade, Seth, what then? Are we going to just continue humoring the family looney? Or are we going to take away the only thing he lives for? Have you even thought about this?" He turned in his chair and faced Joanna, "Have you? Where are we going from here, that's what I want to know." He shook his head slowly and then dropped it into his hands, "Seth, you're going to wish you just left the poor bastard alone." Martin got up, eluded Annie's intervening arms, brushed by Joanna, and walked heavily from the room.

—

SETH WAITED AT THE TICKET WINDOWS until nine-forty-five, half an hour after Eric had agreed to meet him. He made brief, nervous circuits of the newspaper and fast-food places and looked twice, quickly, in the toilets. He waited five minutes more, thinking of reasons for Eric to be late. None of them worked. He worried briefly and foolishly that he'd been involved in an accident or a mugging, but the force of logic triumphed. After surviving this many years, he was pretty likely to survive the last few days.

At ten minutes to ten, Seth went down to the subway and caught a train downtown. It was crowded and he stood, swaying shoulder to shoulder with the huge anonymity of the city into which Eric had once more disappeared. He felt sorrow and despair, that their briefly triumphant search had turned out more or less as he suspected it would. Their quarry had gone to the ground of his own fantasy world and left them behind once more. He rode the train now with only the faintest hope of finding Eric again, tonight or ever. He could not say that he was surprised.

But he was hurt all the same, for Joanna, her brave efforts rejected. And he was hurt for himself, because Eric had lied to him. It opened the one possibility that he did not like to look at: that Eric was no longer the man he had known.

Seth got off at Houston and walked back up Seventh. The Village was lively, a mix of well-dressed sophisticates doing the restaurants and shows, bridge-and-tunnel kids in from the suburbs, and a few originals. Seth walked quickly across Morton Street and easily located the club on Hudson because of the crowd of lavishly costumed patrons waiting outside. He was lucky; it was late in opening. Inside, if it was like other such haunts he'd known, he'd never find anyone in the jam-packed, strobe-lit, dry-ice-fogged dark. Outside he had a chance.

He began pushing forward, peering at faces, stretching up to look over heads. Then he saw Eric. He was standing just outside the locked doors, hunched inside his plaid jacket, his head down. Around him, the cluster of noisy, dreadlocked, nose-ringed, multi-colored youth were like beings of not just another generation, but of another planet. Seth felt a wave of sorrow for Eric's loneliness that overwhelmed the hurt he had felt before.

He wormed his way smoothly through the sidewalk crowd, fending off protests by answering in uncomprehending Italian. He slid around two tall women with pagan symbols painted on their cheeks and lightly touched Eric's arm. Eric turned quickly and then, seeing him, relaxed. He looked regretful, but not apologetic.

"I thought we agreed to meet at Penn Station," Seth said pleasantly.

"I'm sorry, Seth. I changed my mind."

Seth nodded, "Didn't you trust me?"

"Oh, of course. It wasn't that, Seth." There was a noise behind the locked doors, and the crowd swayed. Eric turned to face the doors, but when nothing more happened he looked back to Seth. "I'm sorry," he said again. "But I'd done so much alone . . . I wanted to do this last thing . . . I wanted her to myself."

"You might not have gotten to see her," Seth reminded him. "I've got an interview set up for when they come off."

He realized, surprised, that he wanted a response from Eric, praise or approval, but Eric only said, "I felt I could trust my luck. I've had so many lucky breaks." He was cool and distant, and Seth experienced a hurt of rejection he had not felt in years. His body felt clumsy and his voice sounded awkward in his ears.

He said lamely, "I'll keep out of your way, Eric. I just want to get you through the door."

They were almost separated by the rush of the crowd when the club opened. Eric strode impatiently through the packs of youngsters, and Seth, feeling short and insignificant, pushed hurriedly behind him. The club was a barren, empty, cement-floored space with a high ceiling supported by steel pillars. There was a bar and a few tables and a raised stage cluttered with speakers and microphones and cables. Lights on the stage pulsed quiescent pinks and greens, like dormant jellyfish. Everywhere else was black, but for the two red EXIT signs, one at either side. Seth bought two beers from a bartender costumed as Merlin and took them to a metal table beside a pillar. Eric accepted his beer and started to say something, but music began on the blacked-out stage and blotted out all speech. The lights came up enough to reveal the first performers, four young men in ponytails and plaid shirts. They played a while, too loudly, but not unpleasantly, a bluesy, good-natured sound. All around them the costumed audience danced, packed shoulder to shoulder, hip to hip. Eric watched with well-feigned interest. Seth thought of himself, at long-ago high school dances, scanning the crowd, pretending interest in everybody like that, waiting for the appearance of the one person who mattered.

The lights went down while the band made their exit. When they came up again, five young women were grouped on the stage. They wore jeans and little skinny sweaters and big high-laced DM boots. The keyboard player had a mass of yellow and pink braids tied up in a knot, which she flung from side to side as she began to play. The girl in the center wore her hair stiffly cropped. She was tall and lean. She tilted a delicate, fine-boned face upward into the lights, clasping her microphone with two white hands, shimmied elegantly narrow hips, and began to sing, her voice a sweet whisper that rose with fine steadiness to a crescendo of remarkable power.

Seth started to speak, then stopped. Eric's face, in the flickering light, was frozen in concentration. He sat unmoving, with the shadows of the dancing audience and pulsing lights washing over him. Seth looked back at the stage, and then, out of nothing, a memory came. It was Christmas, a big family secular American Christmas party, at the Carlson house on Long Island, which his Jewish parents attended as they did every year. He was on one of his rare trips home, this time from Amsterdam, where he had lived for a year after India. The big house was full of pine branches and red ribbons, and a huge tree filled a corner of the dining room. There was snow, and it was icy and glittering beyond the windows. The children, Danya and David and Molly, were gathered at the piano, David playing with labored piano-lesson fingers, Danya doing the bottom hand. And Molly was singing "Good King Wenceslas Looked Out." He'd hardly noticed. He was younger then, not really interested in children. But now he could hear that voice, clear and high and whispery at the edges. Molly could sing. She could sing. Seth turned from the stage, to Eric, and then wonderingly back to the stage. He looked at the girl, and he could see it all, the sharp Carlson jawline he so loved on Joanna, the arctic Scandinavian eyes . . . the girl by the piano, that high, sibilant voice . . .

Reality jolted and shuddered. He heard his own voice saying to Joanna, *Don't slide into this.* How many girls in America with blue eyes and Swedish bones? Hundreds? Thousands? How many who could sing? Maybe all Swedes could sing.

The music stopped suddenly. The stage went dark. The kids stopped dancing and moved toward the bar. Eric stood and pushed through them to the red EXIT sign. Seth leaped up and ran after him. "You can't just go in there," he shouted. He grabbed Eric's arm, but Eric pulled smoothly away, swung open the door, and stepped through. Seth caught the handle as it was closing and followed.

They were in a corridor with gray-painted concrete walls and cold strip lighting, white-bright after the darkness of the club. Squinting, Seth said, "The performance isn't over. They're just taking a break."

"I have to see her," Eric said.

"Well, at least wait until they've finished their gig. Eric?"

Eric repeated, "I have to see her," and began walking down the corridor. Seth followed, arguing, and Eric ignored him. He tried one door and found it locked. He tried a second that read FIRE EXIT. It swung open into the night. Eric pulled it shut.

"We'll get thrown out and then you'll never see her," Seth said. Eric found a third door. It opened into another, dimmer corridor on which yet another door stood ajar. Voices and casual laughter drifted through. Eric walked down the corridor until he stood at the opening, his face washed with the warmer light from within.

"Hey," a female voice called sharply. "Who are you?" Eric didn't answer. Seth reached his side, and the voice said suspiciously, "Are you a techie or what?" Again Eric stood silent, and Seth peered around him into the room. The blond lead singer was standing, cigarette in one hand, the other on her angular hip, staring. Two other women stood beside her, and as Seth watched she gestured with the hand holding the cigarette. "Nathan. Nathan, we've got some bozo here." Her voice was pitched evenly between annoyance and fear. A big somber man in denims and a black T-shirt appeared from the depths of the room as the other band members backed warily away.

"Okay, buddy," he said in a surprisingly quiet voice, "back wherever you came from. This is private." Eric stood silently, and Seth saw fear grow in the girl's pale eyes.

"Nathan, get rid of him."

The man stepped forward, and Seth pushed past Eric then and said loudly, "Look, I called you. Alessandro Donatti, remember?" He used again the name borrowed from his village's taxi driver, but didn't bother with the fake Italian accent.

"What?" the girl said. She turned to Nathan.

He said, "The guy's from some European magazine." He looked up to Seth, his eyes glancing uncertainly off Eric, "Can you come back later, okay?" he said pleasantly. "The band's just taking a break. They're going back on in about two minutes." He smiled quickly and said, "Nathan Gittelson," and held his hand out to Seth. Seth shook it. "He your photographer?" Nathan said, gesturing at Eric.

"Photographer. Yeah. He's my photographer." He kept shaking Nathan's hand, half expecting Eric to argue, but Eric said nothing. Then just when he thought they'd made it, Eric lunged forward at the girl. She gave a little yelp and grabbed Nathan's arm.

"Eric," Seth said, "we'll see them later," but Eric stepped closer to where Megan Carmichael cowered visibly against her manager.

"I said *later*," Nathan said, his voice rising. Eric held up his two hands on either side of Megan's face and gently brought them together, cradling the delicate cheekbones and sharp chin.

"Hey," the girl cried, "What are you doing?"

Nathan's hand closed on Eric's elbow. "*Look*," he said. Eric gently opened his hands, so they hovered beside her face but no longer touched.

"Molly," he whispered, "Molly, it's me." She pulled back out of the cage of his hands, cold eyes narrowed.

"Who?" she said.

"It's me, Molly. It's your dad."

"My what?" Seth wanted to close his eyes.

"Your dad, Molly. Your father. You haven't seen me for thirteen years. Not since they took you away."

"Took me? What?"

"From the camp, Molly. You can remember the camp."

"I'm not Molly, mister, I'm Megan," she said. She blinked rapidly, looked at Nathan, who had dropped Eric's arm in astonishment, and looked at Seth. "Is this some kind of joke?" she said to Seth. "Is this meant to be funny?"

"You know this guy?" Nathan said uncertainly.

"Of course I don't. He's a crazy. Get him out . . ." Eric had closed his hands on her face again. Her eyes were wild. Seth caught Eric's arm that Nathan had released.

"Come on," he whispered, "come on, Eric. It's not her. Come on."

"I know it's hard to remember, Molly, but try, try."

"Remember what, you asshole? And I said I'm Megan."

"All right then," Eric said soothingly, "I understand. Megan . . ."

"Get off . . ."

"Eric, come on."

"Okay," Nathan said. "Okay. Whoever you are," he took in Seth as well now, "both of you, just go. Tell your magazine we're not interested, okay?" Eric turned to Nathan calmly, speaking with adult command.

"I'm sorry I'm upsetting her," he said, "but it's a great shock. You see, I am her father. She was kidnapped . . ."

"Kidnapped!" Megan cried. "Oh, for Christ's sake. Nathan, will you get rid of this creep?"

"Megan, I do understand. Whatever's happened. I do understand. You've been through a lot. So have I. But I'm still your dad and I still love . . . oh," he sighed softly, "I still love you so much."

Something in the desperate passion of his voice dissolved her fear, and Seth saw simple cold scorn replace it in her eyes. She ran the straight fingers of one hand mannishly through her scrub brush of hair, tossing her head so the light glinted on the little gold ring at the side of her nose.

"Okay. Okay, mister. Let's start over from the top. One. I'm Megan Carmichael, not Molly What-the-fuck. Two. You're *not* my father. My father's a lawyer in LA. So's my mother. And in a minute I'm going to call them both. After Nathan calls the police. Three. You're leaving. Ten minutes ago won't be soon enough." She turned away. He grabbed her hand. She jerked it back and held it up as if burned. Seth was startled at what a small, vulnerable, girlish hand it was.

Nathan said, "Now. Or I call the police. Let's go nice and peaceful, okay?" Eric still reached toward her with the hand that had held hers.

"How long have you known them?"

"Known who?" she asked, baffled.

"Your 'parents.' The people you call your parents. Can you remember?" Her mouth tightened in outrage.

"My parents? Known them? All my life, naturally."

"Are you sure?"

"Am I sure? What, do you want my fucking baby pictures? Shit. You are amazing." She looked at Seth, all her fear gone now, just disgust and fury left. "Can't you get him back in his cage?"

"Eric," Seth whispered, his arm wrapping around Eric's shoulders, leaning close to him, "come on, pal. We're done here. It's over. We were wrong. Let's just go. We'll talk about it later. Let's go."

Eric stayed, looking yearningly at Megan, a moment longer. Then he dropped his eyes. He stood so quietly that neither the girl nor Nathan moved. When he looked up, he shook his head and said in a faraway, tired voice, "I'm sorry."

Megan Carmichael stared in silence as Seth dragged Eric away. "You sad fuck," she said at last.

———

IT WAS INKY DARK outside the fire door. Seth submerged his instincts and stepped out into the shadows, hustling Eric with him. He shut the door, hearing the heavy latches engage, locking them out into a narrow side alley. Dim light shone from the street at one end. He kept his arm around Eric's shoulders and guided him toward it. Eric moved awkwardly, with neither resistance nor compliance. As they reached the street, music throbbed suddenly through the brick wall of the club at their right, and he straightened and pulled back from Seth's arm. Seth tightened his grip and turned uptown.

Eric didn't resist or argue again, and Seth kept walking up Hudson and then along Christopher to Seventh Avenue, vaguely looking for a cafe or a bar or a cab or just a bench, somewhere to talk. He imagined Megan Carmichael's scorn like a visible aura surrounding them, and yet the streets absorbed them easily. At the corner of Seventh and Fourteenth Street, Seth stopped walking, slipped his arm from Eric's shoulders, and stepped back slightly. He scanned the broad street and turned again to Eric. "Let's get a cab," he said.

Eric nodded, but said, "I'll just walk a bit more, Seth. I want to think a little." Seth shrugged and slid his hands into his jeans pockets.

"Fine. Let's walk."

Eric smiled slightly, "That's kind, Seth, but you don't need to." He held out his hand. "Thanks for coming. I appreciate it. I really do." Seth refused the outstretched hand.

"Eric, we have to talk."

"There's nothing to say. I was wrong." He smiled again. Seth stared, baffled. "It's happened before, Seth," Eric said clearly. "I've handled it before. I'll handle this. But if you don't mind, I really would like to be alone." He held his hand out again. Seth felt the same rebuff he'd felt at the door of the club, the same opening of old wells of insecurity. He stood nodding in unconcious agreement. Eric touched his shoulder lightly and said again, "Thanks, Seth," and turned away.

"No." Eric turned back to face him, and they stared at each other blankly, equally startled. Seth hesitated for a moment, but then said with renewed force, "No, I'm not doing that." He took a quick breath. "I'm not going back to Jo, after all she's done to find you, and tell her I left you in the street. Maybe you can do that to her. I can't."

"I didn't ask Jo to do anything, Seth."

"Oh, come off it. When has anyone ever had to ask Jo for help to get it?"

Eric thrust his hands in the pockets of his jacket and hunched his shoulders, facing down Fourteenth Street into the cold wind off the river. He was silent as Seth watched him. Then he looked up and said solemnly, "I don't want to hurt Jo, Seth. I don't want to do that. I just need a little time . . . look, I'll meet you tomorrow, okay? You say where."

"Like you met me tonight?"

Eric looked away again. When he turned back, his face, lit by the streetlight, was suddenly fierce. "You don't understand," he said. "You don't understand what this family can do to me."

Seth smiled wryly. "Don't I? Give me a few years sometime and I'll tell you what they've done to me." He paused, the smile fading. "They're the only family we've got, Eric." He looked down at the wet, dirty sidewalk. "Let's go home."

Eric shook his head. He smiled again and said, "You're so kind. Always. Always so kind. And the things we used to do to you." He laughed, a faraway laugh from another time. "Seth," he said, calmly laying his hand on Seth's shoulder, "listen to me. I know what you're thinking. I know what you're afraid of . . . but you're wrong. You really don't understand. I can handle this. My way, and alone, but I can handle it. It's not the first time," he said again. "You have no idea, Seth. No idea. The places I've been, the people, the scenes . . . not all good scenes either." He laughed again, a different, sharp laugh. "God, there was one time, a lot of years ago, this little backwater Illinois town . . . I'd gotten a letter from some woman, thought she recognized Molly's picture, a kid at her granddaughter's school who'd turned up out of nowhere, staying with some big Polish family. Nobody seemed to know what she was doing there . . . It's the sort of thing that would happen, Seth. That's the kind of lead I would get. So I went there. Found the school, waited across the road, watched the kids coming out. A lot of days before I even saw her. But when I did, I knew she was the one." He sighed suddenly and stopped talking, running a hand quickly through his hair. "There was a lot of resemblance. I started following her."

"You what?" Seth whispered.

"I followed her."

"What, you mean home from school?" Seth's voice was hoarse.

"That. And other places. She went to a Burger King with her friends most days after school. Stayed out late. I watched . . . I didn't want to approach until I was sure . . ."

"Jesus Christ, Eric."

"I was careful. Really careful. I was sure she hadn't noticed." He glanced away, down the street again and shrugged. "She had, though. Her uncle, that's who she lived with—the old woman had it all wrong—her uncle and three big guys waited for me outside the school."

"Jesus Christ, Eric. You're lucky they didn't kill you."

"Oh, they were going to. They had a gun. They threw me in the back of a pickup and drove to some woods outside of town. But I explained everything."

Seth stared, astounded. "They believed you?" he said at last. Eric tilted his head back and looked at the dark storefronts across the flow of traffic in the street.

"Yeah," he said lightly. "After a while. At first they couldn't decide whether to believe me or not. But in the end they did."

"Eric, I cannot believe you are really this naive."

He looked back and met Seth's eyes steadily. "I'm not naive."

"You have to know what that looked like . . ."

"Oh, I could see that. But I explained. They were okay. Big Polish working guys. Nice guys, really. Yeah, they were angry at first, but in the end, they understood. They were really apologetic." He paused, "They'd been a bit rough." He shrugged again. "In the end they were just kind of bewildered and sad."

"You were lucky."

"I was lucky."

Seth took a deep breath. "You were lucky again tonight."

"Tonight was all right."

"Tonight was not all right. Tonight could have gotten us both in real trouble. Fortunately, that guy Nathan was pretty damned restrained." He shook his head in frustration. "Eric, you can't keep doing this. Following people, approaching strangers. You're going to end up in jail or . . ."

"You shouldn't have come."

"Do you think this would have been any better without me?" Seth asked bleakly.

"I'm used to this. I know what to expect."

"No, you don't. You didn't expect this tonight. Don't try to tell me you did." He gripped Eric's upper arms and forced him to meet his eyes. "You thought that was Molly. You were sure."

"Yes. I was sure. I'm always sure. Each time. It's the only way, Seth. If I don't believe I'm going to find her, I can't keep going. Not at all. Don't you see?" He paused, staring at Seth intensely, "Don't you see why I have to stay away? Don't you see what they can do to me?"

"The family?" Seth said uncertainly. "Eric, they want to help you. They're desperate to help you."

Eric laughed wearily. "Even if it kills me," he said. He dropped his head forward suddenly, resting it on Seth's shoulder. "Not you," he said. "I didn't mean you."

"Not any of them," Seth said painfully. But he thought of Martin's bleak farewell that evening and felt brutally chastened. After a while he said, "I'll take you wherever you want, Eric. It doesn't have to be Annie and Martin's. We can go to my parents' on Long Island. Or your parents' in Florida. Wherever you like." He looked quickly at Eric. "Hey, you want to go to Florida? I've got a car. Come on." Eric looked up and shook his head, but smiled faintly. "Then come home with me."

"Where?" Eric asked, smiling again. "Italy?"

"Sure. We'll ring Jo from the airport." He spotted a cruising cab and stepped off the pavement into the street, raising his hand.

Eric was beside him, laughing softly, "Oh, Seth," he said fondly, "we don't deserve you."

He stood quietly in the street, his arms wrapped around himself, clutching the frayed sleeves of his jacket. The taxi pulled over and stopped. Eric stared at it in silence for a long while. Then he looked back at Seth and slowly released his hands and let them fall to his sides.

"Take me to Jo, please," he said.

Ghosts

"MARTIN," Annie said gently, "go to bed." Martin, slouched half-asleep in his armchair, jerked awake, straightened quickly, and pulled in his sprawling legs.

"No, I'm fine."

"Seth will let us know what happened. We probably won't hear until tomorrow, now." She glanced quickly at her watch. "You have to be up early," she reminded him. She and Martin and Joanna had sat up together all evening, deliberately not talking about Eric and Seth and not wanting to talk about anything else. Merrilee and David went to bed early, as they always did when there was tension in the apartment, and Tess had fallen asleep in the middle of the card game she was playing with her mother. As they spoke, she burrowed deeper into a cushion in the corner of the couch, but did not wake.

"Maybe we should all just go to bed," Joanna said.

"They'll come back here," said Martin.

"I don't think so," Annie said calmly. "Not now."

"Seth will bring him back here," Martin repeated. He paused and added quietly, "If he finds him. If we're lucky, he just won't find him. But if he does, he'll bring him back here."

"If we're lucky?" Annie said sharply. "Martin, what in hell are you saying?"

"Just what you heard me say, Annie." He looked up at her beneath his heavy brows. "If we're lucky, and if Eric's lucky, Seth won't find him." He sighed and closed his eyes, leaning his head back against the chair. "If he does find him, he'll bring him here." He sat for a while with his eyes closed. "I'm too tired for this," he said.

"Then go to bed," Annie snapped.

Joanna said warily, "Seth has his hotel. They've probably gone there."

Martin opened his eyes and looked at her bleakly for a long while. Then he said, "Jo, Seth is not equipped to deal with Eric, and I think he has the sense to know that." He looked around. "None of us are. But Seth certainly isn't. Christ," he said suddenly. "Where are we going to put him even? There isn't any room."

Joanna looked slowly around. "Room?" she said coldly. "There's room in this apartment for twenty people."

"Yeah, yeah." Martin waved his hand airily toward the ceiling. "And after the revolution, sixteen families are going to live here. Get back in the real world, Joanna. Where's he going to sleep?"

"On the floor!" Joanna shouted. "For God's sake, Martin, will you ever get your priorities right? He's been sleeping on the street. Do you think he cares whether you've got a spare room or not?"

Tess woke to her mother's raised voice and sat up, looking around blearily. "Mom? Is Eric here?" she asked.

"No," Annie said quickly. "No one's here."

"He can have my bed," Tess said. "I don't mind sleeping on the floor."

"No one's sleeping on the floor," Annie said soothingly. "Eric can have the couch."

"Tess, go to bed," Joanna said.

"Mom?"

"Now." Joanna's eyes flicked sideways for a brief, dangerous moment. Tess got up in a quick flurry of movement and ran from the room.

Martin stood up slowly. He stretched his big body, winced, and pressed his hand into the small of his back. He looked at Annie and then back at Joanna. "None of you have any hold on reality," he said. "I can't keep cramming more people into this apartment. It isn't even healthy." He looked at Annie. "We've got Merrilee here, pregnant," he said pointedly. Annie blinked, uncomprehending.

"What are you talking about, Martin?" she said. "What's that got to do with anything?" Martin just stood there, his hand pressing heavily against his back, his eyes averted. She felt a surge of anger at his leaden immobility. "Martin?"

"If he's going to spend any time at all here, he has got to have a TB test for a start," Martin said. With his free hand he rubbed the side of his head tiredly.

"TB?" Annie said, astounded.

"Those places are full of it," Martin said quietly.

Annie threw up her hands. "What about AIDS while you're at it?" she shouted. "For God's sake, Martin."

"Yes," Martin said at once. He looked up, meeting her eyes, his own suddenly sharp and intent. "While we're at it." He paused, breathing deeply, and then said, "What gives you the arrogance to assume your family is immune to these things? Have you seen the inside of one of those shelters? Do you know what goes on in there?"

Annie swallowed hard. "My brother isn't a junkie," she said in a hard, cold voice.

"You don't know what your brother is," Martin answered instantly. "You haven't seen your brother for ten years."

"I saw him," Annie said.

"Except," Martin interrupted brutally, "for a couple of minutes on a subway car, and at first you didn't even recognize him. You didn't recognize him."

"I did," Annie said weakly.

"She wasn't expecting to see him like that," Joanna protested.

"You've just made my point for me, Joanna," Martin said. His voice was even and clinically calm. "She didn't know him because he'd become someone she couldn't recognize as her brother. A stranger." He turned back to Annie. "He is a stranger, Annie," he said. "You're asking me to bring a total stranger into our home."

Annie stood up, facing Martin over the coffee table, her delicate hands clasped rigidly before her, the knuckles white. "Joanna and Seth talked to him for an hour." She kept her voice low and as even as his. "He wasn't a stranger. He wasn't a junkie or a wino or a down-and-out. He made perfect sense."

"Perfect," Martin said wearily. "Perfect sense about some West Coast rock singer he's convinced is the little girl he lost in the Adirondacks thirteen years ago. Annie, will you please, please, face reality. Please." She was brought up short by the desperation in his voice.

"Martin?"

He looked away. "Why is this happening to us?" he said sadly.

"Martin?" Annie said again. She stepped toward him, awkwardly, banging her shins on the table between them. As she clambered around it, the telephone rang.

"I'll get it," Joanna said. She pushed by Annie and Martin and reached the phone on the desk before either of them had time to move. She hunched over the receiver as she answered, her shoulders tense, one hand holding back her heavy blond hair. Then her head came up, and she drew in her breath quickly. "Seth. Seth, where are you?" she said. She nodded twice and said, "Yes. Yes. Fine." As she replaced the receiver, she looked up. "That's Seth," she said. "He has Eric with him. They'll be here in a minute." Her face relaxed into a smile of relief. "They're just down the street."

Annie stood silent for a moment before allowing herself to believe what she was hearing. Then she stumbled across the room. "Jo," she said, "you've done it. You've done it. He's coming home." Annie hugged her sister, her soft brown curls pressed against Joanna's shoulder. Then she turned toward Martin. He was watching them both, his face heavy with frustration.

"Yeah, Jo, you've done it. You always were a genius at the grand heroic gesture." He sighed. "And you always did have me to clear up the shit."

Annie lifted her chin and raised one hand and pointed the slim forefinger at Martin's chest. "Right," she whispered. "I've heard it all. Now you listen. I've lived with you for twenty-five years, but I swear to God, if you say one thing, one thing, to make my brother feel unwelcome, even for an instant, then you and I are finished. I'm not joking, Martin. I mean every word."

"Annie," Martin's face went white. "Annie, you don't understand." He raised his hands, palms toward her. "I wouldn't do that. You know I wouldn't do that." His voice was querulous and plaintive at once. Annie stared at him a moment longer and then shook her head. She heard the whirr and rumble of the elevator beyond the wall.

"I don't know what you'd do," she said wearily, "but will you be quiet please? They're here." She turned away and went out of the room and into the hall as Seth opened the front door.

He looked tired and worried as he came in alone. He did not acknowledge her, but said only, "Is Martin here?"

"Of course." Annie stared at him, puzzled by the question, and then pushed past him through the doorway. "Eric?" she said softly, "Eric, are you there?"

He was standing in the center of the landing, arms folded, head down, his face turned away. She noticed distractedly that the long, unkempt hair was freshly washed, glistening ruddily beneath the landing light, and the torn seam of the jacket had been roughly mended. The stooped, tired posture, so at odds with the athlete she remembered, spoke eloquently of change, summoning the image of the stranger on the train. He raised his head. Their eyes met. The brilliant blue of his was the one unchanged thing about him. "I'm sorry, Annie," he said.

"For what?"

He did not answer. Annie reached toward him, but he did not respond. Then Joanna burst past her and flung herself at Eric. He straightened and caught her in his arms and embraced her gently. But although he ducked his head briefly to kiss her hair, he showed no real emotion. He looked up again, and past her. His eyes settled briefly on Annie once more, and on Seth, and then slid away.

Suddenly Martin was there, bulkily filling the doorway, his voice loud and convivial. "Hey," he said, and Annie turned to him, almost in relief. "Good to see you, Eric." He extended his hand and Eric took it instinctively. They shook hands, and Martin said, "Come in, come in," in the same firm voice. Eric obeyed, stepping forward as Martin slipped an arm behind his back. "Good to see you," Martin said again.

Annie followed, bewildered. She closed the apartment door, bent to do the three locks and looked up, catching Seth watching her. "What happened?" she whispered. He shook his head slightly but didn't answer.

"Come sit down, Eric," Martin said. Again, Eric obeyed, going with him into the living room without speaking and without looking at anyone. Martin turned around in the doorway for an instant. "Annie, make us some tea, please," he said. His face was lined with concentration. Annie nodded uncertainly, hesitated for a moment, and then went to the kitchen. She went about heating water and finding cups and milk and sugar with a sense of jarring unreality. When she returned with the tray of tea, Eric was sitting on the couch with Joanna curled up beside him and Seth standing protectively at one side. He seemed unaware of either of them.

Martin was perched on the coffee table, facing him. "Been a lot of years, Eric," he was saying. "A lot of years." Eric's gaze drifted over his shoulder, focusing on nothing. Martin watched, said, "A lot of years" again, more softly, and then looked away. He saw Annie with the tray and said, "Great. That's great." She reached to pour the tea, but he took the pot first, poured one cup and turned back and offered it to Eric. There was no reaction. Martin put the cup in his hands and said, "Drink it."

"Go on," Joanna said gently. He looked at her briefly and then back at Martin. He sipped the tea, looking straight ahead, over Martin's shoulder again. Annie poured tea for Martin. He waved it away. She sat down slowly on the arm of the couch, watching her brother helplessly.

After a long while, Eric said in a quiet, controlled voice, "I was wrong, Jo. It wasn't her." He set the cup down on the table. She caught his hand and twined her fingers with his. "How could I have been so wrong, Jo?" She turned, looking to Seth for help. Seth watched, sadly silent.

"She did look a lot like her," Joanna said tentatively. "In the picture. She did."

"She was afraid of me," he said.

"Eric," Seth said softly, "it was just a crazy scene."

"She was a stranger. And she was afraid of me."

"It doesn't matter," Joanna said.

"I don't understand. How could I be so wrong?" He looked around and his eyes settled on Annie. He stared at her for a long while, as if he had not seen her before. Then he smiled very slightly and said, "You're still so pretty, Annie. You haven't changed at all." She smiled back, fighting tears, and nodded quickly in acknowledgement. He looked at them all then, with quickening awareness, as if he had just awakened. "Where's your little girl?" he said to Joanna, "Where's Tess?"

"Asleep."

"It must be late."

"It's just one," Joanna said.

"I'm sorry. I've kept you all up."

"It really doesn't matter, Eric," Annie said, her throat tight. "It's just so good to see you."

"I'll have to go back," he said.

"Back? Back where?" Joanna sat up straight.

"To the Coast. I'll have to go back to the Coast." He put his hand up to his face and briefly covered his eyes. "I'll have to go back and start again." He dropped the hand. He looked suddenly exhausted.

"Eric," Joanna cried. She tightened her grip on his hand and leaned forward. Martin reached out and gently pushed her back.

"Joanna, leave it," he said.

"What?"

"Leave it. Now."

"I have other leads," Eric said. "I hadn't thought much. This one was so good." He stopped again. "I don't understand. I don't understand how I could have been so wrong."

Martin nodded thoughtfully and rubbed his chin. "Why don't you take a little break first?" he said reasonably. "You could use a break." He sat easily, knees apart, his elbows on his heavy thighs. "Since you're here anyhow. Take a few days. Stay with us. We could go out to the Island maybe. See my parents. Dad would love to see you."

"I'd love to see him," Eric said suddenly. He looked tired again and wistful. "I've missed your dad so much." He paused. After a long while he said, "There was never anyone I could talk to the way I talked to your dad."

"Well, good," Martin said. He kept his voice gentle and even. "Fine. We'll go see him, then." He patted Eric's arm. "Good. That's settled. We'll do that. We were going out there anyhow on Saturday. Sara's got something happening. Wait'll you see Sara. She's real together. Got her own ballet school, even." Annie nodded slightly, watching Martin with puzzled respect. She started to pour more tea in Eric's cup, but heard a noise at the door and looked up. Tess was standing there, still in her jeans and T-shirt, very much awake.

"What is it, dear?" Annie said.

"Can I see Eric?" she asked.

Joanna looked around. "Tess, I told you to go to bed."

"I just want to say hello." She looked warily at her mother, but she held her ground.

Eric turned away from Martin and saw her there. He smiled suddenly, and said, "Hi, kid. How are those roller blades?"

"They're fine," Tess said. She made a small smile. "I'm still crap on them, but they're fine." He laughed softly. She said, "I'm glad you're here." He nodded, watching her. "I've got to go to bed now," she said. She turned, and Martin stood up as she left the room.

After she'd gone he said, "Right. Now we're going to do the same. It's late and everybody's tired. Eric, you're going to sleep here, okay? Annie, can you get him some blankets?"

"You go to bed," Annie said mildly. "I'll do everything."

Martin nodded but didn't move. "Joanna?" he said. "Come on. Everybody's tired." He looked at her pointedly.

"Sure, Martin." She stood up. Eric stood too and then walked slowly across the room to Martin's desk.

"Seth, are you staying or going?" Martin said bluntly.

Seth said, "I'll look after myself." He was watching Eric and not really listening. Eric was standing by the desk, looking down at Martin's collection of family photographs. Molly's fifth-grade school portrait sat among them, but his hand only brushed its frame before he lifted a picture of David in cap and gown.

"They're all so grown-up," he said. "They were kids."

Annie stopped in the doorway and turned back into the room. "They've missed you," she said.

He set the photograph down. "I never meant to be so long."

"Annie," Martin said. "Will you get those blankets? Please."

When she returned with an armful of bedding, Martin had given up and gone to their bedroom. She passed Seth in the kitchen peering into the open refrigerator with familial self-confidence. Joanna and Eric were still in the living room. Joanna had taken Annie's photograph album down from its shelf, and they were standing side by side, looking at it. Annie put the blankets on the couch and went back to the linen closet for pillows. When she came back, they were both sitting cross-legged in the center of the floor, the album between them, their two fair heads bent close. She put the pillows down and went quietly away.

She found Martin sitting on the edge of their bed, setting his alarm. He looked up. "Is Seth still here?" he asked.

"He's making something in the kitchen."

"Is he staying or what?"

Annie sat down and untied her sneaker. "I don't think he's going anywhere at this hour. I left him a sleeping bag and that air mattress Danya's friends use. He'll be fine. You know Seth," she added casually. "He can sleep anywhere." She smiled. "Joanna and Eric are looking at pictures on the floor." She stood up and wriggled out of her jeans. "They look like a couple of kids."

"They're still talking?" Martin said. "Tell Joanna to go to bed."

Annie slipped her nightgown over her head and looked up, surprised. "What does it matter? They don't have to get up. Tomorrow's just Friday. We're not going to your parents' until Saturday morning. They can sleep all day tomorrow if they want."

"He's had a shock. He needs to sleep." Martin sounded grumpily protective. Annie looked at him, surprised, then shrugged and climbed into bed.

"One night can't matter that much," she said.

He said again, "He's had a shock." She leaned over him and put out the light.

"Martin, you really amazed me tonight," she said. "You were so kind. So gentle and kind. And wise," she added slowly. "After everything you said, too." She laid her arm across his big body, and when he turned onto his side, his back toward her, she rested her face against his shoulder. "I couldn't believe what I was seeing."

"You were seeing a doctor and a patient," he said abruptly. She drew back the arm and propped herself on her elbow.

"What?" He didn't answer. "Martin, he's not your patient. He's not sick. He's fine. He looks fine. Doesn't he?" He still didn't answer. "Well, doesn't he?"

"Yeah," Martin said quietly. "He looks okay. You can't tell that much just looking at people, but he looks okay. That wasn't my point. I needed some distance, Annie."

She was quiet. Then she drew back farther and sat up in the darkness. "You mean you needed something to hide behind," she said.

"No. I needed distance. I needed professional distance." He sat up too and switched on the light. He looked at her wearily, squinting in the brightness. "You've never gotten it, Annie, have you? None of you have ever gotten it." He paused and then started again, speaking softly and slowly. "Eric is doing what people do when they can't live in the real world. It's one of the things they do, anyhow. Some of them get a gun and shoot up their workplace, or they jump off buildings, or take an overdose. Some of them just make up their own world. They rewrite the rules so that it works better for them. Everyone's got their own solution. This ghost hunt is Eric's solution. That is what works for him." Annie drew her bare arms tightly around herself. He looked at her for a long while and then said, "Before you try and talk him out of it, think about the alternatives."

Annie dropped her head onto her knees, sitting forlorn and cold in the wide bed. She felt Martin lightly touch her shoulder but did not respond. "I'm sorry, Annie," he said. "But you just have to understand. I can't look after Eric. I'm not equipped. I don't have the skills. None of us have. This isn't the sort of thing you're going to fix with chicken soup and a little pop psychology. Frankly, I don't know what we're going to do."

"Your dad will know what to do."

Martin laughed harshly. "My dad? Annie, I'm a pediatrician. Dad's a retired family doctor. Eric needs a psychiatrist. He needs a whole team. Christ, I wish Jo had left this alone." Annie raised her head again and stared at him through glistening tears.

"What? You mean just left him in the street?"

"It would have been better. I know it. And Annie, Eric knows it. Why did he leave in the first place?" When she did not answer, he said, "I'll tell you why. Because human beings have an instinct for survival, and his was telling him to go."

"But why?" she whispered. "Why?"

"Because he can lie to strangers. And he can lie to himself. He can't lie to us. Annie, we're going to push him over the edge."

She dropped her head and let the tears come. She felt his hand awkwardly patting her shoulder and wrenched away. "Oh, you," she said. "You're always the same. You always have to see the blackest, blackest side to everything."

He was silent for a long time, while she cried. Then he said, "Do you maybe want to show me the bright side of this?"

"Yes." She looked up and glared at him defiantly. "Yes. My brother's home. We're all together again. Like when we were young. We're all together under one roof."

He sighed and then reached for her, enclosing her in his arms. "Oh, Annie," he said, "Annie." Still holding her, he turned off the light and lay down beside her in the dark.

———

ON SATURDAY MORNING, before they went out to the Island, Annie let Martin sleep late. He woke up at ten and came into the kitchen, looking warily around. "Where is everybody?" he asked. "It feels like we're actually alone here." Annie switched on the coffee machine and then held up her hand, ticking off fingers.

"Merrilee's gone to work," she said. "David has gone with her because they're moving some giraffes around. Big ones. Seth has taken Joanna and Eric and Tess out to the Island." She ticked off the rest of the fingers and held up one more. "That leaves just you and me." She smiled and gave him a quick morning kiss.

He rubbed his unshaven jaw and said, "It feels unnatural." Then he said, "They've gone out to my parents' already?" Annie cut a bagel in half and put the two halves in the toaster.

"They wanted to do some malls on the way. We'll probably still get there ahead of them."

"They're shopping?" Martin asked, startled. She poured his coffee.

"They're looking for a costume. For Tess," she said, because he looked blank. "It's Halloween, Martin." As he sat down she added, "Joanna and Eric took her around yesterday but they couldn't find anything."

Martin poured milk into his coffee and said, "In all of New York?"

Annie shrugged. "Kids are particular."

"Damn right," said Martin. He sipped his coffee and raised an eyebrow. "Was this necessary, Annie? Now? I mean your brother's come home two days ago after ten years. Doesn't that maybe take precedence?"

Annie smiled. "Come on, Martin. It's still Halloween. You remember what it was like when ours were little." She put the toasted bagel in front of him.

As he buttered it he said, "I don't really, Annie. You did all that. I was always so busy." He sounded regretful. Annie watched him a moment and then turned away to pour her own coffee.

"Anyhow," she said, "I'm sure Eric didn't mind."

Martin thought a moment. "I don't suppose he would," he said slowly. "Though how you imagine you can tell what he's thinking, I don't know. I talked to him for three hours yesterday evening, and I didn't find him exactly transparent."

Annie looked at him oddly, but she only said, "Well, he's made a hit with Tess, anyhow. She's gotten up at eight o'clock each morning to sit and talk with him. She even ate breakfast. Yesterday was the first morning I've seen that child reach for anything other than the TV remote."

Martin said, "Are you surprised?" She looked at him curiously over her coffee cup. He said, "Have you ever known a child Eric didn't get on with? Our own kids always liked him better than they liked us." He shrugged slightly, "Better than they liked me anyhow."

Annie laughed gently. "That was novelty," she said.

"No. It was more. He's got a thing with them. You remember, up at the camp. He was always teaching them things, showing them things. They all followed him around." He looked moodily down at his plate. "That was one thing Eric always did get right." He paused. "That's what made it all so damned unfair."

———

ANNIE WAITED UNTIL they were in the car and out of the city before she said, "Okay, Martin. Then how did you find him?"

Martin shrugged. "Oh, Christ knows."

"You talked a very long time. You must have learned something."

He shifted his hands on the steering wheel and straightened his shoulders. "It wasn't the best of circumstances. There were people around. Coming in and out."

"We tried to leave you alone."

"I know. I know." He stared at the rear window of the station wagon in front of him. "Okay, Annie. Yeah, sure, we had a long talk. We talked about the practice and what I've been doing and about the kids. And Seth. He has read all Seth's books. Joanna was right. Yeah, okay, he's been living some kind of a life. He's worked. He's found places to live. Most of the time."

"Did you talk to him about calling Mom and Dad?" Annie said urgently.

Martin glanced at her briefly and looked back at the station wagon. "I tried, Annie," he said quietly. "I didn't get very far." He paused. "That seems to be out of bounds."

"Out of bounds?" Annie exclaimed. "How can Mom and Dad be out of bounds?"

Martin sighed and leaned back against his headrest. "They're too close, Annie," he said. "They know him far too well. He can't play this game with them." He paused again. "He's having a hard enough time playing it with us."

"Martin, he's not playing a game."

"Oh yes, he is," Martin looked at her bleakly. "I'm warning you again, Annie. He's fragile. Don't pressure him." He looked ahead and said softly, "Oh sure, fine. He can sound okay. As long as you keep off the whole subject of Molly, he can sound like an all-right human being. Not the person I remember, but all right. But Molly is still there, Annie. We were both talking around her and we both knew it. That's the bottom line."

"What do you mean, not the person you remember?" Annie said sharply. "What's so different?"

"The difference?" Martin was quiet. He pulled out and passed the station wagon. It was a clear, crisp fall day and the Southern State Parkway was filling up. He took a hand off the wheel, wiped the sweaty palm on his trousers, and replaced it. He said, "The difference is that he's following me now. Eric was a leader, Annie. Now he's just doing whatever I tell him. I say we go to Long Island, so we go to Long Island. I say we stay for the weekend, so we stay for the weekend. And while he's doing it, I realize it's really a way of ignoring me. It's like he's acting all the time. And he is. Because the only thing he's thinking about is Molly and this crazy search. I knew it, and he knew I knew it. He's not stupid."

"He's tired, Martin," Annie said sadly. "He's tired and he's very subdued. That's the only difference I see."

"Subdued? He isn't there, Annie," Martin said vehemently. "He's just not there."

Annie looked distractedly out the window. She tugged at the pink silk scarf that held back her hair. "Seth told me all of it," she said quietly. "The whole scene with that singer. It was brutal, Martin."

"What did you expect?" he said coolly. "I did warn you."

Annie sighed. "She could have been kinder," she said. "He didn't deserve that."

Martin floored the accelerator and passed a big four-wheel drive, swerved in sharply in front of it, and braked hard. "She didn't deserve being assaulted by a scruffy middle-aged stranger insisting he was her father," he said. "Imagine if it was Danya, for God's sake. Imagine if it was Danya."

"Danya wouldn't hurt anyone like that," Annie said. Martin turned for a moment to look at her. His eyes were narrow.

"I certainly hope you're wrong," he said. "Women need to protect themselves." He paused. "He scared her, Annie. He said so himself."

"Oh, what was there to be scared of?" Annie said angrily. Martin's eyebrows rose.

"Plenty, Annie," he said. "He's six-foot-two and he looks tough. If I didn't know him, I'd be scared to meet him in a dark street myself."

Annie sat back and closed her eyes. Eventually she said sadly, "He's not tough, Martin. Eric's never hurt anyone in his life."

Martin looked straight ahead. "Wrong, Annie. Eric has hurt people. As a matter of fact, Eric has killed people." Annie opened her eyes and stared at him, momentarily stunned, before he continued evenly, "In Vietnam. He's probably killed a lot of people. I know that doesn't fit your picture of your little brother, but it's real, Annie. It's part of who he is."

"That doesn't count," she said quickly. "He didn't choose that."

"I'm not saying he enjoyed it, Annie. I'm saying he did it. Which means he was capable. *Is* capable. It's all part of who he is." He paused. "You have to start looking carefully at who he really is."

"I know who he is."

"I don't think you do."

Annie turned away abruptly and looked out the window. Her anger with Martin transmuted into an irritation with everything physical, the road, the cars on it, the people in them, the flat Long Island landscape. It all looked mindless and ugly. She fought an onslaught of despair, straightened her back, and set her lips. "It'll be nice to see the folks," she said brightly.

"Will it?"

"Sure." She made herself smile at him. "It'll be fun."

He smiled sheepishly back and then winced. "Yeah, I guess so," he said. "Annie, can you dig those antacid pills out of my pocket?"

"Your stomach bothering you?"

"Nah. Just indigestion." Annie fished around in his jacket pocket and found the bottle. She slipped a pill onto her hand. Martin nibbled it off, like a horse. She put the pills back in his pocket and glanced at her watch.

"We should make it all right," she said. "Sara said lunch at one."

"I don't think it matters a lot if we're late for lunch," Martin said tiredly.

"Of course it matters," Annie said at once. "Sara's got her show later. She really did have enough happening this weekend already. The least we can do now is give her some support."

Martin stiffened. "What do you mean 'the least we can do'?" He turned momentarily from the wheel and then had to look back at once and slam on the brakes.

"You know how I feel about Sara," Annie said quietly. When he made no answer at all, she said, "I see I'm going to get your usual response."

"Annie, do we have to get onto this again? Today? Don't you think we have enough to deal with today?"

"But you always say that," Annie cried, frustrated. "There's always something else more important. But when are we going to deal with this? When is this magic day going to happen?" She shook her head, "Life isn't like that, Martin. You don't get neatly allocated appointment slots for all your problems." She balled her hands into fists on the creases of her linen pants. "Life is passing Sara by," she said urgently. "There isn't time to keep putting this off."

"Putting what off?"

"What we're going to do about your parents."

"Oh, shit, Annie."

"Martin, she's forty-six. If she's ever going to have her own life . . ."

"What, you mean children?" Martin glared at her an instant, then pulled out to pass a battered green Chevy. There was something urgently dismissive in the gesture, and Annie said, "Yes. Children. Why hasn't Sara a right to children—a family?"

"She's too old already, Annie."

"She's not. Not these days."

Martin finished the maneuver. He glanced at her again and said wearily, "Biology is still biology, Annie. Even these days."

"She's still a young woman."

"She's a middle-aged woman, a couple of years off menopause." He shook his head. "Annie, why are you so sure she even wants children?"

"I'm not sure. Maybe she doesn't. But I want her to have the chance to decide for herself. To find someone and get married maybe, and maybe even have a kid. And she's not going to do it running a nursing home. That's for sure."

Martin screwed around in his seat, then looked back and swerved quickly onto the exit to his parents' house. He said, "Look, Annie, I know she's tied down now, but she wasn't always. If she wanted a family, which I wonder actually, she should have thought of it all those years she was running around with that faggot."

"*Martin.*"

"Okay, okay. That gay gentleman."

"Martin, you liked Josh. What's gotten into you? What has gotten into you? You haven't used a word like that in years. For God's sake. We have gay friends."

"I know, I know. Oh, lay off, Annie. Please." He gripped his stomach and winced. After a while he said slowly, "Annie, I just can't take any more. I'm so tired. None of you understand. I'm just good old reliable Martin to all of you. Sara can fulfill herself as a dancer. Seth can wander around India in a dhoti. And all the time good old reliable boring Martin, the family square, works his ass off. And now Sara's not married. Sara has no money. And it's my fault somehow. They had their fun. The sixties kids. You know where I was in the sixties? Working until three A.M. at med school, doing my internship, starting a family, paying a mortgage."

"I was there," Annie reminded him with a small smile.

"And now it's my fault that things are tough with them?"

"Seth's not complaining," Annie grinned cheerfully.

"Screw Seth," Martin shouted. "Screw him. Screw him."

"Calm down," Annie whispered. "Cool it, Martin, we're almost there."

"I can't do it all, Annie. I can't look after everyone. I can't look after Sara. And my parents. And my kid who's having a kid when he's barely out of diapers himself. And now your poor deranged brother as well. I can't do it."

"He's not deranged," Annie said fiercely.

Martin turned to face her as he slowed the car in front of his parents' house. "No," he said quietly. "He's not deranged. All the rest of us are. Annie, please give me a break."

He swung off the road and into the long, curving crushed-shell drive. Annie turned away from him again and looked out the side window. Her anger settled once more on externals, now the unkempt grounds of the big house. The white flagpole in the center of the lawn was streaked with rust and half engulfed by a mountainous rhododendron. Hydrangeas sprawled along a side wall of the house, and lilacs brushed the windows with dry, brown flower heads. A trellis of roses bristled with untamed shoots. Under the big shade maples the grass was stringy and uncut. Annie studied it all with increasing impatience.

Martin pulled up by the kitchen door behind a dark blue Oldsmobile with an Alamo sticker in the rear window. "Seth's here," he said. "They got here ahead of us." Annie nodded. She stared at the overgrown lilacs.

"Is Sara still using that high school kid for the gardening?" she asked sharply.

"I don't know, Annie," Martin switched off the engine and turned to face her. "How should I know?"

Annie gathered her shoulder bag and reached for the door handle. "I think it's time to set up something a bit more regular. Look at the grass. And that lilac. Your dad can't manage the pruning. We're going to have to do something."

Martin sat with hands still on the wheel, staring through the windshield at the rear of the Oldsmobile. "Annie, I have a great idea," he said. "Why not ask Seth to do something?"

"Seth?" Annie looked surprised. Then she shook her head impatiently. "What would Seth know about it?"

Martin released the wheel and sat back. He gave her a small, exasperated smile. "I think a man who can organize his way across the Himalayas might just manage to find a landscape contractor. Don't you?" Annie laughed. "I'm serious," Martin said. She shrugged, opened the door, and got out of the car.

"Oh, take those pastries for me, Martin, will you?" She pointed to a string-tied box on the back seat as she closed her door. She walked around the car and up the steps to the kitchen porch. Martin leaned heavily over the seat, picked up the pastry box, got out, slammed his own door hard, and followed.

Annie found her sister in the kitchen with Martin's mother. Joanna looked up from the sandwiches she was making at the kitchen table. Her hair, plaited into a thick yellow braid, fell over the shoulder of her faded blue shirt. She tossed it back impatiently and hooked one thumb through a belt loop of her jeans. "Hey, you got here," she said, grinning. "We thought you were lost."

"I let Martin sleep late," Annie said, adding, "I thought it might make him less grumpy, but it didn't work." Joanna's grin broadened.

"What's the matter with Martin?" Miriam Levine straightened up by the refrigerator door, holding a big bottle of cranberry juice with both hands. She was a small woman, grown smaller with age, but still impeccably groomed in straight-legged brown trousers, a soft yellow sweater, and strings of chunky beads. Her hair, once black and glistening, was iron gray and cut short, but still thick and strong, more vigorous now than its owner. She had the same deep brown eyes as Sara and Seth, though muddied now slightly with uncertainty.

"Nothing's the matter." Martin pushed aside the screen door with his shoulder and stepped into the kitchen, holding the cake box delicately. "Annie's joking," he said sourly. Miriam looked briefly at Annie and then back to Martin. She shook her head impatiently.

"I don't know. Jokes always. So what's so funny?" She shrugged. "Cranberry juice," she said to the room at large. "Will everyone drink cranberry juice?"

Annie hung her shoulder bag by its strap from a kitchen chair. "Sure, Miriam. Whatever you have." She bent down to kiss Miriam's cheek.

"I have apple too." Miriam looked more worried. She did not seem to notice the kiss.

"Tell you what," Joanna said easily, reaching to take the bottle, "We'll put them both on the table and let people take their pick. How's that?" Miriam seemed momentarily appeased, but then Martin handed her the box of pastries and she became flustered again, opening drawers and closing them, searching for scissors for the string.

"Do it for her," Annie nudged Martin urgently. Martin looked bewildered, but he took the pastry box from his mother and cut the string with a kitchen knife. "So did you get a costume, then?" Annie said to Joanna.

Joanna shook her head. "Three malls. Eight different stores. There was nothing left except the boring stuff kids never want. You know, Snow White and Mickey Mouse."

Miriam took back the pastry box from Martin and lifted the lid. "Last week already in Waldbaum's everything was sold out." She sniffed at the pastries. "These look good, Annie," she said.

"Well, it's our own fault." Joanna slapped mayonnaise on a slice of rye bread, "She only told me she wanted to go yesterday morning. All week long she's been saying she's too old." She shrugged. "We gave up in the end and bought a pumpkin at a farm stand. Seth's helping her carve it."

"Where's Eric?" Martin asked quietly.

"Out on the front porch, talking with your dad."

"With Dad?" Martin looked suddenly hopeful. His eyes settled intently on Joanna's face. "About what?" he asked softly. "Do you know?"

Miriam looked up from the pastry box and lifted her shoulders eloquently. "History. Politics. What do they always talk about?" she said.

Martin raised one heavy eyebrow. "He's been away ten years, Mom. I thought maybe that might inspire some conversation?"

"Sure. They said hello first. Then they start-in about history and politics. What do you expect with your father?" Martin shook his head. His shoulders sagged, and he leaned back against a kitchen counter.

"Go see them," Joanna said. "They're all out there."

"Martin, we only have sandwiches, you know." Miriam looked suddenly panicky. "Will that be enough? All these people."

"Sandwiches are fine, Mom," Martin said tiredly.

"Wait. I have some soup left over. I'll heat up the soup."

"Sandwiches are fine, Mom," Martin said louder. "We've just had breakfast."

"You have, maybe," Miriam said, "but what about the others? What about that child?" She seemed not to connect the child to Joanna, who sliced a stack of sandwiches and said in a calm voice, "Tess is fine, Miriam."

"Kids don't eat soup, Mom," Martin said. "Look, will you stop fussing? We didn't come here to eat. We came here," he stopped suddenly and then said, "we have things to talk about."

"So much to talk about that there's no time for lunch?" Miriam looked unhappy.

"Of course there's time," Annie said. "Come on, Martin, let's say hi to your dad." She took his arm, firmly but not unkindly. As they left the kitchen, Miriam was getting a big soup tureen out of the refrigerator.

In the dark, long hallway leading to the front of the house, Annie stopped and turned to face Martin. "I know it's hard," she said in a firm, even voice, "I know she irritates you and sets you on edge, but you just can't let it show." She smiled and reached up gently and straightened his collar, "Okay?"

Martin looked at the worn strip of carpet on the old oak floor. He said nothing at first, but then suddenly burst out, "No. No, it's not okay. This is nothing new, Annie. She always irritated me. She's made it an art form. Why suddenly pretend I don't notice?"

"Because she's old."

"Is that going to get her off the hook forever now?"

"Yes," Annie said. She walked away from him toward the living room.

It was a big, formal room, made permanently dark by the porch that lined its length and the heavy draperies on its already-shaded windows. It was well furnished, with good old solid pieces standing patiently in the dim light. There was a big, handsome fireplace, but it was empty, swept clean of ash, and looked long unused. Like the room, Annie thought, distantly remembering it as an off-limits adult sanctuary, filled with talk and laughter and the clink of ice in drinks.

One ray of fall sunshine slipped through the French windows at the far end, lighting a rich oblong on the red Persian carpet. Annie looked beyond it, through the open doors into the old winter sunroom that was Sara's dance studio now. On the bare wood floor rows of chairs, gathered from around the house, sat ready for the afternoon's show.

Annie crossed the living room with the soft tread of a child trespassing and opened the front door. Light flooded in with a mix of familiar fall smells, drying leaves, sun-washed wood, salt. She pushed the screen door open and stepped out into the sweet, crisp air. They were all there, Harry Levine talking to Eric as Joanna had said, Seth and Tess carving their jack-o'-lantern, Sara sewing costumes for her show.

"Hey, Annie," Seth looked up and smiled. "We thought you'd deserted us." He knelt on the gray painted planks of the floor, surrounded by spread newspapers, scooping out the entrails of a large and lopsided pumpkin. A pile of stringy, seed-clotted pulp beside him added its vegetable tang to the air.

"We got the last pumpkin," Tess said, looking up for a moment before returning rapt attention to Seth.

"It looks like it," Martin said. He followed Annie through the door, knocking over a decorative cornshock as he did. He stood it up quickly, and it fell over again.

"Leave it," Sara said. "It's just there for my dance kids anyhow." She was sitting behind Seth in a white basket-weave chair, a pile of orange tulle on either side of her. She held a bunch of the cloth on her lap and was stitching it, quickly and expertly.

"It's the Great Pumpkin," Annie said to Tess. Tess looked up again, smiled quickly, and looked back. She was sitting on the floor with her skinny arms linked around her bent legs and her back propped comfortably against Eric's knees. Annie was surprised, though charmed, by the unconcious familiarity. But then, Eric himself looked so natural there, sitting like Tess on the floor, leaning back against the porch railing, listening to Harry. The sharp lines of his face seemed softened, the gauntness less pronounced. Even his worn clothes looked normal, as if he had been working in their parents' yard and just stopped by for a chat. Harry Levine perched on the edge of the wicker love seat, bending forward over his cane, his tanned, bony face animated, eyes alight. He half-raised his hand to Annie in greeting, but kept talking. Annie heard something about Eisenhower and Patton. She stared, slightly bewildered. She had seen them like that in the same places and the same positions so many times in the old days. They seemed to have simply stepped out of the present and into a kinder past.

Her gaze wandered distractedly around the porch, taking in the pumpkin, the cornshocks, Seth and the child, Sara and her sewing, Eric and the intense old man. We look happy, she thought, amazed. We look like a happy family. All we need here is a big shaggy dog.

———

TESS KNEW IT WAS a pretty poor excuse for a pumpkin. It was flat on one side, with a big scaly patch on it, and it was more yellow than orange. But there weren't any other pumpkins, and she wanted to please the adults, because she hadn't found a costume to please them with. So she'd said it was great, and Seth had bought it for her. Now she was making herself as interested as possible in carving it. She was afraid if she didn't look interested her mom would get mad and they'd start arguing like they'd argued in one of the stores about why she wouldn't go out dressed as a princess. She hadn't liked arguing with her mother in front of Eric, and she didn't want to argue in front of him now.

Tess wished they'd just forget about the costume. It was the grown-ups, not Tess, who had insisted on going to all the different stores. She would have given up after maybe two, and she felt sorry for Eric, being dragged around all those stupid malls. But Seth and her mom wouldn't give up. They were doing that thing she'd seen adults do before, making a big deal about some kids' thing when there was a big adult problem around that needed solving instead.

The big adult problem was Eric. She would have to be an idiot not to see that. Though, idiot or not, she couldn't see why. It was like her mom's fights with Sean Kelly. The fact that they were fighting was obvious enough. It was the reasons that never made any sense. Still, in the middle of it, she could pretty well count on someone getting all hung up about her history project, or putting shelves up in her room.

Maybe it was just that kids' things looked easier to fix.

Seth gave her a pencil when he had finished scooping out the pumpkin. While he wrapped up the seeds in newspaper, she drew big triangular eyes, a square nose, and a mouth with lots of teeth on the best side of the pumpkin. Then Seth and Martin got into an argument about the right way of cutting the mouth out without breaking off the teeth. Tess leaned back against Eric's knees again until they'd finished. She closed her eyes with the sun on her face. It was the special kind of sun that came when the air was already getting cold. She liked the feel of it and liked the way Eric steadied her with his hand on her shoulder, quietly and without stopping talking to Harry. She thought she'd like to sit there like that for a while. But then the door opened again; she heard her mom's voice saying lunch was ready, and she opened her eyes. As she did, there was a sharp little gasp. Old Mrs. Levine stood in the doorway with her hand on her chest.

"I got such a start just then," she said. "That child sitting there." Tess saw her mother, standing beside Miriam, wince and shake her head.

Then Martin said loudly, "Yeah, Mom, fine. Let's have lunch."

"But look at her," Miriam said.

"I see her, Mom. Come on, everyone."

"Doesn't she look just like Molly?" Miriam looked around, her hand still on her chest. "Doesn't she look just like her?"

"Jesus, Mom," said Martin. He slumped against the railing, his head down. No one else said anything, and in the silence Tess still felt Eric's hand, gentle on her shoulder, unmoving. Then Harry Levine slid his cane along the floor, making a rubbery squeak.

"Yeah," he said slowly. "She does. She looks a lot like Molly." Tess still sat, rigid, but around her she saw the adults relax, and she knew that somehow Harry's saying it in his old scratchy voice made it all right to say.

"Right," Sara said then, her voice suddenly bright and cheerful on the still porch. "That's done." She threw the last of the orange tulle costumes down on the finished heap. "Now, Tess, I've still got some cloth left over. Shall I make you something after lunch?"

Tess looked up, uncertain. "A costume?" she said. Sara nodded. "You mean go as a dancing pumpkin?" Tess asked warily.

Sara looked down at the orange cloth on her lap and then back to Tess. She grinned wryly. "No. Maybe not," she said. Tess saw her mother looking annoyed.

"Tess. Say thank you at least."

"Thank you, Sara," Tess said quickly, but her mother still looked annoyed.

"If anything, she should make it herself," she said pointedly. "We always did."

Sara only laughed and gave Tess a friendly smile. "Yeah. And every year we went out as ghosts with the same two sheets with eyeholes. It was so wonderfully easy. We must have used those sheets for five years. I bet they're still in the attic now." She put her needle away carefully in a pincushion and set the pincushion, with the scissors, on the arm of her chair. "I used to love Halloween," she said, stretching her arms lazily over her head. "It was such a real kids' holiday. All anarchy and running free in the night." She lowered her arms. "It's not the same now. Now it goes on for weeks and weeks with all the Halloween parties and Halloween decorations and Halloween cards. But it doesn't seem such fun anymore. The adults have taken over. It's all so controlled."

"The adults took over," Martin reminded her, "because it wasn't safe any longer."

"If you ask me," Miriam said darkly, "it's a conspiracy in the card shops. Halloween. Thanksgiving. Mother's Day. Grandparents' Day. Whoever heard of Grandparents' Day? Wouldn't you think Mother's Day and Father's Day would cover everybody? I don't know what's wrong with this country. We can't seem to do anything without it getting bigger and wilder and out of control."

"Do you think they're really still up there?" Joanna said to Sara. "Those sheets?"

"Mom," Tess said, "I don't need a costume. I really don't."

Sara didn't seem to notice. "Go see," she said cheerfully. "Better yet, send Tess to see."

"Send Tess where?" Tess asked.

Seth grinned. "To the attic," he whispered. "The big, black, dusty attic. Full of cobwebs and spiders and . . ."

"Seth," Miriam said, "Be quiet. You'll scare her."

"I'm not scared," Tess said, scared.

"Just up those little stairs by your bedroom door," Seth said.

"Sure. Fine." Tess got up slowly. "Where did you say?" she asked in a small voice.

"She'll never find it," Miriam said. "She'll fall and hurt herself."

"Of course she won't, Mom. We played up there all the time." Seth got up, stepping carefully around the pumpkin. "Wait a moment, Tess," he said. He went out and came back with a metal flashlight. He switched it on and peered at the bulb glowing feebly against the white sunlight. He gave the flashlight a shake and switched it off. "Should last a little while, Tess," he said solemnly. "If you see anything scary, just call us."

"Sure," Tess said. She got up from the floor and took the flashlight from Seth. She looked briefly back at Eric, but Harry Levine had started talking about World War Two again and Eric didn't seem to notice her leaving. She flicked the switch of the flashlight a couple of times for comfort. "Will you hear me?" she asked. Seth tilted his head thoughtfully.

"Probably," he said slowly. "If you scream."

Tess gripped the flashlight and walked determinedly across the porch and through the big front door. As it closed behind her, she heard Eric laughing softly. "Seth, you're a rat," he said.

At first, Tess couldn't even find the stairs. There were so many doors in the upper corridor of the house, some open, some closed, bedroom doors, bathroom doors, one dead-ending at a broom closet. Eventually she found the narrow one, between the broom closet and the bedroom Sara had given her that morning, that opened on a steep, curved staircase. It was as dark as the closet. She reached around with the flat of her hand, seeking a light switch. The wall was rough and unfinished, and her hand touched a soft clump of webs. She yelped and drew back. At last she thought of the flashlight and flicked it on. A fluttering gray beam revealed not a wall switch, but a hanging cord, its frayed end dangling beyond her reach. She climbed a couple of steps and, holding onto the wall with one hand, batted behind her for the cord with the other. Now it was horizontally beyond her reach, flicking insolently across her outstretched fingers, like another spiderweb. She gave up, pushed the door open as far as it would go, and, on shaking legs, climbed cautiously up the stairs.

The light from below dimmed out, and the dark gray attic light above grew no stronger. She stopped, took another step, stopped, took one more, and then stopped again. Slowly, she sat down, feeling around her for the solidity of the bare step. She laid the flashlight sideways across her knee. It clunked softly inside, as the batteries shifted, and went out. Tess screamed, jumped up, and slid clattering, feet first, down the stairs. She tumbled out into the bright, friendly light of the corridor and flailed around instantly to slam the attic door, shutting the blackness inside. Breathing hard, she sat on the strip of patterned carpet, the flashlight beside her, savoring the relief of escape.

The adults were all at the dining room table, talking, when she returned. She crept silently into the room and slithered onto the chair beside Eric, her head ducked low in an ostrich-hope of invisibility. They handed out the sandwiches and poured the cranberry juice. She thought at first she'd escaped, but then Miriam Levine asked, "Did you find them, Tess?" Tess shook her head.

Joanna raised her eyebrows, "You couldn't have looked very long. You've only been gone half a minute."

"It's a big attic, Tess," Seth said, grinning.

"I looked. I did look." Tess screwed her face up in protest, but Seth reached a hand across the table and, still grinning, laid it on hers. She felt again the confusion of like and dislike.

He said, "Your mom and I will find them later, Tess. Eat your lunch." Relieved, Tess took two sandwich halves, one bologna and one cheese, from the platter in the middle of the table and carefully munched off the crusts. The adult conversation went on comfortably over her head, a soothing litany of names she did not know and places she had not been, leaving her free to daydream in peace.

"We miss your mom and dad," Harry Levine said to Eric. "It's not the same with strangers in that house." Eric nodded. Harry watched him carefully.

Eric said, "I always imagined they'd be there when I came back. That everything would be just the same." He looked sad and puzzled.

"You've been a long time, kid," Harry said.

Eric nodded again. "Who bought the house?" he asked.

"Nobody we know," Joanna said. "They came over from the North Shore somewhere."

"Sometimes, you know, I'm out walking in the morning," Harry said, "and I find myself in front of that house. What for? My feet forget your parents are in Florida." He reached to pick up his sandwich, but his gnarled hands trembled and lost it. He tried again and grasped it quickly, brought it to his mouth and bit off a hurried, ungainly mouthful.

"We had a letter yesterday," Miriam said. "It's still very hot. But they have air-conditioning, so I suppose it's all right."

"You'll go and see them now, Eric?" said Harry. Eric did not answer. He sat looking at a point on the wall between Harry and Joanna. "Do you need money?" Harry said. "That's no problem. You know that." Eric shook his head. The room went quiet.

Then Miriam said softly, "Eric, they want so much to see you." Her eyes were dark and wet. "So many years."

"I can't," Eric said at last. "I can't stay." He looked at Miriam for an instant and said gently, "I'd love to if I could." Miriam looked simply baffled. Frustration twisted Joanna's face. She started to speak, but Seth caught her hand on the table. "You don't seem to understand," Eric said, looking up now at Joanna and Seth. "It isn't over."

Joanna sighed. She leaned back in her chair, raised her free hand, and pushed her hair back from her face. "Eric, even after . . ." Seth squeezed her hand tighter. She stopped talking and fought tears.

Miriam said, "What's not over? What is he saying?"

"Eric," Harry Levine said. He smiled, a wise smile that cast deep grooves of kindness across his face. "Eric." The smile seemed to do something that words could not. Eric looked confused. He dropped his eyes, and when he looked up he was suddenly agitated. He stood up.

"Where are you going?" Miriam said. "There's coffee and cake still, isn't there, Sara?" Sara nodded dumbly.

"I've had enough," Eric said. "It was lovely. Thank you, Miriam. Sara." He smiled quickly. "I just want to walk down to our old beach house." He looked around at the serious, watching faces. His eyes fell on Tess. "Would you like to see it?" he said.

"Yeah." Tess jumped up. "I don't want cake either," she said hurriedly.

"No cake? What kind of child is this?" Harry Levine said. He was smiling still, but his eyes, steady on Eric's face, were sad. "You in a hurry, Eric, or can you wait for an old man?"

Eric stood silently behind his chair. Tess, reaching out to take his hand, stopped, looking up at him curiously. He was quiet for a long while, but then he said, "Of course, Harry. Of course I can wait." Harry levered himself erect on his cane. Martin stood up quickly and reached an arm out to steady his father. Miriam stared at them both. She looked around the table, flustered.

"Well, is anybody staying?" she said loudly. Harry ignored Martin's arm. He took two hobbling steps, straightened fully, and then walked purposefully to the door. Martin sat down again and watched his father go out with Eric and Tess.

"It's okay, Mom," he said tiredly. "All the rest of us will stay."

JOANNA FOLLOWED SETH through the attic door. He reached up to tug the light cord casually. The bare bulb at the top of the stairs flashed on, lighting the dusty wood of the steps. They were steep and narrow. Joanna slid her hand up the rough wall as she climbed. They emerged at the top into a dimly lit space beneath high, slanting, cobwebbed roof trusses, gray with age. On either side the roof plunged to dusty darkness, cluttered with the dim shapes of old pieces of furniture.

"I used to think of this place when I had the store in Denver," Joanna said. "I bet there are treasures up here."

"I bet there's a lot of garbage, too," said Seth.

"Oh, probably," Joanna agreed amiably. "All the dress-up stuff is in the back room, isn't it?" she asked.

"Unless it's been moved. And I doubt anyone's been up here since the last time we were as kids." He stopped at the top of the stairs, his hand still on the railing, looking around the dusty interior. Light from the dormer windows of the two half-finished rooms, one at the front of the house, one at the back, filtered through the dim passage. "It's funny," he said, "to think there must have been one day, one ordinary day, no different from any of the others, when we came down these stairs for the last time. Not knowing... it's as if our childhood is still up here ..."

Joanna laughed. "No wonder you're a writer. But anyhow, Martin's kids must have played up here sometimes too. If anyone's left their childhoods lying around, it's David and Danya."

"And Molly," said Seth. Joanna shivered.

"I don't want to talk about Molly," she said. He looked at her oddly, but seemed to accept what she'd said. He went slowly through the passage to the back room, ducking his head where a line of beams swept low. The roof of the old Victorian house was a vast puzzle of peaks and troughs, dormers and chimneys. Inside, it rambled like the skeletal cavities of a prehistoric beast. Joanna followed through its wooden rib cage to the playroom at the back.

The two finished attic rooms had always surprised her. They had linoleum floors and plastered walls, those of the front room papered in a flowered print, those at the back painted an ancient pink. She never could fathom why they were constructed. They were far too good for storerooms, but, islanded at the end of barren corridors of bare beams, clearly unsuitable for habitation. She looked around. The room with its trunk of dress-up clothes, its wooden boxes of erector sets and now genuinely antique lead soldiers, its old-fashioned cupboard, was absolutely unchanged. She stared at the net curtain at the window and could see her own childish hands on the fragile fabric forty years before. To the right was the door to the chimney sweep's passage, the secret room with its perilous open-beam floor where she and Annie, Martin and Eric, Sara and Seth had sworn a lifetime's loyalty. A far-off train whistle sounded on cue to seal the memory. Joanna turned back to the clothes trunk. Seth was sitting, smiling good-naturedly, on its lid.

"We have to."

"Have to what?"

"Talk about Molly," he said.

Joanna stared at him wearily and then flopped down on the linoleum floor. She sat like a kid, her knees drawn up and her arms linked around them. She tossed back her hair and said, "I can't deal with this anymore. Martin's right. Eric's just plain off the wall. You can't reason with him. You can't talk to him. Nothing makes any impression. I thought, surely, after that scene with the singer, he would have to open up to us, but he's just the same. Exactly the same." She shook her head. "I was an idiot, I know, but I somehow imagined I could reach him."

"Jo." Seth was still sitting on the trunk, quietly, his hands clasped in front of him.

"What?"

"Don't give up on him now." She looked up, startled.

"I'm not giving up," she said uncertainly.

"Yes, you are. Don't." He leaned forward and reached out and touched her cheek. "Megan Carmichael reached him. Molly died in that room. I saw it happen."

"How can you say that? He's still looking for her. He just said so."

"He thinks he is. It's a habit. And a buffer. He's not ready to let it go. You have to understand, Eric had the power of life and death over Molly. He's her creator. The real Molly he fathered with his body. This Molly he fathered with his mind. When he lets go with his mind, she dies. He knows that. Give him time."

"I can't, Seth. I can't stand any more. It's breaking me up. I've screwed up Martin and Annie's lives. I've screwed up Tess's."

"Tess is all right. She's learning things."

"I've lost my job." He looked startled.

"How do you know?"

"Oh, my friend Mike called the night you went out with Eric. It's no surprise. I've been away four weeks, and I promised I'd be back in two." She shrugged it off. "I'll find something. Mike offered to give me a few hours in his office if he can get it past his wife."

"Do you need money, Jo?" Seth said quietly.

"Not yours." His head came up and his dark eyes flashed with sudden anger.

"What's *wrong* with my money? What's wrong with me?"

"Nothing, Seth."

"Bullshit. You push me out of your life like I was a pesky high school kid. Jo, look at me."

"I am."

"No you're not. You're seeing your own memories. Look at me really." Joanna laughed. She rocked back, her hands still clasped about her knees.

"All right, I'm looking." She concentrated and found it difficult, as if the shadow of his remembered young self was stronger than the reality before her. She noticed suddenly that his hair, though still richly black, had a few white strands scattered haphazardly through it, that there were thin but definite lines around his eyes, that his unshaved beard would be heavy and full, not the wispy boy's beard she had remembered. Those things in themselves startled her, as if they had appeared suddenly there in the attic playroom. But what surprised her more was the settled, balanced intensity of his eyes, the eyes of a man who knew who he was and where he was going. She grinned.

"What's funny?" he asked.

"Nothing. I like what I see, that's all."

"Well, good," he said uneasily. He stood up from the trunk. "I suppose that's a start, anyhow." He lifted the lid and looked down into the faded jumble of dresses and hats, coats and cloaks. He pulled out an ancient fur stole—two whole, flattened, indeterminate brown animals, the teeth of one clasping the tail of the other, golden glass eyes belligerently staring. He shook it, and fur and dust settled onto the linoleum. "Can you imagine anyone actually wearing this?" he said.

"Give me," Joanna laughed. He tossed it to her and she wrapped it around her neck. "There was a hat . . . a hat I loved." She rummaged in the trunk and found a circle of crumpled black velvet with dark pink satin roses bunched around the crown. She clamped it on her head and waltzed to the mirror-fronted cupboard. She wiped the dust from the glass with the sleeve of her flannel shirt, gleefully studying her reflection. "I used to think I was real hot stuff in this," she said. Seth leaned against the wall, smiling. "There was a wedding dress, remember?" He looked baffled. "Sara and Annie found it hanging in the front room. We just knew we weren't supposed to touch it. Sara and I hid back here while Annie tried it on. Next thing, she came flying through, white as a sheet. She said she heard a voice, a ghostly woman's voice, sobbing . . ." Joanna lifted off the velvet hat and unwrapped the moth-eaten fur. "Sara and I just about wet ourselves trying to get down the stairs. We always loved playing up here, but it was a trial by ordeal getting here, down that cobwebby passage. Funny how kids have these secret rules. We all knew this room was safe, but the corridor . . . oh, the corridor . . ."

"The worst place was the secret room."

"Oh, I hated the secret room. I only went in there because of Annie and Eric."

"Eric and Martin locked me in there once for half an hour."

"Oh, no," Joanna said, her adult, parental self genuinely shocked.

"I'd agreed to it. It was a sort of initiation. I nearly died of fright. They said they'd give me a flashlight, but they took the battery out."

"The rats."

"Oh, that was all part of it. They were pretty good when I came out. Clapped me on the back and shook my hand and told me I was a man." He laughed softly. "I was eight. They were twelve." Joanna dropped the fur and the hat back into the trunk. She stood looking at them and then turned back to Seth,

"I never realized how rotten we all were to you."

"Oh, terrible." He grinned. "You should be ashamed."

"When you're an adult, children seem so innocent. Tess, her friends . . . and then you remember . . ."

"Children are innocent. So is all the natural world. It's just not necessarily nice."

"You make it sound pretty bleak."

"I didn't mean to." He paused, leaning against the faded paint of the wall. "What I meant was it's a time without external morality. Children make their own rules. Their own rights and wrongs, but they honor them. They stick by them. They have a great sense of justice. Martin and Eric wouldn't have dreamed of keeping me in there one second past the half hour." He smiled distantly, "A great sense of justice and a great sense of the heroic. I always think of childhood as Arthurian . . . a time of dragons, and quests, and hidden Holy Grails."

"And ghosts," Joanna said, laughing softly. "Hey, we'd better find these sheets."

"I'm sorry, I get carried away."

"No, I like . . . I don't know anyone who talks like you."

"You were my Guinevere," he said. He had turned from her and was lifting faded, shapeless garments from the trunk. "For you I fought a thousand battles in my mind. I rescued you from storms on the bay, from cars on railroad tracks, from gangs of hoods . . ."

She laughed, delighted and embarrassed, "Oh, Seth."

"I wanted nothing but the chance to look after you. I've wanted it all my life." He held an old coat momentarily in his hands. "Childish, isn't it?" he said and laid the coat down.

"You've never told me."

"Oh, it was far too embarrassing."

"Then why are you telling me now?"

He shrugged, "To lay the ghost? Who knows."

"Is it working?"

"No." He paused. "I've known so many wonderful women, wonderful lovers, wonderful friends. It doesn't make any difference. You'd think it would, wouldn't you?"

Joanna was quiet. A tiny whisper of jealousy arose, unsettling her thoughts. She said, "I've never fallen in love with a friend. Except for Martin, I suppose. I have friends. I mean men who are friends. But they're not the men I fall in love with."

"Who do you fall in love with?"

"People I hardly know. Strangers really. I think that's what excites me." She paused, crouching by the rim of the trunk. She saw the sheets, white and neatly folded from their last Halloween, but did not touch them. "Then I get to know them and I end up sorry."

"Could I excite you?" he said. Startled, she met his eyes. She gave a small nervous laugh.

"Oh, Seth, you're more than a friend. You're almost a brother." His hand touched her arm.

"Let me try."

"Seth, what are you doing?" He laid his fingers on her lips.

"Shh. An experiment. Let me try."

"Seth?" His arm came around her back, the fingers splayed across her rib cage, their tips just brushing the underside of her breast.

"I like the feel of you," he said. "I've never properly touched you."

"Seth, we can't . . ."

"We can do anything we want, Jo. We're grown-ups now."

"WHAT'S A BEACH HOUSE?" Tess asked.

"It's just a sort of shack," Eric said. "With three sides, open at the front. Just bare boards. We used to camp in it when we were kids."

"You and Mom?"

"Sometimes. Sometimes just me and Martin. Or me and Martin and Annie." He paused and smiled, "We didn't always let your mom come. Or Sara. They were the littlest."

"I thought Seth was the youngest."

"Oh, we never let Seth come. Unless our parents made us." He grinned quickly at Harry Levine. Tess considered that, walking between Eric and Harry down the shell driveway that extended back from the house, through fields, toward the marshes and the creek.

She said, "You were all pretty mean."

"Do you think so?"

"I thought so," Harry said.

"If I had a little brother, I don't think I'd be that mean to him." She took two quick strides. "Well, maybe a little mean," she said, looking back.

Eric had stopped and was waiting for Harry. Harry increased his pace, prodding the dry grassy ground with his cane. "Keep going," he said. "I'm not that slow." Eric stayed a moment longer before turning again to Tess. Tess scuffed a sneaker along the ground, waiting for them.

"Where are we going?" she asked.

"Down the lane behind our old house, to the bay."

"Can you see your old house from it?"

"Do you want to?"

Tess shrugged. "If it's okay."

"We'll see it," Eric said.

The lane was narrow and shaded, two strips of crushed shell with a weedy center, bordered by tall, unclipped privet hedges and big maples. The maples were bright yellow and glowed in the sun against the clear blue sky. Fallen yellow leaves, crinkled brown at their edges, piled up at the roots of the privet. Tess walked close to the hedge, scuffing her sneakers through the leaves, sniffing the fall smell.

At a gap in the hedge, Eric said, "Come here," and led her into a space of lawn, with trellises of roses over a path. A few pink roses remained, among spikey shoots of briar flailing in the wind. The grass was mowed velvet short.

"Should we be here?" Tess said. "It's somebody else's now, isn't it?"

"They won't mind," Harry said easily. Tess looked sideways at Eric as they walked up under the trellises. She liked his face. It wasn't really old, like Harry's, but it still had lines in it that made her feel safe.

"Does it make you sad, going to see the house?" she asked.

He turned to look at her. "Not really. Do you think it should?"

Tess considered. "I used to get sad when we passed the road to our ranch house." She paused. "But maybe that's because we don't really have a house anymore. Just a trailer."

"A trailer's okay, Tess."

"It's not real," she said. "It's not a real house."

"It's a real trailer," Eric said. He stopped beside a line of trees with gray branches and shiny purple leaves. He pointed across another wide lawn, with borders of yellow, orange, and red flowers. "There's the house," he said.

It was white-painted, with a dark gray roof, and like all the houses on the wide, shady avenue, it was big. Its three stories went up in tiers, like a wedding cake. There were several levels of roofs and many different-shaped windows, some with little railed balconies. The ground floor was surrounded by porches, like skirts. The highest roof had a little square turret. Tess stared.

"That's where you and Mom grew up?"

"That's it."

"Wow." Tess stared a little longer and said, curiously, "You must have been rich." Eric and Harry exchanged a smile.

"I guess we were," Eric said. He touched her shoulder, "See that window, the last one on the left in the middle section?" Tess followed his pointing finger. "That was your mom's room. And that," he pointed two over, "was mine. Your Auntie Annie had her room on the other side." Tess stared silently at this physical evidence of her mother's childhood.

"Was she really like me?" she said at last.

"To look at? A lot like you." Tess absorbed that, fitting together a picture of a person that was and was not herself, looking out from the window in the big white house. Eric said, "That little round window up high was my father's study. Your grandfather's. It was full of history books." Tess was startled to think of her grandfather as also Eric's father. It made her feel related to Eric in a new way.

"I thought he used to be a scientist."

"He was a physicist. He worked for the government at Brookhaven." Tess nodded, wondering if she was supposed to know what Brookhaven was. "But he loved history," Eric said.

"What did you do?" Tess said as they walked back to the lane. She hesitated and added, "Before."

"Me?" Eric turned around. He looked surprised and confused. "Oh, I did a lot of things." He said it in an offhand, mumbled voice that made her think she shouldn't have asked.

She said quickly, to cover up, "My grandfather came to see us at the ranch one year. He took me rafting on the Fraser River."

Harry said, "Yeah, I heard all about it. He let me know all right." He smiled to himself and turned to Eric. "When you get to our age, you get real competitive about what you can still do, what you're still up to." He paused. "Eventually, even staying alive gets to be a competition." Then he turned back to Tess and said, "Everything Eric ever did, he did well." Eric laughed, but Harry said, "It's true. You did everything well."

"But nothing for very long." Harry shrugged. Eric smiled and then said to Tess, "I wrote for a little while. Then I had a job working with computers. Programming."

"Computers? I like computers," Tess said. "I'm real good at them. I'm the best in my class at school. Better than the boys." She grinned happily. "Mom thinks they're just a waste of time," she added, casually superior.

"Does she?" Eric sounded surprised.

"Yeah, well, maybe it's because of the games."

"You like computer games?"

"Oh yeah," Tess grinned again. "I have Super Mario All Stars and Spiderman Two and Prince Valiant. I've done the lost levels on Super Mario." Harry and Eric both looked vague. "They're the hardest," she explained. "Sean, the man who used to live with us, got me my Nintendo." She was about to explain about the Game Boy, but she stopped. She didn't want to talk about Sean or Mike. Besides, something was missing. Startled, she realized it was the warm yearning for the Game Boy that had suffused her birthday and Christmas wishes for over a year. It didn't seem to matter anymore.

"You must be really good," Eric said.

"Yeah, I'm pretty good," Tess agreed. "Are you going to work with computers now?" she asked.

"Now?" Eric sounded vague again and looked off down the lane toward the blue oval of sky and bay at the end of the green and yellow tunnel of leaves. "No," he said eventually. "I don't think so." Then he looked down at her and smiled quickly. "What about you? What are you going to do?"

Tess was thoughtful. "I'd like to make up computer games," she said. "I've got some really great ideas. I might do educational ones for little kids." She pulled a black-eyed Susan from a bunch growing on the grassy edge of the lane. "Or maybe I'll get a job working with horses. I know how to do that from the ranch." She spun the flower in a circle, like a propeller. "It's real hard work, though. Mom thinks I should go to college," she added dutifully.

"Are you good at school?" Eric asked.

"Yeah," Tess said, "when I work. I'm going to start working soon."

Eric laughed softly, "Why?"

"It gets important."

The lane ended suddenly in a little broken ledge above the beach, where waves had eaten away at the ground during storms. The roots of the last privets were exposed and whitened like bones. The bushes hung precariously, rocking in the wind. Tess jumped down onto a small strip of sand. On either side weathered gray bulwarks ran out into the bright waters of the bay. The air smelled of salt and rotting seaweed.

"You're just like my daughter," Eric said. Tess turned around slowly. Dried seaweed crunched under her sneakers. Eric stood with his arm behind Harry, steadying the old man's balance on the ledge.

"Wasn't Molly good at school?" she asked. Eric smiled. He stepped off the ledge and carefully helped Harry down onto the sand.

"She was always going to be. Next week, or next term, or next year." He smiled again. Then the smile faded and he just stood there, quieter and quieter.

"Maybe she would have been," Tess said.

After a long while, Eric said, "Yes. I'm sure. The shack's over here, Tess."

He walked off abruptly, up the beach, stepping over one of the bulwarks. Tess watched and then looked back questioningly at Harry. He was standing, watching too. When he said nothing, Tess turned away and followed Eric, scrambling onto the broken silvery wood. The bulwark was hollow, and the soft waves breaking on the beach rushed up inside it, gurgling in the darkness. The beach was lower on the other side. Tess jumped down and landed on mounds of brown seaweed. Flies buzzed up, and she flicked them away from her legs. She stood on the crunchy weed, staring out at the bay. The blue-green water was glittering with fall sunshine and flecked with white. There were three distant sails and a speedboat throwing up a white wake. She listened to its hum and thought of the lake in Grand County where Sean Kelly went windsurfing while she and her mom sat on the shore and watched. The lake was dark blue and hemmed in by mountains and trees. "Is this the ocean?" she asked.

Eric had stopped walking and come back to help Harry over the bulwark. "Sort of," he said. "There's an island out there. It's called a barrier island. The real ocean is beyond it." Tess squinted into the bright light at the lumpy strip of island.

"I've never seen the ocean," she said. Eric looked surprised. Then he laughed.

"Poor landlocked child. Of course you haven't."

"We'll show you tomorrow," Harry said.

"Will you?" She looked at Eric.

"Sure. Come see the beach house." He turned away again.

Tess took two steps after him and then stopped, staring. A small brown monster was walking across the seaweed at her feet. It was shelled and plated, hoof-shaped, and dragged a spikey prehistoric tail.

"Eric . . ." she said, watching it. "Eric."

"What's wrong?" He turned back to face her.

"There's a thing here, Eric."

"A what?" He walked back quickly and then stood still and grinned. "It's a horseshoe, Tess. A horseshoe crab." He leaned over and picked it up carefully, his big hands on either edge of its U-shaped shell. Tess jumped back as he held it up for her to see.

"It's nothing to be afraid of," he said gently. "They don't bite or sting or anything."

"I'm not afraid." She kept her feet far away and leaned a little closer. Eric turned the animal on its back. It curled up as far as it could, bringing the tail spike up protectively. Tess saw a lot of scratchy-looking feet and not much else. "I like it better right side up," she said. Eric obediently turned the crab. Then he carried it over the sand and up into the open front of the shack. Its feet kept patiently walking while he did.

"Here we are," he said, as Tess climbed the two sagging steps up onto the sandy floor. Eric set the crab down and sat on the top step. The crab waited for a moment and then began moving very slowly along the unaccustomed wood.

"Shouldn't we put it back?" she asked.

"Eric'll put it back," Harry said. His voice was gentle. He sat down on the step by Eric and looked fondly at the little armored animal between them. "What do you think of the beach house?" he asked. Tess took her eyes from the horseshoe crab and looked around. The shack was square and the size of a small room in an ordinary house. Its peaked roof extended to make a little porch over the steps. There was an empty window at the back, with trees and vines growing up close, and another window at one side. At the other side there was a square opening in the wall, where once there might have been a fireplace. The floor and walls were bare.

"Where did you sleep?" she asked Eric.

"On the floor. In our sleeping bags."

"Weren't there ever any beds?" Eric shook his head. He watched the horseshoe crab again while Tess explored the shack, going quickly from wall to wall, like a wary cat. "We'd light a campfire out on the sand and dig clams and bake them in seaweed," he said.

"In seaweed?" Tess looked at the sodden brown masses of it lining the beach.

"Sure," Harry said. The horseshoe crab reached him and he lifted it and set it down facing the other way. Tess still looked doubtful. She crossed to the opposite wall, examining it for a long while. She stretched up, staring at a single board on a pale patch of wall.

"Eric?" she said.

"Yeah?" He was carefully turning the animal around again, sending it back to Harry.

"There's something written here."

"Is there?" Eric said. "Can you read it?" Tess stared at the wood. There were two neat lines of pencil script. She read, " 'Forty yards East, Two hundred and thirty yards South.' "

"Well, well," said Harry. Tess looked at them both. They both looked back innocently.

"What is it?" she asked.

"Oh, a treasure map," Eric said.

"A treasure map." Her eyes widened hugely. "A real treasure map?" She stared again at the wall. "But if it's a treasure map . . . didn't you follow it and find out? Look, it's real simple. Forty yards east . . . which way's east from here, Eric?" He started to laugh, but Harry leaned forward and pointed with his cane toward his left. She looked at him uncertainly, and he nodded encouragement.

"Watch out for poison ivy," he shouted as she scrambled past them down onto the sand. Her brow furrowed with concentration, she began counting carefully exaggerated paces into the viney woods.

Eric buried his face in his hand. When she was out of sight, he said, "Harry, you never change."

"Ah, she'll have fun. You kids were always convinced you'd find treasure down here." The horseshoe crab bumped its blind brown hoof into his leg. He lifted it and faced it toward the dark interior of the shack. It scrabbled steadily away, and he leaned forward on his cane, prodding the soft sand. "And what about you, Eric?" he asked then. "What do you want to do?"

Eric reached down and picked up a broken shell from the sand. He turned it over, running his fingers across the pearly interior. "I'm going back to the Coast, Harry," he said.

"All right," Harry nodded, pushing the cane through the sand, making a furrow. "And what are you going to do when you get there?"

Eric said, "I know a guy building houses in Sacramento. I can probably get a job with him." He paused, "I'll find something."

"Yeah, I'm sure you will. But I'm asking you what you asked Tess. What are you going to do, Eric?"

Eric looked up, smiling sideways at Harry. "You mean when I grow up?"

Harry laughed. "If that's how you want to put it," he said. Eric dropped the shell, picked up another, and closed a fist around it.

"I don't know, Harry," he said. "I'd been thinking." He stopped suddenly and then started again. "For a while I'd been thinking I'd go back to school. I'd like to teach. I'd really like to teach."

"What, history?"

"Yeah," he said softly. He opened his fist and studied the shell. "I'd love that. History. English." Then he shook his head. "I don't know anymore, Harry." He dropped the shell lightly onto the sand. Harry reached out and tapped it with his cane. He drew it toward himself and picked it up.

"Important thing, work," he said. "The trouble with my kind of work is you got to quit before you get too old to know it's time to quit. So I quit. But I miss it, and I still don't feel old. I am old. But I don't feel old. My body feels old. I don't." He rubbed the shell thoughtfully and looked up at Eric. "Miriam's gotten old," he said. "That bothers me. You get used to the idea of it happening to yourself. I wasn't expecting it to happen to her."

He tossed the shell down into a heap of seaweed. "She goes to a Golden Age club," he said. "They do Golden Age aerobics and they make pottery together. Then they can't think what to do with it. They didn't want to make pottery when they were young, so why do it now?" He smiled wryly at Eric. "Sara brings her home, and she always comes out of the car carrying something. Like the kids, when they were in kindergarten." He paused. "Like the kids." He looked straight ahead at the water. "Your dad's got a lousy heart, Eric. He isn't going to last forever."

Eric put his hands flat on the sandy floor. "I can't stay, Harry," he said. "I told you. I'm going back to the Coast." He drew in his legs and stood up.

"Sit down," Harry said. "I'm talking to you." Eric sat back down, but he turned away from Harry and looked bleakly out at the bay. They sat then in silence. Behind them, the horseshoe crab ran out of floor and resorted to marching in place, its clawed feet scratching, its brown shell pressed doggedly against the wall.

—

TESS CAME RUNNING BACK through the woods and burst out into the bright sunshine of the beach. "Eric," she shouted. "It's impossible. It doesn't work." She stopped suddenly, seeing them sitting there together, but quiet and somehow also apart. "Eric?" she said warily. "Is something wrong?"

He raised his head and looked at Harry for a brief moment before he spoke to her. "No, Tess. Nothing's wrong. What's the problem?"

"The treasure map. It can't be right. It doesn't work." He smiled slightly, but he looked sad. "The treasure would be under the water." She pointed quickly at the bay. "Two hundred and thirty yards south." She paused. "That's south. Isn't it?" He nodded. She furrowed her brow.

"I'm sorry, Tess," he said, "there's a trick." He sounded tired.

"What trick?" She squinted out at the bay and then looked back at him. She suddenly felt childish and silly. "Did you just write it there or something?" Eric shook his head.

"The shack is the trick, Tess," Harry said. "It wasn't here when the message was written. The message belongs somewhere else."

Tess blinked, baffled. "Where was it?" she said. "How did it get here?"

"It floated." She stared at Harry, but he just grinned. "It floated across the bay in the great hurricane of 'thirty-eight. Eric's grandfather found it washed up on his beach the next morning. He had it set up on blocks and used it ever after."

"A house floated?" She looked from Harry to Eric.

Eric said, "Sure."

Tess looked around her at the old wooden walls, the roof trusses above, the shingled roof with chinks of sunlight coming through. She pictured it floating, an ark, the horseshoe crab riding along in it on the bay. She looked back at Eric. "Why didn't you tell me?" she said unhappily.

Harry said, "He wanted to. I wouldn't let him." He shrugged, "Anyhow, you had fun looking, didn't you?"

She tilted her head, looked at the shack and then at the dark woods. She nodded then, slowly, and smiled. "Yeah. It was fun." Then she said, "That thing is stuck." She pointed uneasily at the horseshoe crab pursuing its frustrated course.

Eric looked over his shoulder, saw the animal, and said gently, "We'll put him back now." But he looked at Harry before he moved. Harry returned an amiable grin and raised one hand, palm upward. Eric stood up and walked into the shack to the dim back wall and picked up the horseshoe crab. He turned, holding it in both hands, and looked up at the pale patch of wood where Tess had found the writing.

"Did it really last that long, Harry?" he said. "That's more than fifty years."

"It was covered," Harry said. "There was a cupboard where there's that light patch on the wall. Then somebody took it down, when you were kids, and found the writing behind it."

"That's still forty years."

Harry shrugged. "It's sheltered. Dry. Why not?" Eric still stood, holding the sea animal and looking at the wall.

"I always wondered what it really was."

"A treasure map. I told you."

Eric smiled faintly, "Didn't you just."

"It was, Eric," Harry said earnestly. He rested back on one

elbow, twisting around. "Rum runners. The island was a smuggler's paradise during Prohibition." He grinned suddenly, "You gotta trust me a little, you know. I don't lie to you."

Eric leaned against the wall with the writing for a long while, watching Harry and saying nothing. Then he straightened up and carried the horseshoe crab out of the shack and into the sunlight on the beach. Tess followed him as he took it to the edge of the water, but Harry remained, sitting on the steps, drawing lines with his cane in the sand.

When Eric set the horseshoe crab down, it walked steadfastly into the waves and submerged itself. Tess watched, until it was only a dark shape beneath the water.

"Does he swim?" she asked.

"I think he just walks around on the bottom."

She watched a moment longer and then said, "Good-bye, horseshoe crab."

Eric laughed. He took her hand. "We'd better go back and see if they've found you a costume for Halloween."

"It doesn't matter," Tess said slowly. "I'll use one of Sara's pumpkins or something." She stood holding his hand and looking at the opaque waters of the bay. "Eric?"

"Yes."

"Wouldn't she have called you?" she said.

"Who?" he asked, and then drew in his breath. "Do you mean Molly, Tess?"

"Uh-huh," she said. She held onto his hand very tightly and said in a hurried, unhappy voice, "I've been thinking about it a lot while I was in the woods. A whole lot. And I just kind of know, if it was me, no matter who had kidnapped me, sooner or later, I'd get away to a phone and call my mom."

Eric was silent for a long while, still holding her hand. He said then, "It might have been difficult, Tess. They might have kept her somewhere where there weren't any phones."

"For years?" Tess said in the same unhappy voice. Eric let go of her hand, but in a gentle way that showed he wasn't angry. He turned to face her, looking down.

"Well, maybe for quite a while. Until enough time passed . . ."

"For what?" Tess asked, puzzled.

"Enough time to forget . . . to change the way she felt about us. About them. People do change, Tess. People who are kidnapped are very vulnerable. They come to rely on their kidnappers so much . . . they spend so much time with them, they can actually grow to like them, you know."

"You mean she just forgot about you?"

Eric said nothing. He turned away and looked out at the bay. Tess watched, baffled, and then turned around. Harry was silent too, watching intently. "Well, in a way," Eric said finally. "Part of her mind might forget." He crouched down on the sand, lifting a whitened twig of driftwood from the mound of seaweed. He drew a wavery line in the sand. "Our minds are funny things, Tess," he said. She sat down too, comfortably cross-legged, with her elbow on her knee, her chin on her hand. She studied him a long while before she answered.

"Little kids might forget, Eric. Molly wasn't a little kid. She was almost my age. I wouldn't forget my mom ever." He looked up from the twig and the sand. His eyes were brilliant, mirroring all the blue and sunlight, the pupils tiny.

"You might, Tess. You don't know."

"I do know," she said solemnly. "I'd find a way. I'd sneak out, get to a phone. I'd call my mom. Or if I couldn't find her, I'd call one of those radio stations that ask you to phone in with problems. I'd try anyhow. As long as I was alive, I'd keep trying." He turned away.

"You're different," he said. "You're not like Molly."

"You said I was just like her about school. I bet I'm a lot like her. She was my cousin."

Eric shook his head. "You're different," he said again. He turned his face away, and then quite suddenly dropped his head down onto his folded arms. "You're different," he said a third time, in a choked, muffled voice. Tess watched uncertainly.

"Eric?" He did not answer. "I might be wrong," she said encouragingly. "I'm just a kid. I'm wrong a lot." He still did not answer, and sudenly she became frightened and looked up to Harry for help. The old man sat slowly trawling the sand with his cane and watching them both in silence. When she started to speak, he raised his hand and quietly shook his head. She watched, bewildered. Harry smiled at her gently.

"He's all right, kid," he said, at last.

———

MARTIN PUT OFF TALKING to his mother until late in the afternoon. The family were already gathering in Sara's studio for the show. Little girls in orange tulle, their hair tied back with the sweet severity of dancers, chased each other around the house. Out on the lawn they hid in the rhododendrons, squealed in piles of bright leaves, clambered in and out of the station wagons parked in the drive. Sara, prim in black skirt and sweater, wiped noses and adjusted costumes and greeted arriving parents on the porch. Martin left her separating two warring sisters and retreated down the long corridor to the kitchen.

Miriam was there alone, surrounded by bowls of popcorn and apples, filling orange paper napkins with candy corn. "I forgot the trick-or-treaters," she said as Martin entered. "Tell Sara I'm just coming."

"Mom, you can't use those," Martin said.

"What? What can't I use?" Miriam looked vague, balancing a paper napkin in one hand, a flour scoop full of candies in the other.

"The candies. They're unwrapped. And the apples, for that matter."

"So, I'm wrapping them."

"But they're not wrapped candies, Mom. The parents won't . . ."

"Martin, I've always used these," Miriam said.

Martin shrugged. He took a handful of popcorn and stuffed it clumsily into his mouth. He leaned against a counter and surveyed the array of bowls. "You expecting an army?" He helped himself to more popcorn, watched her moodily for a few more moments, and then said, "Look, Mom, I don't quite know how to put this. I mean, I know it's hard for you sometimes and I know you don't mean any harm, but could you just once maybe think before you say something like that again?"

"Like what?" Miriam dropped a half-filled napkin onto the table. "What did I say?"

"Mom," Martin said wearily, "you know."

"Know? What should I know?"

"About Molly, Mom. What you said on the porch about Molly. About Tess looking like Molly."

Miriam picked up the napkin and shoveled in a scoop of candies. "But she does," she said. "She looks just like her. Anyone can see that."

Martin lowered his head and studied the floor at his feet. "Yeah, Mom," he said. "Yeah." He looked up sharply. "Mom, Eric didn't need to hear that." She met his eyes and her own slid away.

"He must see it too, Martin. He's not blind."

"I know. I know. He sees it. Okay. He still doesn't need us talking about it." She tightened her mouth stubbornly and picked up another napkin. "Mom," Martin said quietly, "Eric's maybe a little unstable just now? Right?"

"Unstable?" Miriam said. "What's unstable?"

Martin gave her another long, weary look and then reached for a third handful of popcorn. His fingers closed on it and then opened again, and his hand came away from the bowl empty. "Mom, why are we tiptoeing around this? You're a professional." His voice cracked. He held his hands up and dropped his face into them for a moment and then looked up at her. "Eric's insane, Mom. We can't treat him like a normal person anymore."

Miriam pursed her lips and looked displeased. She twisted the paper napkin awkwardly and placed it with a sloppy heap of others on a tray. "Because he hasn't given up hope?" Her dark eyes were sharp. Martin looked away. Miriam shrugged. "So when does hope become insanity?"

Martin sighed. He leaned heavily against the counter, his shoulders slumped. He turned his head and looked out the window at the tall, bright trees. "You tell me, Mom," he said. "You tell me." Then he looked suddenly back into the room and met her eyes. "No," he said. "No. I'll tell you. When hope defies all rational logic. All. Insanity begins there."

Miriam stood quietly, her hand smoothing a new paper napkin. Then she shrugged. "So does religion," she said.

"Well?" Martin returned at once. Miriam looked away. "Well?" he said louder.

She put down the napkin, unused. "You're so like your father," she said. "He knows all about God and the universe too." She sighed then, looking down at the napkin. "Poor Eric," she said. "Such a tragedy."

———

TESS, IN THE HALLWAY outside the kitchen door, stopped at the word "tragedy" and, hesitating, stood still. She held the ghost costume bunched up in her arms, a tail of the sheet trailing. She had been looking for Eric to show him what her mother and Seth had found for her while she was with him at the beach. She knew Eric wasn't in the kitchen because they were talking about him, but she stayed there, holding the sheet, outside the door. Whenever the adults talked about Eric, he became a person utterly unlike the person she knew. She felt as if she'd missed something important, like a whole week of school, without even knowing. She leaned against the door, breathing softly, and heard Miriam say in a low voice, "We'll pay for this forever, Martin."

"Pay?" Martin sounded puzzled, "What are you talking about?"

"Over and over I ask myself, what did we do to deserve this?"

"Deserve this?" Martin's voice was louder. "Nobody deserves this. Least of all Eric," he added quietly.

Miriam sighed heavily, "And always I come back to just one thing." She seemed not to have heard Martin at all.

"What is this, Mom?" he said. His voice was low and suspicious, "What are you saying?"

"It was wrong, Martin."

"What?"

"What your father did for you. It was wrong."

Tess wriggled closer to the door. Her ear, flat against it, hurt like it did when she talked too long on the phone. She heard her Uncle Martin mutter something and then say, louder, "Now wait. Wait a moment."

"Nothing went right in this family after that. We all came apart."

"Crap," Martin said. "That's crap. Lots of good things happened. Annie and me. Our children."

"Seth left," Miriam said. "Joanna left." Tess jerked at the sound of her mother's name, her ear scraping against the door. "And then Eric." Miriam sighed once more and then said quietly, "Everyone had such hopes for Eric. Such hopes."

"What about me?" Martin shouted. "Didn't anyone have hopes for me?"

Instead of answering, Miriam said, "We're being punished and we'll pay for this forever." There was a bang, a hand, or a fist, on the table.

"Crap," Martin said again. "Crap."

"We offended God."

"Jesus H. Christ, Mom. You don't believe in God."

"Who ever asked me what I believed? Who?"

There was another bang. Tess winced against the door. Martin shouted, "You pride yourself on your intellect all your life and you still have to find some bastard in the sky to pin this on? What's the matter with you?" There was a silence and then Martin's voice came softer. "I'm sorry, I'm sorry, Mom. Look. Bad things happen. Life's a bitch. But you just cannot believe in that kind of god."

"Who are we to say what kind of god God is?"

"Not a vengeful, petty, ugly god who'd punish someone through their children. And not even get the right person. Why not my child? Why not Danya or David?"

"Hush," Miriam murmured. "Don't say it."

"Or why not Tess? That would be fairer anyhow."

Tess felt something scuttle in her chest, blindly, like the horseshoe crab.

"God forbid. Be quiet."

"Why Eric's child? Eric didn't do anything. Dina didn't do anything."

"Who knows? Maybe God's too subtle for you."

"Or maybe he has lousy aim." There was a clatter, a chair pushed hurriedly against the table. Martin's voice was low and angry. "Don't you do this to me. Don't switch the blame for this onto me. You approved. I know you approved. You wanted me at Ann Arbor like Dad. The whole family did. This was a family decision." He drew in his breath and said bitterly, "You told me it was the right thing. I didn't find it easy, either. You told me it wasn't wrong."

After a long while Miriam said, "I thought a lot of things weren't wrong when I was young."

"And now that you're old and it won't affect you, you're free to join the Moral Majority?"

"I don't know, Martin. I believed in it when I was young. When I was young the alternative was knitting needles and blood." Tess jerked her stinging ear from the door. She clutched the ghost costume tight, her eyes squeezed shut. Then she shook the sheet open and flung it over her head, peering out at the dark hallway from the safety of its eyeholes. "I fought for this thing, Martin," Miriam shouted. "Your father risked his career for you. You can't lecture us about Moral Majorities."

"And now you want to go back to knitting needles."

"*No.* I'm just. Oh, Martin, I'm just tired."

Martin's voice said quietly, "We agreed. We all agreed. Joanna agreed too. She didn't want a baby any more than I did."

Tess stood rigid in her ghost costume, her hands out straight. Then she banged the door hard with her fist and burst through it. "Boo!" she shouted wildly, "Boo! Boo!"

Lovers

JOANNA STALKED THROUGH the kitchen where Miriam and Annie were packing sandwiches, pickles, fruit, and cookies into a row of plastic boxes. "Tess?" she called, leaning through the doorway to the back porch, "You out here, Tess?"

"I haven't seen her," Annie said, closing a box. "I don't think she came through this way." She picked up an open thermos. "I've got one of black coffee, two regular, and one of hot water for tea. Anything you want different?"

"No, fine." Joanna closed the back kitchen door and leaned against it, exasperated.

"What about Tess? Soda, or maybe cocoa; it's going to be cold."

"Oh, anything, Annie. Whatever we choose, she's going to moan about it. If," Joanna added, "she deigns to grace us with her presence at all. Damn. Where is she?"

"She doesn't want the picnic?" Miriam asked.

"Of course she does, Miriam," Annie said soothingly.

"Yesterday she was all excited. She wanted to see the ocean."

"That was yesterday," Joanna said. "Two days of good nature from Tess are apparently more than we can ask." Annie laughed gently. Miriam looked worried.

"Maybe we shouldn't go."

"Of course we're going," Joanna said. "And so," she added with menace, "is Tess."

Joanna ran up the back stairs again and walked down the corridor, glancing quickly into the family bathroom, the shower room, and then the guest bedroom that Eric was using. Eric's small, scruffy sports bag sat beside folded clothes on the ottoman.

The bed was neatly made. One of Tess's computer magazines was open on the floor, as if she'd been lying there reading it, but the room was empty. Joanna crossed the corridor and slammed open Tess's bedroom door. That room, too, was empty. Tess's knapsack sprawled on its back on the floor, like a stranded beetle, clothes tumbling out. Some dirty white sports socks and a pair of underpants were scattered beside it. A half-empty glass of flat Pepsi sat beside the unmade bed. In a corner by the dressing table was a crumpled ball of white, Tess's abandoned ghost costume left exactly where she'd tossed it on the floor. Joanna picked it up, shook it out, and stared at it a moment before gathering it into rough folds.

"You want me, Mom?" Tess was standing in the doorway. When Joanna looked up, her daughter's eyes slid away toward the wall.

"Where were you?" Joanna said, grasping the folded sheet angrily. Tess sidled sideways, slipping into the room, her back against the wall. Her glance flickered to Joanna and dropped away again.

"In the attic."

"The attic," Joanna said. "Great. You're not dressed. You haven't even had breakfast, and the rest of us are almost ready to go." She made another rough fold in the sheet.

"I'm sorry."

"You don't sound it. And while we're at it, since you were going to the attic, why didn't you put this away? I asked you yesterday."

"I was scared."

"What? You weren't scared to *go* to the attic, but you were scared to take this? Tess . . ."

"I was scared yesterday." Tess looked up and suddenly jumped forward and snatched at the sheet. Joanna held onto it. "Well, give it to me, and I'll put it away if it's so important."

"Tess," Joanna said coldly. "It's not important. It wasn't important yesterday. What was important was the fuss you made, the trouble everyone went to, and then the way you behaved."

"I said I was sorry."

"First everyone went all around the stores with you," Joanna said, ignoring her. "Then Sara offered to make you something.

And finally Seth and I got this down from the attic for you. Miriam searched the whole house to find a shopping bag you considered big enough. Seth and I and Eric each offered to go out with you . . ."

"I just didn't want to go any longer."

"That's not an excuse."

"Well, sorry. Sorry. *Sorry.* What else can I say, for crap's sake?"

"I am sick of your damned swearing."

"I'm sick of yours."

Joanna raised her hand and dropped it as Tess slid sideways along the wall. "And that's only part of it," she said. "You were totally obnoxious to Sara, walking out in the middle of her show."

"It was boring. A whole bunch of spoiled little kids expecting everybody to applaud because they could hop around in a circle."

"They're six years old, and it's more than you could do now."

"Thank God. I'd kill myself first, anyhow. I was doing them a favor walking out. I could have sat there and made fun of them instead."

Joanna's eyes narrowed. "Consider yourself lucky you didn't. And by the way, your performance at supper was obnoxious too. Everybody noticed it. Even Eric noticed it."

"He did not," Tess shouted, jolted out of her sullen monotone. "He didn't."

"He couldn't miss it."

"He didn't say I was obnoxious. He didn't. You're lying."

Joanna balled up the sheet in her hands and suddenly tossed it back on the floor. Tess stared uneasily. "Okay. He didn't. The truth is I don't give a shit. I'm sick to the teeth of you, kid. Just smarten up the act. Just do it." She turned wearily. Tess was staring, still, her eyes bright, her mouth trembling. Joanna looked back. She said, "If you really care so much what Eric thinks, I suggest you get dressed and get downstairs. It was Eric who promised to take you to the ocean, not me."

—

TESS CAME DOWN at the last possible moment, shrugging into her pink hooded sweatshirt. She looked around warily, took in the three waiting cars, and scuttled into the one farthest from her mother. Joanna watched a moment and then climbed into the front seat of Seth's rented Oldsmobile.

"Where's Tess?" he asked.

"With Sara and Eric. God help them," Joanna said. "At least that spares your mom and dad," she added as the three cars pulled out of the driveway in convoy. Martin and Annie were in the lead with the elder Levines side by side in their backseat.

"Having a rough time?" Seth asked.

"Horrendous. I just don't know . . . she was perfectly all right, and then . . . is this adolescence? Already?"

"They say it starts younger and younger. Particularly in America. Good nutrition."

"I'll stop feeding her."

He reached across the seat with his right hand and clasped hers. "Hang in there. It's just another ten years."

"Oh, shit." He laughed and kept holding her hand. She thought suddenly of Mike Hewitt pulling his hand away when they walked in the mountains, and felt oddly pleased to be holding Seth's. Pleased also to be riding, relaxed, in the passenger seat. "Oh, nice," she said, enjoying the fall sunlight. He didn't look toward her, but she saw a smile twitch at the corners of his mouth. "When are you going back, Seth?" she asked.

"Back?"

"To Italy."

"Oh." He turned the car easily, one-handedly following Martin through a junction. He shrugged. "I haven't thought."

She was quiet for a while and said eventually, "It must be lovely to be that free." She closed her eyes, thinking what it would be like to have enough money to stop worrying about it, a job from which you could come and go, no one's needs but your own. "It's like being perpetually young, isn't it? Like we all were once." He laughed again.

"I'm not complaining," he said honestly. But after a while he added, "Freedom's the flipside of loneliness, Jo. It's that, too." She opened her eyes and lifted her head slightly to look at him.

"Hardly for you, Seth."

"Sometimes," he said with the same candor. "Between projects, when I'm not traveling or working. When Maria-Luisa and her children go to Milan to stay with her sister."

"Maria who?"

"Maria-Luisa. She's my housekeeper, Jo. I love her. And her children. And her husband. But they have their own lives."

"So have you."

"Mine isn't as real as theirs." He paused and said, fastidiously correct, "It is, sometimes. It depends . . ." He slipped his hand free to steady the wheel on a corner. "I'm making things sound a bit bleak. I'll be honest, Jo. The woman I was living with walked out at the beginning of July. I'm a bit lonely just now, that's all. You're getting me at a bad time."

"Oh. Oh, I see." Joanna looked out the window at the marsh-and-reed approach to Smith Point, but saw instead the pink-painted walls and linoleum floor of the attic room. She could feel the subtlety of Seth's hand through her flannel shirt as if he were touching her now. She said in a stiff, bright voice, "Was she Italian?"

"Who, Julia? No, American, actually."

"Oh, American," Joanna said, disappointed somehow, as if an Italian lover was perhaps less consequential.

"I met her at Cannes, two years ago. She was in a film a friend of mine was showing."

"An actress?"

"Yes. Yes, she is. Quite a good actress too." Joanna felt another disappointment, a foolish one. Seth Levine was hardly likely to take up with a bimbo, American or Italian. "Sweet girl," Seth said, a little regretfully.

"So what happened?" Joanna heard an undeniable edge in her own voice. If Seth heard it too, he didn't acknowledge it.

"Oh, the usual. I'm a bastard to live with, Jo."

"Are you?" she asked, looking back at him.

"Oh yes. There's the traveling for a start. And when I'm working I'm pretty antisocial. And, oh, I don't know, sometimes I just need to be alone . . . she found it hard."

Joanna thought and said evenly, "Since the traveling is your work and you can hardly write in the middle of a party, it doesn't sound totally unreasonable."

"Try telling that to a twenty-year-old."

"Twenty!" She looked up, eyes wide. "*Seth.*"

"Well, twenty-one. When she left." He looked embarrassed. "Still."

"Well, I didn't know what age she was. You know those Valley girls, they grow up fast. By the time she told me, we were already in the sack." Joanna looked at him again and then laughed softly.

"What's funny?"

"You. I've never heard you on the defensive before. You sound like Martin." She smiled. "Would it have made a difference if you'd known?"

"Oh, of course it would. But once we were involved . . . to tell the truth, Jo, we got on quite well. If the place wasn't so isolated, and if I had a different job . . ." He shrugged. "Who knows? The truth is, that's the way life works. If you're still single at my age, you find yourself with younger people."

"I know," Joanna said.

He looked up, curious. "You too?" She nodded.

"Same problems. A lot of good sex. And not enough of anything else." She sighed, "I don't really blame Tess for resenting them. At best, they haven't got a lot to offer her. At worst, they treat her like a rival."

Seth glanced sideways and then back to the road. "She needs a father, Jo."

Joanna turned to stare at him. "Now you really sound like Martin."

"Don't get angry. I'm not passing judgment. Just making an observation."

"A pretty flawed one, Seth. Tess needs men like she needs a hole in her head."

"You haven't given her men. You've given her boys. You've just said so." He reached to take her hand. She pulled hers away. "Jo, I'm trying to help."

"Well, you can't. No one can. She's my daughter and my problem. I had her alone and I'll raise her alone and to hell with you all."

Seth laughed quietly, "Yeah, Jo, nothing ever changes."

"What?"

"Nothing." He put both hands back on the wheel as the car mounted the bridge, soaring over the white-capped waters of the bay and onto the windblown strip of barrier beach.

———

"I LIKED IT BETTER when there was the ferry," Miriam said. "Remember, Harry?"

"Sure."

"What ferry?" Martin said.

"Before they built the bridge. We used to take the ferry."

"We never came here before the bridge," Martin said.

"Yes, we did."

"We went to the *Pines* on the ferry. Or Leja Beach. We went to Leja Beach on the ferry. Not here."

"We went here," Miriam said. "You forget."

"You've confused it, Mom. Why would we come all the way here for a ferry?"

"We did, Martin."

"We didn't."

"Martin . . ." Annie said gently. "Your mother says you did."

"Sure, Mom," Martin said. "I remember."

"You think I'm wrong . . ."

"I said I remember."

"This isn't something I've forgotten. Harry? Tell him."

"Your mother's right."

"I said . . ."

"How should you remember, anyhow? You were just a little boy," Miriam said sharply. She leaned forward and tapped Annie on the shoulder as Martin parked the car in the center of the beach parking lot. "Your mother and I used to come here during the War, when Harry and your Dad were overseas. We'd pick beach plums for jelly. We'd take the carriages over on the ferry, Eric and Martin with a canopy from the sun. You toddling with a little sun hat . . ." She paused and said softly, "To think, Sara and Jo and Seth not even gleams in their daddies' eyes."

"*I* had a gleam in my eye," Harry said. "All across the South Pacific." Miriam giggled.

"Oh, there's Sara and Eric. They've parked way over there."

The parking lot was huge and empty, with a gathering of seagulls in its center and a strong north wind rippling pools of standing rainwater. Annie helped Harry out, and they walked slowly across the tarmac to where Eric and Sara were unloading picnic baskets and blankets from their trunk; but Miriam sat in the car with Martin. She watched Tess standing idly to one side, head down, one toe prodding something on the ground, her blond hair whipping in long, tangled strands. "That's a very unhappy child," Miriam said uneasily.

"Are you surprised?" said Martin.

"She didn't hear anything. How could she hear anything?"

"She heard every word." Martin opened his door wearily and stepped out into the wintery wind.

—

THEY GATHERED IN A GROUP by Martin's car, taking out the picnic baskets and shopping bags, the old army blankets and the two folding chairs for Miriam and Harry.

"I've brought a couple of towels, if anyone wants to swim," Sara said.

"Swim!" Martin said. "You're crazy."

"Tess might want to," Sara said. "Kids don't feel the cold."

"This kid does," Tess said, wrapping her arms around herself and tucking her elbows in tight. "It's freezing."

"You want a sweater?" Miriam said. "I brought an extra sweater." Tess shook her head. Miriam turned to Joanna. "She should have a sweater."

"She'll tell us if she's cold," Joanna said. She watched her daughter.

Tess looked away. They walked, clustered together with their various burdens, toward the underpass that led to the beach. Tess, running to warm herself, orbited them like an unstable asteroid, swinging out to avoid Joanna, ducking close to brush familiarly against Eric's arm. She stopped and looked out to the water they had crossed.

"Is *that* the ocean?" she asked.

"No," Eric said, "that's still the bay. The ocean's over on this side." He grinned as she jogged in place, slapping her hands against her upper arms. "Come on, I'll race you."

"Yo!" Tess shouted. "All right." She ran off down the path. Seth took Eric's shopping bag full of thermoses and six-packs, and Eric sprinted after Tess. He caught up with her in three long strides, then lagged carefully behind. Tess looked over her shoulder.

"Don't look back," Sara shouted. "Keep going."

"Go for it," Seth called. Tess bent forward and put on a burst of speed, disappearing into the underpass. Eric loped easily after her.

"Well, he's not feeling *his* age," Annie said. Martin looked grumpy.

"Good little runner, your daughter," Harry Levine said to Joanna.

"She is," Joanna said, surprised. "God knows how. She just lies around her room all day."

"At that age, you can get away with anything," Sara said wistfully. "I have to train two hours a day just to keep up with yesterday." She was watching Tess and Eric, distant figures, glimpsed between sand dunes, still running. "How nice, the way she gets on with Eric."

"At least she gets on with somebody."

Sara glanced sideways, shifting the folded blankets she carried to the other arm. "You're having problems, aren't you?"

"Shows, does it?" Joanna said wryly. She reached for the basket. Sara was juggling with the blankets. "Here, let me, I've only got this bag." Sara smiled and acquiesced. Joanna readjusted her own load, tossed her windblown hair back, and said, "There's usually some problem, but it's generally pretty obvious what. This time I'm in deep shit and I have no idea even, what I've done."

Sara shrugged. "Probably hormones," she said easily.

❦

"THAT'S THE OCEAN," Tess said. She stopped running and stood on the empty terrace of the big, darkened snack bar, holding her hair back with her hand and staring at her first glimpse of rolling blue surf. "That has to be it."

"That's it," Eric said.

"Oh, wow. Oh great. It's great."

"Big."

"Yeah."

"Come on down." He took her hand and they walked past the deserted, wet picnic tables, raising a flock of screaming gulls. At the foot of the steps leading down to the beach, Tess broke into a run again. Eric followed, walking across the wide, wintry strand.

He watched her dart across the sand, race down to the surf, and run back up just ahead of the curling white foam. She stopped, sat quickly, pulled off her sneakers and her socks, flung them carelessly aside, and ran barefoot into the surf. Eric walked to where she'd left the shoes and picked them up. She ran off down the shining wet sand, the pink of her tracksuit shimmering in the reflection of the blue and white sky. He walked on, patiently, carrying the shoes, and she flitted back and forth, in and out of the water, until they were far down the beach and the only sounds were the surf and the mewing of gulls.

⚓

"Do you think it bothers him?" Miriam asked, "Coming back here again? They came here a lot, you know, Eric and the little girl. And Dina." She pronounced Dina's name oddly, isolated by a little space of silence.

"Yes, of course they would have," Joanna said thoughtfully. She finished setting up Miriam's yellow and red deck chair on the sand, and before she began on Harry's, straightened and stood watching her brother and her daughter, two dark figures against the sun, far down the bright beach. "No, I don't think it will. He's not like that. You remember, when I came back East with Tess as a baby, we all spent a week up at the camp. If ever there was a place he might never want to see again . . . but he was quite happy . . . maybe it's because he doesn't really believe . . ." She shrugged and turned back to the second chair. Harry watched her silently a while, and then joined in, wrestling with wood slats and canvas.

"That Dina," Miriam said coldly, settling herself in her chair. Harry sat down in his and patted her hand.

"Nice day," he said. "Nice day for a picnic."

"It's cold," Miriam said.

"Nice day for a November picnic," Harry said, grinning.

"November already," Miriam said, and Martin echoed, "November. Thanksgiving next, and then Christmas. Christ, where's the year gone?"

"Where have any of them gone?" Harry laughed.

"It's all Dina's fault," Miriam said.

"Miriam." Harry Levine smiled gently. Joanna was struck by how little he needed to say to get an effect. They were all quiet now, watching him. Miriam pulled her hand from under his.

"Don't Miriam me," she said. "I never liked her. She was a selfish girl. She thought only of herself."

"That's a bit hard," Annie said mildly. She stopped in the middle of setting out the plastic lunch boxes in a neat row. "You know, I forgot the mustard. I hope no one minds."

"Your mother agrees with me," Miriam said to Annie.

"She had nothing against Dina," Annie said, so lightly as to remove any sense of contradiction, but Miriam pursued.

"She agrees with me."

"What does it matter?" Martin said abruptly. "It's all history now. Who cares?"

"I care," Joanna said. She sat on her haunches, looking out across the sand, at the spray-misted horizon, where Tess and Eric were now so far away she could no longer define them among the lone figures of fishermen playing the surf. Seth stopped spreading a second army blanket and, still kneeling in the sand, looked up to her.

"Why?" he asked simply.

"Because," Joanna said, thinking carefully, "I think Miriam's right."

"See," Miriam said quickly.

Joanna continued evenly, "Not so much that anything's Dina's fault, but that Dina is the cause." Martin started to argue, but Joanna shook her head quickly and said, "She turned away from him. When he needed her to forgive him, she turned away."

"What was there to forgive?" Seth said. "Eric didn't do anything wrong. He didn't do anything Dina wouldn't have done. Or you, Jo. Or Annie and Martin. He let his kid go out to play. Who wouldn't?"

"But it *was* Eric," Joanna said. "It wasn't Dina. Or Annie. Or me. It was Eric. Eric lost her."

"That's crazy," Martin said. "No one ever said they blamed Eric for that."

"Dina did," said Sara. "Dina blamed Eric."

"She was jealous," Miriam said.

"What?" Martin said sharply. Annie saw his mouth tighten with the nervous irritation Miriam's confusions always triggered. "Jealous of who? Who had she to be jealous about?"

"Molly. She was jealous of Molly."

"Oh, Mom. She adored Molly. She was a devoted mother."

"She was jealous," Miriam said, unbudging. "She was always trying to get them apart. When Eric hugged his daughter, she'd push her way in between like a jealous three-year-old." She paused. "Selfish."

"Molly was Dina's own little girl," Martin said angrily. "She loved . . . Christ, if Dina could hear this, after everything she's been through."

Miriam sat firmly on her deck chair, her feet side by side, her shoes flat on the sand. She looked straight ahead at the blue ocean. "She was sexually jealous of her daughter," she said.

"Mom!" Martin's voice was thick with disgust.

"Martin," Annie said softly, "let your mother alone."

"Me? She's . . ."

"Leave her *alone*," Annie said.

"Mom, you want a sandwich?" Sara asked brightly. "Or a cup of coffee? How about a cup of coffee?"

"I'm right, Martin." Miriam patted Sara's arm absently, but looked at her son. "You can't dismiss everything I say just because I'm old. I haven't forgotten everything I ever knew. I was a clinical psychologist for thirty years, and I'm telling you, that relationship was dysfunctional. I saw that. I always saw that." Martin met her eyes, then dropped his and stood up. "Where are you going?" Miriam said.

"Down to the water."

"Martin."

"I want to look at the water." Annie tapped Miriam's arm, and when she looked around, handed her coffee in a plastic thermos cup.

"Let him go," she said with her wise smile. "He's tired. Things upset him."

"So? I'm tired too. I'm *old* and tired."

Seth got up quietly and followed his brother, jogging lightly so that he caught up before Martin reached the edge of the surf. They stood talking, mismatched in shape and size, as the sea ran in and out again. Annie, Sara, Joanna, and Miriam remained, handing coffee and sugar lumps and plastic spoons around in a circle. Harry sat in the middle. He grinned suddenly.

"Now, I like this. Four women all to myself. It's what I deserve."

———

"How far are we going?" Tess asked.

"As far as you want." Eric had taken his shoes and socks off too and was now carrying his as well as hers, walking barefoot along the cold white edge of the ocean.

"How far does it go?"

He laughed. "A long way. Longer than you'd want to walk. At least before lunch."

"How does it end?"

"It joins the mainland again, and then it goes out along the South Fork to Montauk Point. There's a lighthouse."

"Is Europe out there?" Tess said, pointing out over the incoming Atlantic.

"No. That's South that way. The next thing that way is Brazil. Europe's there." He pointed eastward into the white haze of spray and morning sun.

"Have you been there?"

"Europe? No." He paused. "I'd love to go."

"My mom hasn't either. The only place she's been outside of America is Canada. And Mexico. She went to Mexico once," she said. "But that's all."

"America's a big place, Tess. You can spend a lot of time going around America."

"Yeah," she said, unconvinced. "Have you ever been out of America?"

Eric laughed softly, "Not aside from Uncle Sam's guided tour of Southeast Asia," he said.

"I forgot about that." Tess stopped walking. She looked at him curiously. "Weren't you against the war?"

"No."

"You were for it?" Tess asked, slightly incredulous.

"I wasn't for it, Tess." He leaned over and picked up a flat white stone, turning it over in his hand. "I believed in my country. If it asked me to do something, I thought I should. Like my dad in World War Two."

"My mom was against the war," Tess said. Eric laughed again and threw the stone, flat-sided, skipping it across the back of a wave.

"Oh, I know that," he said.

"Did you fight about it?" Tess asked.

"Yes."

"Did she try to stop you going?"

"Oh yes."

"And you went anyhow."

"Yes."

"Was she mad at you?"

He sighed and picked up another stone, "I suppose she must have been." He studied the stone carefully, finding its weight and balance before throwing it with a sharp flick of his wrist. It skipped three times. Tess cheered. "She moved heaven and earth to stop me, Tess, until the day I went. Then for two solid years she wrote the letters that kept me alive." Tess stared at him, her forehead lined, her eyes squinting against the sun.

"Eric?"

He didn't look at her, but said, "Yeah, Tess?"

"Who was right about the war?" He was quiet for a long while, then turned and smiled, just when she thought he was going to be angry.

"No one, Tess. We were all of us wrong."

They continued walking, still eastward, away from the others. She said then, looking down at the sand, "Where was Martin during the war?"

"At med school. They were exempt." He paused to pick up a third stone. "But Martin agreed with me. He'd have gone if they'd asked him to." He studied the stone, then tossed it, discarded, into the sand. "Seth went to India. He had a bad knee," he added mildly. Once he had resented that, but now he was just glad that Seth had been so simply spared.

"Where was my mom?" He looked down at her, startled.

"Here. And at college. Why?"

"Eric, did my mom used to go out with Uncle Martin?" There was an intensity in her voice beyond the detached curiousity of her earlier questions.

Puzzled, he said casually, "Sure."

"He went out with my mom," Tess repeated. Her eyes were cold.

"For a year or two, Tess. Why?"

"I just wanted to know." The coldness remained, and she turned away and looked out at the sea.

"Tess, it was a long time ago. They were kids." He paused. "Nobody cares, now. They're all really good friends."

"That's okay," Tess said. She turned to him quickly. Her eyes were wet. She brushed them angrily with her pink sleeve. "I want to go back now," she said. She took her shoes from him so she could hold his hand. As soon as they faced westward again, they saw two figures walking toward them on the beach, but it was a long time before they could see who they were. Eric peered into the white glare.

"It's Seth and your mom," he said.

"Uh-huh," said Tess. He glanced down quickly. She was looking straight ahead. As they drew closer. Seth waved. Eric let go of Tess's hand briefly to wave back, then caught it easily again.

Then they stood together, a little group of four in the emptiness of sand, sky, and water. "How do you like it, Tess?" Joanna said.

"All right."

"All right." Joanna put one hand on her hip. "It's the *Atlantic Ocean*, sweetheart . . ."

"I said, all right." Tess, still holding Eric's hand, pivoted around so she was facing the water. Joanna said, "Annie and Sara have the sandwiches if you're hungry." Tess said nothing.

Seth clapped his hand lightly against Eric's arm as they passed each other. Joanna turned once to look back at her brother and her daughter as the two couples drew apart again. "This is a joke," she said. "This whole weekend was planned with one purpose—to try and give Eric some time to sort himself out. So far, all I've managed to do is dump my kid on him." Seth's hand brushed hers, their fingers tangling.

"The trouble with real life, Jo, is you never get a chance to do anything with just one purpose. There's always a hundred other purposes, and people, and needs in the way. I spend my life thinking if I could just get a clear run at things, I'd sort myself out." She looked across to him, surprised. His eyes, hidden behind his gold-rimmed sunglasses, gave no clues.

"I don't think of you needing to sort anything out, Seth. You seem to have things set up just fine."

"I'm drifting, Jo. The same as I've always done. Drifting in a richer sea, maybe, but drifting all the same. That's the real thing that went wrong between Julia and me. She wanted that simple, fair thing, a commitment, and I was too detached, too selfish and too uncertain to make one. And so she left."

"Maybe she wasn't the right one."

"Oh, I know she wasn't the right one, Jo, but maybe it's time to stop hanging around for the right one. Maybe it's time to take the bird in hand and be grateful."

"Not you," she said quietly. "You're an idealist."

He smiled wryly. "So what then? Am I condemned to a life of monkish solitude as a reward?" She laughed and punched him lightly with her free hand.

"Oh, stop, you're breaking my heart."

"Ah, fair return," he said with another slow smile. Joanna stopped walking. Their hands broke free as she turned to face him.

She stood, smiling slightly too, rubbing her chin with bent fingers, her hair blowing across her face. She caught it with her hand, holding it back.

"Let me get something straight, Seth," she said. "You keep tossing me these fishing lines and I just know if I pick up the bait I'm going to look pretty stupid, so why don't you stop, okay?"

"Why?" he said. "Why should you look stupid?"

"Because you're not serious, Seth."

He looked at her for a long while and then sat down, cross-legged, in the sand. He said, "When I'm dead and buried, you know what it's going to say on my gravestone? 'You're not serious, Seth.' Especially if you have anything to do with it."

"Come on," she said, smiling and kneeling in the sand beside him, "That's not fair."

"I say I'm lonely, and you don't believe me. I say I don't know where I'm going, and you don't believe me. I say I'm in love with you, and you don't believe me. Yes, I'm serious. I've always been serious. I was serious when I was sixteen years old."

"You were not."

"*See*," he said, almost angrily.

"When you were sixteen you were passionately in love with Marsha Lang. You used to commandeer me for long, pointless walks around town that always ended up going past her house. You were not in love with me."

"She was a cover. I got the walks, you see."

"Crap. After Marsha there was that blonde cheerleader, Patti or Peggy or whatever. You were going through your Aryan period."

"She looked like you."

"Oh, I wish."

"She did. Only more ordinary. I made love to her in the back of Martin's car and pretended it was you."

"You didn't."

"How the fuck do you know?" He took off his dark glasses. His eyes, lively and good-humored, were still full of sharp challenge. "How do you know? Tell me, huh?"

"You're making this all up."

"Am I? All of it? And why?"

"I don't know why." She looked away. "I wish you'd stop. You're upsetting me."

"I always did upset you, Jo. That's what you're trying to forget."

"I'm not trying to forget anything. There's nothing to forget."

"Oh yes, there is. There was a lot. Not just the walks, Jo. That whole year . . . sure, you were going out with Martin. But Martin was away at school, and that whole year we hung around together."

"You were like a brother."

He put his glasses back on and looked out to sea. "Well, Jo, I hope you never got up to with Eric what you got up to with me."

"That happened once."

"It happened more than once."

"Once. And it was no big deal. A bit of necking . . . Christ, I bet Tess has been up to more."

"I hope not," he said seriously.

"Well, really, Seth, there was never . . ."

"It doesn't matter, Jo. I still say there was a bit more than you're choosing to remember, but I know it didn't mean anything to you." He paused, stretching out on the sand, staring moodily at the surf through his dark glasses. "I knew it then. You were playing with me. You were horny and young. I was safe. I wouldn't tell Martin, and I wouldn't take it any further than you wanted . . ."

"You make me out to be some bitch."

"Oh no, Joanna," he said fervently. "It was harmless, innocent. We were so young. But I knew something else, and I knew it even then. I turned you on. And I turned you on again, yesterday, in the attic. And whatever went on between you and Martin, it was nothing, nothing compared to what you and I could have." She laughed lightly, half annoyed, half flattered.

"Well, are you that great a lover, Seth?"

"No. I'm quite an ordinary lover, Jo. But I love you the way no one ever has." He leaned over quite suddenly and kissed her. Surprised, she did not think to resist, and then did not want to.

It was a good kiss, thoughtful and sensual. It had been a long time since anyone had kissed her that way. She'd grown so used to the impatient kisses of perfunctory lovers, brief preparatory asides, with no more significance than a man throwing a saddle on a horse. She had pretty much given up on the pleasures of kissing.

"Let me make love to you," Seth said.

"What, now?"

"Sure." She looked around at the emptiness around them, astounded.

"Here?"

"Up in the dunes. Come on. They won't miss us."

"Seth . . ." she said, her eyes widening. "I don't believe you." She felt an abrupt and carnal yearning as she said it.

"Oh yes, you do," he said. He grinned, teasingly, and then stood up, extending his hand. "Come on," he said, "It's time for lunch."

They walked back down the beach, hand in hand. As they drew nearer the others she worried briefly about Tess seeing them like that, but dismissed the worry in a surge of rebellion. She was tired of Tess, tired of trying to please the unpleaseable and lift the endless deadweight of her moods. For one brief moment she longed for freedom—the first time ever since Tess was born. Ashamed, she pushed the thought out of her mind.

"Hey," Seth said suddenly. He bent quickly and lifted something from the sand. "Look at that." He held it up, a green glass wine bottle with something inside. She took it and turned it, holding it against the light.

"It's paper. Oh, Seth, a message. A message in a bottle." She laughed, charmed.

"A castaway," he said, taking it back. "Or maybe . . . a treasure map."

"Oh, sure. A treasure map. That's it. Come on," she said, laughing, "get it out." He had removed the cork and was holding the bottle upside down, giving it a tentative tap. "Here, my fingers are smaller." She took the bottle again and fiddled delicately with the extended corner of the rolled paper, pressing it against the smooth interior curve of the glass She turned it successfully, but could not withdraw it. Seth watched and then bent down, searching the sand. "Get a stick," she said. He handed her a length of dry reed, sandy and splintered, and she tried for a while to curl the paper around it. "It won't move." She had become utterly intent upon the task, and he watched, amused, as she slapped the bottle twice more. Then he took the bottle and the reed from her, snapped the reed in half and, slipping the two halves into the narrow neck, and using them like chopsticks, clasped the paper neatly and drew it out.

"Hey, you're smart."

"Just a little trick I picked up in the Orient." He handed her the rolled paper. She opened it carefully and smoothed it with her hand.

" 'Erin and Pete Forever,' " she read.

He smiled, "Oh, lovely."

She stared at it a moment longer and then burst out laughing.

"What's funny?"

"The date. It's yesterday. So much for romance." He took the paper and studied it, still smiling. Then he curled it, tucked it back into the bottle, and corked it firmly. He raised his arm and tossed the bottle far out into the surf.

"Good luck, Pete and Erin," he shouted over the wind. Joanna watched, hands on hips, smiling wryly.

"At least, anyhow, we can be pretty sure they're still together."

"Unless," Seth slipped his arm through hers, "something awful happened last night."

"Yeah," Joanna said, "You have to think of that." She looked out to the water again, shielding her eyes. "Good luck, Pete and Erin," she whispered, "Forever, USA."

———

THE LITTLE ENCAMPMENT of deck chairs and blankets tucked high up the beach, sheltering beneath the dunes, said "winter" as much as the north wind rippling the shining beach grass. Joanna approached it through layers of summer memories. Childhood ball games on the sand were overlaid by days of adolescent dreaming beneath the cool shadows of the boardwalk. And over that, the hot September afternoon she strode for sandy miles, arguing with her brother, Eric, bound for a Maryland boot camp the following day.

As she and Seth drew nearer, she saw her daughter's familiar shape huddled beside Eric at the foot of Miriam Levine's deck chair, her pink hood drawn up over her hair. She was eating a sandwich and seemed at first oblivious of their approach, but she got up suddenly, still not looking their way, and walked off pointedly down the beach, the sandwich still in her hand.

"Tess," Joanna called.

"I'm finished." Tess's voice sounded thin and faraway against the wind. "I'm going for a walk," she called without looking back.

There was a silence as Joanna stood watching her walk away westward, and then Annie said, "Come have some lunch, you two, before we eat it all."

Harry patted the wooden arm of his chair, "Sit here by me, Joanna," he said. She turned from Tess and became aware of them all watching her, and aware too that she was still absently holding Seth's hand. She let it go.

"Sure, Harry," she said. She settled on the sandy, curled edge of the khaki blanket, by his feet. Sara passed her a red thermos cup of coffee, and Annie held out a plastic box of sandwiches. She took the first at hand and passed the box to Seth.

"She ate three halves," Sara said. "So it can't be that bad." Joanna smiled weakly. Tess had gone far off down the beach, but even at such a distance, Joanna could read the hunched, unhappy shape of her body. She took a bite of her sandwich and turned to Eric, who was staring out to sea.

"Did she say anything to you?" He looked around quickly. His eyes had a vague, distracted look, and she knew instantly he had been thinking of Molly.

"Nothing particular, Jo. We just talked."

"She didn't say what she's angry about."

"She didn't seem angry."

Joanna sipped from the plastic mug. The coffee was cold already, in the chilling wind. "Well, she's not, with you."

"We talked about the past. She's curious. She's very bright."

Joanna laughed. "I suspect you're right, Eric, but that just makes the report cards harder to take."

"School isn't everything," Sara said, comfortably.

"These days it is," Martin returned at once. "Look at David. And he had a college degree..."

"Oh, so what," Harry Levine said suddenly.

"So what? So he's unemployed and about to be a father, that's so what."

Harry shrugged, "He'll manage."

"Oh, really? And just how well is he managing at the moment?"

"He's managing fine." Harry spoke in the same slow, patient drawl he used to settle Miriam. "He's got a beautiful, wonderful wife. They're going to have a beautiful baby. He'll manage." Martin stared at his father bleakly.

"Well you've sure changed your tune," he said at last.

Harry shrugged. He smiled again, imperturbable. Then he said suddenly, "Eric, I need a favor."

Everyone looked up, startled—except, oddly, Eric, who only nodded and said, "What can I do for you, Harry?"

"You remember that new roof we put on the privy up at the camp, summer after you graduated?"

"Sure," Eric said easily.

"Well, you remember that old white pine with a kind of lean to it, beside it? The one your dad always said was going to fall on that roof if we didn't cut it down?"

"I said so too," Eric said, laughing. "Don't tell me; it did."

"Yeah. It did." Harry grinned. "I don't care. I liked that old pine. I liked the shape of it."

"Take the roof off?" Eric said, grinning back.

"Nah. It came down gently, in the snow last winter. Lot of branches. Nice and cushioned. Just dented it a bit. Cracked some shingles." He smiled, proud of his tree even in its demise. "Still," he said, "It needs fixing." He looked for a moment at Miriam and then said, "I've been meaning all summer to get something done about it. When your folks came up in July, your dad and I were all set to work on it, but as soon as we got the ladder out, you couldn't hear yourself think for fussing women..."

"And I should think so," Miriam cut in. "You on a ladder.

You can hardly manage the stairs. And your dad isn't fit for climbing around rooftops either, Eric, whatever he thinks."

"I thought I'd get the MacKenzie boy to do it," Harry continued placidly, "but he hasn't had any time since he got married . . ."

"He's married?" Eric said. "Little Donald MacKenzie?"

"Married last year. Got a kid on the way. Anyhow, he's started up a business, and I haven't found anyone else. I'm going to have to do something before we open the place up for Thanksgiving, otherwise it's going to be damned uncomfortable sitting on the can with snowmelt dripping down your neck." He looked at Eric steadily. "How'd you feel about going up there for a few days and fixing that roof?"

Eric drew his knees up and hooked his arms around them loosely, one big hand clasping the other wrist. He looked toward the white beach, then closed his eyes and leaned back, his Viking profile sharp in the cold light. "Harry, I'd love to do this for you," he said.

"But?" Harry asked.

"I haven't a lot of time."

"Won't take a lot of time, Eric."

"Harry . . ."

"There's a few other things need doing, as well," Harry said. "The screens are still up, even. They need to come down and the storms go up. The pipe to the header tank's clogging again . . ."

"I was going to fix that," Martin said, "I told you I was." Harry nodded pleasantly toward his son, not taking his eyes off Eric.

"I know you were. But you're busy. That big place in Connecticut to look after." He paused. "Everybody's busy. Just the way things are these days." He smiled to himself and said, to Eric, "Your dad and I got to wondering what we're doing with the old place. Nobody has time for it. By the time we haul our asses up there, none of us have any energy for anything more than some geriatric skinny-dipping." He laughed.

"We use it," Martin said. "We try to use it."

"I know you do," Harry said mildly. He turned back to Eric. "Your dad tried to sneak out last summer. Old rascal. Started talking of giving me their share since they were down in Florida, and all that. Damned if I was letting him off that lightly. Anyhow," he shifted his bony hips in the deck chair and winced briefly. "It was in your family first. And we've shared it now for a generation. I like it like that. I want it to stay like that between the two families. It sort of holds things together."

"Martin and Annie are married," Miriam interrupted. "Surely that holds things together."

"Sure it does. Sure it does." He grinned slowly. "But I like the feel of land. Land is forever." He patted Miriam's hand and smiled again. "What about it, Eric?" Eric looked up uneasily. Harry said, "I know you're short of money, kid. It's not going to cost you anything. I'll pay for your time and whatever." He held a hand up against protest. "I'd have to be paying someone. Better someone I can rely on."

"It's not the money, Harry."

Harry nodded and was quiet. But after a moment he said, "Working with your hands leaves your mind free. You need some time with your mind free. You need to think. The trouble with people today is they don't give themselves time to think." Eric smiled and shook his head, looking down at his knees.

"You're hard to argue with, Harry," he said.

"So don't argue. Joanna," he looked around and caught Joanna's eye, "you go with him."

"Harry, I . . ."

"Do what I say," Harry said, mildly, but without concession.

"Harry, don't tell her what to do," Miriam protested. "She's a grown woman. She has things to do."

"Oh, everybody has things to do," Harry snapped.

"Tess has to get back to school," Annie said, evenly. "No matter what Joanna would like to do." Harry looked at her with narrowed eyes.

"When any of the bunch of you were growing up, and somebody offered you a couple weeks off school to go to the mountains, would you mind?"

Joanna leaned forward. "Harry," she said, "of course we wouldn't, and of course Tess won't. She'd like nothing better at this point than to never go back to school. But when we do get back and she's miles behind in everything, she will mind. We've been away a month already."

"Has she got any books with her?" Joanna looked around, startled, to Eric, who had asked the question.

"Well, yeah, of course she has. She has them all. At the bottom of her knapsack." She paused and smiled. "The usual place."

"We could maybe do some work together," he said. Joanna looked at her brother, her eyebrows raised in quizzical silence. Harry leaned forward and put his hand on Eric's shoulder and gave it a gentle, affectionate squeeze.

"Good kid," he said, "Good kid."

———

SARA PASSED THE LAST of the sandwiches around, and Annie followed, dividing the dregs of each thermos among their cups. The wind, rising, flipped up corners of the army blankets and rippled the canvas of Miriam's deck chair as she leaned forward, struggling into the spare sweater she'd brought for Tess.

"You cold, Mom?" Seth said, helping her with it.

"No. I'm fine." Miriam straightened the sweater, then wrapped her arms around herself. "Some fall this, feels more like winter," she said. Seth smiled.

"Time to go, I think," he said quietly to Joanna.

"I've got to find that kid," she answered, looking distractedly past him down the beach.

"She's gone quite a ways," Eric said. "I've been watching. She was by that fisherman for a while, but then she went farther." He paused, "I can still see her though," he added softly. "She's not out of sight." Joanna looked in the direction he was pointing, startled to realize that he had been so carefully watching all the time they talked.

"I'll go get her," she said. She stood up, brushing the sand off her jeans, and started walking down the beach. Behind her, Annie and Sara began packing up the picnic. When she drew closer to Tess she waved her arm, beckoning her daughter, but there was no response and she continued walking. She reached the fisherman, standing at the surf's edge, his long line trailing out over the breakers, the delicate arc of his rod quivering in the wind.

"Catch anything?" Joanna said.

"Not yet." He lifted his chin toward Tess. "That your little girl?"

"Yup," Joanna said. "Hope she's not been bothering you."

"No. Nothing like it. Real bright kid. Full of questions. I like bright kids."

"Thanks," Joanna said, smiling ruefully. "Tess!" she shouted. She could see that Tess could see her, but there was no answer and, to her surprise, the girl turned around and began walking the other way. "You little shit," Joanna said, under her breath, and broke into a jogging run. Tess had the sense not to run as well, but she didn't stop walking away until her mother, breathing hard and angrily, had caught up with her. "What kind of a game are you playing?" Joanna demanded.

"Nothing."

"Why'd you run away?"

"I didn't. I didn't run. I'm walking. See. Walking." Tess made two elaborate steps. Joanna grabbed the hood of her sweatshirt, spinning her around and pulling loose strands of her hair by accident. "Ow."

"I was calling you."

"I didn't hear. Ow, you're pulling my hair."

"You saw me. I waved. We're going home. Everybody's waiting for you. Though why, I can't imagine. You've hardly been nice company."

"Yes, I have. I was nice with Eric. I was nice with Sara and Miriam and everybody."

"I haven't seen it."

"Well, you weren't there, were you? You were off with Seth." Joanna let go of her hood. She turned half around, glancing back to the distant picnic site, the cluster of dark shapes moving around it, the fisherman in the foreground.

"That's what this is about then, is it? Me and Seth?"

"No." Tess stared stoney-faced down the beach, into the haze of blowing surf.

"Tess," Joanna began quietly, "I don't know what you imagine is going on between me and Seth, but I can assure you . . ."

"I don't give a shit. I don't give a shit about you and Seth."

"Watch your mouth."

"You can screw Seth all over this beach and I wouldn't care. You can screw Mike and Sean and anybody else you want. Big shit."

"Tess, you make me sick," Joanna whispered.

"You can screw Martin if you want," Tess whispered back.

"What?" Tess looked up, suddenly nervous. "What did you say?" Joanna's eyes were slits.

"I said you can screw Martin," Tess shrugged, trying to make something inconsequential out of the words. It didn't work.

"Why'd you say that?"

Tess shrugged again, "I don't know. I just said it."

"What gave you such an idea?"

Tess ducked away, feeling like she'd felt on the attic stairs, scared to go on, scared to go back. "Nobody."

"What do you mean nobody? Have you been talking to somebody? Who?"

"Why would I talk to anybody? I haven't. I just thought of it."

"Crap," Joanna said.

"Look, I didn't mean anything. I just said it."

"Did Eric tell you something?" Joanna said, her voice queer and troubled.

"Eric?" Tess shouted. "*Eric.* Eric's the nicest person in this family. I like him better than any of the rest of you. So don't blame Eric."

"I'm not blaming Eric. But you were talking to him."

"All Eric said was you went *out* with Martin. He said it was fine and nobody cared and it was long ago. But he didn't know, did he?"

"Know what?" Joanna said flatly. Tess turned suddenly, jerked free of Joanna's hand, and bolted down the beach. She ran fast and well, and Joanna had trouble catching her. When she did, it was like catching a wildcat. Tess fought and screamed, kicked and bit. Joanna wrestled her onto the sand and pinned her at last, her arms wrapped around her daughter from behind. "What *is it*, Tess?" she cried. Tess gave one more kick and gave up.

"You had an abortion," she whispered. "You bitch. You fucking bitch."

———

THE PICNIC WAS ALMOST cleared away when Joanna got back up the beach. Annie and Eric were at the far end of the boardwalk, deck chairs under their arms, escorting Harry Levine back to the car. Seth was down at the water's edge, rinsing cups in the surf. Only Sara and Martin and Miriam remained. Sara helped her mother pack the picnic boxes into shopping bags and carryalls, and Martin stood holding the two army blankets and looking around for something to do.

Martin had seen her coming a long way off, striding swiftly across the sand, her eyes blazing, the child following a long way behind. He knew he was in trouble, and he read in Tess's reluctant slouch and downcast gaze, exactly the cause. "Oh, shit," he whispered softly to himself, and then Joanna reached him. She caught the sleeve of his jacket with her left hand and brought her right around hard in a fierce slap across his jaw. Martin staggered.

"You bastard," she cried. "You *bastard*."

"Jo!" Sara looked up from her shopping bag, her gentle eyes wide with astonishment.

"You told her!" Joanna shouted. She swung her hand back and slapped Martin again. He accepted the slap, unmoving, his face white. "You told her."

"I didn't, Jo," he murmured sadly.

"Then how does she know? How?" Martin shook his head. He put his hand up to his face. Joanna raised her arm again. Sara jumped forward, catching her sleeve.

"Jo, stop it," she said. "What are you doing?"

"Leave me alone." Joanna shook her arm free. "I'll beat the shit out of the bastard." Her face crumpled but she did not cry. She saw Tess watching numbly from a distance. Miriam's old hands were raised in protest.

"What's he done?" Miriam said. "Somebody tell me, what's going on?" Martin swung around and glared at her coldly.

"*You* tell her," he said.

"What? What am I supposed to tell?"

"She heard us, Mom, I told you she heard us." Miriam looked sideways at Tess. Tess turned around and bolted toward the ocean, colliding with Seth. He dropped his handful of wet cups and caught her in his arms. She stood frozen there, her eyes squeezed shut. Martin turned back to Joanna, his big palms upraised. His mouth was trembling, his upper lip cut and smeared with blood.

"Jo, I'm so sorry. I'm so sorry. She overheard."

"What? You talked about it?" He nodded.

"Me and Mom. In the kitchen."

"With my daughter in the house?"

Martin's hands flew up in frustration. "Well, how was I supposed to know she was sneaking around?"

"She wasn't sneaking. My daughter doesn't sneak."

"Okay, okay. I didn't mean . . ."

"You talked about it," she said again, stunned. Miriam folded her hands in front of her.

"Was I right, Martin? We'll pay forever."

Martin whirled around and raised his fist at his mother, "Cut it. Cut your damned Jewish dramatics. *You're* the cause of all this."

"Martin stop it," Sara shrieked. "Don't talk to Mom like that."

"She is. She's the cause."

"That's right," Joanna said coldly. "It's everybody's fault but yours. As always. You've learned nothing. In thirty years you've learned nothing. You couldn't take responsibility then and you can't take it now . . . you're such a shit, Martin."

"Jo," he turned to her, hands outstretched, "please, Jo, can't we talk later? The family's here. The whole family . . ." Joanna hunched her shoulders, swept her hair back with one hand, and stared at him. The presence of the others, Sara, Tess, Seth, strengthened in her awareness like figures emerging from a mist, but she could not care.

"You tell my daughter I aborted your child, and *you're* worried about family? Screw you, Martin Levine." She turned her back and strode toward the boardwalk and saw then the small, graceful figure of her sister Annie, standing on the windswept steps, looking silently down.

—

THEY WERE ON THE Southern State. Martin was driving, fast and hard. Annie sat stiffly beside him, the leather console between them an insurmountable barrier.

She said in a queer, strained voice, "I think I deserved to have been told."

"What does it matter now, Annie?" he said wearily. "It's thirty years ago."

"Not now. Then. I deserved to have been told then."

"It had nothing to do with you." He slammed on the brakes. A horn blared. Martin screeched out of his lane, pulling past an old black Cadillac, whipping in again in front of it.

Annie said, as if nothing had interrupted, "It had a lot to do with you, though, Martin, and I was marrying you."

"I didn't marry you just because Jo left me," he said stiffly.

"I know that, Martin," Annie turned to look at him. "I know why you married me. You married me for exactly the reason you could never have married Jo. Our ideals were the same, and they were light-years from hers. I knew that when I was seventeen. You haven't learned it yet."

"Yes, I have. I have now."

She looked straight ahead, out the windshield, "You'll never understand her, Martin. She belongs to another generation. You'll never understand her at all."

"I know," he said impatiently. "Look, Annie, can we just drop this? It's all past and done with. It was before there was anything between you and me. I can't understand how you can be this jealous over something that happened thirty years ago."

"Jealous?" Annie's head whipped around again, and she stared at him with glittering eyes. "I'm not jealous, Martin. I wasn't jealous then, and I'm not jealous even now, of your fawning over Jo. Sometimes I find you pathetic, but I'm not jealous."

"Okay, okay." He took both hands off the wheel, then slammed them back. "You're jealous, you're not jealous. I don't care, Annie. I just want peace."

"I don't care what you felt about Jo, Martin," Annie said quietly. "But what you did . . ." She gulped suddenly and then burst out, "You did *that* to my little sister. You put her through *that*."

"Wait a moment. Wait a moment. She was in this too. It takes two, remember?"

"*You* got her pregnant. *You* made her have an abortion to save *your* career."

Martin looked straight ahead at the tail of the blue Ford he was harrying down the parkway. "She didn't want my baby, Annie," he said coldly. "She wanted her sandals and her love beads and her freedom. Her precious fucking freedom. That's all that ever mattered to Jo." He glanced at his wife and gave a brief bitter smile. "Look," he said, "it was no big deal. All right, it wasn't legal then, but you know, and you knew then, that if you had the money it was always available. My father . . ."

"No!" Annie shrieked and covered her ears. "I don't want to know. If your father did it, I don't want to know. I'll never be able . . ."

"Oh, for Christ's sake, Annie. My father didn't do it. He arranged it. That's all. He arranged it. A friend. Colleague. Totally professional. She got the best treatment . . . at least as good as she'd get today." He sighed wearily. "Now will you lay off before I crash this car?"

"Your father. Your mom and dad. I can't believe . . ."

"Annie. This happens all the time. Legally. A law you'd fight to defend. I don't see where you're coming from . . ."

"*My little sister*," she said savagely. And then whispered to herself, "Poor little Jo."

Trust

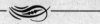

"CAN I HELP, ERIC?" Tess said. He looked down from the roof of the cabin and saw her, in jeans and a red and black checked shirt, standing in the bright sunshine of the clearing. Her hair was braided into two practical pigtails, and she looked younger and happier that way, as if the anonymity of the North Woods allowed her a respite from adolescence.

"That depends," he said. He sat easily on the gently sloping roof, a pile of new shingles beside him. The privy roof had had the excuse of a falling tree, and was mended in a day. The roof of the original old cabin, now one large end bedroom, had no excuse but age, and—with the crumbling mortar of its unused chimney, the pine-needle-clogged gutters, and the rotting window frames—it would take a lot more time than that.

"On what?' "

"On have you finished your history?"

"Yeah! Do you want to see it?" Eric lifted his hammer and a nail and lined up another shingle. "I'll see it later." He glanced down at her. "It better be longer than the last one."

"It is. It's real long. A page and a half."

"Big writing?" Eric asked.

"Little writing. Real little. Tiny."

"I bet." He fastened the shingle with two quick hammer blows. "Okay. Come on up. Bring those nails in that bag, okay?"

Tess scrambled up the ladder, the paper bag full of nails in her hand, and started up the sloping roof.

"Walk," Eric said. "Don't run." She tiptoed with demonstrative slowness up to where he was working and settled astride the ridge, her sneakered feet dangling. "If you're going to fall off, fall this way," he pointed to the way she'd come. "That side's too high."

"I won't fall off."

"Your mom gone to the store?"

"Yeah," Tess said. "I almost went with her, 'cause I like riding in the back of the Jeep." She thought momentarily of Mike Hewitt's pickup at home. It seemed so far away now. "But then I decided to stay and help you."

"Lucky me," said Eric.

"I'm a big help," Tess pouted little-girlishly.

"Wonderful. Pass me a nail." She picked one out of the bag carefully and handed it down to him.

"See."

"Irreplaceable," he said.

She sat contentedly in a spot of sun dappled by the shadow of a tall pine at the back of the cabin, watching the bright new course of shingles grow. She liked watching Eric because nothing seemed to bother him. She used to watch Sean Kelly working around the ranch, but he was only fun until something went wrong. Then he'd start fuming and saying "shit" and "fuck" and yelling at her that she was in the way. But Eric just kept working and talking, and when a shingle split, or a nail bent, he'd just pull it off calmly and start over with a new one. She thought about Sean Kelly and the ranch a little longer. Then she said, "When we go back to Colorado, are you going to come too?" He stopped working and looked at her. "We can make room in the trailer," she said. "There's a fold-up bed where the kitchen table is. Or I could go in with Mom and you could have my room."

"That's very kind of you, Tess," he said with a gentle smile.

"You could stay with us," she said quietly. "We could be a real family then."

"You are a real family, Tess."

"No, we're not. There's just Mom and me."

"Single-parent families are still real families. There's all kinds of families, Tess."

"I know, I know," she said impatiently. She looked away, frustrated, her blond pigtails flicking across the collar of her shirt. "I know single-parent families count. I mean, I know lots of kids whose parents are divorced and all that. But it's different for us. Mom and me. We just aren't good at it. We aren't big enough, just the two of us. We can't make it work." Eric laid his hammer down carefully beside the pile of shingles. He shifted his position on the roof, bracing himself with one foot, and looked at her steadily.

"Tess, if it's not working between the two of you right now, having me around is not going to be a whole lot of help. I'd just get in the way." She started to protest, but he continued, "I think, though, that it's probably working quite a lot better than you feel at the moment. It looks pretty good to me. I also think," he said, after a careful pause, "that your mom maybe needs something more than just her big brother around."

Tess's forehead wrinkled into two worry lines. She said, disappointed, "You mean she needs someone like Seth."

"I didn't say that."

"I know. I did."

Eric looked at her quietly for a moment. Then he said, "Don't you like Seth?" Tess shrugged uncomfortably. She wiggled around on the roof, bringing her foot up, balancing it on the ridge, picking at her laces. "Watch it," Eric said.

"I'm okay." She tugged at the lace again and then suddenly looked up. "Oh, what's the point?" she said.

"What do you mean?" Eric asked. He stood and moved up the roof until he was close enough to catch her if she wriggled enough to fall off, then sat down again just below the ridge.

"I liked Sean," she said. "Sort of. I really like Mike. But what's the point?"

"Okay, Tess," he said easily. "I've got the general idea." He looked down the roof at his tools and, with satisfaction, at the neat course of new shingles. "What makes you so sure Seth would leave too?"

Tess shrugged again. "Let's get real here. People fall in love and then they fall out of love and then they go away. That's just what happens. Except in the movies," she added, grinning cockily.

"Not always," Eric said. "Look at Annie and Martin." Tess shot him a wary look. He returned it with a bland smile.

"Well, that's not exactly a great example," she said coolly. "They sure weren't all lovey-dovey that weekend."

"No. They were having an argument. They often have arguments. They're human. But they're together after twenty-five years. That's real life, sweetheart, not the movies."

"Okay." Tess threw her arms up in capitulation, and Eric reached instinctively to steady her. "Look, I'm not going to fall off," she said, but lightly, without annoyance. "Right, you win with Annie and Martin. But they're an exception. Statistically, I'm right. At least where me and Mom are concerned." She held up her hand and began ticking off fingers as she spoke. "There was Larry, and he went away. There was Ben, and he went away. There was Sean, and he went away. There's sort of Mike, and the only reason he's never gone away is because he's married to some lady up the valley and he hasn't really arrived enough to go away."

"Finished?"

"They all go away."

"Except your mom. She's never gone away. Never. Right, Tess?"

"Yeah . . . so?"

"So don't forget it." He sounded just slightly gruff, and she shut up, unnerved. He stretched out comfortably on the roof, leaning on one elbow, studying her. She sat astride the ridge again, head down, perusing a hole in the knee of her jeans. He leaned closer and sniffed. "You been smoking?"

"No." She looked up innocently.

"I can smell it from here." She looked confused, deciding whether it was worth trying to deny it again. He said, "Got any on you?"

"Yeah," she said, puzzled.

"Can I see?" She fished into the deep pocket of her plaid shirt and dug out her squashed pack. She handed it to him diffidently. Eric turned the pack over, studying it. "Where'd you get them?" he asked.

"Home. My friend Bobby gets them from his brother. This is my last pack." He looked inside, giving the pack a shake.

"Can you spare me one?"

"You want to *smoke* one?"

He laughed. "That's the usual idea. You haven't got a lot . . ." he said politely.

"Sure. You can . . . I didn't know you smoked." She looked disappointed.

Eric shook out a cigarette. "Haven't for years, Tess. But it sounds pretty good right now." She watched him uneasily.

"Maybe you shouldn't . . ." she blurted. "I mean if you have quit." She leaned down toward him, her eyes scrunched up in lines of protective concern.

"Oh, once a smoker, always a smoker, Tess. Unless you quit when you're young. You got a light?" Worriedly, she produced a book of matches with "Edelweiss Cafe" printed on them. He took them, struck one, and lit the cigarette. He drew on it thoughtfully and then handed her the matches and the pack.

"You joining me?"

"No thanks," she said, still worried. "I don't want one right now."

He nodded. "Then you better put those away," he said. "Your mom will be home soon." She shoved them roughly down into the bottom of her pocket and buttoned the flap.

Eric had finished the cigarette and gone back to work when they heard the rumble of the Jeep approaching. Sound preceded arrivals by a long interval on the rough, steep track, but at the first distant gear change, Tess got up and slid down the roof to the waiting ladder. Eric put his tools down and followed her. By the time he reached the ground, she was walking away.

"Where are you going?" he asked casually.

"Down to the lake."

"You want to wait and say hi to your mom?" he asked with slightly more force.

"No."

"Might be the friendly thing to do."

"I'm not friendly," she said. She turned and smiled slightly. He gave up and watched her go, head down, hands thrust in pockets. When Joanna, in the old blue camp Jeep, pulled up in front of the cabin, she was far away, her red checked shirt a bright splash amidst the pines by the water's edge. Joanna sat in the Jeep staring at her out the open window. Eric walked around to the driver's side and opened her door.

She said, looking after her daughter, "I see I'm still not exactly flavor of the month."

Eric smiled wryly. "What can I carry?" he said.

"There's a gas bottle in the back," she said distractedly, still looking toward the lake. He went around to the rear and lowered the tailgate of the Jeep. Joanna slid down from the high driver's seat, her arms around two paper bags. She watched as he lifted down the green metal cylinder and hauled it to its place beneath the kitchen window.

"Remember when there was just the old wood range?" he said.

"Roughing it," she answered, in their father's voice, and laughed. "And Mom and Miriam cursing and trying to cook a Thanksgiving turkey in that oven? I think if the men hadn't capitulated over that, this camp would have been history."

Eric said seriously, "It nearly is, anyhow, Jo."

"What do you mean?"

"Just that. It's falling apart." He paused. "There's a *lot* of work needing doing."

"Well, you can't do it all yourself," she said hastily. "I'm sure Harry didn't mean that."

"Oh, I know he didn't, Jo. I doubt Harry even realizes. Or Dad. They've gotten old and the place has gotten old with them." He smiled, thinking of Harry and his father, and then added, "I don't think any serious work has been done here in years."

The stubborn hinges of the screen door screeched as he opened it, as if in agreement. He held the screen and the inner plank door for her, and she edged in sideways with the grocery bags. She set them heavily on the oilcloth-covered table and said, suddenly morose, "Maybe Dad was right, trying to pull out. Maybe they should just sell it." He looked surprised.

"It's nothing that can't be fixed, Jo. And I'm happy to fix it. I'm going to need a hand with some stuff, that's all. Is David coming up for Thanksgiving?"

"I think they're all coming," Joanna said. "I spoke to Annie the other night. She said we'd see them all." She paused and added, "Harry talked to Mom and Dad. They know you're here." He said nothing, just stood looking out the window at the old Jeep parked among the pines. "I think you should call them."

"I know," he said. She got up quickly and began unloading the two paper bags and shoving things into the refrigerator. "I'm not ready, Jo," he said. She nodded tiredly and continued unpacking. When the table was clear she folded the brown bags for recycling and sat down again in a kitchen chair.

She said, "Are you staying for Thanksgiving, Eric?" He sat down across from her, looking at his hands.

"I might as well."

"And then?"

"I don't know, Jo. I just don't know." She traced a pattern with her finger among the red and yellow swirls of the table covering.

"This is the same old oilcloth," she said. "I remember it when we were kids. I remember when we had card games and I got too sleepy to play, I'd just sit here leaning against Dad, listening to the grown-ups talk over my head and making up pictures from the pattern." She paused, smiling. "I liked it before we got power up here and there was just the kerosene lamp, the smell of it and the way it drew you all in close, away from the shadows."

"So did I," Eric said. "Though I'm not sure I would now. The handy thing about being a kid is those things don't make a lot of difference. Except that there wasn't any TV, our lives were just the same, power or no power, gas range or wood stove."

Joanna laughed. "We never noticed. How did things get washed? How did they cook on that thing? Or clean up? There was only the hand pump, out back, too."

"I remember carrying water. That much I do remember. That was a kid's job. And chopping kindling. But the rest of it was no problem of ours." He leaned back in his chair, stretching his arms over his head. "We're a real funny country. We build the most elaborate technologies in the world and then spend all our time dreaming of running away from them."

"Speaking of high technologies," Joanna said suddenly, "there's a revolution brewing. Annie wants a flush toilet." Eric laughed, shaking his head.

"Oh no. No way. That's heresy."

"You should hear Dad."

"Never mind Dad. What would Grandpa Carlson have said?" He grinned at her, and the grin faded slowly into a distant smile. "Remember him going off each morning with his book and his glasses and that cane he used to prop the privy door open and let the sun in?" She nodded. "This place is packed with memories," he said slowly. "It's nothing but memories. I think that's what's holding it together, not those rusty old nails."

Joanna studied the oilcloth thoughtfully and then said, with care, "Does it help, Eric?" He looked startled. "Does it bring you closer to her?"

He looked around the pine-clad walls, the battered red-painted chairs and table, the paint-spotted linoleum floor, all familiar beyond expression. He said, bleakly, "I haven't felt further from her in years."

Joanna's head came up. She stared at him, amazed, "Why, Eric?" she whispered. "Here?"

He shook his head and looked away from her. "I don't know. I don't understand it." He paused and then said, in considered words, "Everything's so real here. So concrete. The past. The way it happened. How everything looked. I can see her standing there that morning . . . and suddenly she's just my ordinary, ten-year-old daughter and I know she couldn't have done one of the things I've imagined her doing over the years. She's just Molly, and one day she goes out that door and she's gone. That's all."

Joanna sighed deeply. Her voice came out thin and stretched when she spoke. "Eric?"

"Yes?"

"You know you're not going to find her, don't you?" He looked at her steadily for a moment that seemed to teeter toward revelation, then he turned and looked out the window again. She gave up and started to rise to leave. He gestured her to sit.

"No, wait," he said. After another long pause, he added, "There's something I never told you, Jo." She faced him again, and some deep, treacherous part of herself gave a little jolt of fear.

"What?" she said, her voice unnaturally calm.

He kept his eyes on a distant branch across the clearing, noting as he spoke how long it had grown, its feathery fingers brushing the roof of the Jeep. "That morning, the morning Molly disappeared . . ." Joanna nodded, sitting rigidly still . . ."Dina called me from Lake George." He turned to her suddenly, breaking off what he was saying. "Jo," he said urgently, "she was so clingy, so protective . . . she often did that; leave us for a day and call me, twice, even . . . maybe you don't remember. You were away a lot . . ."

"I do remember she was very cautious when we went up a mountain or anything."

" 'Cautious,' " he repeated softly. He leaned forward. "Joanna, I had to fight for every ounce of freedom that child had. If Dina had had her way, Molly would never have ridden a bike, or learned to swim, or to skate, or to ski." He shook his head, stopped, and then continued, almost conversationally, "She was the same about me. She had to know where I was all the time. Not jealous, you understand, just needing to be sure I was safe. It let up a bit after Molly was born, but only because it was all focused on Molly instead." He stopped talking again, looking down at his hands, stretching his fingers out, studying the nails.

"It was hard," he said simply. "I always had to be so laid back, to balance her. If Molly was sick, or hurt herself . . . I couldn't allow myself to worry, I was so busy dealing with her mother. She really would never have let Molly out of her sight if she could avoid it. She didn't trust anyone. Not the school, not my parents, not even her own parents. And not me." He paused. "That hurt, Jo. She lumped the whole outside world into this threat against her child. Our child. And I was part of the outside world."

"Is that why she never went back to teaching? I often wondered."

"Oh, certainly. Even for that time when I was out of work, taking that course at nights, and we could have used the money. She came up with all kinds of excuses, but the bottom line was it meant leaving Molly with me."

"Eric, I had no idea."

"She was a devoted mother," he said without irony, "and that's all anyone outside ever saw." He paused and gave a small, wry smile. Then he fixed his eyes on the branch beyond the window and began again. "That morning, Molly wanted to go fishing, but I couldn't go with her because I had letters to write and some bills to pay. Things that seemed urgent at the time," he added slowly. "So she decided to go berry picking. She asked me if she could take a picnic. I said yes." Joanna watched his face change as he spoke, softening with memory and growing somehow younger. "She ran around collecting her things. Then Dina called from Lake George. She said she'd had a 'bad feeling' about Molly. A premonition. Dina was really into psychic communication. She had books . . . she was always having these 'feelings.' She said I shouldn't let her go out." He sighed, "Jo, I'd just said yes to the kid. I'd said yes. She had all her stuff together. Her bucket for berries, and she'd made a picnic. She was all excited. She was going alone. She wanted to go alone." He broke off. "You remember that feeling, the first time Mom or Dad let us do something alone, something we'd always needed an adult for before." Joanna nodded, helplessly. He closed his eyes. "I couldn't take that away from her." He sat for a long while in silence. "And I knew," he said at last, "this was safe. So far from the city. The safest place in the world."

"Oh, Eric." Joanna whispered. He opened his eyes.

"When Dina came back and Molly was gone, she looked at me . . ." His voice broke suddenly. Joanna reached to touch him. He drew back and said distantly, "I remember when we were about ten, Martin and I were in the woods with the Frazer kids from the farm, Pete and his big brother, Dan." Joanna nodded, puzzled. "We found a fox's den," Eric continued. "Dan shot the fox and drove the vixen away and killed the cubs. She watched us. She watched from the woods. That's what Dina looked like, looking at me. She hates me, Jo. We were married once. And now she hates me more than anyone on earth. More than whoever it was who took Molly. She hates me more." He sat then in silence, looking out at the branch of the pine, and Jo, without words, sat in silence too.

The door banged open and Tess burst in, and then stopped, seeing them sitting there. Eric looked up. "Come in, sweetheart," he said gently, "we're just talking." Tess looked from him to her mother and stepped back toward the doorway.

"It's all right, Eric," she said. "I'll wait for you outside."

Joanna watched bleakly as she slipped out the door, closing it and the screen gently behind her.

"I'm not making a lot of progress," she said.

"She'll get over it," Eric answered in the same gentle voice.

"I would have thought she'd have gotten over it by now. I really don't understand this. Why should it matter so much? It was so long ago."

Eric shrugged. "Kids are funny, Jo," he said, adding, "talk to her. Keep talking to her. She'll tell you eventually."

"She won't, Eric. She dodges off. She even sort of pretends it never happened. Yesterday she came on all sunny and cheerful for a while when we were painting those window frames. Then it was like she suddenly remembered how angry she was. She just stopped talking, left her brush, and walked away."

"Did you call her back?"

"Yes. I did. She acts like she doesn't hear." Joanna stood up and went to the window, looking out. Tess was standing with one foot in the rubber tire swing that Martin had hung for his own kids from the branch of a big, leaning birch. Joanna watched her swing slowly back and forth, dragging her other foot through the dry leaves. "I'm lost on this one, Eric. She's a nineties kid. She's hardly grown up sheltered. She isn't even antiabortion. We've talked about it. Kids these days have strong opinions on everything. They're well informed. You should see the Letters pages of the magazines she reads. It's not exactly acne cures and shall we kiss on the first date anymore."

"Talk to her," Eric said. Joanna looked at him queerly.

"Has she talked to you?" she said suddenly. "I mean, don't break a confidence . . ." Eric shook his head.

"I wouldn't, Jo. But she hasn't." He thought a moment longer and then got up from his chair. Joanna followed him outside. He stood looking at the roof, and Tess came down from the swing.

"Are you ready?" Tess asked.

"I'm going out for some nails and stuff," he said casually. "We'll finish it when I get back." He got into the Jeep, and Tess ran around to the passenger side.

"Can I come?" she asked hopefully, as he started the engine.

"Keep your mom company," he said. She made a face, but he

only grinned and waved as he pulled away. Disappointed, she watched the Jeep disappear down the track, then turned around and saw Joanna watching her.

"How about going canoeing, Tess?" she said. Tess looked again down the track.

"I'm helping Eric."

"We'll be back in time."

"Shouldn't we be fixing something?"

"I think Harry would allow us an hour off." Tess looked around for something else to say in objection, but thought of nothing. "Get the paddles and the life jackets," Joanna said. "They're in the shed."

She went ahead, down the sandy path through the pines to the lake. The canoe was lying, inverted, on the grassy shore beside the dock, where Eric and Tess had left it the day before. Joanna turned it upright and then sat down on a flat gray rock beside the lake to wait for Tess. She drew up her knees and locked her arms around them dreamily, breathing in the cold smell of the lapping water, in which purity and decay, oddly intermingled, were counterpointed by the spicy sweetness of balsam. She closed her eyes and thought suddenly and romantically of Seth and realized, to her surprise, how much she had been missing him.

"I'm here," Tess said. Joanna opened her eyes and looked up. Tess was standing in front of the canoe, wearing a faded red life jacket, a paddle clutched faintly belligerently in each hand. A second life jacket lay at her feet. "Are we going or what?"

Joanna got up calmly. She slipped into the life jacket and pushed the canoe halfway into the water. "You get in" she said. "I'll push you out." She waited patiently as Tess climbed in gingerly and picked her way down its length.

"Don't tip me!" she shrieked, clutching the aluminum sides.

"God, you're trusting." Joanna waited until Tess had seated herself, the paddle held uneasily across her knees, then stepped neatly in over the curved stern, and gave a final push with her damp sneaker. The canoe slid into the lake, the water rippling gently. "What are you worrying about, anyhow? You were swimming here yesterday."

"It was warm yesterday. And I didn't have my clothes on.

Mom!" She shrieked, as Joanna gave the craft two quick wobbles with her knees. "It's not funny." Joanna grinned and resisted a devilish inclination to do it again.

She lifted her paddle and stroked the silken black water, twice, and the canoe glided out into the lake. It was a big lake, with several islands, its shores thickly grown with birches and maples and poplars, on their branches a scattering of red and yellow leaves, the last of the glory of the fall.

"We've just missed the colors," Joanna said, regretfully, to Tess's immobile back. "We're a little too late."

Tess dipped her paddle and said nothing. Once out in the water, Joanna could pick out a distant dock and boat landing and even just make out the roof of another cabin, hidden, like theirs, in the woods. That cabin always surprised her and reminded her that the remoteness of the camp was to some degree a myth nurtured by all of them for their own romantic purposes. "There's another cabin," she said to Tess. Tess turned around to see where she was pointing, but made no response. She plied her paddle mechanically and quickly, as if it were a job to be done with.

"Ease up," Joanna said. "We're not racing anyone. Oh, look," she pointed. "A loon." The bird made a ponderous takeoff and flew away, low over the black waters, disappearing behind a shrubby island. Tess never looked. Joanna paddled steadily, steering the canoe behind the island. Overhead a fine and evocative honking called her to look up to where a thin, wavering V of geese wended south. She thought of home, of the early snows whitening the bare tops of the mountains and turning their piney slopes back into a winter playground again. She thrust her paddle deep into the dark water and felt the canoe surge outward toward the next island.

"Where are we heading?" Tess asked querulously.

"Right there," Joanna answered. "Let's beach her there."

"On that island?"

"Yeah, right there, by that fallen log. You jump out when I tell you." Tess lifted her paddle clear and hung onto her seat, and Joanna aimed the canoe at a sandy patch and ran it up onto the shore. Tess clambered out over the bow, absurdly determined to keep her feet dry, and pulled the canoe up the sand, tugging on the length of frayed blue rope tied to its prow. Joanna stepped easily onto the sand and hauled the canoe higher up onto the island.

"What are we stopping here for?" Tess asked. Joanna looked around. The island had only four small birches and a single pine to hide behind in all its fifteen-yard length.

"Let's talk," she said, with satisfaction.

"About what?" Tess asked, her voice pitched between indifference and belligerence.

" 'Family Values,' " Joanna said. Tess stared at her, puzzled, looked around the island, and, finding no ready source of respite, settled her eyes on the canoe.

"I don't get it," she said.

"Neither do I, Tess. I don't get where you're coming from or what you're wanting. And I don't get why, ever since you had the misfortune to overhear something that happened in my life almost twenty years before you were born, you have been unable to grant me a single civil word."

"I don't want to talk about it."

Joanna sat down on the fallen log beside the canoe and wished distantly for a cigarette. She said, "You know, kid, I'd picked up on that. I really had."

"Look," Tess said, suddenly animated, "you're right. It happened before I was born. It's nothing to do with me. I'm sorry about being rude. I'll stop."

"Uh-uh. Not that easy, girl."

"I don't want to talk about it."

"Are you that much against abortion?" Joanna said. Tess put her hands over her ears. "This is new to me, kid. I used to get a pretty liberal line from you. A little too liberal, if you want my honest opinion." Tess sat, her face reddening, her ears covered. Suddenly she flung her head up, her arms flailing outward.

"You ruined it," she cried.

"What?"

"Everything. You ruined everything. You ruined your life. And mine."

"Yours?" Joanna asked, startled.

"You could have been married. You could have had a husband and a house and a real family."

"You mean with Martin?" Joanna asked, incredulous. Tess ducked her head. Joanna leaned closer to her, and she brushed her eyes and looked away.

"That was my brother or sister, you know."

Joanna looked at her for a long quiet time and then said evenly, "No it wasn't, Tess. It was nothing of the sort."

"Yes, it was. That was our chance. And you missed it. We could have been a real family. You could have married Martin and had the baby and then you could have had me and he'd have been my father too." Joanna stared and began to laugh, tried to suppress it, and gave up.

"No, he wouldn't, Tess. That's an alternative universe. Everything would have been different. Including you, if you even *were*, which you wouldn't have been." Tess looked up tearfully. "Come on, surely you can see that." Joanna reached out and gently tangled her fingers in one of Tess's snarled and fuzzy braids. "Christ, kid, this hasn't seen a brush in days," she said gently. "Besides," she added, "would you really want Martin for a father? I didn't think you were all that wild about him."

Tess shrugged philosophically. "He's all right. A bit grumpy. But he's a real father, at least. Better than nothing." She paused and said, "Better than some ski-bum whose name you've forgotten."

"I haven't," Joanna said indignantly.

"Yeah? What's his name then?" Joanna looked up at the blue perfect sky.

"I'm not telling you, anyhow."

"See? Jeez," Tess rolled over on her stomach on the grass. Joanna got down from the log and lay flat beside her.

"Look," she said. "His name didn't matter because he didn't matter. I didn't have you for him. I had you for me. Because I wanted you. And okay, I'm shit with men. I admit it. But I wanted my baby, my daughter, and being shit with men wasn't going to stop me, okay?" Tess looked at her sideways, the trace of a hopeful smile starting at the corners of her mouth. She started to speak and then suddenly stopped. She turned her face aside and pulled up a clump of grass.

"I used to like that story," she said.

"It's not a story. It's the truth."

Tess turned again to face her with her cool blue gaze. "I don't believe you anymore," she said. "You just got pregnant again like you did with Martin. You probably wanted to have an abortion again too, but for some reason you didn't, so I'm here."

Joanna pushed herself up on one elbow and gripped Tess's arm, "I did not want an abortion. I got pregnant by choice and I did not want an abortion."

"I bet you thought about it," Tess said.

"*No.*" Joanna flopped back down and then rolled onto her back, looking up through the last few yellow leaves of a birch to the unchanging blue sky. "I've told you so many times," she said wearily. "I wanted you. I chose to get pregnant with you. I planned it."

Tess sat up suddenly, "You know, that's the part that really gets me," she said. "I'm supposed to be grateful for that? Some plan. If it was an accident, maybe I could understand, but you planned it this way? You knew I'd never have a real dad, right from the start?"

Joanna closed her eyes, shutting out the birch tree, the blue sky, and Tess. She smiled sadly. "I thought we'd be happy," she said. "Just the two of us. I really did."

Tess was quiet. After a while she said, in a suddenly adult voice, "Maybe we would have been." Joanna opened her eyes again and raised her head, puzzled. Tess looked at her steadily. "But it's never been just the two of us, has it?" She leaned forward. "You always say you just wanted me, but it's never true. You always have to have some man around as well." She met Joanna's eyes with a look of such bitterness and frustration that Joanna could not respond. She shook her head, sat up, and stared bleakly across the black lake. "Are you sorry?" Tess said.

Joanna glanced at her quickly, then looked back to the water. "I'm sorry I've made you so unhappy; of course I am."

"No, not that," Tess said quickly. There was a trace of surprised gratitude in her voice, though, and she paused before she said, "I didn't mean that, I meant are you sorry you had me."

Joanna looked around and smiled, "Of course not."

"Were you ever?" Tess persisted.

"No."

"Never?"

"*No.*"

"You could have been real free," Tess said persuasively. "You could be real free now. You could do what you want without me in the way."

"You're not in the way."

"You could marry Seth."

"What?"

"Or something," Tess added weakly, giving Joanna a wary sidewise glance.

"Jesus, Tess, is that what this is leading up to?"

"Why does everything always have to lead up to something? Why can't I just say things . . ."

"Tess, do you really dislike Seth that much?"

"I don't dislike Seth at all," Tess shouted. "Why do you always think I dislike people?"

"Because you treat them like shit, maybe?" Joanna said mildly. "Seth has been number one in the firing line since he arrived. No," she said fairly. "Number two. I'm number one." She grinned. "I don't give up first place that easy." Tess looked at her, still warily, and then grinned back.

"I like Seth," she said. She kept grinning while Joanna stared at her in consternation. Then she jumped up and picked up her paddle. "Should we get back? Eric'll be waiting for me." Joanna stared at her a moment longer and then stood up as well.

"Sure, we'll go back," she said. "I got to fix supper anyhow."

The sun was lowering as they paddled back across the lake, lighting Tess's hair a ruddy pink. Tess hummed to herself cheerfully as she paddled, and now and again flipped deliberate splashes back at her mother. She turned around each time, slyly, to assess the effect.

"Once more, and I'll capsize her."

"You'll get wet too."

"I don't care. It'll be worth it." Joanna jammed her knees out against the sides and gave the canoe a hearty tip.

"No!" Tess shrieked, "I'll stop. I promise." She paddled with exaggerated care, touching the surface as gently as if it were glass. "See?" she looked around.

"Just watch it," Joanna said. "I'd like a swim." Tess scrunched her shoulders in mock terror.

She dipped her paddle delicately and said, "When's he coming back?"

"Seth?"

"Mmm," Tess said casually.

"Today or tomorrow. Whenever he's finished."

"Finished with what?"

"Work. He's working." Joanna thought a moment and added, "Contrary to what your Uncle Martin thinks, Seth works."

"I thought he wrote books," said Tess.

"That *is* his work," Joanna said sharply.

"Well, he's not writing a book now, is he?"

"No. He's writing a travel article for an in-flight magazine."

"A what?"

"An in-flight magazine. You know, one of those magazines they stick down the back of airplane seats."

"I don't know," Tess said pointedly. "I've never been on an airplane. We came on a train, remember?"

Joanna grinned wearily. "I remember."

"Is Seth going to come see us in Colorado?" Tess asked suddenly.

Joanna lifted her paddle and held it motionless for a moment. She dipped it again and said, casually, "I don't know. He might visit, I suppose." She paused warily. "Would you mind?"

Tess didn't answer at first. Then she said, "You really like him, don't you?"

Joanna hesitated again and then, making two quick strokes that thrust the canoe determinedly forward, said firmly, "Yes, Tess. I do."

"Would you like him to do more than visit?"

Joanna sighed softly to herself. She thought about Seth being there, if not with her, at least near her in some way, their easy companionship going on beyond this brief interlude of reunion and ripening smoothly and naturally into more. She said tiredly, "Would that be so awful?"

"No," Tess said, surprising her. Then she added coolly, "If he stayed. I mean really stayed."

"If Seth came," Joanna said slowly, "he'd stay."

"How do you know?" Tess challenged instantly, and Joanna realized that although she did know, she didn't know how she knew. "You'd have said that about Sean once."

"No," Joanna seized the realization. "No, I wouldn't. Or about Ben. Or anybody. But I am saying it about Seth." A warmth of longing for him filled her. "You'll just have to trust me," she finished.

She expected argument, but to her amazement Tess only nodded. Her attention shifted to a beaver whose dark, smooth head appeared in the marshy shallows. She pointed and shouted happily as he passed them, pushing a captured branch proudly before him as he swam. Two mallards crossed their path, and Tess amused herself pursuing them with the canoe, until, irritated, they rose and flapped away into the sky.

"You're a little rat," Joanna said easily.

"Yeah. I know." Tess looked over her shoulder and grinned. "I didn't hurt them," She added, "Besides, you helped." She splashed backward with her paddle.

"Pushing your luck, kid."

"What's it about, anyhow?"

"What?"

"Seth's article."

"Oh," Joanna mentally jumped back. "Bed and breakfast places in New England."

"What's there to write about that?" Tess asked, unimpressed.

"Well, he has to go and stay in some and see what the rooms are like, and the service, and the food . . ." Joanna said, lining up the canoe with the sandy yellow strip among the dark pines that marked the camp landing.

Tess turned around briefly, "Sounds pretty boring," she said.

"Oh, I wouldn't mind being bored with a nice bedroom and

a beautiful big breakfast cooked by somebody else. But anyhow, Tess, it's a job. It doesn't have to be exciting all the time. All jobs are boring sometimes."

"Especially yours," Tess said. She turned around and gave Joanna a superior grin. "You must have the boringest job in the world." Joanna stopped paddling. They were a few yards from the landing, but she carefully back-paddled until the canoe swung around broadside to the shore and then into reverse. "Why are we going this way?" Tess said. "Are we going out again?"

"No," Joanna said smiling. "We're just going in backward."

"Why?" Tess asked suspiciously.

"No reason." Joanna stroked her end of the canoe in toward the shore. "I don't think it's the most boring job in the world, Tess," she said, still smiling. "What about the time George ordered chili instead of a hamburger and fries? That was exciting."

"Wha . . . ?"

"And," Joanna continued, stepping adroitly backward out of the canoe, onto the flat gray rock, "there was the time Dan forgot he was a cheap bastard and left a tip. That was a red-letter day."

"Mom? What are you doing?" Joanna braced one foot against the rock, planted the other firmly on the sand, and with both hands gripped her end of the canoe. "Hey, pull me in."

"And what about the wonderful day the toilets flooded . . ." she lifted the canoe.

"Mom, *Mom* . . ."

"And we all nearly drowned." Joanna gave an expert toss. The canoe lurched broadside, and Tess hit the water with a smack and a resounding splash. Joanna sat down, laughing, on the rock, kicking her feet out gleefully, clapping her hands in delight. Tess floundered in the mud, got to her feet too quickly, and fell back in, butt first. Joanna buried her face in her arms.

"Mom, you rat. It's not funny."

"Yes, it is, Tess."

"Why? Why'd you do that?" Tess demanded. She got up, more carefully, and plodded toward the shore, her dripping jeans sagging, her feet squishing in water-filled sneakers.

"I don't know," Joanna giggled. "I guess I was just bored."

"Bored?" Tess looked stunned. "That's your excuse? Bored?"

"Shocking, isn't it, Tess?" Joanna whirled around to the voice behind her. Seth was leaning against a big white pine above the boat landing, his arms folded across his chest.

"Seth!" Tess cried, still knee-deep in the lake. "Look what she did."

"Terrible. To an innocent child. A completely innocent child."

"See," Tess said, self-righteously, "I'm an innocent child." The trace of a grin crossed her face. She saw Eric walking down the path from the cabin and called out, "She threw me in, Eric, did you see?"

"Threw her in," Seth repeated solemnly. He unfolded his arms and took a step down the bank.

"Wait a minute," Joanna said, "You want to hear what she said first . . ." She kept her eye on Seth and backed away along the shore.

"Yeah, yeah. She started it. I've heard it all before."

"Shit." Joanna bolted toward the trees.

"Get her," Tess shouted, as Seth caught her on her second stride. "Right in," Tess chanted, "in the deep part."

"That's where she's going," Seth said, struggling to hold on. "Damn it, Jo, you're strong," he added, impressed. He gave up trying to lift her and settled for an ungentlemanly manhandling onto the dock and a final vigorous shove. Joanna splashed into the lake and, still wearing her life jacket, bobbed spluttering to the surface.

"Great," Tess bounced up and down. "The deep part." She shook Seth's hand as Joanna swam soddenly ashore. She climbed out onto the gray rock, shaking her dripping ponytail, and looked around to where Eric stood now, leaning against the pine tree.

"Eric?"

"Yeah?"

"What are big brothers for?"

"Uh-uh," Seth said. He stood grinning on the dock. "That won't work, Jo. Men stick together in the woods. It's the Iron John thing. Right, Eric?"

"Sorry, Seth."

"Oh, fuck." Seth backed to the end of the dock. Eric followed him, strolling easily along its length. "Christ, you're big," Seth said. "You were always too big. Tess?" he called. "Tess? I helped you." Tess watched, thoughtfully.

"Yeah, but Eric's my friend."

"Oh, great." He looked up at Eric. "I'm a desperate man. I'll take you with me."

"Doubt it."

Seth held up his hands, hopefully. "Can you be bought?" Eric shook his head. Seth sighed, looked around futilely for rescue, and stepped resignedly off the edge like a pirate walking the plank. He went under, then came up spitting water and shouting, "Shit, that's cold." Eric was leaning comfortably against the end post of the dock, looking down.

"You shouldn't have done that, Seth. I was only joking." He grinned and waved, and Seth suddenly grinned back, looking past him. Eric turned around just as Tess, bolting down the dock, tackled his knees. He hit the water full length, went under, and came up beside Seth, shaking wet hair out of his eyes.

"I wasn't joking," said Tess.

"You're my friend," Eric cried, sadly.

She shrugged. "Changed my mind." She looked at her mother. "I decided I'm Mom's friend," she said. She shook Joanna's hand, and they walked off together up the path.

———

AFTER SUPPER, Seth lit the woodstove and got out his laptop computer, setting it up on the kitchen table. Tess came from drying the dishes and hung over his shoulder, her eyes on the little fold-up screen.

"Leave Seth alone, he's working," Joanna said, flicking a dish towel at her.

"I'm not bothering him."

"She's okay, Jo," he said. "I'm just sketching out my piece for the airline. It's hardly great art."

"It doesn't matter. She has her own work to do anyhow."

"I've done it."

"The history?" Tess nodded vigorously, still watching the screen. "And the arithmetic?"

"I gave it to Eric. I finished it."

"Then brush your teeth and get ready for bed. Go on."

"Oh, Mom," Tess moaned, "I haven't even seen a computer in weeks. I've forgotten what they look like."

"Bed. And don't bother Eric either."

"Why do you always think I'm bothering people?"

"Because you are. You're bothering me at the moment." Tess made a face, but sidled toward her bedroom resignedly. Seth got up and went out to the woodshed. He came back with an armful of logs and dumped them heavily on the cement hearth. He opened the stove door and clapped his hands together before the glow of the flames.

"It's freezing out there," he said. "I can't believe we were all in the lake this afternoon."

"It's November," Joanna said. She watched him load the stove and fasten the door. "The nights are getting cold. Besides, I don't remember anyone going into the lake deliberately this afternoon."

Seth sat back down in front of his computer and grinned, "I did. Didn't you?"

"You," she said, sitting down across from him, "were a craven coward."

"Damn right. You think I'm standing up to Eric? I learned better when I was six." His fingers drifted lightly across the keyboard, and a few sentences grew across the screen. He said, without looking up, "Where is he?"

"In his room. I think he's reading."

"What's this, some big brotherly discretion? Leaving me alone to seduce his little sister?" She smiled slightly, but shook her head. She touched the white casing of the computer, sitting so incongruously on the ancient oilcloth.

"This looks pretty handy."

"Cute, isn't it?"

"Expensive?"

"A bit." He looked up. "Is he all right?"

"Eric?" He nodded. She fingered the computer lightly. "He needs to be alone a lot. I let him. He gets up at six and goes up on the ridge by himself. Then he comes down and works all day." She paused. "He's some workman."

"I've noticed. Dad's going to fall over when he sees the place."

"Eric was always so good with his hands. He could do so many things . . ." She sounded wistful.

"Is something wrong, Jo?"

She shook her head again and quickly brushed a sudden rush of tears from her eyes. "I get so close. So close. Today when we were talking I thought I was there. But there's always this last little chasm to cross, like a cleft in a rock, very narrow, but very deep. I can't get over it. He turns in on himself, and I've lost . . . I'm afraid to pressure him. I'm afraid I'll wake up in the morning and find him gone."

"Would he do that?"

"He did before."

Seth stared at his computer screen a moment longer, then pressed a couple of keys and switched the machine off. He closed the lid and studied her quietly. "I don't understand. He seems so . . ." he paused and said eventually, "solid. Today at the lake, he was playing. Did you realize . . ."

"I realized."

"I haven't seen Eric like that since before it happened."

"I know. So close." She stood up and crossed to the wood-stove, holding her hands over its warmth. "I have to see Dina," she said.

Seth leaned back in his chair, stretching his legs out under the table. After a long while, he said, "Has Sara told you what she's like?"

"Yes. I have to see her anyhow." She paused. "He told me today what Dina did to him."

"Did?" he asked puzzled.

She leaned forward, her voice suddenly angry, "She blamed him, Seth. She made it his fault."

Seth shook his head impatiently. "That was years later, she started doing that. He was long gone. She was blaming a shadow by then."

"No. She did it right from the beginning," Joanna said. "She put every ounce of it on Eric's shoulders, and he's carried it ever since. He told me." Seth stared, not comprending. She brushed her hair back and raised her chin, wiping more tears away defiantly, "It seems she had some kind of premonition that Eric ignored. Look, I remember Dina way back, when she was still Sara's roommate at college. She was into every bit of sixties supernatural crap you can think of. Tarot and Ouija and all that stuff. Apparently, she kept it up. Anyhow, he ignored it this time, and this time she was right. It was just terrible luck. Like when somebody shouts 'I hope you die' to someone, and they do. It's just one of those nightmare things that shouldn't ever happen. But it did happen, and it's warped both their lives. I have to see her."

Seth sighed, "From what I hear, Jo, you'll get nowhere. She's very bitter."

"I don't care," Joanna whispered hoarsely. "I don't care how bitter she is. She's destroyed my brother's life. He can never accept he's lost Molly until he can accept he's not to blame. And how can he when the one person who matters most has told him from the start, from the very start, that he is?" She paused and took a deep breath, "I want Dina to tell him she's forgiven him."

"Jo," Seth said soothingly, "Jo. She's a wounded, damaged woman. You can't expect reason from her."

"She has a new husband. A child. She has a life. Eric has nothing." She crouched down by the woodstove, opened the door, and prodded the ashes angrily. Sparks flew up, and the heat dried the tears on her face. "If he leaves, none of us will ever see him again. I know that. I just know it, Seth."

"I'll take you down tomorrow," he said. She looked up, surprised. He was watching her solemnly.

"Tomorrow?"

"We can be back in a couple of days."

She nodded and then said, "What will I tell Eric?"

"The truth."

"What? That I'm going to see Dina?"

"No." Seth paused, looking down at his hands for a long while. "No. Jo, my father's been having some tests . . ." She turned away from the stove, surprised, and stepped toward him.

"Oh, Seth. I didn't know . . ."

"He's had some problems." He shook his head quickly. "I think it's going to be nothing, but it's hard to tell with Dad. He keeps serious things to himself."

"You're upset."

"Yes. Yes, I am. I know it's odd, because he's an old man and anyhow I live so far away, and have for so long. I don't even see him that much." He stopped. "Still, I'd like to be there when he gets the results. That is the truth. I was going down anyway on Thursday. So come with me tomorrow and tell Eric that."

"Seth," He looked up. She was standing very close. "Are you sure you want me along then, if that's what you're going for?"

"Oh yes." He reached out quickly, fumbling for her hand. "I wanted you with me anyhow, but I wasn't going to ask." She stepped closer and put her arms around his shoulders. He leaned against her, hugging her briefly, and let her go.

"I'll tell Tess in the morning," she said, with a wan smile. "I can't face the fight tonight."

———

TESS STARED INTO HER CORNFLAKES at the breakfast table and pushed a sodden brown mound of them around her cereal bowl.

"We'll be back in three days," Joanna said, turning the egg she was frying in a black iron pan. She lowered the gas and looked over her shoulder at her daughter.

"But we've just got here," Tess said. "Why do we have to leave already?"

"I've told you. Seth's dad had to go into the hospital. We want to see him." Tess looked sideways at Seth. She wanted to say he should go alone, but she felt sorry for him because he looked sad and worried. He even looked a little like Martin, just for a moment.

"But it's boring on Long Island. And anyhow, Eric said he was going to take me to climb a mountain when we finish the roof. What about that?"

"Three days, Tess. We'll be back in three days. You can climb a mountain then." Joanna slipped her spatula expertly under the egg and slid it out onto a plate. She lifted the bacon she'd laid out on a paper towel, put it next to the egg, and set the plate in front of Seth. "Where this desperation to climb mountains comes from I'd love to know," she said. "We live in the Rockies, kid, and I've never been able to move your butt up one there."

"This is different," Tess said. "It would be fun with Eric." She ate the last mouthful of cornflakes.

"You sure know how to make me feel good."

Tess looked up under her eyelashes. "Sorry," she said in a small voice.

"I'm sure Eric will wait for you," Joanna said, dropping another egg into the pan.

"He'll be busy when we get back. He'll start another job and he won't have time."

"Won't have time for what?" Eric said, coming through the door with an armful of split logs. "Do you want this lit, Jo?" he said as he laid them on the hearth.

"Only if you want it yourself," she said. "We won't need it. We'll be going in an hour." She turned from the pan and said, "Get your things ready, Tess." Tess got up reluctantly, tossed her pigtails back wearily, and slouched away. "Take your plate to the sink." Tess came back, lifted her bowl and spoon, and carried them like an overbearing burden to the sink. She set them down with a grating clunk and slunk off to her room.

"Problem?" said Eric, watching with a small smile. He sat down beside Seth.

Seth poured coffee for him and said, "It would appear the young lady doesn't want to go."

"So leave her."

Seth set the coffeepot down, "With you?"

"Sure."

"You want her?"

Eric laughed. "Poor Tess," he said. "Of course I do."

"No, you don't, Eric," Joanna said. She set a plate in front of him. "Not in the mood she's in."

"She's only in it because she's having to leave."

"Even so." She dropped her own egg into the pan and watched it sizzle. "You don't know what you're taking on."

"Of course I do." He looked up. Tess was watching hopefully from the door. "Tess is my friend. Most of the time." He looked at her, and she giggled. "Vanish, kid," he said, "we're talking about you." She nodded and tiptoed away. He turned to Joanna and said seriously, "She's actually quite a nice kid, Jo."

"You mean they come worse?"

Eric laughed softly. "When was the last time you were apart?"

Joanna stopped and thought for a long while. She said eventually, "Shortly before she was conceived."

Eric smiled. "Leave her with me. Have yourself a little break. You need it. Maybe she needs it too." Joanna looked doubtful. Eric turned to Seth, "Take her out somewhere. Take her to dinner. Somewhere nice." Joanna smiled and got up from the table.

"I'll go tell Tess," she said.

When she had gone, Seth grinned, clasping his hands over his head. "Thank you, pal. Thank you, thank you. You going to slip me a pack of condoms as I go out the door, as well?"

Eric sipped his coffee and fought a smile. "Seth, old friend, I kind of hoped, at your age, you'd gotten around to carrying your own."

Night

"SETH LEVINE, where are we going? Do you mind telling me? I haven't recognized anything for an hour. This is the weirdest route."

"We're going . . ." he paused, glancing in his mirror before yet another turnoff, onto an even more obscure road, "nowhere. We've been driving in circles for five hours and we're actually just ten miles from the camp."

"I can believe that. I really can. Where are we?"

"Massachusetts."

"Massachusetts! When did we cross the line? I didn't see . . ."

"When I told you to look to your right at that pair of non-existent deer. The sign was on our left."

"No wonder I couldn't see them. I thought it was my eyes. Seth, what precisely are you up to?"

"Pretty drive, isn't it?"

"*Seth.*"

"I'm waiting for dark, and then I'm going to run out of gas on one of these country lanes and ravish you on the backseat."

"Lovely, but if you really mean that, how about filling up now and finding a nice motel instead? I like to be ravished in comfort these days."

"I'm so glad you said that." He turned off again at a small white sign and drove up a well-tended dirt track. It ended in a meadow, beyond which was a handsome, gray-painted farmhouse. Two fine bay riding horses trotted across a white-fenced paddock at the front. Behind the house a hill rose, drenched in late autumn color. Seth drove up to the house and parked in front of the long porch. Seven tables, covered with red checked cloths and attended by white wicker chairs, lined its length. A rustic painted sign, BIRCHWOOD BED AND BREAKFAST, hung over the door.

"Seth, I was joking."

"Big brother said I should take you out to dinner."

"In Massachusetts?"

"This place is a gem. Wait till you taste the *crème brûlée.*" He grinned, opened his door, and stepped out.

"Seth," Joanna followed him out of the car into the white fall sunshine, "it's three in the afternoon."

"We could take a walk first. There's a lake. And a swan."

"A swan," Joanna said. Seth nodded. "And then dinner." He nodded again. "And then we drive to Long Island?"

He shrugged. "We can if you want to," he said easily. "But no one's expecting anybody until tomorrow." Joanna stepped up on the porch, looking at the tables, the green shutters, the milk churn filled with white impatiens at the side of the green door. She turned and looked out over the meadow. The horses stood side by side, entwining their necks, biting at each other's manes.

"Would I possibly be right if I guessed you've already booked a room?"

"I've booked them all, actually."

"What?"

"I called from that gas station on the Northway, this morning."

"This morning. All of them. How many are there?"

"Eight. I thought it would be nice to have it all to ourselves. I've booked the dining room as well."

"Seth how much . . ."

"They gave me a special rate," he said encouragingly.

"*Even so.*"

He grinned suddenly. "I thought of driving to Boston and flying you to Paris, but that would have been a bit extravagant. And we'd never have gotten back in time."

She shook her head, smiling, "No, I imagine not. Well, Seth, all I can say is, it's a big step up from two beers and a package of salted nuts. That's the usual offer where I come from."

He got suddenly serious. "Jo. This is just for fun. You can sleep in any one of those rooms you like. You don't even have to tell me which, okay?"

She leaned her shoulder against the white pillar of the porch, looked up, curiously, at the roof above, and then down at Seth, standing at the foot of the steps. She smiled again, fondly, shaking her head.

"Seth, I'd love to . . ."

"But?"

"I just feel so awfully guilty. We're supposed to be seeing your father."

"We'll see him. There's no point today. He won't know anything until tomorrow."

"And Dina?" she said quietly.

"Jo, whatever you do get from Dina—and I warn you again, don't expect to get anything much—a day won't matter. Not to Dina or you or Eric. Not after thirteen years."

"I feel I'm using him, Seth."

"He asked you to. Jo, you've trekked halfway across the country for him. You've scoured the streets of New York for him. You've lost your job and what little security you had. Do him the kindness of letting him give something back." She closed her eyes briefly, nodding. "Jo," he said.

"Yes?"

"When was the last time you did something just for yourself? Just for fun?"

"I have lots of fun, Seth. I don't know what impression I've given, but my life's not some sort of purgatory. Tess and I have had a lot of good times."

"No. Not you and Tess. You. Something for you. Just for you."

She shrugged, "You don't expect to, Seth, when you've got a kid."

"Tonight. Just for you. No kid. No duties. Just you. One night. Okay?" He held his hands out to her, gently, palms upraised. The sun glistened on his black hair and won a kind light from his sharp, dark eyes.

"Show me the swan," she said.

THERE WERE THREE SWANS circling silkily on a landscaped artificial pond. Joanna and Seth found a white stone bench, put there, clearly, for swan watching, and sat side by side. "Three for the price of one," Joanna said.

"I had the others flown in. I thought one looked lonely." They sat for a long while, talking in the gathering cold of the afternoon. Seth put his arm around Joanna's shoulders, and they leaned against each other, peacefully, for warmth. The sun shifted westward, sinking to the horizon, and they fell quiet. After a long silence, he said, very carefully, "Jo, there's something I have to know."

She could tell from his voice exactly what it was, and said, in answer, "I'm surprised you waited so long."

"I just want to know when, Jo, that's all."

"Does it matter?"

"I want to know where I was."

"You were there, Seth. It was my senior year. Martin had come home for Thanksgiving, and what with being apart so long, we just got careless. You remember what sex is like at that age." He was silent. "I guessed right away. I was always regular as clockwork, and then I wasn't. I wrote Martin. He came back. We had this big family conference. His parents. My parents . . ."

"I don't remember any of this," Seth said.

"Why should you? Martin came home for a weekend. That's all there was for you to remember."

"I can't believe I didn't realize what was happening."

"We weren't exactly broadcasting it."

"But I felt I was so close to you. I felt you told me everything."

"I was ashamed, Seth. I didn't want anyone to know." He nodded, troubled.

"So when . . . ?" he asked painfully.

"January . . . Seth, I really don't like talking about this."

He slipped his arm from her shoulders and slid it between them, capturing her hand. "I'm sorry, Jo, I'm being terribly selfish." He sat in silence for a while, holding her hand. When he spoke his voice was distant. "It's just so humbling to realize that while you were going through the biggest crisis of your life, I was talking to you about Bob Dylan and imagining myself your one true soul mate. What fools we are."

She laughed gently. "I think you were my one true soul mate," she said. She cocked her head sideways, smiling at him, and then said more seriously, "It sure wasn't Martin, anyhow. If there was a lesson learned that winter, it was that." She paused and said hurriedly, "Oh, he was right, Seth. We'd have made a hell of a mess, married, with a kid, at that age. He was right and sensible, and if I'm really honest, he gave me the escape I desperately wanted. But I couldn't love him anymore. We were just too different. He'd shown me caution where I'd wanted . . ." She paused. "I don't know, Seth, recklessness? Courage? He wasn't a man I could love."

"But you didn't break up then, Jo. It was years later. I was in India . . ."

"Oh, I know. I know." She twined her fingers comfortably in his and watched as the swans drifted in an intricacy of triangles, toward the shore. "Still, it was over that winter. We'd got rid of the baby for the sake of our future, and then, once it was gone, there wasn't any future left. But the habit of love is hard to break, and it's the habit of love that makes us blind. Then we had our big fight and I took off for the Coast. Inside himself, I think Martin was just as relieved as I was." She smiled gently, "And after I left, he turned around twice and saw what I had seen for years."

"What was that?"

"That it was Annie, not me, that he loved." She looked up wisely. "I think he still gets a little romantic about me from time to time, when he's feeling forlorn, but it's only because he sees me as a sort of icon of his youth." She stood up slowly, still holding Seth's hand. "Which is funny, because the one thing I remember clearest about Martin was that he was never really young."

Seth stood up too, and put his arm back around her shoulders as they followed the grassy mowed path around the pond, back toward the house. The swans drifted toward the center of the water again, and he wanted to ask if she, freed, too, from the habit of love, had thought of him, far off in India. But he said nothing, not wanting to hear her say no.

———

THE GUEST HOUSE served them dinner with utmost discretion, in front of a big log fire. Candles flickered on the white cloth and glowed from wall sconces above the mantel, leaving the rest of the room, with its shadowy, empty tables, in gathering darkness. "It feels like it's our own home," Joanna said.

"That's what I wanted." He passed her the menu and studied the wine list. When she made her selection, he raised his eyes over his reading glasses and gave her a dark look. "Joanna, you're picking the cheapest things on the menu. Will you stop? I'm paying."

"That's what's worrying me."

He took the glasses off. "Fine. I'll sell the place in Italy maybe, but I'll manage to pay this bill. Have what you want or I'll order it all. Seriously." Joanna looked up nervously.

"Like the rooms?"

"Like the rooms. I'll do it, Jo."

"Yes," she said, watching him. "Yes, I'm sure you will." She picked up the menu again and drew in a quick breath. "Right. I'll have a steak. A huge, red, juicy, environmentally scandalous, unhealthy, expensive steak. With mushrooms and fries and onion rings," she added in a rush.

"Fine." He took the menu from her. "Good girl." He gave their orders, and chose wine, and handed back the two leatherbound folders to the instantly attendant waitress. When she had gone, he said to Joanna, "I think I should tell them I've already written my piece, before they collapse from the strain."

"It's not that, Seth. It's the thing with the rooms. They probably think you're richer than God."

He laughed gently and brushed back his hair with the side of his hand, "Right, Jo. Would you like to come to Italy for Christmas?" he said.

"Seth. Stop it." Her eyes were wide. "I've ordered the steak. That's enough."

"Okay, okay." He brushed back his hair again. "We'll talk about that later."

"No, we won't," she said, firmly enough that he didn't dare. Yet it didn't stop his describing the villa to her in such sensual travel writer's detail that she could feel the sun on her bare shoulders, smell the dusty grapes on the arbor, and taste the cappuccino served in its dappled shadow.

As she finished her *crème brûlée,* she stretched luxuriantly and then folded her hands across her stomach. "Oh, Seth, that was gorgeous. I'm going to split my jeans if I move."

"Don't move," he said. "I'll order liqueurs."

"No. Nothing. Honest," she begged, laughing. "You'll have to carry me upstairs."

He grinned ruefully, "This is where I always wish for some height. I'll probably have to drag you, Jo."

"I'll walk." She lifted her cuff to see her watch.

"Nine-thirty," he said. "Do you want to call?"

"Tess? No." She shook her head quickly. "I was just wondering how poor Eric's managing."

"Just fine, Jo. He's good with kids anyhow, but he's got a no-lose scenario with Tess. She worships him. She'll do anything he asks, probably before he asks it. She'll be tucked up angelically in bed, schoolwork done, dishes dried. She's probably even brushed her teeth." He paused. "But go on and call and put your mind at rest."

She shook her head again. "No. She'll hate it if I do. I'll leave them alone." She smiled wanly. "Isn't it silly, what mothers are like?"

"I think it's enchanting," he said. He smiled fondly and then said, "It'll be good for her, Jo. And good for him as well."

"I know." She studied the sleeve of her shirt thoughtfully. "It was the funniest thing," she said. "When we were driving away, looking back at the two of them standing there together." Seth nodded, thinking he knew what she was going to say. "She looks so much like Molly, doesn't she?"

"Yes."

"I remember," Joanna said, "Eric used to say, at the beginning, that he had this tremendously powerful feeling that it was all still redeemable somehow, that if he could somehow just go back to the day before it happened . . ."

"That he could do the day over and get it right."

"Yes."

"I remember. He told me too. It's a common feeling, apparently, during grief . . . after an accident, a death."

"I know," she said urgently. "But don't you see, I looked back and I saw them and I thought somehow, *we've done it*. It was like looking into the past. Like we'd won back that day." Seth raised his wineglass, but did not drink from it.

> " 'Though lovers be lost love shall not;
> And death shall have no dominion.' "

She looked up, startled. "Is that you?" she said.

He laughed softly in self-mockery. "Oh, I wish." He drank the wine and set down the glass. "Dylan Thomas," he said.

"Oh." She smiled. "It's been a while since I read anything like that." She paused. "Seth, do you believe in God?" she asked.

"Not yet. But I keep trying." He smiled sweetly, rose, and reached for her hand.

The big front hallway of the farmhouse, with its small, well-disguised reception desk, was empty. On a low table, eight sets of keys with discreet brass tags were fanned out like a hand of cards.

"There's no one here," Joanna said.

"They seem to have taken my desire for privacy a little over-seriously. You'd think I was Howard Hughes, back from the grave. Or the *Capo del Capos* of the Mafia. That's it. They've seen the Italian address."

Joanna giggled, "It's kind of nice, actually." She looked around at their lonely reflections in a big maple-framed mirror. "A little spooky too. Like one of those fairy-tale castles where all the work is done by magic and you can stay a year and never see a soul."

"Wonderful. Let's stay a year."

"I think Eric would get a bit tired of Tess by then."

"Maybe not. Maybe we'd come out and find no time had passed in all the outside world." He gestured expansively with both hands. "Or maybe she'd have turned into an enchanted princess."

"Pretty strong magic," said Joanna.

"Hey," Seth said, sweeping up the keys. "You remember that story we had at school . . . the woman who had to choose between two doors for her lover to enter?"

" 'The Lady or the Tiger?' "

"The tiger behind one, a beautiful princess to marry behind the other. Either way, she loses him forever." He held up the keys. "Which is it, Jo?" She laughed and gave him a gentle shove as they started up the stairs.

"It's a wonderfully young story," she said. "Can you imagine actually thinking there was a choice? We actually puzzled over it. Can you imagine?"

"Oh, I've known women who would choose the tiger," he said solemnly. "It's amazing in this world what passes for love." He stopped on the stairs and held out the eight keys. "Pick a key, any key," he said.

"You first." He shrugged and, without looking at them, separated one from the group and slipped it into his pocket. "Why, Seth," she said, with a disapproving smile, "you've taken mine."

———

TESS WOKE UP, knowing something was lost. She even searched around the outside of her sleeping bag, until she remembered she had been dreaming and the lost thing was part of her dream. Relieved and disappointed at once, she flopped back down on her bunk and pulled the puffy warmth of the bag up to her chin. She had been dreaming about her pet cat that she lost three years ago when she was eight. In the dream she'd been just at the point of finding it. In reality, she'd looked for it for days, up and down the road, in the barn where it hunted, in the woods where it liked to play with dry leaves, but never did find it. Even now, all this time later, and living away from the ranch, she still looked for it sometimes, just for a day or two, when she thought of it again and got that feeling of something lost from her life.

The looking-for-something feeling remained, left over from her dream, and she lay quietly in her bunk, watching the cold sun filtering through the frost feathers on the window. She puffed a breath out, saw it condense into a wispy cloud, and pulled the sleeping bag in close. Then she remembered her mother had gone away yesterday with Seth, and she sat up in her bunk.

It was the top bunk of a pair built into the pinewood wall of the cabin, and Tess had chosen to sleep in it after carefully considering both the bottom bunk and the metal-framed double bed that sat against the opposite wall. Between it and the bunk beds, a faded rug made of braided, multicolored rags was spread on the linoleum floor. Tess crawled out of her sleeping bag and jumped down onto the rug and, keeping her feet on it, leaned over her knapsack, quickly hauling out clean underpants and socks. Clutching them, she grabbed her shirt and T-shirt and jeans from the bottom bunk and scrambled back up into her sleeping bag. She wiggled out of her pajamas and into her clothes inside its warm, dark nest. If her mother was here, she would have run with her clothes to dress by the woodstove, but she was shy with just herself and Eric.

The whole cabin seemed different now that they were alone in it. Yesterday, after Seth and her mother had driven away, it was exciting and adventurous, working on the roof and making meals and in the evening doing her schoolwork, with Eric reading a book while he waited to check her spelling. But in the night, in bed, she got suddenly gigantically lonely, missing her mom, and actually cried before going to sleep. In the bright, cold morning light, she was ashamed at the memory. She stayed inside the sleeping bag even after she was dressed, ejecting her pajama top and bottoms onto the floor and then watching the sun melt the layer of ice from the window. She made bargains about getting up, when the sun touched one patch of frost, or another, but broke them all, looking around dreamily through half-open eyes.

After a while she heard the scrape of the poker, as Eric cleaned out the woodstove and the bang of the door when he went out for logs. Then there was the smell of wood smoke drifting in from outside, through the cracks by the window, and the smell of coffee from the kitchen. She stretched out straight in the sleeping bag, feeling wonderfully safe, as she had on winter mornings at the ranch in the days before Sean Kelly and her mom had stopped being in love.

There was a knock on her door, and then Eric came in and

brought her coffee in a thick blue mug. She sat up in her sleeping bag and took it, thanking him, though she didn't drink coffee. She sipped it, experimentally, and didn't like it any better than she'd remembered.

"You want sugar?" Eric said. She shook her head.

"I usually take it black," she said, which was a total lie, but had a good sound to it. "But this is fine," she added before he could offer to change it.

"Did you sleep in your clothes?" he asked, smiling at her, sitting there in her shirt and jeans. She shook her head again.

"I'm getting up, really," she said. "Only it's cold." She saw he was wearing the old woodsman's jacket that he'd found in the cabin when they arrived, and said, "Have you been up the ridge?"

"Not this morning."

"You can go if you want. I'm fine alone," she said quickly. "I could make breakfast maybe." As she said it she had a mental image of her mom with her mouth open in astonishment. The image made her smile. Side by side with it was a picture of her usual morning at home in the trailer, slouching around in her pajamas, arguing about everything, and never even knowing quite why. It all seemed pretty silly, and she started to giggle.

"What's funny?" Eric asked. He had been looking out the frosty window at the sun on the trees, one hand resting on the upright of the bunk, and he turned, surprised. She shrugged.

"I was thinking of something." He looked curious, and she said suddenly, "Do you ever have arguments with someone for no reason at all?" He smiled thoughtfully and held her coffee mug for her as she scrambled down from the upper bunk.

"All arguments are about something, Tess, even if the something is hidden by other things."

"Do you think so?" she said seriously.

"I know so."

She pushed her feet into her unlaced sneakers and shuffled toward the door. "You know, I just thought of something real funny."

He followed her. In the kitchen she set her coffee mug down on the table, where he had already laid a place for her breakfast. "What was that?"

"It was Mom and Sean Kelly. You know what they fought about?" Eric shook his head. He opened the refrigerator and got out bacon and eggs, but she could see he was listening just the same, and she said, "Steps."

"Steps?"

"There were two back steps by the kitchen door, and one of them had a hole in it. A real hole. The board was rotten and someone's foot had made a hole. So it did matter," she said conscientiously. "And from the beginning of school until Christmas, Mom kept saying to Sean, 'Will you fix it?' and he kept saying yes, but not doing it. Then one day Mom was coming up the steps with the groceries, and she tripped and dropped everything and the dog—it was Sean's dog—jumped right in and pulled out a package of steak and ate it in about two seconds. And Mom was so mad, because we hadn't had steak for months, but she didn't get mad at the dog. She got mad at Sean. She sure yelled at him." Tess sat down at the table, staring at her place setting thoughtfully.

"Is that when he left?" Eric asked.

"No." Tess looked up. "That was the funny part. He fixed the step, and the next night he brought home three big steaks and we all ate them, with candles on the table, and they were all lovey and everything. And then the next day he left." She was quiet. "It was like, once the step was finally fixed, there wasn't any point in staying." She watched as he laid strips of bacon in the frying pan. "You know what I used to do?"

"What was that?"

"I used to try to make the hole come in the step again. I'd kick at it every time I went in or out. Which was pretty stupid, because it was a real good solid board."

"You miss him, Tess?" She wrinkled her face and then shook her chin up and down in fierce affirmation. "I don't know why. He used to yell at me and send me to bed early and he cheated on promises all the time." She felt her eyes wet and buried them in her sleeve. He put his arm around her, casually, still cooking her breakfast with the other hand.

"We're made to love people, Tess," he said, "whether they deserve it or not." He fried an egg and put it and the bacon on a plate for her. "It's not your fault," he said and then added, as he sat down across from her, "It's not your mom's fault either, you know."

"I didn't say it was," she said quickly.

"Yes, you have, Tess. You say it all the time."

"I don't."

He smiled. "All arguments are about something, Tess." She looked confused. "Eat your breakfast. We're going to climb a mountain," he said.

"What, today?" She looked up eagerly, but felt duty bound to add, "We haven't finished the roof yet."

"We can finish it tomorrow. It's a good day. We'll go today."

"Oh, right on!" She jumped up and then sat down quickly, gobbling her breakfast. "A big mountain?" she asked, stuffing in two strips of bacon. He nodded, laughing. "Marcy?"

"Maybe not Marcy," he said, "We'll see. Something big anyhow. How fit are you?"

"Real fit. You saw me run, right?"

"Right," he said, still smiling. "Okay. How about you make some sandwiches, while I find us some gear."

"Sure, Eric," she said. She took her plate and cutlery to the sink and washed them. Then she got bread out and started spreading it with peanut butter and jelly. She heard herself saying, "Sure," to her mom in the same way, like a revelation. It was so simple. The sandwiches took next to no time to make, and it was even fun, stacking them up neatly in a plastic bag.

Eric came in from the lean-to shed where they kept skis and sleeping bags, winter clothes, and the two family tents. He tossed her a red wool hat with snowflakes on the rim and two pairs of mittens, one white and one yellow. "You have a sweater?" She nodded. "And your jacket. The warm one."

"I'll go pack," she said, still carefully employing her new adult mode. She didn't even argue about the big padded jacket that she always refused to wear at home because it made her look fat. In her room she emptied the contents of the knapsack onto the rag rug and began replacing them with things for the mountain.

She put the padded jacket at the bottom, with a resigned shrug, added the hat and the mittens Eric had given her, and covered them with a green wool sweater she'd begged from her mom because it had really good holes in the elbows and one in the hem. Then she looked around the room for other things that might be useful.

She found a squashed Snickers bar and shoved it in on top of the sweater, and her bathing suit, in case it got warm and they found a lake or a stream to swim in, and a pair of socks in case the ones she was wearing rubbed a blister. She toyed with her personal stereo and thought how nice it would be to listen to Michael Jackson on the top of a mountain. She unzipped the top pocket of the knapsack and stuffed the stereo and headphones and three cassettes inside. There was something squashy there already, and she pulled it out, curiously, and then grimaced. It was the unopened pastel-wrapped pack of sanitary napkins her mother had given her six months ago, "just in case." For the first few weeks Tess had dragged them around everywhere, smuggling them along whenever she went to the bathroom, but after that, when nothing happened, she forgot about them. She turned the pack over in her hand, dropped it with the rest of her stuff on the rag rug, then picked it up again and hastily shoved it back in, beside the stereo. Just her luck if *it* started on top of a mountain in the middle of nowhere. She zipped the pocket closed and lifted the knapsack. It wasn't very heavy and she carried it, slung over one shoulder, into the kitchen of the cabin.

"I'm ready, Eric," she said, dumping the knapsack on the kitchen floor beside an old khaki-colored one that belonged to the cabin, into which Eric was packing the sandwiches and two thermos bottles.

"I've left one black for you," he said, and she grinned weakly and said, "Great."

"You have enough warm clothes?"

"Sure."

"It'll be cold."

"I've got lots," she said, though not really believing him. The sun was pouring down now, and the cabin felt too warm with the fire burning in the woodstove. Still, Eric opened the door and added two big logs and shut down the draft before they went out to the Jeep.

He loaded the knapsacks in the back and asked, "Where are you riding, Tess?"

She thought about sitting in the back, watching the road twist away dreamily behind the tailgate, and was briefly tempted. But she said, "In front with you, if it's okay."

"Of course," he said. "Why wouldn't it be?"

"Because I'll probably talk a lot. Mom says I bother people."

"You don't bother me." He sounded as if he meant it, but she was still quiet at the beginning of the drive, in case he was being polite. But then he asked her about her friends at school, and she ended up telling him everything, really everything, about Bobby, who always wanted to play games that ended with people taking their clothes off, and Cathy, who smoked hash as well as tobacco and had given her some to try, which she'd hidden up in the woods.

"I can't tell my mom any of this stuff."

"Have you tried?"

"Are you kidding? She goes ape-shit over tobacco!" She paused, "She's real strict, my mom. You'd be surprised." She put her feet up on the dashboard and said, consideredly, "I think it's being a single parent. She thinks she's got to be double-strict to make up, or something." She looked across at Eric. "Were you strict? I mean with Molly," she added awkwardly. He was quiet, and she looked at his big hands on the steering wheel rather than at his face.

"It depends on who you ask," he said eventually. "Parents are only strict because they love you, you know."

"That's not true," Tess said at once. "Oh, it's true mostly for Mom, I know that. But sometimes she's strict to prove a point to somebody. Like I have the earliest bedtime of all my friends, and I have to be home sooner than anybody if there's a party or anything at school. And that's because everyone knows I haven't got a father."

"It might not be."

"It is," she said with easy certainty. "Bobby's mother is strict when his dad goes out to see his girlfriend at the Slalom Bar. Suddenly Bobby has to stay in and clean up his room and everything." She paused. "That's really unfair. My mom's fair, anyhow," she added.

Eric said, "Tess, your mom's a savvy lady. Trust her."

She smiled shyly. "I do, really," she said. "Most of the time. Most of the time she's pretty great. Though," she paused, seriously, "some of the time she's a real pain in the ass."

"Some of the time, sweetheart," he said with a smile, "so are you."

THE FIRST SIGHT of the mountain they were going to climb made Tess forget all about Bobby and Cathy and even her mom. "Is that it?" she pointed at the hazy blue outline rising above the wintry brown foothills.

"One of them is it," Eric said, keeping his own eyes on the winding road.

"It looks real big."

"Well, it's big for here, Tess. Hardly the Rockies, though. Small stuff for you." She was quiet for a moment, thinking.

"I never really look at them," she said, honestly. "They're just there."

He laughed. "That's supposed to be the best reason for climbing them." She looked puzzled. "Because they're there. Never mind, Tess, it's an old story."

"Well, I guess you wouldn't climb them if they weren't there," she said, after thinking about it.

"That's it, kid. Right the first time." He turned off the road, down a dirt track and into a broad, empty parking lot with a big timber building at the far end.

"What's this?"

"Where we start."

"Where's the mountain gone?" she asked, jumping out and looking around, disappointed.

"Behind those trees." He pointed toward the trailhead as he climbed down from the Jeep.

"Great," she said, hopping from foot to foot. As soon as he'd lowered the tailgate, she grabbed her pack, slung it onto her shoulders, and set out for the trail at a run.

"Take your time," he shouted. "It's a long way." She kept running, joyfully oblivious. Locking the Jeep quickly, Eric shouldered his own knapsack and jogged after her, catching quick glimpses of her blue shirt and yellow hair between the bare gray tree trunks. He hesitated at the visitor's logbook at the trailhead, but passed it by, rather than lose sight of her, and broke into a run, the old-fashioned pack bouncing awkwardly with each step, his feet sliding a little in Martin's old hiking boots. When he caught up with her, she was standing alone in a circle of lofty birches, staring up at their white trunks against the rich blue sky.

"I think maybe I should look at things more," she said in a serious, adult voice. She began walking then, carefully, treading the dry brown leaves with a pilgrim's hesitant respect, a slight, blond wood sprite beneath the towering trees. Eric followed at a distance, leaving her in a solitude of discovery.

The first half of the climb was easy, a well-worn trail mounting steadily through gray winter oaks and maples and luminescent birches, dipping down to cross streams and, once, a waterfall, where they stopped for a snack. Tess wrinkled her nose and drank her black coffee and grinned proudly when Eric said she had grown-up taste.

Past the waterfall, the trail turned upward more sharply, the trees thinned, allowing glimpses over distant brown hills, and the air turned cold. Surprised, Tess put on the mittens and hat Eric had given her, and climbed faster, to warm up. The trail was rockier, and the wet patches in the shadows shone blackly with ice. Eric showed her how to cross them, keeping her hands and feet on paler dry rock. She liked the feel of the rock, smooth and solid, and took off the mittens again, stuffing them into her jeans pockets so she could get a better grip. The trail got suddenly steeper, and on either side, the pine trees grew in a thick greeny-black wall. She looked back down the canyon it formed to far vistas of blue hills.

"We're real high now, aren't we?"

"Slower, Tess. Watch the ice." He climbed up, just behind her, as he'd done on the roof.

"I'm not going to fall," she said, as she'd said then, but here she wasn't quite as sure. He said nothing, but followed closely, and she didn't even pretend to herself that she minded. After the steep part, the trail rounded off, the pine trees were smaller and smaller, and the sun hit the gray rocks, melting away the ice. Tess straightened up and began to run, following the yellow paint splashes that marked the way. Eric let her go, staying well back so that she could find the summit alone, seeing himself and Martin, forty years before, on this same unchanging mountain, with the same conquering eagerness of youth. Only then it had been Harry Levine who had ambled, hands in pockets, behind.

The top of the mountain was bald, bare rock and golden grass and juniper. This climb had always surprised Eric: the trail coming out suddenly from the dark embrace of endless pine into an alpine barrenness, filled with air and sky. He saw Tess at the highest point, standing on a hump of gray-brown rock, her feet planted wide apart, her arms hanging loosely at her sides. She turned slowly, taking in the perfect circle of mountains and valleys, lakes and blue receding hills. When he reached her and put his hand lightly on her shoulder, she did not even respond at first, then looked up suddenly, as if startled from sleep. "Have they got names, Eric?" she asked.

"Mostly."

"What are they called?"

He smiled, slipping off his knapsack and lowering it to a grassy patch of ground. He sat beside it, cross-legged. "I'll need the map for that, Tess. It's been a while." He pulled a map from the knapsack, spread it out on her rock, and showed her how to read contours and to form mountain shapes in her mind from their curving brown lines. She nodded quickly, absorbing each point.

"So this is the one we're on. And that's the trail up. And there's that lake," she said.

"That's right."

"And that's the funny one over there with the gray stripes on it."

"Mud slides. That's it." She looked back to the map, her fingers tracing shapes, her eyes intent. Looking up again, she pointed to the skyline ridge.

"That's Marcy, then."

"Right. Good."

"The biggest," Tess said.

"The biggest," Eric agreed.

"I want that one next." He looked down and started to laugh, but stopped. Her forehead was lined with concentration as she stared at the distant peak.

He said softly, "Well, well. A mountaineer." She looked up. The pale blue eyes were narrow and serious, with the same demanding honesty as Jo's.

"Don't laugh at me, Eric," she said. "I just want to climb the biggest."

"I'm not laughing, Tess. I meant it." She studied him carefully and then smiled. Her eyes went back to the mountain.

"It's beautiful."

"Okay," he said. "We'll climb it. But not today. Let's have some lunch."

"Lunch. Yeah. Right on." She jumped down off her rock, a little girl again, and leaped to the knapsack, burrowing for sandwiches and chocolate bars. "I'm starving." After three sandwiches and all the chocolate, Eric intervened.

"You'll want something on the way down. If I'd ever seen you eat like that before, I'd have brought a lot more food."

"Climbing mountains makes me hungry," she said, with satisfaction. But she relinquished the last two sandwiches, dutifully, and drank the rest of her coffee, thirsty enough now to not care about the taste.

"There's a couple of cans of Diet Pepsi," he offered. But she shook her head, deciding to have outgrown Diet Pepsi.

"How long can we stay?" she asked. Eric looked at the sun in the bright, high sky.

"A little while longer."

"Great." As he packed away the lunch, she got her own knapsack and took her Walkman from the top pocket. She slipped the headphones on and climbed up onto her big rock. Eric watched her, amazed.

"You carried that all the way up here?"

She looked shy. "There's a song I like. I wanted to hear it on top of a mountain." She shrugged. He smiled, but did not laugh, because he had carried his folder of pictures of Molly in his knapsack, just as he carried it everywhere, and he understood the nature of homage.

"Enjoy it," he said quietly. She nodded and sat down solemnly then, cross-legged, eyes closed, an electronic buddha swaying her blond head to her secluded song. Eric stretched out in the sun on a patch of dried grass, listening to the wind in the pines below. The sun felt like summer, but the air in every shadow was already winter cold. Having thought of the folder, he thought then of Molly and realized, startled, that although Harry and Martin had come into his mind on this old familiar mountain, Molly had not, though he had climbed it with her twice. The realization brought a strange relief, as in awaking from a frenetic, exhausting dream at the gray edge of dawn. Now he quite consciously put her from his mind and thought instead of Harry Levine in his familiar territory of hospital corridors, transmuted from invincible doctor to vulnerable patient. It unsettled him, more than if it were his own father, who had had two bypasses and for whose death he had long prepared.

"Are you asleep, Eric?" Tess asked.

"No," he said, still keeping his eyes closed. "Is your song finished?"

"Yeah. Do you know what?"

"What?"

"When I get home I'm going to climb every mountain there is."

"Every one? All the Rockies?"

"Well, all our Rockies." He opened his eyes then, squinting against the sun, and sat up.

"Good. Be sure you take someone with you. Someone grown-up. Not Bobby."

"Bobby!" she shrieked. "He wouldn't get up a mountain. All he does is lie around and listen to rap. He's real unfit." She added, "He smokes too."

"And you don't."

"I don't really smoke," Tess said defensively.

He drew one knee up and rested his elbow on it, his chin on

his hand. "You know, sweetheart," he said. "I've been a lot of places in the last few years, and the worst of them were full of people who once thought they didn't really do things, like smoke, or drink, or use crack."

"I don't do anything like that," she whispered, wide-eyed.

"Good. Keep it like that." He stood up.

"Is it time to go?" she asked cautiously, a little afraid, as always, of the sudden serious side he sometimes showed her. He looked at the sun. It was hazy now and a gray band of cloud had mounted along the northern horizon.

"Yeah, Tess, time to go."

"Can I see the map?"

"Sure." He withdrew it again from his pack and opened it for her carefully. It was old and stained and cracked at the folds, like all the camp maps. He spread it out again on the rock and she knelt over it, studying it carefully, her small fingers drawing experimental lines across the paper.

"We can go down that way," she said. He leaned in close, and she traced a new trail, leaving the summit opposite to the way they had come. "See, around the lake and around that hill, back to the parking lot."

"Good. Yes, we could, Tess." He paused. "But I think it's too long."

"No, it's not. Look." She took a measure from the mile chart at the base of the map against her index finger and worked it around the winding line of the trail. "Only a couple of miles, maybe."

"More than a couple, Tess, and even a couple of miles are a lot when you're tired."

"But I'm not tired. And it's all down. Down is easy."

"Down is hard. No."

"Please, Eric. I'm real fit. I was running up." He smiled.

"Yes, you were," he acknowledged fairly. "It's a bit late." He looked back at the sun, still high in the sky, but tipping slightly toward the western horizon, and the bank of cloud that had spread in from the north. "And the weather's changing," he added.

"It won't change that fast. And it doesn't matter if we're late.

Mom's not there. There's no one there," she said. "So we won't get yelled at." He grinned.

"Well, as long as we won't get yelled at," he said, "it must be all right." He picked up the map and folded it with the necessary section uppermost and handed it to Tess. "Okay, but we'll have to move fast. No fooling around."

"I don't fool around," she said.

He lifted his knapsack and nodded in concession. "Fair enough. I apologize."

She looked solemn for a moment longer and then smiled quickly, "It's okay." She slung her pack back on her shoulders, looked carefully at the map, and set off down the trail at a run.

"Tess. Slow down."

"You said we had to move fast."

"I didn't say run, Tess," he called sharply. "Moving fast doesn't mean running." She turned around, jogging backward and grinning, but saw he meant it and slowed down to a fast, determined walk. He followed, glancing once more at the fading sun as they left the summit behind.

"Is Marcy the highest mountain on the whole East Coast?" Tess shouted back, between the fir trees that had closed in almost at once.

"No."

"What is, then?"

Eric scrambled down a ledge of wet rock and caught up with her. "I don't know. Mount Washington maybe."

"Where's that?" she shouted, jumping down the next ledge.

"New Hampshire." He pointed vaguely eastward. "Out that way. Tess, slow down."

"What's the highest in America?"

"Counting Alaska?" He reached her ledge, but she was already scuttling down a narrow spine of rock beyond.

"Not counting Alaska."

"Mount Whitney."

"Counting Alaska?"

"Mount McKinley. Tess, you're running." She swung one-handed around the trunk of a thin fir.

"No, I'm not. In Europe?"

"Mont Blanc. You are."

She giggled and jumped from one side of the trail to the other, avoiding a sheet of ice. "In the world?" she said.

"Everest."

"I knew that." She made another quick jump and skidded, clutching a fir branch for balance.

"Watch the ice."

"I'm watching. I think I'll climb Everest," she said.

"How about concentrating on this one for a moment?" She turned and gave him a cocky grin.

"I am." She bolted off again, and he smiled in spite of himself, watching her dart, sure-footed and rabbit quick, and hearing with the ears of his own youth his father's voice shouting, "Slow down, Eric," far behind. He slipped his hands into his pockets and eased his own pace, letting her go on, just out of sight, secured to him yet by a string of shouts and questions drifting back to him.

"Eric, there's a waterfall . . ." Her voice sounded thin and far away in the cold air.

"Leave it. Wait for me." He freed his hands and scrambled hurriedly down the steepening trail, leaping the ice patches with quick expertise. "Tess . . ."

"It's fine . . ." she shouted. "Oh. Oh, shit." He heard the rough scrape of boots slipping on rock, a snapping of branches, and a thud.

"Tess. Tess?" He leaped forward, running down the trail, skidding on the heels of his boots, fending off fir branches with an upraised arm. The waterfall was ten feet high, a narrow trickle, surrounded by ferns and black moss and delicately encased in sheets of white ice. Tess was at the bottom in a small, awkward heap. She turned her head and looked up.

"Oh, shit, Eric," she moaned.

"Sweetheart . . ." He scrambled down the icy drop, jumping half of it. "What is it?"

"I think I've busted my Walkman," she said, feeling for her pack.

"Oh, Christ, kid, is that all?" She bit her lip, twisted around experimentally.

"And maybe my leg," she added, with a wince.

—◆—

IT WAS ONE O'CLOCK when Seth and Joanna turned into his parents' curving shell drive. He parked the Oldsmobile in front of the long gray veranda and looked at his watch. "That took longer than I'd thought," he said.

Joanna smiled, "What was I saying this morning when you wouldn't get out of bed?"

He stretched his arms over his head, working stiff shoulders. "Bed was nice."

"Very nice. When's your dad seeing the specialist?"

"He said three. I want to be there by two. We'll make it." He leaned across the front seat and kissed her gently, then straightened and reached to open his door, but stopped. "I have this awful, awkward feeling going in," he said. "Like when I used to bring a girl home from a movie and it was after midnight, because we'd been down at the beach. The house would be dark, and then you'd see the light going on in the bedroom and you knew her parents were on their way down the stairs." He covered his face with his hand, "Christ, it all comes back."

"If it's any comfort, Seth, this isn't my house. It's yours."

"It doesn't seem to make any difference. Do you think anybody'll guess?"

Joanna laughed gleefully. "Come on, Seth, the real question is, do you think anybody'll care?" She punched his shoulder. "I don't believe you," she said. He grinned but still looked wary as he got out of the car.

"My mother," he said, as they mounted the porch steps, "my mother will guess."

But Miriam, when they found her in the kitchen, seemed only flustered and confused, and quite uncurious about either Joanna's presence, or indeed, Tess's absence. She kissed them both and went back to chopping rounds of carrots.

"Is it enough, do you think? Sara's making chicken and

dumplings. I said I'd do the vegetables while she went to the store . . ." She chopped away, with worried, shaky fingers.

"I'm sure it's fine, Mom," Seth said.

"You'll both stay for lunch, Joanna?" Joanna looked at Seth.

Seth said, "Mom, are we going to the hospital?"

"Why should we go to the hospital?"

Seth paused and looked at Joanna. "To see Dad, Mom," he said warily.

"Where?"

"At the hospital, Mom." Seth's voice strengthened. Joanna touched his arm.

"Your father's in his study," Miriam said. Seth drew back, his eyes darkening, watching her uncertainly.

"He's where?"

"In his study." Seth glanced again at Joanna. She shook her head, bewildered.

"You mean he's home?"

"Where else is his study? Of course he's home," Miriam said.

"He told me afternoon, Mom. He told me three o'clock. He was seeing the specialist."

"So, he told me afternoon too. Then he calls your sister this morning and says he's seen the specialist, everything's fine, she should come and pick him up. That's it. No explanations. That's your father." Her hands stopped chopping and she looked up at Seth, and he saw to his relief and his surprise that the murkiness in her eyes was not confusion, but anger. "You want to go see him? Maybe he'll tell you something." She shrugged.

"Go see him," Joanna said. "I'll help your mother." She slipped her denim jacket off and hung it over the back of a chair, then picked up a paper bag of corn. "You want these, Miriam?"

"Oh, I suppose. That Sara. She never says what she wants."

"We'll just do a few," Joanna said soothingly, stripping the green husks from an ear. "She can always use a few." She smiled at Seth, and he slipped gratefully out the door.

His father's study was a little, dark room at the back of the house. Its one, north-facing window was overgrown by an aging lilac whose branches tapped and scratched against the glass in the wind, shutting out what little could be seen of a dull gray sky.

The walls were lined with shelves stacked with two generations of medical texts, rows of hard-backed western and mystery novels, and a forty-year collection of *National Geographic*, the yellow spines fading back into time like the layers of an archaeological dig.

In the middle of the room Harry Levine sat at his big oak desk, under the light of a maroon-shaded brass lamp, the *New York Times*, folded to the editorial page, before him, a glass half-filled with Scotch beside his hand. He put his finger on the page to keep his place when Seth opened the door.

"Dad?"

"Tell me this," Harry said, keeping his finger on the paper and tilting his head, the index finger of the other hand resting against his strong hooked nose. "Why is it, for all those years I wanted a Democrat in the White House and now we've finally got a Democrat in the White House, so maybe I should be happy for a change, and still somehow I don't feel so good about it. Is it just because he's younger than my kids?"

"He's younger than me?" Seth mocked horror. "I feel old."

"You? You're a baby."

"Kennedy was even younger."

"So was I in 1960. That felt all right. So how are you, Seth? You want a drink? Sit down."

"I'm fine." Seth sat on the edge of the broken-down leather sofa in front of the desk. "No, thanks," he said as Harry lifted the Venetian glass decanter that sat beside the lamp. Absently, he remembered the birthday when he had sent it to his father, in lieu of his presence, for which he now felt ashamed.

"How are you?" He said evenly. He watched his father's face. Harry took his glasses off and rubbed the bridge of his nose.

"Oh, fine, Seth, fine."

"What did they say?"

"The usual garbage. What do I expect at my age? It's nothing, Seth."

"It didn't sound that much like nothing before you went in."

"Well, it is. I told you. Old man's stuff. Prostate. It's embarrassing. I don't want to talk about it."

"Dad," Seth said clearly, "you're a doctor."

Harry put his glasses back on and glared at Seth over their gray rims, "Does that mean I can't be embarrassed in front of my son? Come on, give me a break." Seth shook his head, frustrated.

"Have you talked to Martin about what they said? Is Martin happy?"

"When is Martin *ever* happy? No, I haven't talked to Martin. I just got home. And there's nothing to talk to Martin about." He waved his hand dismissively and then leaned forward, "Now, you tell me, how's Eric and Joanna, up at the camp? How's he doing?"

Seth sighed and leaned back in the sofa, giving up. He said, his voice still distracted, "Good. He's doing real good." He paused. "He's rebuilding the place from scratch as far as I can see. You're going to be amazed."

"Ha. That Eric. Isn't he something?" He put his hand flat on the paper. "I could always rely on Eric," he said and then added slowly, "and how is he?"

Seth shrugged. "I can't tell. He doesn't talk to me. I'm a kid to Eric still. He wouldn't dream of confiding in me." He closed his eyes for a moment, then opened them. "Jo's come down with me. She's going to see Dina." His father looked up, surprised, and then took his glasses off again, swinging them loosely by one earpiece. He rubbed his eyes.

"I don't think this is a good idea," he said.

"Neither do I," said Seth. "But what can I do?"

"Oh, I know. I know. Women. They always have to have everything out in the open. Show them a scab, they have to pick. You can't convince them. One day the thing is as clean as it's ever going to be, and then you just have to let it heal and accept the scar." He tapped the glasses on his paper and lifted them back onto his face and said abruptly, "So, how's the weather up there? Any snow yet?"

"Cold. No snow."

"You came down this morning?"

Seth hesitated, unable to say the simple, uncomplicated lie. "No. Not from the camp. We left there yesterday." He paused and added deliberately, "Joanna and I spent the night in a place in Massachusetts." His father smiled.

"That was nice."

"It *was* nice," Seth said. "One of these bed and breakfast places. I'm doing an article . . ."

"You and Joanna, Seth. That's what's nice."

"We've always been good friends," Seth said quickly.

"And now you're more than good friends. I tell you, it's nice." He leaned back in his leather chair, folding his bony arms behind his head and looking at Seth over the rim of his glasses. "What? I'm not supposed to notice? You're too grown-up now?" He laughed quickly, then released the clasp of his hands, waving Seth away with one, and picking up his *Times* with the other.

Harry was holding the paper folded to the sports section when he came into the dining room for lunch. He walked slowly, his reading glasses down on the bridge of his nose, using the cane with each step. He sat at his place, with Seth and Joanna on either side, and continued reading until Sara and Miriam came in with the meal.

"Put your paper away, Harry, we're ready to eat." Miriam sounded sharp and distracted at once, the way she did when the thing that was annoying her was different from the thing she was talking about.

Harry ignored her and said to Seth, "Ice hockey. That's a good sport. Everyone moving all the time, no time to get bored."

"Except when they stop and hit each other over the head," Miriam said. "Chicken, Joanna? Have some chicken?"

"So, even then, it's a good sport. It's honest. You think when they play football, or basketball, they don't want to hit each other over the head?" Seth laughed, and Harry touched his arm. "Remember when we used to play on the lake, at Christmas, up at the camp?"

"I remember clearing the ice," Miriam said. "Pushing a snow shovel up and down all afternoon. Some fun."

"Aw, it was great. Remember Martin getting so mad when Eric scored a goal, he'd kick a hole in the ice with his skate, and just about fall in?"

"Dangerous," Miriam muttered. "I hated it, everybody fooling around on that ice." She dumped two chicken thighs on Harry's plate.

"No. Too much," he said, but she ignored him. Sara passed vegetables, smiling benignly, while her parents argued. When everyone was served, she herself sat down, shaking out her cloth napkin.

Seth smiled at her. "*Buon appetito.*"

"Oh, *grazie*," she said. She smiled quickly, warmly back. "Everyone talking about ice skating already, and all I can think of is sunshine on the Med. Send me a box of it when you get back, Seth, hey?"

"I just might do that," he said. He looked at her fondly.

Miriam watched them, then said to Sara, as if to tug her back from some wayward digression, "So, tell me, how's Bill?" Sara turned away from Seth.

"I don't know, Mom," she said cheerfully, "I haven't seen him since you asked me last."

"You haven't seen him?" Miriam said, alert. "Is something wrong?"

"Mom," Sara laughed lightly, "I saw him yesterday. Yesterday he was fine. That's all I can tell you."

"So don't get angry. I'm only interested. You'd rather I wasn't interested?" Sara maintained her gentle smile. Miriam turned to Seth and Joanna. "Sara has a new boyfriend."

"Mom. He's not a boyfriend."

"So what is he?"

"Well, if anything, he's a manfriend. He's forty-two."

"A little younger doesn't matter these days," Miriam said complacently.

"Miriam," Harry said.

"I said it doesn't matter."

"So, you two," Harry said loudly to Joanna and Seth, "you're going to stay a while?"

"Oh no," Joanna said quickly. "I've left my poor brother with Tess, God help him. I've got to get right . . ."

"Younger men are more sympathetic, I think," Miriam continued, unabashed. "*New Men*, they call them now." She paused, making sure that she had full attention again, and gave a small, smug smile, for Harry's benefit, before continuing. "Still, three little children's a lot to take on." She nodded her head solemnly.

"Mom," Sara said, "I'm not taking anything on."

"But you're always a generous girl."

Sara balled her hands into fists and gave an exasperated little sigh. Joanna and Seth were both looking at her curiously.

"Have we missed something?" Joanna said at last.

Sara shook her head, but she smiled again, kindly, and said with a quick glance at her mother, "Those two little girls in my class, the sisters Cally and Karen? Well, I've been out maybe twice with their father."

"More than twice," Miriam said.

"He's a widower. I knew his wife first, actually. She died last year."

"Breast cancer," Miriam whispered. "A young woman. With three little children. The things people get these days."

Harry laid his fork down. "People have always gotten these things, Miriam." He paused. "Now suddenly it's not supposed to happen anymore. We think we've arrived at a place where death isn't allowed." The room went quiet. Miriam folded her hands in her lap and looked at her plate. Sara stood up, breaking the silence with a clatter of dishes as she began clearing their places.

Joanna followed, carrying the big white china tureens out to the kitchen. When they were alone, scraping plates for the dishwasher, she said, "Is this something nice?" Sara tilted her head, the heavy weight of her bound hair seeming to labor her slender neck.

"Yeah," she said tentatively. "It's nice." She smiled quickly and turned away as if afraid of too much hope.

When they were back all together in the dining room, passing Miriam's banana cream pie around in a circle, Joanna said, "I've come down to see Dina. That's why I'm here."

"So Seth has been telling me," Harry said in an even, thoughtful voice. He dragged each word out, leaving a lot of room for reconsideration in between.

"I have to," Joanna said.

"Jo," Sara began. "She's just not able to help. Even if she wanted . . ."

"She doesn't want, Sara," Miriam interrupted. "She wants to hurt."

"Miriam, let Joanna talk, please," Harry said. She looked up to her husband, frightened by his sudden politeness.

"If I don't at least try, I'll never forgive myself," Joanna said simply. "What can she do, other than say no?"

Harry shook his head slowly and put his hand on top of hers. "This is over, Joanna. Finished. Their marriage is dead. Their daughter is dead. Let it rest."

"I can't." She turned away from his fierce, exacting eyes. "Sara, can you give me her number?"

Sara watched her, still troubled, and then said, "Don't call. I'll give you the address. Just go there."

"Just go? Wouldn't it be fairer to at least call?"

"If you call, she'll say no," Sara said bluntly. "It's as simple as that." Joanna still looked doubtful. "Look," Sara said, "I know her. Believe me."

"Just turn up on her doorstep and hope she's there and nobody with her or anything?" Seth said, equally doubtful.

"She'll be there," Sara said. Her voice was tired and strained. "Gary will be at work and she'll be there. She's always there. She and that poor little kid."

———

THE PRETTY LITTLE white-painted frame house was set well back from a road curving steeply up the North Shore bluffs, with a view of the harbor and the Sound. Seth pulled up cautiously in front of it, studying the plain, open porch, with its rocking chair and yellow wicker summer furniture still in place.

"This it?" he asked uncertainly. Joanna looked down at the map Sara had drawn for her and then up at the closed green-painted door.

"Number sixteen. It must be. It's real nice, isn't it?" she added, surprised. Her long association of Dina with sorrow seemed incongruous in such a pleasant setting. And yet, as she looked, she recognized touches: the wind chime of white birds hanging from the porch, a wreath of red and yellow Indian corn on the door, a row of candles in green wine bottles on the step. They instantly recalled the airy, artistic girl who had danced with Eric at their wedding in a white muslin dress, flowers in her long black hair. She felt a pang of yearning for that lost happy day.

"You sure this is right?" Seth said, adding after a moment, "It doesn't look like a house with a kid in it."

"It's right," Joanna said, at the same time seeing what he meant. There were no toys scattered on the silky old grass of the lawn, no swing hanging from the low branch of the big maple by the driveway, no tricycle to trip people at the foot of the steps. As they got out of the car, she peered around the clump of fir trees screening the backyard, looking for a jungle gym or a playhouse. There was only a big chain-link fence, cutting the back off firmly from the front, tall and solid and out of place.

"Christ, look at that," Seth said. "What have they got back there?"

"Dog?" Joanna said.

"Must be a big fucker," Seth answered, staring at the fence. "They've got barbed wire all along the top." Joanna looked to where he pointed. Three thin, spiked, outward-leaning strands trimmed the high fence. "It looks like the Bronx," he said, bemused.

Just for a moment, as she stood on the porch, Joanna didn't want to go on. She hovered there, Seth two steps behind her, surrounded by Dina's pretty handiwork, an intruder from Dina's grievous past. She wanted to turn and run and leave the woman alone in her hard-won peace. But in the same moment she realized that she had dragged herself and Tess all the way from Colorado for only one purpose, and that purpose was unachievable without this. She reached out and rang the bell. It chimed, a small, vaguely familiar tune, far away in the depths of the house. In answer, there rose a child's high-pitched wavering wail. Then there was silence, a silence that lasted so long that she turned to look at Seth in confusion.

"She must be there," he said. "The child's there." Joanna shrugged and rang the bell again, harder, holding it longer and letting the little tune jangle its full length. She heard a door slam and the rapid, sharp staccato of hurried feet. The door rattled and clicked as a series of heavy, unsuburban locks were released, and then was flung open.

"For God's sake, why keep ringing it? I heard you, you know." She stood half in the shadow of the house, leaning tensely out the open door, a thin, fine-featured, nervous woman, her smooth black hair drawn back in a heavy, practical clip. Her makeup, the pale lips and heavily darkened eyes of their youth, now gave her that look of fading, girlish surprise that marked their generation's awkward entry into middle age.

"Dina?" Joanna whispered. The richly decorated eyes narrowed, and the woman looked at her properly for the first time. Then she blinked quickly and half turned away.

"Oh, Christ," she said tiredly. "Joanna." She looked down at her feet, then raised her eyes and met Joanna's without a trace of warmth. "I suppose you'd better come in," she said. She stood back, allowing just room enough for Joanna to enter. Seth, behind her, reached out his hand.

"Hello, Dina," he said.

"Seth." It was an acknowledgment, but scarcely a greeting, and she did not take his hand, only stepped back a little farther to let him pass. Then she bent over the door, carefully refastening each heavy latch before turning and leading them into the interior of the house.

She took them to a large room at the back, a garden room with tall patio windows that would have provided a view of the backyard, were not the pale beige vertical blinds drawn almost shut, leaving only bare, thin slices of light. Joanna stepped closer to the blinds and parted them slightly, without thinking. She glimpsed a big square of grass enclosed by the chain-link fence.

"You can open them," Dina said. Joanna, embarrassed, dropped her hand.

"It's okay. I was just curious."

"That's Ben's play area. I close them when we have lessons. It's important to minimize distraction."

"Oh. Oh, of course," Joanna said uncertainly. Seth was staring bleakly out through the narrow slits at the enclosure beyond.

"I should make some coffee," Dina said. Her voice was far

away, as if she were standing at some distance, speaking quite consciously to her own self.

"That's all right," Seth said quickly. "We're fine. We don't want to interrupt."

"No. No, I'll make coffee." She became suddenly animated. "I won't be a minute." She turned to leave but stopped at the door. "Please wait for me here," she said.

"Sure," Joanna said, puzzled.

"It's Ben. He's very sensitive. He might be frightened if he suddenly saw you . . ." Her voice trailed off.

"Where is he?" Seth said. Dina looked wary.

"He's having his rest. Please, I really mean it."

"We'll stay right here if you want, Dina," Joanna said evenly. "But can't I help?"

"No." Dina backed to the door, watching them, and then went hurriedly out and shut it. Seth half expected to hear the click of a latch. He turned to Joanna and, in silence, raised his expressive black brows. She met his eyes and shook her head slowly and shrugged. Together, without speaking, they returned to the window and stood silently waiting there. Seth parted the blinds with his hand, as Joanna had done, and looked out for a long while.

"His play area?" he said in a soft, strained voice. "What do you think he plays? KGB and dissidents?"

"Shh," Joanna said.

"The whole place is a fortress. Did you see the locks on that door?" Seth's voice was rising.

She took his arm. "Seth," she said softly, "can you really blame her for being afraid?"

"Jo, there's a child in here. You can't make a prisoner of a child . . ." She gripped his arm suddenly, and he thought it was to silence him, because there was a sound at the door. But when he turned, it was not Dina standing in the entrance, but a dark-eyed little boy in purple denim dungarees. Seth glanced quickly at Joanna, then crouched down, at eye-level with the boy, and said smiling, "Hey, hello." He held out one hand, gently, the fingers curved. "Come here. What's your name?" The child looked at the beckoning hand for a full ten seconds, staring. His eyes widened almost comically, then he shut them tight, opened his mouth in a wide, dark square, and shrieked—a wordless, rising, terrified scream.

A door banged down the hallway, and Dina appeared instantly, wild-eyed, still holding the coffeepot she had been filling. She set it down, mindlessly, on the floor and fell to her knees beside the child, sweeping him into her arms. He continued shrieking while she embraced him, clinging to her with frantic, kneading hands. Joanna and Seth stood watching, astonished. The screams trailed off, slowly, to little gasping shouts and, finally, silence. Dina looked up over the child's dark head.

"I told you," she whispered. "I told you to stay."

"Dina," Seth said coolly, "we did stay. He came in. The kid came in."

"You're blaming him?" Dina whispered more hoarsely. "You're blaming the child?"

"Dina, we're not blaming anybody." Seth's voice rose and Joanna tugged at his arm. The little boy wriggled around and opened one eye, surveying them, to Joanna's surprise, with simple curiosity.

"Look," Joanna said soothingly, "it's a real shame he got such a fright. Why don't you take him back to the kitchen until he's ready to see us."

"Strangers, Mommy," the little boy said. He was still staring with the unblinking intensity of his age, and his voice had yet the tremor of latent tears.

"No," Dina said. She paused. "Mommy's friends."

"Strangers."

"No, Ben. Friends. This is Mommy's friend, Seth," she pointed carefully, "and this is Mommy's friend, Joanna." She smiled when she said it, and Joanna found the manufactured warmth of her manner almost more upsetting than her previous hostility. "You can say hello," Dina said to them then, with the same brittle smile.

"Hello, Ben." Joanna kept her voice soft and gentle.

"Hi, Ben." Seth smiled winningly. Ben unhooked his arm from his mother's neck and stepped cautiously across the room. He smiled back at Seth and walked right up to him. Seth crouched down again and very carefully extended his arm. Ben looked at the arm. He looked at his mother. Then he raised his small hand and slapped Seth's face. Seth jerked back, and Joanna caught a flash of small triumph in the child's dark eyes. She looked at Dina and was amazed to see no reaction beyond the same fixed smile. "Why'd you do that, Ben?" Seth said gently. The child giggled and ran coyly to his mother's side.

"Bad strangers," he said.

"No," Dina repeated calmly, "Mommy's friends." She left them then abruptly, picking up the coffeepot and walking back to the kitchen, Ben running giggling at her side.

When she returned she was carrying a tray with the coffee, cups and saucers, a plate of Danish, and a glass of orange juice for Ben. She set the tray down on a low table, and Ben, who had shadowed her legs as she walked, now hung over the tray, picking pieces off each of the pastries. Ignoring the juice, he took one pastry and sat on the floor, crumbling it into a sticky heap. Dina poured the coffee and handed Joanna a cup. Ben stood up, crossed the room, and snatched at it.

"Careful," Joanna said, "it might spill." She held it from his reach and pointed at the tray. "Look, there's your juice." He opened his mouth and began to shriek.

"Give it to him," Dina said. "I'll pour you another." Joanna looked at her, uncertain she'd heard right. Dina nodded urgently. With a glance at Seth, Joanna handed the child the cup and saucer. He gave his triumphant grin again and carried away his trophy, setting it, spilling freely, on the floor. Seth opened his mouth to say something and then shut it with a quick shake of his head. Dina looked at him coolly.

"Ben's psychiatrist says we should avoid negative input," she said.

"Come again . . . ?" Seth's eyebrows raised sharply.

Joanna said quickly, "I'm sorry Dina, I didn't realize you were having a problem . . ." She looked at Ben significantly and let her voice trail off.

"I'm not having a problem," Dina said instantly. "Ben isn't a problem. The problem is that we live in a society that's totally hostile to children. I'm only doing what's necessary to protect my child." She looked quickly from Joanna to Seth. "Do you have a problem with that?" Seth looked at her steadily, started to speak, and then shook his head again. He waved his hand abruptly, in dismissal.

"No, Dina. Fine. Whatever." He looked back with troubled eyes at Ben, playing on the floor, pouring coffee from the cup into the saucer and back to the cup.

Dina finished serving the coffee, went out to the kitchen for another cup, and passed the plate of child-tattered pastries. Then she sat down in the chair nearest her son, who was making a pattern with pastry crumbs on the rug. Joanna waited until she had settled, somewhat stiffly, in her chair. Then she said quietly, "Dina, Eric's come home." Dina's head snapped up. Her eyes widened, her mouth opened, the lips pale and trembling.

"Here? Eric's here?" She looked wildly from Joanna to Seth.

Seth said quickly, "He's come back east, Dina. That's all."

"You haven't brought him here?" she cried, looking back to Joanna.

"Of course not, Dina," Joanna said smoothly. "We couldn't do that without asking first."

"I don't want to see him," Dina said. Ben turned around to the fear in her voice and began to whimper. She held out her arms and he ran into them. "If he's out in the car . . ." She turned toward the door, panic in her eyes.

"Dina," Joanna said firmly. "I told you. He's not here. He's miles away."

"He's with your parents," Dina said, accusingly, to Seth. "You've got him there."

"No," Joanna said exasperated. "Dina, listen to me. He's nowhere near here. He's up at our Adirondack camp with my daughter. Okay?" She tossed back her hair, irritated.

"Your daughter?" Dina whispered.

"Yeah. My daughter, Tess. You remember . . . you saw her once when she was a baby, at my parents' house." She shook her head, finding it hard to conceive now that in those early years Dina still came occasionally to her husband's family home. "She's eleven now," she said tiredly.

"You've left your daughter with Eric?"

Joanna stiffened. "He's her uncle, Dina. Of course I have," she said in a cold, angry voice. Dina turned her head away. The little boy clung closer and whimpered noisily. Dina stroked his hair. When she stopped, he whimpered again. After a long while, she turned back to Joanna.

"I do not want to see Eric ever again. I do not want even to hear his name. If that's why you've come, you may as well go. And if I were you," she added quietly, "I'd go back to my daughter. Right now."

"My daughter's fine," Joanna said icily. "My brother's not fine. And you're responsible."

"I am responsible for him?" Dina said. She tightened her grip on Ben's shoulders until the boy wiggled in annoyance. "That is sick."

Joanna struggled with her anger and deliberately calmed her voice, making it kind and persuasive, "Dina, look, I know you've grieved terribly for Molly, and I know you'll never forget her, but time has passed."

"I don't grieve for Molly," Dina said. Her voice was suddenly bright and she gave a small airy smile. Ben wriggled out of her arms, and she let him go. "Molly is fine now." Joanna looked at Seth. He shrugged slightly.

"Good," Joanna said, stretching the word out soothingly. "I'm glad you're able to feel that way now." Dina turned and gave her a remote, superior smile.

"I don't grieve for Molly anymore, because Molly is alive." Joanna gripped the cup she was holding so hard it rattled on its saucer. She flung Seth a wild look.

Seth leaned forward. "Dina?" he said warily. "But you . . ."

"She is alive in a new existence. My teacher made contact." She paused. "Spiritual contact," she added a little loftily.

"Your teacher?"

"I follow the Buddhist Way now." She stopped and a wary look flitted through her eyes, as if she had only just remembered who she was talking to. "You're a Buddhist, aren't you Seth?" He shook his head slightly. "Oh, I thought . . ." She sounded confused and a little relieved.

"It doesn't matter, Dina," he said softly. "Tell me about Molly." Her eyes brightened dreamily.

"Oh, she's so happy," she said. Ben turned, in the middle of the room, and looked at his mother. He gave one of his little whimpers, but when he got no response he went instead to Seth. Seth held out his hand, instinctively, his eyes still intent on Dina. This time Ben took his hand and held it with both of his, and then flopped over Seth's arm, sagging there. Seth patted his back gently. "She's been born into the body of a little girl in a village in Tibet. Everybody in Tibetan villages loves children of course, but they love her particularly because she's a special child. They call her 'the blessed one,' and they bring her flowers and special food."

Ben swung on Seth's arm, twisting around to watch his mother. She sat joyfully entranced with her own words. "She's very beautiful, with dark skin and long, shining black hair." Ben released Seth's arm and scrambled up onto his chair, leaning on his shoulder. Seth circled him with his arm to steady him, watching Dina with gentle compassion. "Her eyes are blue, though, like they were. Something always remains of the past existence." Ben prodded Seth's face, tangled his fingers in his hair and tugged roughly. Seth turned his head slightly so he could still see Dina, still supporting the child with his arm. Ben lunged forward and brought his hand around in a sharp, solid punch, his small fist leaving a bright mark across Seth's cheek. He swung back, grinning and giggling, and slipped to the floor. Seth sat staring at him, rubbing his face.

"You all right?" Joanna said. He did not answer, but looked at Dina.

"Bad stranger," Ben said loudly to his mother. She made no response. Seth leaned forward and gently took the boy's shoulders in his hands, turning the child to face him.

"Why'd you do that, Ben?"

"Do it again." Ben giggled sharply.

"No, sweetheart," Seth said firmly. "It hurts. That's enough." Ben stared. His eyes went wide and he swiveled around to look at his mother. He made his square mouth and shrieked, loudly and insistently, and flung himself free of Seth's hands. Dina leaped up from her chair, and Ben rolled over on the floor, arms and legs punching the air, screaming. Dina reached him, and he scrambled up into her arms, still shrieking, his body held rigid. Dina stood up, holding him to her, and over his thrusting head and flailing arms whispered hoarsely, "I can't believe this. I can't believe you tried to discipline my child." She spun about and stalked out of the room, and they heard her sharp footsteps and Ben's fading shrieks retreating down the hall and up the stairs.

Joanna sat in stunned silence and then turned slowly to Seth. "This is a madhouse," he said.

Dina was gone a very long time, so long that Joanna began to imagine that she would not return but would remain cloistered somewhere in the upper regions of the house until—who knew? Until they left? Her husband returned? Night fell? "Should we go?" she said to Seth. He shook his head. He stood up then and crossed to the shaded window, looking out at the fenced-in rectangle of grass beyond. Joanna went and stood beside him. He sighed and put his arms around her and held her to him.

"This is so sad." He rested his head on her shoulder, closing his eyes. "Oh, why is it always a goddamned 'village in Tibet'?" he said wearily. "Maybe if some of these bozos could see a Tibetan village they might relocate their paradise. 'The blessed one.' Oh, Christ."

Joanna stroked his hair gently, "What does it matter?" she said. "She's happy believing it."

"I don't call that happy," said Seth.

———

WHEN DINA RETURNED she was calm and composed. She sat down with dignity and poured more coffee for each of them and then said, "I'm sorry I was so long. I had to lie down with him until he went to sleep." She paused, speaking in even-voiced abstraction as if they had taken no part in the earlier events. "I think he'll settle down now, but if he's still disturbed later, I'll call the doctor."

"The doctor?" Joanna whispered.

"Ben's psychiatrist." She paused and looked at Seth coolly.

"It's all right. We often have setbacks. It's been a difficult day for Ben. Starting with the doorbell . . ."

"The doorbell? What about the doorbell?" Seth asked.

"My son is afraid of the doorbell."

"Oh, I see," Joanna said numbly.

"Dina," Seth said incredulously, "why not just disconnect the damned thing?" She shook her head.

"We did for a while. The psychiatrist says we should re-introduce it. But he has to be familiarized slowly with external experiences. I'm afraid you don't know much about children, Seth. You haven't any of your own."

"Is that what it is, Dina?" he said bleakly. "I didn't realize."

"Dina," Joanna interrupted, casting a worried glance at Seth, "now that Ben isn't here, I want to talk about Eric."

"I told you . . ."

"No. That's not enough. Look," Joanna leaned forward, reaching out to the woman, "you've said yourself, you're happier now. You have Ben. Your husband. And you're at peace about Molly. Why begrudge Eric the chance . . ."

"I'm not happy, Joanna," she said coldly. "I'm just not in hell anymore."

"But Eric's in hell," Joanna said fiercely. "You've put him in hell . . ."

"He deserves it."

"You shit."

Seth stood up as Joanna crouched forward on her chair, but she waved him away. Dina looked from one to the other.

"You're such a fool, Joanna," she said. "Can't you see I'm doing you a favor?" She paused. "He does deserve it. Whatever you think."

"What? Because he once ignored one of your silly premonitions, he deserves this?"

"Is that what he told you?" Dina said. She crossed her legs and folded her hands on her lap.

"He's not responsible for Molly's death. All he did was let his daughter go out to play."

"That's not all he did, Joanna."

Seth stepped forward and said, softly, "Jo, come on, this is leading nowhere."

"So what, you called him . . . you were always calling him. You called him whenever you left them alone. You never wanted to leave them alone at all."

"Joanna." Dina's eyes were deep and dark, her white hands very steady, resting on her lap.

"What?"

"Joanna, why do you think I didn't want to leave them alone?"

"What?"

"Why?"

"Jo, let's go," Seth said. "We're all just upsetting each other."

"Joanna, have you ever thought why it's only Eric who won't admit that Molly is dead?" Dina raised one hand coolly. "You accept it. I accept it. You, Seth. All the family. Only one person has to keep pretending that Molly's alive."

"Yes. Because you've put so much guilt on him he can't ever face it . . ."

"No," Dina said. "Because he knows."

"He doesn't, Dina. We know." Joanna turned to face Seth, in confusion. Seth was reaching to her with one gentle hand, the way he had reached to the child, Ben. His eyes were pleading.

"No," Dina said. "We assume Molly's dead. Eric knows. Eric's the only person who knows. The only person in the world." Seth closed his eyes. "Eric killed Molly, Joanna. She was going to tell me, at last, and so he killed her. That's why he can't say she's dead."

Joanna moved fast, but Seth moved faster. He was across the room and between them, and when Joanna's flailing hands struck flesh, it was his, not Dina's, they struck. He ducked her blows and wrapped his arms around her and held on tight.

"You bitch. You bitch!" she screamed, her hands clawing for Dina's face. "I'll kill you, you bitch."

Dina sat still, almost serene, her deep brown eyes remote. "It won't change anything," she said. There was something of Ben's small triumph in her voice. "It won't change what happened, and it won't change what Eric is."

"He's not a murderer, you bitch. You fucking bitch," Joanna sobbed. "How can you. How can you? You knew him so well. He loved you. You knew him . . . he's the gentlest, kindest man, the gentlest . . ."

"Most child molesters are," Dina said smoothly. "How do you think they get what they want?"

"May you rot in hell."

"You're right, you know," Dina said. "I knew him so well." Upstairs a thin wail arose. She stood up. "I have to go to my child." She paused. "But we've said all we want to say, now, anyhow." She looked back at Joanna. "Haven't we?"

—

JOANNA HEARD THE THREE LOCKS click behind her as Seth hurried her down the walk. He kept his arm tight about her shoulders, led her to the car, and opened her door, stopping briefly to squeeze her hand as she sat numbly in the passenger seat. He slammed the door shut, ran around the car, jumped into the driver's seat, and started the engine. He threw the car into reverse, screeching backward into Dina's driveway, spun the wheel and then tore off down the road the way they had come.

Joanna sat, hands clenched into fists, staring out the windshield, blindly oblivious of where he was going, or why. Suburban streets flashed by, then marshland, a glimpse of the Sound. As suddenly as he'd started, Seth pulled the car off the road and stopped. They were at an overlook on a bluff beside the water, with only one house in sight, a small brown Cape Cod tucked away in the distance. He switched off the engine, turned and reached out his arms. Joanna grasped them with trembling hands and leaned across the console into an awkward embrace. He held her while she cried, and after a long while she straightened up, still holding his hands, and looked bleakly into his eyes.

"Why?" she asked. "Why did she say that?"

"This is why Dad didn't want us to go," Seth said, almost to himself.

"What? Do you think she's told him this? She's told other people?" Rising fury shook her voice.

"No, Jo," he said, shaking his head, reaching to gently stroke her face. "No. I think he probably guessed. It was the final end of where she was heading." He paused, his fingers brushing tears from her cheekbones. "Pity her, Jo. Pity her and pity that poor little boy." She closed her eyes.

"I can't, Seth. She said that. She said it. She's poisonous. Evil."

"She's not evil, Jo. She's a woman whose nightmares have come true. Have pity."

She shook her head, "But why that? Of all the things, why accuse him of that?" Joanna was very cold and her hands were shaking. Seth slipped his jacket off and put it around her shoulders.

"Let's go home," he said.

"Why would she say such a thing? Why would she want to believe that?" She heard her own voice rising into hysteria. Seth gripped her shoulders through the clumsy bulk of the jacket.

"She's crazy, Jo. Now forget you heard it. She's a poor, crazy woman."

"She said, she said . . ."

"Forget it, Jo."

"About Tess. I'd left Tess . . ."

"Jo." He shook her abruptly. "Don't listen to it. Don't let it get a grip on you."

"But why would she say it? I don't understand . . ." Seth pulled back. He held her at arm's length.

"Joanna, be careful."

"What do you mean? What do you mean, be careful?"

"You understand me." She stared at him desperately, clinging to the steadiness of his voice, the solemn intensity of his gaze.

"Yes. Yes," she murmured, but everything was sliding, unfathomable, slipping from her grasp. She turned away and closed her eyes.

"Seth . . ."

"He's your brother. You know him. You love him. You trust him."

"I want my daughter, Seth."

"ERIC?" TESS SAID, "am I holding on too tight?"

"No, sweetheart. You're doing fine." He stopped at the top of a ledge and carefully readjusted her weight on his back, wary of the left ankle he had roughly splinted with strips of his shirt and two trimmed lengths of fir. She loosened her arm around his neck. "You hang on," he said.

"I am. Eric, if my ankle isn't broken, it's all right to walk on it, sure?"

"I don't know that it isn't broken, Tess. I'm just guessing." He stepped sideways off the ledge, found a footing, and worked his way gingerly down. Tess swayed outward, the weight of the two packs, one compressed into the other, swaying out with her shoulders, unsettling his balance. He stumbled and caught his footing again. Tess gave a little yelp.

"Sorry, sweetheart."

"It didn't hurt," she said. "Look, if you make me crutches, I could hop."

He laughed softly, "Take a while, Tess."

"Eric," she said firmly. "You can't carry me all the way down this mountain. I'm too heavy." He stopped at a level spot of track.

"We'll have a break." He gently lowered her to the ground and then steadied her as she sat down, stretching the hurt leg in front of her.

"Look, it isn't really even swollen. I'm sure I can walk." He sat down beside her.

"Tess," he said, "you're a real toughie and I like that, but no. You're not heavy. I've carried a lot more, a lot farther. I was in the army, kid. They did things like this to us for fun. Now stop worrying."

"I'm not worrying." She paused and looked at him carefully. "You're worrying," she said cannily.

He smiled. "You're just like your mother." She looked surprised and pleased. "I could never get much past her either." He stretched out on the pine needle carpet and squinted up through the trees. The sky was overcast, and the angle of the thin gray light low. In the shadows of the woods, darkness was already gathering. "Okay, Tess. Yes, I am worried. It's getting late, and we're not making very good time." She thought carefully.

"We could leave the pack. Then I'd be lighter to carry."

"We could, Tess. But if we're going to spend the night out here, we're going to need what's in it."

She was silent for a long while before saying, "Are we?"

"Are we what?"

"Going to spend the night out here."

"Not if I can help it." She thought again, prodding at the splint he'd made around her hurt ankle.

"Don't you like sleeping out?" she asked. He laughed again, a quiet, private laugh.

"Not quite as much anymore as I used to," he said. Then he got serious. "Sleeping out's fine, Tess, with sleeping bags and maybe a tent. We haven't got those things."

"No," she said, still thinking. "I guess it's not a great idea."

"Nope. Not great. Come on, kid. Let's see what we can do." She linked her arms around his neck again, and he lifted her easily onto his back and started down the trail. It was harder now, in the dim light, to pick out the patches of ice. He warily felt his way. When he had gone another mile, the trail itself was getting hard to see. He turned briefly and looked back through the pale trunks of the close-grown birch. It was difficult to judge, but he felt they'd made most of the descent, and the flattening angle of the trail winding into the darkness gave confirmation. At least they'd be spared the worst of the cold. He set out again, on the softer, leaf-strewn path, in an easy, long-legged lope that brought them to the edge of the lake, silvered in the last of the light. As he had fervently hoped, a small three-sided log lean-to sheltered in the trees by the shore.

"Tess," he said, lowering her to the ground at its entrance, "this is our lucky day."

"It is?" she said, rubbing her leg and looking dismally at the dark open entrance of the hut.

Eric laughed, "Okay. Imagine the same place without it." Tess nodded.

"I got you," she said.

"Lucky?"

"Lucky."

"Not," Eric said then, walking around the inside of the lean-to, patting its walls, "that I deserve it. Not one little bit."

"Why not?" she asked curiously.

"Because, sweetheart, I have been stupid and I don't deserve any luck at all. But maybe the luck's for you." He patted the solid timber fondly. "I've been monumentally stupid," he said. Tess looked worried.

"Won't we be all right?" she asked.

He smiled.

"Oh, we're going to be fine, sweetheart," he said. "Only we could have been a whole lot more comfortable if I hadn't made a couple of really stupid mistakes. Three. Three stupid mistakes."

He was talking to himself more than her, but she said, "I guess the first was taking me along." He looked up from the log wall he was admiring, back to her, laughing.

"No, Tess. That wasn't a mistake. Maybe I should have kept you a bit closer to me, but no, it wasn't you." He came and sat down cross-legged beside her, taking the knapsack from her and opening the straps. "No. The first was going by the trailhead without logging our names in, so no one knows we're out here and no one's looking for us." Tess nodded. "The second," he said, pulling her little pack out from the larger one and tossing it to her, "was I didn't bring a lantern or a flashlight, which would have gotten us out of here, even now." She shrugged; they seemed like little, unimportant things to her, still.

"What was the third?"

"The third is the stupidest, but I think it isn't going to matter."

"Why not?"

"Because the third is, I haven't got any matches. But I have got you, and the one thing you can count on a smoker for is they'll always have a light." She was quiet, thoughtful.

Then she took a deep breath and said, "Eric, there's a problem about that." He looked at her intently, and then his features relaxed into a wry, weary grin. He covered his face with one hand.

"Tess, if you're going to tell me you've quit, all I can say is this is a piece of news I'd love to get tomorrow." He was laughing as he said it, but she tugged urgently at his sleeve.

"I haven't quit, Eric." He looked up, hopefully. She said, "But you remember yesterday when Mom threw me in the lake? They were in my pocket. My cigarettes. And my matches."

"Ah."

"Sorry."

"No. No, we'll manage." He stood up, "I'm going to cut some pine boughs before it's dark." She nodded, but as he stepped out of the shelter, she suddenly shouted, "Eric, Eric, wait." He turned back. She was clawing in the top pocket of her pack, hauling out her little collection of tape cassettes. He watched curiously, as she opened one after the other, shaking them. "There," she said triumphantly. From one plastic box she carefully extracted not a cassette, but two battered cigarettes and, beneath them, a book of Edelweiss Cafe matches. "My secret supply," she said, "hidden from mom . . ." He grabbed the matches, grinning.

"Tess," he said. "You're a devious little shit, and I'm glad I'm not your father, but as a friend, you're just fine." He slipped the matches into his pocket. "Now," he said, "we're really okay." He turned away from her and went out again, into the darkness. "I'll just be a moment, Tess."

He was gone so long she began to get scared. "Eric?" she shouted.

"I'm right here." He sounded far away. He moved so quietly in the woods she couldn't tell where he was until she heard the snapping of a dry branch or the sound of his hunting knife sawing at a pine bough, like the ones he'd cut to splint her leg. She called his name twice more, and each time he answered he sounded farther away. She bit down hard on her lip, determined not to cry. Then he appeared suddenly from nowhere, a dark shape in the paler darkness beyond the hut, rough and scraggly, with the load of branches he was carrying. She cried out in surprise.

"Just me." He dropped a load of crackly sticks in front of the shelter and took a dark, shaggy armful within.

"What's that?"

"Your bed."

"I'm going to sleep on those?" She poked at the scratchy, sweet-smelling fir.

"On them and under them."

"They're sharp," she said doubtfully.

"Complain to the management. I'm going to light a fire."

"Oh, great," she said, suddenly aware of being really cold.

But he wasn't quick about it. He took a long, meticulous time clearing a space in front of the lean-to, sweeping away twigs and pine needles, and then going to the lake shore to bring back rocks. He laid them carefully in a ring.

"Do you have to do all that?" she said, folding her hands in under her arms.

"Put your mittens on. Yes, I do." He paused. "We don't want to set the woods on fire."

"Jeez," Tess said. "Who cares? It's better than freezing to death."

"We're not freezing." He looked up. She could not see his face, but she sensed he wasn't pleased. "We're not the only things that matter, Tess. The woods have been here a long time."

"I was joking," she said.

He laughed gently, "Besides, my dad would kill me if I burned the woods down. And I'm not joking." She wrapped her arms tighter, watching his gray shape bent over his little stone hearth.

She said, awed, "Would Grandpa mind that much?"

"That much, Tess, and probably more." He could hear his father's voice. "You got yourself into this, Eric, now minimize the damage and get yourself out." He sat back, brushing earth from his hands, peering at his handiwork in the thick charcoal dusk. "But it's okay, because I'm not going to burn the woods down. Now, have you got any paper Tess? Anything at all that might burn?"

She thought carefully. "My cigarettes."

"Well, that's a start."

"Wait a moment," Tess began rooting in her pack. "There's these. These are paper." She had her cassettes out again, and quickly snapping each case open, she pulled out the title cards. "These'll burn." Then she dragged a fistful of chocolate wrappers from her pocket. "And these."

"Well done." Eric took them, laying them carefully beside his neat heap of small, dry twigs.

Tess sat tugging at one of her pigtails. "That's all. I'm sorry," she said. But then she stopped, in the midst of putting the cassettes away, and winced. "Eric," she said in a small, embarrassed voice. "I'm not sure if they'll burn, but I've got these." Her hand closed reluctantly on the squashy package she'd stuffed in beside her Walkman.

"What, Tess? I can't see."

"I don't want you to see," she said. "There's these things." She handed them over and said quickly, "Mom gave them to me." She wanted to crawl into the pine boughs and hide.

Eric took them, felt the package with his hands, and said, puzzled, "Your mom? Oh. Oh, Tess. Oh, Tess, I'm sorry. I didn't realize you . . ." he stopped respectfully. "I didn't realize you were so grown-up."

"I'm not," Tess said miserably. "They're just in case." She paused. "I don't think I'll need them tonight. If they'll burn." He put his big hand on her shoulder and hugged her for a moment.

"They'll burn," he said. He took the book of matches out of his pocket. She felt a little better then and went back to thinking of what was in her pack, but there wasn't anything else.

"I don't have any more paper, Eric," she said. He was holding the match book delicately between his big fingers. He opened it, feeling for the matches in the darkness. "Ah," he said softly.

"Do you?" She asked. He was silent for a moment.

"Yes, I've got paper, Tess." He said it quietly, as if he were thinking of something else. He'd laid her package beside the cards and the cigarettes and the twigs, and now he reached into his pack, searching by feel. He took out the lunch bags and the thermos bottles, and a wool hat and gloves, laying each thing carefully aside. The folder was smooth and cold in his hands. He laid it down by his stone hearth and opened it to the first page. He could see nothing but the dark oblong of its shape, but he knew the pictures so intimately, their order and their place. He drew out the first, sliding it carefully from within the plastic envelope. Tess peered at him in the darkness.

"What are you doing, Eric?" He didn't answer, but gently crushed the picture between his hands, making it into a soft ball. "Eric? Are those your pictures?"

"It's all right, Tess."

"No, it's not." She reached for the folder, grabbing at it quickly. He stopped her hands gently with his own. "You can't burn those."

"I've got copies, Tess. It doesn't matter." His voice was infinitely gentle. He continued through the folder, removing page after page. The small mound of crumpled white grew in front of him, palely visible in the night.

"It does matter. They're special. They're . . ."

"Just paper, Tess. They're just paper." He closed the empty folder and laid it down.

He made his fire with the pictures at its heart, piling gently around them the cards, the napkins, Tess's two cigarettes and, then, above them, a little tent of twigs. He did it blindly, with hands familiar from a hundred campfires in his youth. Around the twigs was a little stockade of squaw wood, and securely balanced above, a neat, interlaced square of dry, dead birch. He sat back, took out the matchbook again, folded it, and withdrew a single match. He struck it, a sudden sparking glare, shielded by his curved palm, held until a full-formed flame rose and flickered. He laid flame and match at the center of his tinder. It flared blue and gold, caught, red and orange, licking the edges of the paper, curled upward, wrapped itself around the card, the cotton, the twigs. Wood sparked and shifted and, with a soft whisper of warmth, flamed into fire. Eric watched as yellow light spread out, revealing a circle of brown needles and earth beyond his cleared hearth, the shadowy log walls of the lean-to, and Tess's face, lips parted in surprise and delight.

"Eric! You did it." She cheered and clapped her hands and held them in her mittens out toward the flames. He laid two more larger dry branches across the hearth stones and two across those, and sat back. They caught, good and true, and he was satisfied.

"Make a fire right," he said, hearing his father once more, "and it lights with a single match." He smiled. "Which, Tess, is just as well, because as it turns out, that's exactly what we had." He turned the matchbook over in his hand and showed her its empty stubble of match stalks, then grinned and tossed it into the flames.

With the fire there, it didn't seem so lonely when he went

back to the woods for more dead branches to burn. He came back with armfuls and made a big pile beside the lean-to. Then he got out the remains of their lunch and made her eat the rest of the sandwiches and the last apple.

"What about you? Aren't you hungry?"

"I'm bigger than you. I don't need to eat as often. Finish it." She did, reluctantly. "Now get your spare clothes and put them on."

"I don't need them. I'm not cold."

"You will be later. It's easier to stay warm than warm up once you're cold." Tess dutifully put on her extra sweater, the spare mittens, and her hat. "And your jacket."

"I can't move already. I've got a T-shirt and a shirt and two sweaters, and my denim jacket."

"And the big jacket."

"I hate that jacket. I feel like a robot in that jacket."

"Put it on. By morning you're going to love that jacket." Tess sighed, hauled out the big padded winter jacket, and pulled it on.

"Okay?" she said, irritated. Eric said nothing. He put more wood on the fire and then went into the shelter and spread half the pine boughs evenly on the ground. Tess pulled herself upright, keeping her hurt ankle clear of the ground, and hopped in to watch. "Are we going to bed now?" He picked up the two empty knapsacks, laying them on the pine boughs.

"Well, I suppose we could watch a movie first. Anything good on?"

Tess leaned against the shelter wall. "Is this what life was like before electricity?"

He laughed aloud. "Oh, Tess. I think you've missed a few stages of history, but, yes, entertainment was limited." He beckoned her into the shelter, reaching to steady her as she lowered herself. She sat on the flattened knapsacks on top of the branches, bouncing tentatively up and down.

"Well?"

"It's all right," she said.

"Thanks a lot."

"I mean it's nice. It's real nice," she said hastily. She stretched out. "It smells wonderful." He smiled.

"Put your feet inside the big pack. Feet get cold quickest." Gingerly Tess obeyed, stretching the sore ankle down inside the canvas carefully. "How's that?" he asked.

"Great." She stretched her arms over her head and looked at the fluttering light of the flames on the log roof. She held up her hands, casting shadows. "I like this," she said. He rolled up the wrappings of their lunch and threw them on the fire, then sat down beside her, drawing his knees up, and resting his back against the rough wall.

"What we need now is Seth," he said.

"What for?" Tess asked, raising her head, curious.

"To tell us a ghost story. Whenever we slept out, he used to tell us wonderful ghost stories. Even when he was a real little kid." He laughed softly. "All us big ones, Martin and me, and Annie and Sara and your mom, all hanging onto every word. Scared shitless." He smiled, "It was the only reason we'd let him come along."

Tess thought a moment and said, "I think I'm scared enough." Her voice was small and serious.

"There's nothing to be scared of out here, Tess."

She looked unconvinced. "Bears?"

"We've got nothing they want. We've eaten all the food and burnt the wrappers."

"Maybe they want us," Tess said.

He laughed quietly and shook his head. "Wild animals have their own world. Nothing to do with ours. And," he turned and smiled comfortingly, "they don't like the fire."

"What if it goes out?"

"It won't go out."

Tess lay back flat and sighed. "That's a relief." She was quiet for a while but then said, "It's still scary."

"Why?"

She thought again. "We're all alone." Eric stood up. He slipped his plaid jacket off his shoulders.

"That's just why we're safe, Tess," he said. He carried the jacket across the shelter and spread it over her.

"Eric, what are you doing?" she said. She sat up. "No. Uh-

uh." Her eyes were narrow, like her mother's when she was serious about something. Her voice was very adult. "No. You'll freeze."

He smiled. "I wouldn't do it if I thought so, Tess. I'm not that stupid." He smoothed the jacket out carefully and laid a soft layer of pine boughs on top of it. "Warm enough?" She lay down, looking at him uncertainly.

"*I'm* fine," she said.

"I'm used to the cold, sweetheart. I've had a lot of practice." She nodded.

After a long while she said, "This is the best bed I've ever slept in."

He went out again and got a further load of wood for the fire, piled three solid pieces onto the flames, and then came in and stretched out on the pine branches beside her. She curled around toward him. "Eric? Can I snuggle up?" she said in a sleepy child's voice. He slipped one arm beneath her and she tucked herself in against his shoulder. He lay looking at the shadows on the roof and listening to her breathing. "Eric?"

"What?"

"Are you really glad you're not my father?"

"No, Tess, of course not. That was a joke." She made a small sound of affirmation or contentment and began to drift off to sleep again. But then suddenly she sat up, staring out at the blackness beyond the firelight.

"Eric. It's snowing."

"It's been snowing for a while, Tess. You just couldn't see it before."

"What if it snows a lot, and we can't get out?" She sounded really scared.

"We'll get out." He wrapped his other arm around her and she held on tight, trying not to cry. "First snow," he said. "There's a poem about first snow. Robert Frost."

She raised her head quickly. "I know it. 'Stopping by Woods on a Snowy Evening.' "

He smiled. "Good for you. But not that one. There's another one. It isn't maybe so famous." He paused, listening, and said, "It tells about the sound snow makes the first time it falls, before there's any snow yet on the ground. It only happens once each winter, up here. Listen, Tess. That's the sound. You can hear it. Listen." She did. A faint dry rustling filled the night woods. "Hear it?"

"Yeah," she said politely and then added, "I think I'd like to hear it some other time." He laughed. She stretched out again and closed her eyes. "I did 'Stopping by Woods' for assembly at school. With Amanda Quigley. We did it in parts." She chanted the first lines in a sleepy singsong voice and then stopped. "Eric? Whose woods are these?"

"These?" He paused, content with the warmth of the fire on one side of him, her small child's warmth on the other. "The state of New York has them on a long lease from God."

"Really?

He laughed quietly. "Do you know any more of it?" She shook her head.

"I didn't learn it very well. Amanda always had to poke me whenever we got to one of my parts. I did the first part and then Amanda did the second. Then I did the part about the horse and the harness bells . . ." she trailed off. "I like it," she said, "but it's sort of creepy. And I don't know why it's creepy, because there's nothing creepy in it. Just the snow and the woods and the horse . . ."

"It's about dying, Tess," he said. He paused. "It's about choosing whether or not to die." She lifted her head.

"Choosing?" she said. "But there isn't any choice."

"Oh yes, there is," he said.

She lay back down, disconcerted. After a long while she said uncertainly, "There isn't, Eric. That's the whole thing about dying. If there was a choice, everybody would choose living. Then the world would get so crowded up with all the old people not wanting to leave, there wouldn't be room for anyone new."

Eric looked up again at the flickering firelight on the wooden roof and smiled. "It could be a problem, Tess. You've got a point."

"A real problem." She thought, then said practically, "I suppose there'd have to be a rule. Like the get-out-of-jail rule in Monopoly."

"What, three rolls of the dice and you've got to go?" He laughed gently.

"Something like that," she said. She snuggled closer, warm and sleepy. "You'd probably need someone like Uncle Martin to make sure everyone played fair. Otherwise, people would cheat."

Eric laughed again, gleefully. "Uncle Martin as the Grim Reaper. What a wonderful idea. You're a genius, Tess."

She looked up at him and smiled and then buried her face against his shoulder and closed her eyes. "It isn't a real choice, Eric, is it? Not if everybody chooses the same thing."

"It's a real choice," he said quietly.

She kept her eyes closed tight. "Well, who would choose dying?" she said uncertainly.

After a long while he said, "Someone who'd finished living." A few cold flakes of snow blew in past the fire, and he tightened his arm around her, smoothing the jacket up around her ears. "Someone who'd finished all they had to do."

She thought for a moment and then raised her head, "Well, that rules us out," she said cheerfully.

He smiled. "Does it? How's that?"

"We haven't finished Harry's roof."

He laughed aloud. "Oh hell, we haven't. And there'll be a foot of snow on it in the morning." He laughed again, wearily. "Go to sleep, Tess. I'll worry about that tomorrow."

She curled against him contentedly, and he gently stroked her head in its woolly hat. "Are you going to sleep too?" she asked. He lay beside her looking dreamily out into the snowy darkness beyond the fire.

"Not yet, Tess. Not for a while."

—

THE SNOW WAS FALLING heavy and fast when Seth fishtailed the Oldsmobile down the curving, steep track to the cabin. He'd been skidding and sliding for the last fifty miles as he pushed the car, his skill, his luck. Once he'd shimmied across two lanes, mounting the median strip, a hideous accident in the making. Fortunately, it was two A.M. and the Northway was empty. After that, he'd slowed down. Killing himself and Joanna certainly wasn't going to help anything.

She sat stiffly beside him, exhausted, yet tense and alert. She had hit the floorboard with her braking foot so many times that he had thought of handing her the wheel. But she wasn't in any condition to drive. She silently peered into the confusing white maze where his headlights probed the swirling flakes. They had hardly spoken since they left his parents' place. There wasn't anything he could find to say that didn't end up making it worse. And Joanna didn't want to talk, anyway.

His headlights picked up the dark bulk of the cabin, its roof cloaked thickly white. She leaned forward, gripping the dash. "The Jeep's not there," she said.

"Maybe it's around the back. Maybe he was unloading timber or something." Joanna said nothing. Seth kept moving in the deep snow in front of the cabin, easing the big car around in a circle so he was facing back out the way he'd come. When he stopped, it settled heavily into the drifts. He opened the door with difficulty, plowing a soft arc in the snow, and climbed out. His feet, in street shoes, felt naked and inadequate. Wind-borne flakes touched coldly against his face. The cabin was dark, with only the faintest scent of wood smoke, as if left over yet from yesterday's fire.

"There's no one here," Joanna said.

For some reason he couldn't understand, Seth felt obliged to argue and answered sharply, "Well, you didn't expect to find them awake, Jo, it's three-thirty, for Christ's sake."

"They're not here," she repeated.

He went to the door, tried it, and found it unlocked, which meant very little. They only locked it when they left to go south, but still he said, "It's open," aloud, as part of his argument. Joanna pushed past him and went in, switching on the light. She walked stiffly, holding herself upright, as if literally holding herself together. The kitchen and living room were half open to each other, divided by a partial wall against which the woodstove sat and above which its metal chimney rose through an asbestos collar in the roof. Though they seemed like separate rooms, it was instantly possible to see at a glance through both. Seth had not expected to find anyone in either and yet their emptiness seemed a reproach to his optimism. That, and the knowledge that since Vietnam, Eric woke at the slightest sound and would never have slept through his tire-spinning approach through the snow. Still, he said in an ordinary voice, "Try the bedrooms, Jo. Quietly. Let's not give them a fright."

"There's no one here," she said again tiredly. But she went obediently to the room Tess had slept in, opening the door and turning on the light. She stood staring a long while at the empty, mussed-up bunk, finding the reality of her own fears still a stunning shock. "Maybe she used my room," she said numbly. Now Seth was looking at her with the same weary pity with which, throughout the journey, she had regarded him. Still, she opened that door and another and another, through the warren of bedrooms in the rambling, low building that once had housed their whole happy clan. She opened Eric's door last, reluctant still to make her accusation fact. The room was neat, tidy, empty, and cold. She closed the door and turned back to Seth, who was watching her from the narrow, pine-clad corridor.

"Where are they?" she said. Her voice was shaking and the accusation in it seemed almost to be leveled at him. He drew back from it, shutting in on himself.

"I don't know, Joanna," he said, reasonably. "Perhaps he took her somewhere."

"Where?" She demanded fiercely. "Where would he take her? Why didn't he tell me?"

"Jo," Seth said. "He wasn't expecting us back. He didn't know we'd drive all night, for God's sake." He paused and stepped closer to her, taking her shoulders. Her body felt rigid. "Look," he said persuasively, "maybe they went camping or something. They talked about climbing something . . ."

"Camping? In this weather?"

"Sure, Jo. We used to camp in the snow. Remember?"

She shook her head sharply. "He shouldn't have . . . I didn't give him permission to take her camping."

Seth tightened his grip on her shoulders. His eyes darkened. "He doesn't need your permission," he said angrily. "You entrusted your daughter to his care. That was enough. Whatever decisions he made you entrusted him to make." He released his hold and went out to the kitchen, with Joanna following. He looked around quickly for anything that might give some clue, but found nothing. He opened the door of the wood burner, crouching in front of it, and stirred the white ash with the old broken poker. A few frail sparks flew up, still. "He left a good fire."

"So?"

"I don't know. Maybe they meant to come back tonight."

"So where are they?"

"I don't *know*, Joanna. Maybe he was just keeping the place warm for tomorrow. I can't tell." He looked around angrily, and finding some kindling in the box beside the stove, thrust a few pieces in. "We'd better have a fire, anyhow," he said. He looked up after closing the door. "Are the tents still kept in the same place, Jo? Do you know?"

"I think so," she said numbly. He went out to the lean-to shed and came back after a short while, looking troubled.

"Are there still just the two family tents?"

She nodded, "Are they there?"

"They're both there." He sat down at the kitchen table wearily and looked up at her. "Could there be a new one maybe, something I don't know about?"

"I don't know, Seth. The place is all different now. The shed's full of things I don't recognize. David and his friends used the cabin a lot. They've left their stuff here. Skis and things." He nodded.

"I was trying to see if anything's missing. I just can't tell." He paused, the troubled look returning. "The tents are definitely there."

"So where are they?" Joanna said fiercely.

"They could have got late, coming back, stopped somewhere, a motel . . ."

"He hasn't any money."

"He's got money, Jo. Dad gave him money . . ." He stopped because he wasn't believing it himself and saw no reason then why she should. He took a deep breath. "Look, Jo, I hate saying this, but the Jeep's gone. The roads are pretty terrible. Eric's a good, careful driver . . ." he paused. "Anyone can have a crash, Jo. I almost had one tonight. I think I should phone the police and check it out." He paused again and added softly, "And maybe the hospitals."

She sat down across from him at the table, facing him bleakly. She nodded then, saying nothing, and looked away. He stood up. "Jo," he said quietly, "if you don't mind, I'd like to do this alone. Could you make me some coffee, please?"

She looked up, blankly, but then said, "Sure. You go phone." She stood up too, picked up the coffeepot from the counter by the sink, and began filling it mechanically. He went through to the living room and sat down at the desk beside the bookshelves that lined the far wall. He half lifted the phone and then set it down and dropped his head into his hands instead.

Once, some years before, a British friend, coming to stay at the villa, had run a Lamborghini sports car off a bend on the *autostrada*, just south of San Remo. Seth had spent three hours making this kind of phone call in Italian, amidst Italian bureaucracy, before getting, at last, the answer he didn't want to hear. It was an experience he had no wish to repeat. He raised his head, looking around the desk. His father's address book sat in one pigeonhole, a pretty cloisonné pen of his mother's in another. There was a stack of Tess's schoolbooks, neatly piled in one corner, and beside them a battered old copy of *Doctor Zhivago* from the cabin shelf. A receipt from the lumberyard marked Eric's place. Seth set the book down and picked up the phone.

From where Joanna sat at the kichen table, listening to the bubbling of the coffeepot and the sparking of the two pine logs she'd added to Seth's kindling, his voice beyond the half-wall and the chimney was just a slow murmur, the words, perhaps deliberately, too soft for her to distinguish. She shut her mind to them, tracing a swirling pattern on the oilcloth with her finger, too scared and tired to think.

When he came back, he was smiling, buoyant with relief. "Nothing," he said, holding up one hand. He poured himself a cup of black coffee as he passed the stove and sat down, slouching in the wooden chair, resting his head against its back, eyes closed. "Thank God." Joanna stared.

"Nothing," she repeated uncertainly.

"No vehicle of that description in any accident. No one of that description at any of the hospitals. We're clear."

"Clear? Seth, why are you sitting there grinning? The place is abandoned. It's snowing like shit. Where's my daughter?"

"With your brother, for Christ's sake, Jo." She jerked back, stunned by his outburst. "Have you ever been in a hospital morgue? No, you haven't. I have. That's why I'm sitting here 'grinning' as you put it. 'No' was the only word I wanted to hear." He drank from the coffee in an angry gulp, burning his mouth. "Shit," he said, slamming the cup down.

"I'm sorry, Seth."

"It's all right." He reached across the table and took her hand. "I'm sorry too. I'm tired." He sat for a moment looking at the table, then said, "Look, Jo, the Park Rangers aren't looking for anyone either, for what that's worth."

"Not looking? What does that mean?"

"It means they haven't signed in at any trailhead and failed to sign out again. That's all, Jo." He paused, looking up and meeting her eyes. "It doesn't mean much," he said.

"Well, let's call the Park Rangers . . ."

"And tell them what? Jo," he leaned forward, "they could be anywhere. Anywhere. On any mountain, or no mountain. Even if we could find the Jeep, and it could be anywhere, in some parking lot or just at the side of a road somewhere, even then, we've no idea where they've gone. This is a big, big place." He paused again, then straightened up, still holding her hand, "If they're out in the woods, no one's going to find them tonight. They're on their own."

"In this weather?" Joanna said bleakly.

"Yes, in this weather. Eric's the best woodsman in the family. The best woodsman I know. He'll look after her." He smiled, "Have some faith, Jo." She let go of his hand and wiped her eyes.

"I'm trying, Seth," she said, "I'm trying." She stood up, walked around the table, and went to the window, staring out at the falling snow. "Oh, fuck it," she cried, "Why can't it stop."

"Jo . . ." She whirled around.

"I'm sorry Seth. You're right, I should have faith and be rational and be glad they've not had an accident and all of it. But she's my little girl and I don't know where she is and you just can't understand."

"So everyone keeps telling me," he said wearily.

"I'm sorry, Seth." He said nothing, looking down at his cup of cooling coffee. He wobbled the cup, watching the rings widen and disperse.

"Do you want me to report them missing?" he said. She turned from the window.

"But you just said there's no point."

"There isn't, if they're out in the woods. But it's not the woods you're worried about, is it, Jo?" he said quietly. He looked up. His eyes beneath their dark brows were intense. Joanna turned away. She shook her hair back angrily, running fierce fingers through it, tugging roughly at the tangle at the ends.

"I don't *know*, Seth. I'm worried about so many things I don't know what I'm worried about. Oh, where has he taken her?" she cried desperately. He stood up and crossed the room and stood behind her, his arms linked around her body. He rested his chin on her shoulder.

"It doesn't matter where, Jo. She's with him. She'll be safe with him. This is Eric we're talking about. Not some stranger." Joanna stood very still.

"He is a stranger, Seth. I don't know who he is anymore."

"Yes, you do, Jo," Seth pleaded. "He's the person you believed in. He's the person you believed in enough to give up your job and disrupt your life and cross half the country and search those wretched streets . . ."

"But was I right?" she said sadly.

"*Yes.*" He released his hold and turned away. He walked to the table and stood looking down at the oilcloth and his cup. Then he turned abruptly and walked out into the living room. She followed him and stood by the dividing wall. He was sitting at the desk, his hand on the phone. He looked up as she came into the room. "Jo," he said, "I know this is a grievous decision. I can't make it for you, and I can't tell you what to do. But I want you to think very carefully. And I want you aware of the consequences. Your daughter is legitimately in your brother's care, and we really have no logical reason to assume anything is wrong at all. If you're asking for a police search, you will have to articulate your doubts." He stopped and drew a long breath. "You do realize that there are people up here who are going to remember who Eric Carlson is? Thirteen years is a long time, but police files stay open a long time." He paused. "Joanna, I'm not sure you were aware at the time, but when Molly disappeared, Eric was their first suspect."

"*What?*"

"Male relatives always are, Jo. It was procedure. They were pretty decent about it and fairly discreet, but there was no question what they were doing." He sat quietly then and after a while said carefully, "You've worked heroically building your brother a bridge back to the family. If we make this call, at the very least, we'll knock that bridge down. At the worst, we'll give that poor, sick woman he was married to the chance to make her accusations public."

"Oh, Christ," Joanna said. "Seth, Seth, what about my daughter? Where's my daughter in all this? You told me my daughter came first."

"And so she does." He was very calm, studying her without expression, his hand still resting on the phone.

She cried angrily, "Have you *no* doubt? No doubt at all?"

"I have no doubt," he answered instantly. "Is that because I have no children, or because I trust my heart?" He lifted the receiver and held it up. "Do you want them reported missing?" She stood in silence, listening to the soft batting of snowflakes, innocent as a child's Christmas, against the cabin windows. "Do you, Jo?"

She sighed softly. "No."

———

GOLD SUNLIGHT WAS TOUCHING the top of the snow-laden pines as Eric turned the Jeep into the camp track. Sun-warmed, a bent branch sprang free, releasing a small soft avalanche onto the roof as they passed. He had doubted the Jeep would make the track, but the tire marks of another vehicle preceding them, though rounded and half filled with snow, broke the trail.

"Somebody's been down here," he said to Tess, casually.

"Who?"

He shrugged, "Hunters, probably. Must have been early though. It stopped snowing before dawn." He glanced briefly at her, then back at once to the track. "How are you now?"

"Great," she said. She had her hurt foot out in front of her, the boot and sock off, stretching the toes experimentally. She was still wearing all her clothes and was snuggled under his jacket. "My foot's lots better. I bet I can walk." He gave another quick glance. It was swollen around the ankle, the slender, delicate bones hidden in puffy flesh.

"I think you'll know about it if you try," he said.

"I don't think I need a doctor at all, Eric," she said practically. "Maybe when Mom comes home . . ."

"We'll see." He ran the Jeep down a little dip to buy some momentum for the next climb. "We'll get you warm first, anyhow."

"I am warm. I'm great. How about you?"

"Just fine, Tess." He spun the wheel into a little skid and centered the Jeep again on the track. Invigorated by the dawn walk out of the woods, and with the heater in the Jeep turned up as high as it went, he was savoring warmth as a richly sensual pleasure. He slid a little on the last bend, bringing the Jeep slithering down the steep dip to the cabin, and shimmying to an unexpected stop just short of the blue Oldsmobile blocking the road.

"That's Seth's car," said Tess.

"I know," Eric said, quietly puzzled, and then worried. "Christ, they must have come back last night."

"Did they say that?" Tess looked at him, curious.

"No. No, they didn't." He switched the engine off. "Come on, Tess, we'd better get in." He jumped down into the snow and ran quickly around the Jeep, opening her door and reaching up for her.

"Please, Eric," she said, suddenly very adult. "Let me hop. I'm really embarrassed."

He nodded, "Well, carefully then, and let me get you down first . . ." Then the cabin door banged open and Joanna ran out, in stocking feet, into the snow.

"Tess . . ."

"Hi, Mom!" Tess shouted. She had one hand on Eric's shoulder, and she waved the other as he lifted her down. She stood on one foot, holding up the bare, damaged one delicately, like an exotic wading bird. "Look what I did," she said. "I fell off a waterfall and Eric carried me down the whole mountain and we got stuck in the woods overnight. In the *snow*. And Eric made a fire and a wonderful bed out of pine branches and it was great!"

"Tess," Joanna whispered. She took two stumbling steps through the snow. Seth came out the door behind her, shaking sleep from his head, his hair in a tangle over his eyes. Joanna extended her arms to her daughter, her fingers trembling. Tess wobbled on her one good foot.

"*Mom,*" she said, half eluding the embrace. "Jeez, what's the fuss?"

Joanna felt Seth's arm come around her shoulders, tightening. "Yeah," he said, "What's the fuss, Jo, hey?" He gripped her harder and gave her a little shake. "Just a little unplanned camping trip." He extended his hand to Eric. "Been having fun, pal?" he said.

"You could call it that," Eric said. He smiled slightly at Seth and took his hand, but his eyes, on his sister, were somber. "I'm sorry, Jo, I must have worried the hell out of you." She stood with the melting snow soaking into her socks, her hand held up, pushing back her hair.

"Yeah, Eric, but I should have known better. Seth kept telling me you were the best woodsman he knew." She smiled and stepped forward, wrapping her arms around him. He held her briefly, then turned back to helping Tess.

"Seth's generous," he said. "I made enough mistakes to get thrown out of the Cub Scouts."

———

INSIDE THE CABIN, Tess sat in front of the woodstove, eagerly examining her ankle. "Look, it's turned purple," she said happily. Eric crouched beside her, looking it over carefully.

"You may want an X-ray, Jo, but I really don't think it's broken. I did at first."

"That must have been cheerful," Seth said, "considering where you were."

"I've had better moments." Eric sat down on the hearth and leaned up against the wall. "That smells wonderful," he said, as Joanna poured him coffee. "You want some, Tess?"

"Yeah," she said.

"What?" Joanna looked at her.

"Black," said Tess, confidently. Joanna shrugged and poured it for her, then opened the door of the wood burner, letting the heat blaze out. "You should have seen the fire Eric built," Tess said. "And he had only one match." She was glowing with pride.

"Half a match, Tess," he grinned. "Let's make this story good."

She grinned back. "Then he made me the best bed in the world." She paused. "He gave me his jacket, too." She looked at him with worry and love. "I told him not to, but he did anyway."

Seth said seriously, "That must have been a bit chilly." Eric shook his head. He leaned back against the wall again and closed his eyes. "Are you all right?" Seth said.

"I'm fine. *You* know, Seth. When you light a fire in the woods, you don't keep warm by sitting over it. You keep warm running around all night looking for enough dead wood to keep it going. That's a very tidy piece of woods, now, I can tell you."

Seth laughed, "Good wood warms you twice." Eric laid his hand on the stack of firewood beside the stove and stroked it fondly, still with his eyes closed.

"As far as I've ever been able to see, it warms you about six times, Seth. Finding it, cutting it down, sawing it up, stacking it, *un*stacking it, splitting it. It must be the best energy source in the world. Or the worst. I'm not sure which." He felt himself drifting. "I think I could use some sleep."

Seth stood up and reached out a hand. "Come on," he said gently, "bed." Eric looked up and smiled and took the hand, but jumped up easily, suddenly alert again.

"Seth, I'm sorry. I'm not thinking very clearly. You were down to see your dad. Is something wrong? Is that why you're back early?"

"No," Seth said. "No, he's fine. Or at least he's saying he's fine, and that's all we're going to get." He shrugged. Eric nodded. He looked at Joanna.

"So why are you back so soon?"

"Oh, I caught the CNN forecast," Seth said casually. "And they were saying a lot of snow. I thought we'd get back up ahead of it, but I got it wrong." He paused. "I nearly wiped us out on the Northway. Stinker of a drive." Eric, still looking at Joanna, put his hand on Seth's shoulder.

Joanna opened her mouth, but said nothing. She shook her head and brushed her hand across her eyes, the honest blue eyes whose honesty he'd always loved. They stood looking at each other in solemn silence. Tess watched them both from her chair.

"Premonition, Jo?" he asked softly. She did not answer. He turned away from her and leaned his forehead briefly against the hand on Seth's shoulder. Then he raised his head and grinned, "Hey, Seth, I was telling Tess last night about your ghost stories. What a great storyteller you were. You could make me believe anything." He laughed softly. "But the thing about Jo, Seth," he said, turning back, "is I always knew where I stood with her. She'd lay down her life for me, but she could never, ever, tell me a lie." He brought the other arm around Joanna and embraced them both fiercely. Then he released them, leaned back against the wall, and closed his eyes. "I've got to call Mom and Dad."

"What, right now, Eric?" Joanna said. She laughed, happy but puzzled.

"Before I fall asleep. What's their number, Jo?"

"It's in Dad's book," Seth said, watching him. "Call them later, Eric. The world's not going to end in the next couple of hours."

Eric smiled and opened his eyes, "Ah well, Seth, you never know. Martin might get grumpy about the rules."

"Martin?" Seth said. "Martin?" He paused uncertainly. "Are you really all right?"

"Fine, Seth. Just fine." He straightened up from the wall and patted Seth's shoulder as he went past him into the living room. Seth looked at Joanna. She raised her hands and shrugged. They heard the scrape of the desk chair as Eric sat down and picked up the phone. There was a long pause, and then he said softly, "Dad? Yeah. It's me. Yeah, long time." He paused again, "Home, Dad. I'm calling from home."

Home Free All!

ANNIE THOUGHT SHE'D DONE a good job. She'd found David's missing socks and located Danya's spare hiking boots for Merrilee. She'd rounded up all the shopping bags in a neat row on the landing. She'd remembered towels—there were never enough at the camp—and she'd packed all of Martin's clothes. It was an hour since she'd come in from work, and now they were all out the apartment door.

Martin leaned on the elevator button and glowered at his watch. When the doors opened he picked up his black medical bag in one hand, their canvas weekender in the other, and said plaintively, "Why are we never, ever, out of here before six?" Annie knew he was tired and needed soothing, but since that day on the beach she was finding it hard to care. She shrugged and pushed past him into the elevator. Merrilee and David gathered their shopping bags and followed warily behind.

"I don't understand it," Martin said as they packed the trunk. "Why is there always more stuff? Every year there's more stuff."

"There's more people?" Merrilee suggested.

"I said we could wait for Danya and Aaron," David said pointedly. "I did say we could go tomorrow with them."

"That would be silly," Annie squeezed a final brown bag into place. "To have them come all the way down from Providence first. And anyhow, there's plenty of room. Just four people and a couple of bags, for Pete's sake." She looked sharply at Martin.

"Yeah, plenty," he said. He watched as Annie took the front passenger seat and Merrilee and David climbed into the back and sat, expectantly patient, like little kids. Then he got in behind the wheel and pulled out around the red Toyota that had boxed him in. When they hit the traffic on the avenue he said, "This is going to be a great drive."

"The roads were fine this afternoon," Merrilee said. "It was just four when Seth called. They got up there real fast."

"Sure, they were fine this afternoon," Martin said. "Maybe he should try rush hour sometime like the rest of the human race."

"I just meant there wasn't any snow." Merrilee sounded hurt.

"He took your parents," Annie said coldly. "That's always a job."

"They're his parents too."

"I know." Annie shook her head impatiently. Then she said, "Martin, would you pull over in front of that deli a moment? I need to get the sweet potatoes."

"I can't stop here."

"Just for a moment, Martin."

"Annie."

"Well, pull around the corner. Come on, Martin."

Martin swung into the cross street and crammed the big car in close to a fetid looking truck. "If I see a cop, we'll see you Monday," he said.

"Fine. Suits me." Annie grabbed her purse and jumped out onto the sidewalk. She slammed the door and ran into the store, bagged a great mound of sweet potatoes, threw some celery into her basket on top of them, and then collected milk and some more beer. By the time she got back to the car Martin was sitting with his shoulders hunched, sporadically slapping the steering wheel with his palms. "If we don't get on the road soon we might as well wait till tomorrow," he said.

"We're on it. That's it, Martin. I just needed sweet potatoes." She handed the two bags of groceries over the backseat to David, who set them on the floor. Martin gave her a jaded look.

"Couldn't Sara and Seth have got sweet potatoes? They'd have passed about a million supermarkets along the way."

"They've got the turkey," Annie said.

"So?"

"Thanksgiving's meant to be a family effort. Remember?"

"Oh, it is, Annie." He pulled away from the truck and began a circuit of the block, back to the avenue. "It's an effort, all right."

Annie ignored that. "Merrilee's done the stuffings. And your mother's made the pumpkin pie."

"Again? Annie, no one has eaten my mother's pumpkin pie for twenty years. We all hate pumpkin pie." Annie shrugged. Martin pulled back onto the avenue. "Everyone in America hates pumpkin pie." He gestured wildly with one hand as he drove. "Why do we inflict this on ourselves?"

"It's a tradition," said Merrilee.

"So was burning witches at the stake," Martin shouted. "We managed to give that up." He put his hand back on the wheel. He looked at Annie accusingly. "I thought we agreed we could quit this when the kids were grown."

David said, "I don't want to quit. I like Thanksgiving."

Martin looked sour but only said, "There's a lot of work, David."

"Okay," David said slowly. "So I'll do the work." He paused. "I'll tell you one thing, though. I'm sure as hell not going to bitch about it in front of my kids."

Martin got quiet then, and they drove the rest of the way out of the city in silence. When they were on the thruway, he said suddenly, "Did I always bitch about it, David?" His voice was sad, and Annie looked at him, startled.

"Yes." David said.

"Oh, not always," Annie put in quickly.

"Always," David said.

"Daddy was joking a lot," she said.

David said, "No, he wasn't." She looked briefly at Martin, who drove on in bleak silence.

"Yes, he was. We all joked and teased. That was all." She turned around and grinned at them in the flickering light. "You kids used to have a song about it even. Remember?"

David smiled slowly. "Yeah." Then he shrugged. "I still wish he wasn't always complaining."

"Oh, damn, Annie," Martin inclined his head with sudden alertness. "There's that noise in the transmission again. Just what we need."

"See?" said David.

Annie listened a moment and said, "It'll be all right, Martin."

"It better be."

"What was the song, David?" asked Merrilee.

David laughed quietly. "Just a song."

"Sing it," Annie said.

"I don't think Dad wants me to."

"Yeah, why not?" said Martin. "We can have a little cabaret when we break down on the thruway."

"We won't break down," Annie smiled.

"Listen to the mechanic," said Martin.

David sat back in his seat. He paused briefly and then sang,

> "Up the Northway and through the woods
> To Grandfather's house we go.
> Dad knows how far to push the car,
> Through the deep and drifting snow-oh!"

Merrilee giggled.

"Stephen Sondheim you're not, David," said Martin.

"There used to be a verse about the privy, but I can't remember it." David paused. "Danya will know."

"I'm holding my breath," said Martin.

"Oh, the privy," Annie moaned. "Four days of frozen behinds. Why do we do this?"

"That's what I was saying, and you all jumped all over me," Martin protested.

Annie sighed. Then she said seriously, "Oh, I don't know. To tell you the truth, if it weren't for Joanna and Eric being up there, I really don't think I'd go."

"Well, Eric could have come down to us," Martin said, "and that would have been lovely." He paused, "As for Joanna, I'm not looking forward to a weekend of trying to hang onto my balls."

Annie was instantly icy. "Well, I want to see my sister, Martin, whatever. They're going home on Tuesday." She said then, more quietly, "You can't be surprised that she's angry."

"I did apologize."

"A lot of good that did for Tess."

Martin shook his head and peered past the oncoming headlights. He raised one hand clear of the wheel and then dropped it. "I always screw up," he said sadly. "I don't know why."

"Miriam said that too," said Merrilee.

"What? That I always screw up?"

"No," Merrilee sounded surprised. "About not going up to the camp. She's only going because of Eric and Joanna, too."

"What?" Martin turned around and stared for an instant. He looked back at the road and demanded, "She said that? Then what are we doing this for?" He pounded the steering wheel twice with his fist.

"Grandpa likes it," said David.

"Oh yes," Martin said grimly, "Grandpa likes it." He slammed his foot down on the gas and the car bucked forward, but he let it off almost at once. "Of course he likes it," he said. "All of us up there and endless opportunity to be a pain in the ass. What could suit him better?" He shrugged philosophically. Annie looked over at him and smiled. Martin drove on in silence for a minute and then said, "Remember, what was it, the year before last? I caught him out on David's skis. Skis, for Christ's sake."

"It wasn't the year before last," Annie said, a little sadly. "It was before he had the stroke."

Martin said quietly, "Well, no wonder he had it. He was a stroke waiting to happen. I could just see myself dealing with a seventy-five-year-old's broken leg, three miles from nowhere, with him criticizing every damned inch of the way. He's like a three-year-old. He'll do anything for attention." He glowered at the night.

David said, "I thought it was great that Grandpa wanted to ski."

"Did you?" said Martin. He glanced in the rearview mirror and caught the dim outlines of his son and daughter-in-law snuggled up together on the backseat, their heads together. Then he looked at Annie. "No more," he said. "This is it. Read my lips. No more Thanksgivings at the camp."

Annie laughed softly.

"I've got it." David raised his head from Merrilee's and sang,

"Hurrah for New York, where the toilets work,
Hurrah for Thanksgiving Day!"

By the time they had passed Albany, Merrilee and David were both asleep. It was a cold, still night and the road was dry. Annie offered twice to take the wheel and then gave up. Martin had slipped into his frontier patriarch mode, leading his family into the wilderness. Driving the whole way was always part of it. She closed her eyes, resting her head back, relaxing. She really wanted to stay angry with Martin this time, but she never could hold out long. She always ended up feeling sorry for him instead.

"I wish my parents were coming," she said.

"It's too far for a weekend, Annie. The flight and the drive. It wipes your dad out."

"I know," she said softly, keeping her eyes closed. "But they want to see Eric so much."

"We'll get them up at Christmas. It's just a couple more weeks anyhow." He paused and said carefully, "Give him a little space, Annie. He's done so well."

She nodded and after a while asked, "Did your dad say that?"

"Yes."

She was quiet for a long while, feeling safe and warm in the car, with Martin's big solid shape beside her in the darkness. She said then, "Your dad knew what he was doing, didn't he? Sending Eric up there."

"He did," Martin said. He paused and shifted his hands on the wheel. "I certainly didn't think so at the time," he said fervently, "but I was wrong, thank God." She opened her eyes and looked across at his silhouette. Martin looked up at the mirror and then screwed around briefly and glanced at the backseat. "Are they asleep?" he asked.

Annie looked behind her and smiled fondly. "Sound," she said. "Like babies."

Martin sighed. "I was so scared, Annie," he said. She looked back at him, startled. "All I could think of was the shotgun sitting in the closet in Dad's room. And Eric up there working on his own."

Annie drew in her breath. She said in a small voice, "Joanna was there too."

"She couldn't be with him every minute." The car filled with silence. Martin shook his head. "I shouldn't have said that," he said. "I'm sorry, Annie."

She said again in the same small voice, "You didn't tell me."

"I told Dad." He paused and then said quietly, "I wanted him to get Seth to get rid of the thing."

"Did he?" Annie whispered.

Martin shook his head again. "He said you have to trust people. That's all he said." Martin looked at her briefly. "And he was right. I was wrong and he was right." He let out a long breath. "Annie, for the rest of my life I'll celebrate every time the old bastard proves me wrong."

He took his hand off the wheel, took hers, held it for a moment, and let it go.

━

IT WAS AFTER MIDNIGHT when they reached the camp. There was snow on the ground, and the outdoor light, left on to greet them, cast a wide, white glow. Martin switched off the engine and stared. "Goddamn your brother," he said.

"What?" Annie looked abruptly from the cabin to Martin.

"Look at the place."

"I am. It looks great. What's wrong with it? Look, he's even straightened up the shutters on that end window. They've been sagging since we were kids."

"That's what's wrong with it, Annie." He sighed and leaned back, stretching his arms, his eyes closed. Then he opened them and glared again at the cabin. "For all these years my one joy up here has been watching it all fall down. He's fixed the whole damn place. Now we're stuck with it for another fifty years."

━

THE SUN WASN'T UP YET when Tess followed Eric out to climb the ridge. The sky and the ground were both the same cold gray-white. The snow that had fallen the night they slept in the woods had thawed back until there were dark circles at the bases of trees.

Then it had gotten really cold, and what remained turned hard as rock. The lake froze and glistened dark blue-gray, and her mom and Eric were going to skate, but then it snowed again the next day and the lake was covered velvety white.

Outside the cabin the snow was churned and flattened from the boots and cars of all the people who had arrived yesterday. Tess walked silently behind Eric in the deep, icy ruts up the track. She had asked permission the night before, but she wasn't too sure he really wanted her along. She thought the ridge might be something private.

They walked single file along the track, a long way, until it climbed up to the tarred road that led away from the camp. The road had been plowed, scraped black and bare. They crossed it together and went into the woods on the other side. The ridge was a lot farther than she'd thought, and she realized that Eric must usually run most of the way to get there and back in the time he did.

"Am I going too slow?" she asked. He looked back over his shoulder.

"I'm not in any hurry." He smiled. "You're awfully quiet. Something wrong?"

"I like to be quiet sometimes."

He slowed down a little so they were side by side. "Your ankle okay?"

"Yeah, it's fine." She kicked at the snow to show him. It flew up, dry as dust. The ridge rose ahead of them, the shape of the land visible now that the trees were bare. There wasn't any path, and they scrambled up through the snow, using trees for handholds. The top was bare and open, with only gray bristly bushes and a few young trees. At the highest point they could see, between the trees, down to the white of the lake and the dark pines by the cabin, discernable only by its blue drift of wood smoke. There were big stumps of trees and one fallen log. Eric brushed the snow from it, and they sat down side by side.

"It was cleared for timber when I was eight," he said. "Ever since, we came up once a year to keep it clear." He looked out over the vigorous scrub. "I think we're losing now." He paused. "The woods always win in the end."

"It doesn't seem like that," Tess said. "What about the rain forests?"

"That's different. They're losing there because someone wants the land. This land is too hard. No one wants it anymore. There are farms under that," he said, waving one hand toward the thick-grown trees. "Sometimes you find them. Old foundations. Apple trees. All grown over. It doesn't take long. If we left the cabin tomorrow and didn't come back, in a few years the roof would come down. Then the walls. Next, there'd be saplings finding their way in. Then trees." Tess sat on the log, thinking of trees growing up through the cabin floor, by the woodstove, by her bunk bed, by Eric's desk in the living room.

"I don't want that to happen," she said. He smiled suddenly. "Then see that it doesn't."

"Me?"

"Who else? You're the young one."

She thought carefully. "Well, it isn't just me, really. There's David and Merrilee. And maybe Danya. And maybe even her boyfriend. They'll help."

"I'm sure they will," he said. "But I'll count on you."

They sat quietly, then, neither of them moving, the land around them silent and stark, the bones of it showing, black trees and gray rock, and white snow. Then the sun broke over the next ridge and the snow turned pink, and where it clung to the trees, gold.

"Pretty place," Eric said. Tess nodded, still wanting to be quiet. "It's pretty in the summer too. Hot and sunny and covered in blueberry bushes. It even smells of blueberries."

"That must be nice," Tess said, thinking about the blueberries. Then an idea came into her head so fast that she'd said it before she even thought. "This is where Molly was coming to, isn't it?" He didn't say anything, but he closed his eyes briefly and nodded in acknowledgement. She hunched over, studying him, and then asked finally in a small, troubled voice, "Is that why you come here, then?"

He didn't answer at first, but sat thinking, looking down at his boots in the snow. Then he turned to her and smiled and said lightly, "Sometimes. But there's a lot of reasons. Sometimes I come here to think. Sometimes just because it's pretty. I've always come here, Tess. Long before Molly was even born." He smiled again, and she felt relieved and sat back on the log, stretching her feet out.

After a while she said, "I've got a place up in some pine trees behind the trailer. That's where I go to think." She looked at him shyly. "We're going home on Tuesday."

"I know that."

"I don't want to go." He turned to face her. The sun had reached them, touching his face and casting a red light over his hair.

"You will once you get going, Tess," he said gently. "You'll see your friends. School."

"I hate school."

"You do not."

"I don't have any friends."

"I think you do." She scuffed at the snow with the heel of her boot, digging a hole down to the frozen leaves. The sun glared white in her eyes when she looked up.

"I don't want to leave you."

"I'll come see you."

"Will you? Will you really? You're not just saying that."

"I don't just say things, Tess. Ever." She sat for a moment longer until she was certain she believed him, then she turned and flung her arms around his neck and buried her face against the rough wool of his jacket.

"I love you," she said, and held on with all her strength.

———

WHEN THEY CAME BACK DOWN from the ridge, the kitchen of the cabin was full of people and smelled of coffee and frying bacon. There were so many of them sitting around the big round table that there weren't enough chairs, and Martin was sitting on the edge of the kindling box, and Tess's mom, in a sweater over her pajamas, was sitting on Seth's knees, eating breakfast and talking to Miriam at the same time. She had one arm looped around his neck as casually as if he were a brother, and Tess found she liked the way she looked there, happy and unconcerned. She squeezed in beside them and found a place on the edge of Merrilee's chair.

"Hey, you're up early," Merrilee said.

"I climbed the ridge."

"Good for you." Merrilee shifted her weight, planting her feet solidly and laying her hands on her big stomach. "Maybe one day I'll climb the ridge again, too." She grinned. "Though it's pretty hard to believe."

"You'll climb it," Harry said. "And soon. Three weeks you got. Maybe two and a half."

"My obstetrician says four."

"Your obstetrician was in diapers when I was practicing medicine. Three." He grinned. "Then, one, two, three, push, and you're a free woman."

"Oh," Merrilee moaned, "I can't wait. I can't wait." Tess looked at her with shy admiration. "Hey, kid, eat your breakfast. We're on call for turkey stuffing in half an hour."

Tess felt the warm chaos of the kitchen begin to envelop her, the snowy peace of the ridge slip away. She ate her breakfast and let Miriam give her two extra pieces of toast, then got up to wash her plate.

When, after breakfast, Eric went out to cut wood, she half wanted to follow, but instead she stayed in the kitchen, where the smell of the turkey giblets boiling up for stock was already making her think of dinner. Martin went out with Eric, and Harry got up and went too, picking his way across the crusted snow, using a ski pole instead of his cane.

"What's that old fool up to?" Miriam asked, peering through the still-frosty window.

"Nothing, Mom," Sara said. "He'll just sit at the side and watch."

"It's cold."

"There's good sun. He'll sit in the sun." Sara watched her father's progress, smiling gently, and then went back to her cooking.

Seth and David came in from the lean-to shed, carrying ski poles and cross-country skis. Seth picked up a piece of the celery Joanna was chopping and took a bite before handing it back.

"We're just going to see if the old track around the lake needs clearing," he said.

"We'll be back later if you want any help," David added, his eyes on Merrilee. He looked guilty. Seth looked oblivious.

When they'd gone, Annie wiped her hands down her jeans and said, "God, it doesn't take long, does it? We sure do revert to type up here. Men in the woods. Women in the kitchen."

Joanna laughed, leaning back from the table, "Oh, I've split enough logs to keep me for a lifetime. Let them have it." She grinned at Tess. "And they're washing all the dishes, whatever they think." Sara took the big turkey out of its cardboard box and wiped it with a wet paper towel.

Miriam watched and said worriedly, "What are we going to do about what's-his-name?"

"Who, Mom?"

"What's-her-name's boyfriend."

"Aaron?" said Annie.

"That's right," Miriam said. "What are we going to do about him?"

"Who's Aaron?" Joanna asked.

"Danya's boyfriend," Annie said. She turned back to her mother-in-law. "What's the problem, Miriam?"

"Martin was saying maybe he keeps kosher."

"Oh, Mom," Sara said.

Annie smiled. "Martin's teasing you, Miriam."

"Teasing? What's teasing? Why should he tease about that?"

"Because it gets your hackles up. Miriam, aren't you used to him yet?" Joanna was watching, puzzled. Annie lifted her hands from the bowl of stuffing she was mixing, and said, "He's a real nice boy, Jo. It just so happens he went to synagogue when he was staying with us and Martin saw him in a yarmulke, with the predictable results."

"His family, are they very religious?" Miriam said warily.

"They're religious. Not very religious. Look, what does it matter? Danya would have told us if there was any problem." Miriam nodded but still looked unhappy.

Sara said, "Mom, do you remember where that big tablecloth is? The one we always used?"

"Sure. In the chest of drawers in the big bedroom at the end. No . . . now, did we move it? Annie, did we put it in that closet in your room? Or did we put it up above?"

"I can't remember, Miriam." Annie looked around, "Tess, how about you go help Miriam find it. You might have to go up in the roof space, over the end bedroom. Ask Eric or Martin for a ladder if you need it."

"I know where the ladders are." Tess smiled and carefully took Miriam's hand. "You show me what I'm looking for and I'll do the climbing," she said.

They went out the door, and Annie turned to her sister-in-law, "Thanks, Sara. I could strangle Martin. As if Miriam and religion weren't enough of a minefield without him making jokes." She sighed, giving the bowl of turkey stuffing a last stir, "You know, unreligious people are every bit as bigoted as religious people when they get down to it. It won't hurt Danya to go to synagogue, whatever Martin thinks."

"Is Martin that antireligious?" Joanna asked.

"Oh yes," Annie said. "How can he help it? Look at his father. Wait'll he gets going on it."

"Oh, I know. I've heard him. But Martin . . ." She shrugged awkwardly. "I never was sure what he thought. He might have rebelled against Harry, after all."

"He didn't. Martin never rebelled against anything. That's what's wrong with him now. Aside, of course, from just being an asshole." Merrilee looked up, wide-eyed, from peeling potatoes.

Joanna said, "Oh, Annie. He's not."

"Yes, he is."

"Annie," Joanna stopped working and looked sadly at her sister, "I'm sorry I ever said what I said, and I'm sorriest of all that you heard it. It was never meant for you to hear."

Annie shrugged stiffly, "I can handle truth, Jo."

"Okay," Joanna said, breathing deeply. "Then handle this. He was no more guilty than I was. His biggest sin was he couldn't stand up to his parents. Well, neither could I stand up to mine. That's the way we were." She smiled wryly. "Now we've both raised children who defy us at every turn. So there's our victory, I suppose."

"David doesn't want to defy Martin," Merrilee said fervently. "David would like nothing better than to please him. Really."

"I know, sweetheart," Annie said gently. "Don't you worry about it. I'll handle Martin." She leaned over and kissed the top of Merrilee's head, then looked back to Joanna. "He was a shit to you, Jo, and now he has the presumption to be a shit to David, because, quite frankly, David has shown him up. What gets me is the damned hypocrisy. I've had half a year hearing what a fool his son was, and now I learn what's really bugging him is knowing David had more guts than he had himself."

"Not more guts," Joanna said, "different priorities."

"Better priorities."

"Different. Different values." She smiled. "Forgive him, Annie. He's never once in his life deliberately done anyone harm. He can't be that bad a man." Annie balled up a fistful of stuffing and rammed it into the turkey, smiling grimly back.

"Oh, give me a year," she said.

The kitchen door swung open, and Tess and Miriam came back into the kitchen. Tess was wearing the tablecloth draped over her head like a veil, two bunches of yellowed linen caught up under her chin. Miriam held it fanned out behind her, a circular train. "Here comes the bride . . ." she sang in her quavery voice.

"Short, fat, and wide," Joanna joined.

"Thanks a lot, Mom," Tess grimaced. She giggled as Joanna took her hands in her own, the cloth grasped between them, and waltzed her around the kitchen, stumbling into chairs, stocking feet slipping on the worn linoleum floor. Miriam danced a few steps, behind them, then stopped.

"That's an heirloom. Harry's mother gave us that for our wedding. Imagine. All these years and here it is." She hummed the tune as Tess whirled faster with her mother, the linen cloth rippling in a ring. "I never liked it much," she said.

———

"Is that my tree, Eric?" Harry asked.

"That's your tree." Eric straightened up from wrestling the big log up onto the sawhorses. Martin leaned against the log, breathing hard. "Sorry to do this in front of you, Harry, but I'd been kind of waiting for another hand on the saw."

"What about Seth?" Martin said. Eric leaned a hand against the log and looked up at Martin.

"That's funny, I never thought of it," he said, surprised.

"No one ever does think of work when Seth's around," said Martin.

"Yeah, yeah," Harry said. He was sitting on a tree stump they'd left for a chopping block, his feet, in his old climbing boots, planted in front of him. He leant on the ski pole the way he leaned on his cane. "Well, get on with it. If you're going to cut my tree up, you may as well get it over and done."

"You'll be glad of it next winter. There's a few warm nights in this," Martin said. Harry didn't answer. He watched Eric wax the saw with an old piece of candle.

Then he said, "You've done a beautiful job, Eric. Thank you." Eric looked up and nodded.

"My pleasure," he said softly. He bent once again over the saw.

Harry laughed quietly to himself. "Little Donald MacKenzie's in for a surprise. He told me last summer it would take two months, and maybe a couple of guys working on it. Ha!"

"He *was* surprised," Eric said, not looking up.

"He been up here?" Eric finished with the saw and put the wax in his jacket pocket.

"He came by a week ago. I'd met him a couple of times at the lumberyard, and I guess he got curious."

"Impressed?" said Harry.

"Must have been," Eric said. He stepped behind the log and held out one end of the two-handed saw toward Martin. "He offered me a job."

"He what?" said Martin, his hand lightly touching the saw.

"He's running a little construction company," Eric said. "They've got a big renovation job, some hotel down at Lake George. He needs more people."

"Little Donald MacKenzie offered *you* a job," Martin said. "That's a bit of nerve." Eric looked up from positioning the saw and studied Martin.

"I don't get you."

"He's a kid, Eric. He used to run around here bare-assed with our kids. Now he's going to be your boss?"

Eric smiled and drew the saw lightly toward himself, marking the soft bark of the log. "He's a kid with a good head for business, which is more than I've got. Why shouldn't I work for him?"

"Eric." Martin looked pained. "It isn't right. You don't have to . . ."

"What's wrong with that?" Harry said sharply. "What's wrong with someone working with their hands? That's what made this country. People making things, not just moving them around. No wonder everything's going to pot if we're ashamed now of working with our hands."

"Not ashamed," Martin said hurriedly. "I didn't . . ."

"He's a bright kid, Martin," Eric said. "He employs ten people already. I'll do fine with him."

Martin nodded sadly. He raised his hand, half in protest, half in apology. "Let's cut this wood," he said.

It was green and sappy and resisted the saw, and they worked hard at it, taking a length off, stopping to shift the rest along the sawhorses, taking off another length. Eric shrugged out of his jacket and hung it across a branch. Martin pulled his heavy fisherman's knit over his head and stood sweating in a gray turtleneck. Harry reached up and patted the roll of flab above the top of his jeans. "You're getting fat," he said, grinning.

"So who has time to exercise?"

Harry laughed, "Well, you're getting some now. Don't complain."

"I'm not," Martin said testily. He turned back to the saw. They cut another length and started the next. Harry sat in the sun, grinning, with the comfortable enjoyment of a well-settled cat.

"Don't lean on it, Martin," he said. "A two-handed saw, you gotta let it run." Martin nodded, wiped sweat from his face with his sleeve, and turned back to work. "Look, you've got Eric pulling your weight as well as the saw. Let it run."

"I am," Martin said. Harry grumbled something and sat back quietly. But in another moment, he leaned forward, waving his ski pole.

"Jeez, kid, where's your sense of rhythm? Didn't I teach you anything?"

"You taught me," Martin said grimly. He gave the saw a sharp shove.

"Martin, you're doing it again. Loosen up." The saw caught solid. Martin felt the jerk right up his arms, into his neck.

"Shit."

"Well no wonder it jams."

Martin dropped his end of the saw, leaving it sticking in the wood. He held up both hands, clear of it. "Okay. Okay. You do it. Okay?"

Harry shrugged, grinning amiably, "What do I want to saw up my own tree for?" He rocked back on the stump, his grin spreading.

Eric jiggled the saw lightly and released the blade. He swung it free and rested one end on the ground and smiled. "Harry, lay off," he said. Harry put his hands on his knees. He grinned again but said nothing, then sat back, watching once more good-naturedly.

After a few minutes, he said, "Maybe I'll go kibitz in the kitchen." Martin grunted something. Harry got to his feet, awkwardly, prodding at the snow with his ski pole. Eric reached to steady him. Harry clasped his arm, regained his balance, and then released his grasp. He patted Eric's shoulder gently as he passed. Martin watched and then turned back to the saw. They finished one section of tree and dragged a new one up onto the sawhorses.

Martin said, plaintively, "How do you get away with saying that?" Eric laughed.

"Same way you do with my dad." He raised the saw and then laid it down lightly, sideways on the log. "I love him, Martin, but he's not perfect."

"Oh, I know that," Martin said wearily.

"The trouble is, you don't. He has his flaws. Like never getting used to having a son who might beat him at things, for a start. What the hell do you care how well you can saw up a log? Why let him rile you?"

"He always riled me."

"I know. That's what I'm saying. You still see him the way you saw him when we were kids."

"He'd always get at me so. Never Seth. He never got at Seth . . ."

"He doesn't notice Seth. It's you. You're the first son. You're the competition."

"He could always do everything. He always knew everything."

"He put up a good smoke screen, Martin." Eric lifted the saw and marked the log. "So do you," he said. "You can't see yourself the way David and Danya see you." Martin gripped his end of the saw. He drew it, scraping, along the rough bark, trying to let it slide easily as Eric pulled it back. It cut, white, into the wood. Piney sap scented the cold air.

"David thinks I'm a fool," he said.

"Does he? Then why is he so desperate to please you?" Martin shook his head. He ran the saw blade twice more through the wood and then dropped his hands from it and just left it, halfway through the log. He turned away and sat down on Harry's stump.

"Eric, I'm so sick of being on the wrong side of everybody." Eric watched him for a moment and then carefully slid the saw free of its groove and leaned it against the log, one end in the snow. He perched on the edge of one of the sawhorses and looked down at Martin.

"Like who?"

"Like Annie. Joanna. David. Merrilee. My father. My mother. Enough for a start?"

Eric inclined his head thoughtfully. "Pretty good list."

"It was bad enough, before this thing with Jo."

"Don't worry about Jo."

"She hates me," Martin said. "I can't live with that. I have to believe there's still some part of her . . . I can't bear her hating me."

Eric waved a dismissive hand. "Jo doesn't hate anybody, Martin. She's volatile and she says what she thinks, sometimes a little before she thinks it, but she can't hold a grudge and she can't tell a lie. You gotta just take her for what she is." Martin looked uncertain. "She doesn't blame you, Martin," Eric said bluntly.

"The rest of them do. Mom blames me for everything that's

gone wrong in this family. She's got me carrying everyone's sins into the goddamned desert. They've rewritten our history. I don't recognize what they're remembering. And what they're forgetting. Did I imagine all that pressure back then? And Dad. Now he turns around to David, like having a kid at twenty-three with no job and no prospects was the greatest idea in the world. What's happened to all that shit about career and responsibility they laid on me? Now suddenly they're a pair of octogenarian hippies. Tune In, Turn On, Drop Out. And I'm the old stick-in-the-mud adult defending family values."

"He's indulging himself, Martin," Eric said, smiling. "He can afford to. He's got his son following in his footsteps, keeping up the family tradition. His own father's dead and not looking over his shoulder anymore. Now he can indulge himself. And David."

"At my expense."

"Parents use grandchildren when they want to apologize to their own kids. Listen hard, Martin, it's the only apology you're going to get."

Martin shook his head. "They laugh at me," he said at last.

"And they lean on you. They always did. *We* always did. Whose couch did I sleep on when Seth brought me home? And you didn't need that. At all."

"You're always welcome," Martin said, his voice muffled.

"Oh, I know," Eric said. "I do know. All of us know. None of us ever forget." He picked up the saw, looked at the log, and shrugged, swung the saw over his shoulder and turned away. "Come on."

"We're not finished," Martin said.

"Leave it there. Let's give the old so-and-so something to think of, come spring."

———

THEY PUT THE SAW AWAY in the toolshed, dusting it clean of snow before hanging it in its place, and walked together down the slope to the cabin. A pair of snowy skis stood on either side of the kitchen door, a cluster of poles on the packed snow beside them. Inside, David and Seth lounged in kitchen chairs by the woodstove, stocking feet up on the hearth, while Annie and Sara and Joanna stepped over and around them preparing the meal. Tess and Miriam sat at the table, peeling and slicing apples. Seth swung his chair around on its back legs, as they came in, and took his feet down.

"Hey, great. We were just going down to clear some ice to skate. Want to come?"

"Maybe when I've had a chance to catch my breath," Martin said sourly.

"You been working?" Seth looked up, curious.

Eric stepped behind his chair and stretched his hands out over the stove. "Just sawing up your dad's favorite tree," he said. "How's the skiing?"

"Good," Seth said. "We should have a little tour before it's dark. Maybe Jo and Tess would like to come."

Martin said, "There *is* work to do around here, Seth." Annie lifted her hands from the piecrust she was rolling on the table.

"Come on, Martin. It's a holiday. How often do we get to see Seth here?"

"Is that my fault?"

"Why not just clear the lake, and we can all skate before dinner."

Martin shoved his hands into his pockets, standing with his shoulders hunched. Then he shrugged and said, "Do you think there's enough ice? It's early."

"Should be," Eric said. "It's been cold. We'll get a rope and test it, anyhow."

"Harry's gone to test it," Tess said.

"He's what?" Martin took his hands out of his pockets.

"No, he hasn't," Sara said. "He wouldn't do that."

"He said he was," Tess looked at Eric.

"He's just talking," Annie said.

"What's he doing?" Miriam asked. "Has he gone out on that ice?" She got up and went to the window and peered out worriedly.

"He always used to." Seth stood up, looking around for his boots. "He'd never let any of us on it until he'd been on it first."

"Stupid old fool," said Miriam.

"Oh, great," Martin said. "Now I've got to run out and get him. *Shit,* I hate it up here."

Eric stepped past him and laid his hand on Martin's forearm in passing, "I'll get him, Martin. Have a break." He smiled, and Martin smiled back sheepishly. "It's his game," Eric said, "and you can't win. So don't play it with him."

"So what then? He ups the ante and falls through the ice? Then who wins?" Martin cried in frustration.

"Not Harry," said Eric, going out.

He went back up to the toolshed, got a length of rope, and trotted down the steep snowy path between the pines with the rope coiled over his shoulder.

The lake was wide and white and silent. Snow was drifted around the feet of the dock, and in the distance the surface blurred gently into the snowy shoreline beneath a now-gray sky. Harry was walking across the little indentation they thought of as their bay, leaving a wavering trail of dark prints in the snow. From time to time he stopped and tapped the frozen surface with his ski pole. He looked small and bowed, a dark question mark against the white emptiness.

"Harry," Eric called. Harry looked up. He waved. Eric stepped closer to the shore and stood on the snow-covered gray rock at its edge. "Harry will you get the hell off that ice?"

"I'm testing it."

"I'll test it. And I'll use a rope. Just like you taught us," he added, grinning. "Now get off before you fall through." He stepped back from the shore and knotted the rope around a tree.

"It's thick, Eric," Harry stamped on the ice. "I'm not falling through anything."

"Yeah, well, if you do, I'm going to get damn wet and cold getting you out." He slipped the coiled rope onto his shoulder and walked out onto the ice.

"So leave me, Eric. Who needs an old man?"

"Don't tempt me, Harry. I might." He followed Harry's footsteps across the lake. "Come on, you're worrying Miriam. Go sit on the dock until I'm done." Harry tapped the ski pole on the ice. He looked at Eric, then shrugged playfully and tapped his way slowly back toward the shore. When he reached the dock, he sat down stiffly on its edge.

Eric walked in a wide arc, as far out as they'd want to skate. He scraped the snow with the side of his boot. It swept cleanly away, leaving the dark surface glistening and dry. He knelt on it, studying the cracks that revealed its depth. It looked almost six inches. He stood up, stamped on it, and then jumped up and down. "You *want* to swim or something?" Harry shouted.

"It's fine."

"What did I tell you? Come here," Harry called. Eric recoiled the rope onto his shoulder and walked back to the dock. He sat beside Harry and lay the coiled rope between them. "Want to talk to you, kid." Harry said.

"What about?"

Harry drew a line in the snow between his feet with the end of the ski pole. "Eric, you told me you wanted to go back to school. You said you wanted to teach."

Eric shrugged. "I said I'd thought about it. I wasn't sure."

"I meant what I said about people working with their hands."

"I know."

"I want you to understand that. It's a plenty good enough thing to do." He drew another line beside the first.

"I understand."

"Now I've said that, I'm going to say the other thing. You were born to be a teacher, Eric. I always knew that. I told you that when you were fourteen."

"Did you?" Eric looked up surprised. Harry crossed his two lines with a third.

"Sure, I did. You didn't listen." He crossed the lines again. "Now. You want to go to school, you want to take courses, whatever. You do it. I'll pay for it."

"Harry . . ."

Harry drew a cross in the center of his crossed lines, "Your dad'll say the same, but I'm saying it first, so you take it from me."

Eric laughed and shook his head. "I think both of you have

put enough people through school already," he said. Harry drew a circle at one corner of his little grid.

"What do I need money for, Eric? I'm an old man." He drew a second circle, and a second cross. "Think about it. Go work for Donald a while if you like. Just promise me you'll think about it. Okay?" Eric nodded slowly. He looked down at the snow and Harry's drawing. "You might as well say yes, you know. You're just getting it in my will if you don't."

Eric said, exasperated, "Harry, do you *ever* take no for an answer?"

"Sure I do. I've lived with Miriam for fifty years. Now, come on, what do you say?" Eric laid his big, rough hands flat on his knees and studied them, smiling gently. Then he looked up at Harry and nodded again.

"Okay."

"Good kid." Harry drew a third circle and a triumphant connecting line. "Tic-tac-toe solitaire," he said.

"Solitaire?"

"Yeah. You can't lose. Good game."

Eric smiled, "We'd better go up to the cabin. They'll think we've both fallen in."

"Ah, let them. Give Martin something to complain about. Double funeral. All that expense."

"Harry," Eric said softly, "come on."

Harry grinned devilishly. "When you starting with Donald?"

"New Year's. After New Year's. It'll all be interiors now until spring."

"Can you come down at Christmas? I got a reason for asking."

Eric looked up curiously. "Sure, if you want."

"Seth wants to take Sara to Italy."

"Oh, bless him," Eric said softly. "She'll love it."

"Yeah, she'll love it if she goes. It's getting her to go. You know what she's like. You come stay in the house, maybe she'll feel she can go."

"Oh, sure, Harry. That's easily done. A pleasure."

"Yeah, well, it's a pleasure for me too," Harry said, "Whether or not Sara goes. But I want her to go. I want her to have this.

Things aren't going to get any easier." He fell silent and drew another tic-tac-toe board in the snow. "That thing I was in for, Eric." He looked up. "It's cancer, actually."

Eric sat looking down at the drawing at their feet. "I'm sorry to hear that," he said.

"Yeah, I'm not thrilled about it either." Harry filled in two circles and a cross on his new board. "You guessed anyhow, didn't you?"

"Yes."

"Thought you would." Harry added another cross and then another, stacking the odds against himself. "I don't know about the others. Miriam's mad at me. I don't know if she's mad at me for not telling her or she's mad at me for getting cancer." He paused. "I don't want to say it to her yet. The moment I say it aloud, that's it, everything's finished, I'm an invalid. After I had this stroke," he tapped his leg with his ski pole, "I was *half* an invalid. You know, a big fuss over food and getting enough sleep and not falling. And no more sex. That made me mad. I mean, just for argument, say I was capable once in a blue moon, why shouldn't we try? But no. After the stroke that was out. I think she was bored with it, to tell the truth." He paused, and smiled a faraway smile. "God, she used to love it, too, when she was young." He shook his head and drew a quick winning circle on his board.

"I can't tell Martin," he said. "Not yet. Martin's going to want intervention. I don't blame him. I raised him that way. Martin's a good doctor." He sat silent, thoughtful, and then looked up, squinting at the flat gray sky. "But, you know, I can't be bothered," he said.

"Is that wise?" Eric asked softly.

"What's wise, Eric? I've been in medicine all my life. I know how these things work. A few months in and out of hospitals tied up in tubes, and then the same result. I'm an old man. I'd rather enjoy myself. See my new great-grandson. Have a little fun." He dragged his ski pole through his games in the snow and then ruffled them up, blotting them out. "I'll tell Sara when she gets back. If I tell her before, she just won't go." He paused, tapping the pole against his boot. "I can't bring myself to tell Seth." He scraped the side of the pole along the leg of his jeans, looking again at the sky.

"You should tell him before he leaves, Harry," Eric said.

"I know. I can't. Seth's the baby. I can't tell Seth." He looked at the sky a moment longer and then turned back. "Hey, you look sad."

Eric laughed weakly. "Well, what do you expect?"

"Ah, don't be. Going to happen sooner or later anyhow."

"It's going to happen sooner or later to all of us, Harry. But it's you, and it's now, and I don't want it to be." Harry waved one hand lightly in the air.

"Yeah, but that's the difference. The later's still a lot later for you. Once you get here, it looks different. It's like climbing a big mountain. When you finally get there and look back from the top, all the ups and downs, all the insurmountable parts, look like nothing much." He shifted one leg and winced. "I remember during the war, when I learned I was being sent overseas, Miriam and I just hung onto each other in bed, crying and crying. There she was with a little baby and I was leaving her, and you can be sure, Eric, we knew we weren't going to see each other ever again, after that night.

"And here we are all these years, all these *people*, later. Who'd ever have thought it?" He closed his gnarled hand over Eric's on the dock. "Trust me. You'll be amazed yourself one day." He looked up. "Ah. There's the rescue party," he said.

Miriam, in boots and jeans, stood halfway down the track, her eyes shaded, peering at the dock. "Eric? Have you got a stupid old man with you?"

"Ha," said Harry.

Eric looked at him quickly, laughing. "I can't answer that, Miriam," he said. She trudged down through the snow. Eric stood up and reached a hand out to her, and she stepped warily onto the ice and sat down on the dock, taking his place beside Harry.

"Very funny," Harry said. She looked straight ahead, fighting a smile. Martin, Tess, Seth, and David came down the track after her and gathered on the shore with snow shovels and brushes.

"How's the ice?" Martin asked.

"Solid. You could probably drive a car on it," Eric said, adding, "though I wouldn't, just in case."

"I wasn't planning on it." Martin looked at his father. "Want a snow shovel, Dad?"

"Nope. Want to watch you instead."

"Just what I thought," Martin said with a smile. He walked out onto the ice and set his shovel down. The snow curled away, light and smooth, and he began clearing a broad black strip.

After ten feet, Harry said, "Come on, Martin, you're leaving as much as you're clearing. Can't you keep it steady at least?" Martin kept smiling, grimly, as metal scraped on ice. They cleared a big, wide semicircle, banking the snow in a wall around its rim, and then went back to the cabin to find skates. Martin stayed behind and built a fire in the stone fireplace by the water's edge. He lit it on the first try. Harry watched it blaze up, disappointed, and said, "Don't see what you need a fire for. We'll be having dinner in an hour."

"Well then, you sit over there and freeze your butt off. The rest of us would like to be warm." Miriam got up from the dock and came and sat on the log seat by the fire. Then Harry got up, too, ambled across the ice, and sat down on the other end of the log. Martin was standing to one side, glowering at him, when Eric came back down the track with their skates. They sat together on the dock while Martin tied his laces and Eric waited for Tess, a pair of white girls' skates lying beside his own.

"His game," Eric reminded Martin with a smile. "His game. Just don't play." Martin picked up one of the clutch of hockey sticks David had brought down from the shed. He balanced it familiarly, tapped it on the ice, and skidded a hard lump of snow across the clearing.

" 'New York Physician Clubs Elderly Father to Death with Hockey Stick.' How's that for a headline?"

"I wouldn't bother," Eric said. "These days it wouldn't even make the news." He looked up. Tess was walking down the track in jeans and a sweater and the red snowflake hat she'd worn on the mountain, pulled down over her pigtails. She walked gingerly out to the end of the dock.

"It's safe, Tess," Eric said. "We've tested it."

"Yeah." She looked uncertain, stepping lightly on the black ice. "Mom says you have skates for me?" she asked shyly. He stood up as she sat on the dock beside Martin.

"You never skated, Tess?" Martin asked. She shook her head, looking at the white skates, thinking. "Well, you've got the expert to teach you," Martin said. He stood up on his blades and took a couple of sure gliding strokes, circled, picked up the hockey stick again, and headed out into the lake. Tess watched. Martin, who always seemed so heavy and slow, looked powerful and fast on the ice. Eric looked over his shoulder to see Martin, then went back to untying Tesse's boots.

"He's not so bad himself," he said.

"Yeah," Tess kept watching, a little awed. "Are you better?"

Eric slid her boot off and slipped on a skate. He glanced back at Martin again and said, "I'm fancier. He's stronger. It depends what's needed." He removed her other boot and replaced it with the second skate. She watched as he laced them, her forehead lined. He looked up and met her eyes. "These were Danya's or Molly's, Tess," he said. "I honestly can't remember which." She nodded solemnly and swung her feet gently while he sat beside her, tying on his skates. "You ski, Tess, don't you."

"Oh yeah."

"It's the same as skiing. You've got two edges on each skate." He swung one of his legs across the other at the knee to show her the blades. "It's all about moving from edge to edge. Watch Martin now. See, inside edge, now he's turning, outside edge. Simple."

"Simple," said Tess warily.

Eric smiled suddenly, "I'm telling you this, but the truth is, I only found out after I'd been skating for years. It comes naturally."

"Sure," said Tess.

"It does," he said. "It's really just like your roller blades, only it's easier." Tess said, "Sure," again. Joanna came and sat down beside them, her own skates slung over her shoulder.

"Look at the loving brothers," she said. Out on the ice, Martin was battling Seth for a flat stone puck, sticks clattering, blades scraping great gouges of ice. She watched a moment longer and then began untying her boots.

Eric said with a quick grin, "This should be interesting. I haven't done it in a lot of years."

She looked up and said dryly, "I somehow don't think you'll have forgotten how."

He stood up, looking out at the lake. Martin drove Seth into the edge of the cleared ice, tripped him with his stick, and toppled him into the piled snow. "Not a lot changes," Eric said with a smile. He took a few long, easy strokes out across the ice and then stopped, trying his edges, circling gently one way and then the other. Seth got to his feet, and he and Martin stood at the side, leaning on their sticks, watching. Sara and Annie, coming down from the cabin with their own skates over their shoulders, stopped by the shore.

Eric began skating in a wide circle, using the whole of the ice, slowly at first and then faster, crossing one leg smoothly in front of the other with each stroke. He flipped around, skating backward, faster still, arms lightly extended, glancing over his shoulder, gathering momentum. He turned and then jumped a half turn clear of the ice, landing facing backward again. He skated another circuit, increased his speed, and jumped a full turn, landing easily on one leg, the other gracefully extended. Harry cheered. Eric did two more quick turns, accelerated again, and leapt a circle and a half, landing on a backward-reaching skate, stayed on it, spun in a circle, and stopped. Sara applauded with mittened hands.

"Will you look at him," she said wistfully. "Who'd believe he was fifty?"

"Show-off," said Annie. Seth came skating in from the snow border and skidded to a hockey stop in front of Joanna.

"Oh, Christ, I hate the bastard," he said.

Eric skated slowly back to join them. He was sweating and breathing hard, and he grinned at Joanna and said, "I remember." He held out his hand to her. She took it and skated with him back to the center of the ice, and he waltzed her gracefully around in a circle before returning to the dock. He released Joanna's hand and held his out for Tess. Tess sat unmoving.

"You lied to me," she said. He looked at her seriously, dropping his hand slightly.

"I've never lied to you."

"You lied to me about the roller blades."

"What?" He looked puzzled.

"You said you couldn't do them. You said you tried them in San Francisco and spent four hours on your behind." She paused, solemnly. "Not if you can skate like that, you didn't." He looked confused, then his eyes crinkled at the corners as he remembered, and he laughed.

"Well, maybe I exaggerated." He held out his hand again, smiling winningly. Reluctantly, Tess slouched off the dock and onto her skates. She gripped his hand and took a couple of scraping steps. "Good." He took her other hand and skated backward, leading her out onto the lake, his hands beneath her wrists. "Just like you're walking, but turn your legs out a little. Nice and smooth. Let them glide. That's it, that's it. Fine." She giggled and pushed harder with one foot. The other slid forward and she flailed with one hand. He swung around, steadying her easily, his arm behind her waist.

"I can't."

"You can. Come on, Tess, trust me, trust me. You won't fall." She took a deep breath and leaned into his arm and felt his balance and his grace flow from him into her.

"Hey," she said, "I can."

DANYA AND AARON stopped halfway down the track from the cabin, seeing the fire, the skaters, and the watchers, bright splashes of color against the white of the lake and the grays and dark greens of the shore.

"Oh, look at this," Aaron said. "This is unreal. This is Currier and Ives country." He was a tall, angular boy with curling black hair, his metal-framed glasses adding intensity to sharp, blue-gray eyes. His eyes were like her father's, and Danya acknowledged the complexity that added to his attractiveness. "Oh, this is great, Danya. I've never seen anything like it." She shrugged closer into her Navaho-patterned duffle coat, keeping the hood up over her head, half concealing her face.

"I used to hate coming back here," she said. He turned to look down at her, his hand instinctively tucking in behind her arm.

"I know," he said gently. "You always told me that. I mean," he stopped, "I do understand, but it seems, I don't know, such an innocent place."

"Yeah." She pushed the hood back and ruffled her tangled brown hair with one slow hand. "I guess it really is." She looked at the lake again, hearing shouts and laughter, and her smooth young forehead wrinkled as she studied the skaters. "Oh," she said softly. "Oh, look."

"That blond guy teaching the kid can skate," Aaron said.

"It's Eric," Danya said. "That's my Uncle Eric. I haven't seen him for so many years." She smiled slowly, watching, and then turned to Aaron. "That's Molly's dad," she said.

"*Oh.*" He looked down at the lake for a long while. "Oh. I see." He was quiet, and then, taking her hand, he said, "He's sure some skater, anyhow."

"He taught us all," Danya said softly. She hesitated, then tugged Aaron's hand. "Come on, I've got to see him," she said. Holding his hand, she ran, giggling and sliding in the snow, down to the shore. "Uncle Eric," she shouted, waving, "Uncle Eric, it's me." He stopped, turning toward her, his arm still supporting Tess. He looked uncertain. She ran down from the shore, out onto the ice, her heavy black boots skidding.

"Danya." She nodded and stood smiling, looking up at him. "Danya, you've grown up so beautifully." His voice was very soft. He turned to Annie, who'd skated out from the fireside. "She's just like you."

"Oh, I was never that pretty, Eric," Annie said. She hugged her daughter and shook Aaron's hand. Danya reached up shyly to Eric and he leant down, awkwardly, to kiss her, still balancing Tess.

"Is this my baby cousin?" Danya said, staring at Tess. Tess looked at her warily from under the shelter of Eric's arm.

"I'm eleven," she said, and then she grinned and added good-naturedly, "but I guess I'm still the littlest."

"Don't tell me about it," Seth shouted, skating in from the hockey game with Martin and David in pursuit. "Tess and I are forming a Youngest Child Liberation Army. Membership, two. Danya!" He flung his hockey stick, letting it clatter on the ice, grasped her in his arms and spun on his skates, swinging her in a wild circle before setting her down.

"Uncle Seth." She hugged him and kissed him, the reserve she'd shown to Eric having vanished. "How are you? How's Maria-Luisa?"

"Fine!"

"And Antonio and Lucia?"

"Fine. Great. They missed you terribly when you left." He paused. "So did I."

"I missed you," she said quietly. "Seth, this is Aaron Feldstein." She reached her arm out to the boy. He stood silent, a foot from the shore, staring at Seth. When he moved, it was with a sudden awkward jerk, as if startled awake. He stepped gingerly across the ice. He shook Seth's hand carefully, and then Eric's and Tess's. His eyes went warily back to Seth.

"Is anybody else maybe hungry?" Miriam said. Danya turned quickly.

"Hi, Grandma. Grandpa."

"Only there's a turkey cooking away up there by itself, and maybe it would be a good idea to eat it."

"Right, Miriam," Annie said. "Okay, work party. Up to the cabin, everyone. Kids, run ahead and set the table. Don't wake up Merrilee yet if she's sleeping. We'll be up in a moment." She began untying her skates. Martin skated around collecting hockey sticks and discarded hats and gloves from the ice. Eric led Tess to the dock and helped her untie her laces. Sara joined her parents, pulling her skates off and stuffing her feet into boots before helping her father to his feet.

Danya and Aaron walked ahead up the snow-filled track. At the top, Aaron turned and looked back toward the lake, hidden now by trees. "Danya, I've got to get something straight," his dark brows lowered. "That's your *uncle*?"

"Who, Eric?"

"No. No. Seth," he said carefully.

"Yeah, my Uncle Seth. Come on, I want to see Merrilee."

"Now wait a moment, wait a moment. Is that *Seth Levine?*" Danya looked blank.

"Yeah," she said again. "I told you about him. I stayed with him in Italy last summer."

"Well, yeah. I know that. I mean, I know you're a Levine and you had an Uncle Seth, but I didn't know he was Seth Levine." Danya widened her eyes and tugged at a curl of brown hair.

"Well, what else would he be?" she said. Aaron slapped his palm against his forehead.

"I don't know why I'm asking. I've seen enough pictures, for God's sake. He's your uncle. Seth Levine is your uncle."

"Aaron, have you got a problem with this?"

"Seth Levine who wrote *Hotel Tibet* is your uncle?"

"Yeah," Danya said. "I guess he did."

"I don't believe this. Your uncle." He shook his head, glasses jiggling, wild hair tumbling. "Seth Levine."

"He's my dad's little brother," Danya said.

—

BY THE TIME EVERYBODY gathered in a crowded ring around the round table, dragging in chairs and a couple of old crates to sit on, it was dark, and a new flurry of snow swirled against the window. The meal was laid out, and Martin carved, quarrying the big turkey down to scraped bone. Harry argued at every cut. Argument pursued the vegetables around the table, waxing stronger as the meal progressed. Aaron sat, awed, right across a table from Seth Levine. But whenever Seth said anything, Martin and Harry talked over his words. Aaron ended up talking with Eric and David about roof joists, instead.

The women retreated as soon as dinner was finished, leaving the kitchen full of piled dishes and pots and male disputation. Tess, deciding to be a woman, followed Miriam and her mom and Annie and Sara into the living room. Merrilee was already sitting on the couch, her feet up on a chair, her hands on her stomach, while Danya sat cross-legged on the floor at her feet.

"I could go to sleep," Merrilee yawned luxuriantly. "All I've done all day is sleep, and still I could go to sleep."

"Enjoy it," Annie said, stretching out beside her, "In three weeks you can kiss sleep good-bye."

Tess thought she could go to sleep too. She lay on her back on the rug, her eyes closed, blond pigtails splayed out either side of her head. She crossed her hands over her full stomach and soaked in the good stuffed feeling and the comforting murmur of voices flowing over her head. The women's sounds were soft and contented, the men's boisterous and quarrelsome. She drifted off, warm and dozy.

When David and Aaron came in, stamping snow off their boots, announcing a sled race, Joanna and Annie groaned and waved them away. But Danya got up, and then Merrilee, and then Tess, until they were all in the newly scrubbed kitchen, clambering back into coats and mittens and boots. "I need the john first," Danya said cheerfully.

"The lantern's right by the door," Annie said. She paused. "Do you want company?" She made her voice casual, but she watched her daughter's face.

"I've got Aaron," Danya said happily. She grabbed his hand and tramped through the lean-to shed and out the back door. When they were outside, in the dark, she said. "I used to be so scared out here. I'd lie to everybody. I'd sneak out and squat down and pee by the door, then hide in the shed until it was time to go back. I used to have a nightmare. It was awful. It was about Molly and me at the same time, and a dark place, just past that scary tree." She pointed and then saw, in the dim light beyond the circle of yellow thrown by the lantern, that the tree she was pointing to, the tree that leaned over the privy, was gone. "That's funny," she said, still holding Aaron's hand.

He stood at the back of the privy as she went in. The lantern sent light glowing out through cracks in the planks. "Keep talking," she said. He stood dumbfounded.

"What about?"

"Anything. I want to be sure you're there."

"I wouldn't go anywhere, Dan. I know you're scared."

"I'm not that scared anymore. But talk anyhow."

He was silent for a moment and then he said, "I love your family."

"Do you? You can have them."

"No, really. I can't believe this Thanksgiving. It's like you read about in books. All those amazing, authentic people. The skating and all. Sort of the American dream family."

"The American nightmare family. Did you hear my dad and grandpa?"

"Yeah. Still."

"I like *your* family," Danya said fervently. She meant it. They went to synagogue and kept the customs her own family had abandoned two generations ago. Aaron's mother had showed her how to light the Shabbat candles, and it had pleased her in some deep-rooted place within her she hadn't known existed. "They've kept their roots."

"They're pretty boring," Aaron said. She was silent. "You okay?"

"Yeah. I'm having a crap."

"Oh, fine," he said. He waited patiently. They had no embarrassments. They camped and climbed together all the time, and he knew her body intimately, though they hadn't had sex.

"Well, that was nice," she said. She came out of the privy, holding up the lantern, lighting his face. "Mom says if we don't have a flush toilet next year, she's never coming back."

"Does she mean it?"

Danya shrugged. "She says it every year."

———

MARTIN AND ERIC came down from the toolshed carrying the second sled between them. The first lay on the snow in the circle of light in front of the cabin, with Merrilee sitting prettily in the center of it, her feet drawn up a little awkwardly, her cheeks colored by the cold air. Each was a big four-man toboggan of polished wood with a graceful curl at the front. They looked simple, but could run stunningly fast.

"Hey, what are you doing?" Martin said, setting his end of the second sled down. "She can't ride on that."

David picked up the sled rope and said, patiently, "I'm

just giving her a little tow around, Dad. Do you think I'm an idiot?"

"I don't know sometimes. Come on, David, be careful. She could fall off."

"I'm going two miles an hour, Dad."

"I'm fine," Merrilee said cheerily. Martin grumbled something, stood back a moment longer, and then rushed forward and clambered clumsily onto the toboggan behind Merrilee. He folded his big knees around her, steadying her with his arms.

"Okay, now you can pull."

David leaned against the rope, panting. "God, Dad, it's like pulling an elephant." He dug his boot toes into the snow. Then Eric ran and joined him, grabbing a loop of the rope, and they towed Merrilee and Martin carefully up and down in the circle of light.

"Slow down," Martin shouted. "This is my grandchild here. Slow down." Merrilee leaned back against him, laughing.

"Fine, fine," she said easily. "That's my thrill for the day. I'm going in by the fire." She got up carefully and stepped off onto the snow, with David holding her hand. He took her into the cabin and then came back out again. He stood in front of the sleds and clapped his hands together.

"Right, teams. Ben-Hur toboggan race, from the cabin to the lake, no rules—pushing, shoving, collisions, cheating all allowed. Let's go." He grabbed his father's sleeve. "Come on, Dad, you're on mine. Let's use that weight for something, for a change."

They made teams, mixing and swapping, piling extras onto overloaded toboggans, and raced each other chaotically down the steep track, colliding and spilling, burying themselves in snow. The run, polished by the sleds, got faster and faster, until they were skidding far out onto the lake at the end. One by one, people dropped out, seduced by the warm lights of the cabin after the long trudge up the hill, until eventually only one toboggan was left, with Seth and Eric, Joanna and Tess to man it.

"One more run," Seth pleaded, climbing the last few feet to the cabin. "It's great now. Really fast."

Joanna shook snow from her jeans. "Oh, I've had enough. You go."

But Seth said, "No, look, Dad and Mom have come out to watch." Joanna looked up. The two old people, seeming small and vulnerable, stood side by side, silhouetted by the lights. "Let's give them a show."

"Oh, my legs," Joanna moaned. She smiled wryly and nodded. "Okay."

"Right," Eric said, "Seth in front, Tess on behind. You and I push. Let's see some real speed now." Seth braced his legs against the curve at the front, and Tess tucked herself in behind him. Joanna and Eric put a hand each on Tess's shoulders and the wood of the toboggan.

"Come on, push, push," Tess shouted. They ran together, accelerating the sled down the slope. Joanna leapt on, wrapping her legs around her daughter, and Eric gave a last shove and jumped on behind her. The toboggan streaked down the track, rumbling and crackling on the ice. Tess shouted, "Great!"

"Go for it," said Joanna.

"Steer," shouted Seth from the front.

"Steer?" said Eric.

"Come on, Eric, steer. Steer!"

"You steer, Seth."

"I can't steer. I'm at the front. The guy at the back steers, Eric. You know that."

"Does he?" Eric asked innocently.

"Will one of you steer?" Joanna said.

"There's a tree, Eric," Seth jammed his feet against the sled, ducking.

"I'm sure it's the guy at the front who steers."

"It's the guy at the front who hits the fucking tree, Eric. Steer!"

"Okay. Here we go." Eric braced himself, jammed his boot heel into the snow and threw his weight to the opposite side. The toboggan swerved ferociously, missing the tree.

"Shit," said Seth. Then it missed the bend in the track as well, slewed up the bank, ploughed over a birch sapling, brushed a scrub maple and flipped, and threw all four into the snow. There was a brief snowy silence.

Then Eric said warily, "Everybody still alive?"

"Christ, I hate you," said Seth.

"Sorry about that. I misjudged. You okay, Tess? Jo?"

"I've got snow down everywhere," said Tess from the darkness. Joanna reached out and clasped Eric's hand on one side and Seth's on the other and lay grinning up at the sky.

"I love you both," she said. Eric gripped her hand. He looked up through the pine branches. The clouds had blown off and the clear sky was whiter than it was black.

"Oh, Jo, look at the stars," he said. He tightened his grip and then let her hand go and jumped up. "Come on, Tess, time to get warm." He righted the toboggan. "Hop on. I'll pull you up." Tess climbed on the toboggan, brushing snow off as she did. Eric picked up the rope and trotted lightly up the track, the sled gliding easily. Seth lay back in the snow and closed his eyes and smiled. Then he rolled over, on top of Joanna.

"You know," he said, looking down at her dim face, "that guy does this discretion thing well."

She laughed, looking fondly after Eric in the starlight. "Oh, he does everything well," she said.

Seth shook his head. "No, he doesn't, Jo," he said seriously. "For a start, he can't steer a sled." She looked back at Seth. "I love you, too," he said. He dropped his head, found her mouth, and kissed her long and gently. "Can I make love to you again?"

"Here? In the snow?"

He winced. "What I had in mind was tonight and in my room."

Joanna raised her head. "What, you mean just tramp right through the cabin, in front of everyone, and into your bed?"

"No." Seth smiled in the darkness, kissed her again, and sat up. "Why do you think Dad put me in the big end bedroom, Jo? With the double bed? And the outside door?"

She sat up too. "I was wondering about that. It seemed a bit odd, Martin and Annie crammed into that little room by mine. I heard Martin grumping about it too."

"All you have to do, Jo, is go out to the privy and come around that side. Dad's probably wondering why you haven't. Or, at least, assuming you had."

"The old devil," she said, smiling.

"Martin imagines I get the room because I'm the prodigal son, of course. But the truth is, I'm forty-five years old and Dad still thinks I need help getting laid." He stood up, held out his hand, lifted her to her feet, and wrapped his arms around her body, worming them in beneath her coat. He kissed her again, slowly and sensuously, fingers slipping expertly beneath her clothes. "Jo, what about Italy?" he said. He paused when she did not answer, and said carefully, "I'm not pressuring you for anything. Sara's coming anyhow, so it will be real easy and comfortable. Just a family Christmas. Nothing even Tess would mind. I promise."

She stood still for a moment and then withdrew reluctantly from his embrace. "No, Seth. I'm going home. I've got to get my daughter back into school. Though to tell the truth, I think she's learned more in four weeks with Eric than in the last two years there. And then . . . " she paused. "I'm going to the Edelweiss Cafe and tell that asshole John to give me my job back. And a raise." She grinned as she said it, but Seth was solemn.

"And that's it then, is it, Jo? You're going to be a waitress in Colorado for the rest of your life?"

She shrugged. "Not for the rest of my life, Seth. For a while. Until I get some money together."

"About how long will that take, Jo? On a waitress's pay?"

Joanna stepped back from him, her boots crunching on frozen snow. She said unhappily, "I know what the problems are, Seth. You don't have to point them out."

"Will you accept some help?"

"No."

He sighed and stepped away from her too. His shoulders touched a fir branch, bringing down a soft cascade of snow. "What are you afraid of, Jo?" he said.

"Nothing. I'm not afraid."

He laughed softly and ran his gloved hands down his sleeves, brushing the snow off. His hands stilled and he stood quietly. "I've never known anyone so fearless," he said. "You'd have gone to the gates of hell for your brother. But now you're afraid. What do you think will happen, Jo, if you just once take a little bit of the help you're always so willing to give? What are you so scared of?"

She turned away from him and began walking up the snowy

hill. He ran after her and stopped her, his hand on her arm. "Answer me, Jo."

"It's not for me. I'm scared for my daughter."

"It's for you. Don't hide behind Tess."

"I'm not." She pulled away from his arm. "Seth, I've been here before. I know the signs. I'm getting too involved with you."

"Because I offered you money?"

"Because you're offering me love." She shook her head angrily. "Aren't you?"

"Yes. But you can have the money without the love if you prefer. I really want to help." He took her shoulders in both hands, peering at her in the starlight. "I'm perfectly capable of doing that, Jo. I'll put it in the hands of a lawyer, and you'll never hear from me. I promise. If you really want me out of your life, I'll go. But you have to tell me that, and you have to say it to my face. Otherwise, I'm staying."

"I don't want you out of my life," she said. "But I'm still afraid for Tess. You don't understand. I get involved and then I get hurt. Tough shit, that's life. But Tess gets involved too. Each time. And each time, Tess gets hurt. And Tess gets harder. She's eleven going on forty. It's no accident that the only man she's ever gotten along with is my brother."

"She gets along with me."

"Wait till you try to get closer."

"That's just what I'm planning to do, Jo. I'll wait. I'll wait until she wants to get closer to me."

"What if she never does?"

"Then I'll accept that. But I don't think that's what will happen. And you don't think so either. It's you you're scared for, Jo, not Tess." She tried to turn away, but he still held her arms. He tightened his grip suddenly. "Do you remember snow angels?" he said.

"What?"

"Snow angels. You know, you fall back in the snow and wave your arms and legs."

"Seth?" she said, laughing. "What are you talking about?"

"Don't you remember? It makes a picture of an angel in the snow."

"I remember, Seth," she said, still laughing. "But why are you asking me now?"

"Make me a snow angel, Jo." He smiled encouragingly in the pale light.

"What, here?"

"You always used to, when we were little. You always made great snow angels. I used to love to watch you, the way you'd let yourself fall straight back into the snow." He paused and then said, "I never had the nerve. I used to try and just sit down and drop back, real carefully, but not you. And yours were always beautiful. Make me a snow angel, Jo."

Joanna stood in the starlight, a drift of untouched snow behind her, the shadowy firs above. She held her arms out from her sides, experimentally, and glanced back over her shoulder. Then she grinned and stood up straight, closed her eyes, and leaned back onto her heels. Holding herself rigid, she tipped back toward the snow. She slipped through air for an instant and then into the warm circle of his arm. He held her firm, and she lay straight across his arm for a moment. Then she stumbled, gripped his shoulder, and pulled herself erect. "What'd you do that for? I can't do it unless you let me fall."

"Just showing you I could catch you," he said. He released her and then caught her hand. "Come on, let's do it together. Double snow angels." He stood beside her, the drift behind them, extending his free arm out to the side. She laughed delightedly and stood straight again.

"Ready?" she asked.

"No. Not ready." She looked at him and smiled, and he laughed. "This is idiotic, but I really find this scary. I really do."

"Seth," she said patiently. "You've done a few scary things in your life. What was that thing you climbed in Nepal? And what about the little foray into Afghanistan?"

"That's different. I didn't do them backward. I like to see where I'm going."

"Don't be a baby. Come on."

"What if there's a stump or a rock or something?"

"Then you'll probably die. Come on." She jerked his hand.

"Okay, okay, don't rush me."

"Jesus, I remember this always took half an hour when you were a kid."

"Right. Right. I'm ready." He took a deep breath, closed his eyes, and clutched her hand. They fell backward together, through darkness, into the snow. "I did it, I did it," Seth said.

"Great. Now wave your arms and legs."

"How's that?"

"I don't know. I can't see until we get up."

Seth sat up. "We can't see anyhow. It's pitch dark." He shrugged and fell back into the snow, dragging her down into his arms. "I'm sure they're beautiful," he said. "Yours will be, anyhow. That's you, Jo. That's how you did everything. That's how you've lived your whole life. Wonderful and beautiful and free."

"And look where it's got me," she said.

He tightened his grip and then rolled over on his back, pulling her on top of him. "This is where it's got you, Jo. Trust yourself." He put his hands behind her head, drew her down, and found her mouth. He kissed her, his gloved fingers catching in her snowy hair. He released her and said, "Let's get married, Jo."

"Married?" She lifted her head, startled.

"Take the plunge. Make a snow angel. Let go."

"But married?"

"Yeah. You know. That thing our parents did that we got too grown up for?" She laughed softly. He said, "I don't feel so grown-up anymore." She smiled down at him and then rested her head gently on his shoulder.

"I guess I don't either," she said. She snuggled closer and then raised her head again and peered at him. "Did you really mean that, about waiting for Tess?"

"Of course."

"How long, Seth?" she said solemnly. "It could be a pretty long time."

He reached up and stroked her hair clumsily and smiled. "Well, Jo, I've waited forty years for you already. I suppose I could wait another forty. It really depends on how you feel about older men."

She laughed, and dropped her head down again, holding him closer. "Just fine," she said. "Older men are just fine." She sighed. "I would love Christmas in Italy, Seth."

He tightened his grip and grinned, "Oh, good girl."

"No. Wait. I can't. I just can't." She paused. "Kids need roots, Seth."

"I know that," he said, puzzled.

She shook her head quickly. "People think kids are wonderfully free and spontaneous, but they're not. They need roots. Even if it's only a crummy trailer in a dirt backyard. I took Tess away from there. I took her away from her school and her friends. And that's what matters to kids. They don't live in our world, Seth. They live in their own. I took her away and I promised I'd bring her back. Before I do anything, I have to keep that promise. It's more important to a kid then a wonderful vacation in a foreign country." He nodded. "Do you understand?"

"I think so." He smiled gently. "No Christmas in Italy."

"No." She brushed snow from his hair with her mittens. "Seth, could you come to us after the holidays?"

He grinned again and rolled over, kissing her in the snow. "Jo, Jo, I thought you'd never ask." Then he stood up and reached down his hand for hers. They walked up the snowy starlit path and he stopped to kiss her once more before the yellow glow of the cabin intruded through the dark wall of pines.

⟨━⟩

IN HER BEDROOM, Tess wriggled gingerly out of her snow-crusted sweater and jeans, dropped them in a sodden heap on the rag rug, and then kicked them under the bunk bed so they wouldn't be in anyone's way. She pulled off her dripping socks and kicked them after the sweater and jeans. Then she got into her pajamas and sat down on the lower bunk. It suddenly seemed easy just to climb into her own bunk and go to sleep, but Sara was making her cocoa. She pulled her mom's green sweater with the holes in the sleeves on over her pajamas and went sleepily out to the kitchen.

There were fewer people there now, since David and Merrilee and Harry and Miriam had gone to bed. She found a chair by the woodstove and pulled it over to the table. Sara set her cocoa in front of her. She sipped at it slowly, but she was so tired it tasted too sweet and sickly, and she left it, half drunk. Martin brought a game box in from the bookshelves and said, "Monopoly, Tess? We're going to play." She shook her head. But she didn't want to miss anything either; so she stayed by the table, and when Eric came in with wood for the stove and sat down, she pulled her chair in next to his and sat half on each chair, curled up against him. He slipped his arm around her while he, Martin, Seth, and Aaron set up the game. Danya hung over the back of Aaron's chair, whispering suggestions, and Joanna came from washing the cocoa pot and leaned over Eric's shoulders, her arms linked around his neck. Tess curled closer, tracing patterns with her finger in the yellow and red swirls of the oilcloth, while they talked and laughed and rolled dice and moved property cards and houses and hotels around the board. Once or twice she fell asleep, but somebody always woke her, shouting or laughing—usually Martin, complaining about the rules.

"What's that?" he demanded suddenly. Tess straightened up. Eric and Seth were making something out of two matchboxes and a piece of wood. It looked like a bridge and extended across the board from Eric's property to Seth's.

"Shopping mall," Eric said.

"Monopoly doesn't have shopping malls," Martin grumped.

"Has now," said Seth. He drank from a can of Coke, draining it and setting it down on the table. "Want to buy in, Aaron? Fifteen houses buys a shopping mall."

"What?" said Martin.

"Yeah, come on, Aaron, help us wipe Martin out." Eric picked up the dice.

"These partnerships aren't allowed," Martin said.

"Sure they are. Rule Four Hundred and Two. Any party or parties can form any cooperative union that may be deemed advantageous to aforesaid party or parties."

Seth dropped his Coke can on the floor and stamped on it. "When," he said, "you land on *our* shopping mall, you have to spend everything you have on consumer crap, represented by this squashed Coke can." He picked up the flattened metal and slapped it down in the center of the board.

"So who gets the money?" Martin asked suspiciously.

"We do," said Eric.

"Why you? Wait a minute. Who makes up all these rules?"

"I do."

"Why you?" Martin demanded again.

"Because," Eric said patiently, "I'm the biggest. Come on, Martin, you know how life works by now. Stop arguing and play."

Annie wandered through the kitchen with an empty cup, stopped, and watched as Martin sat fuming. "Getting rich, Eric?" she said, studying the table.

"Soon will be. And," he added with satisfaction, "the best way I know. At Martin's expense. Oh, that reminds me." He leaned back in his chair, reached into his jeans pocket, drew out a bunch of coins, and pressed them into her hand. She looked down, puzzled.

"What's this, Eric?"

"Yours." He folded her fingers closed and wrapped his big hand around hers. He smiled without looking up. "Thanks for the loan."

Frank Delaney

A Stranger in Their Midst

INNOCENCE IS NO DEFENCE . . .

In village Ireland of the 1950s, Thomas and Ellen Kane's daughters, Helena and Grace, are gullible young women. Then, into their lives slinks Dennis Sykes, a brilliant and driven man, with a secret history of emotional mayhem and scandal. The Kane girls, lovingly close in fear of their disturbed father, have no defences against this sexual terrorist. As the decades roll forward, the outside world comes to Deanstown. Rural electrification, intended to illuminate the land, brings instead a tragedy as dark as Thomas Kane's moods.

Using great dramatic themes – the drowning of traditional houses in an ancient valley to build a dam, the destruction of a family's inner life – Delaney draws you in deep, into a time, and place, and family, in a novel that will keep you thinking long after you've finished reading.

'*A Stranger in Their Midst* is a dramatic novel. Written in clear, dry prose, it seldom loses its conviction.'   *The Times*

'Blast Frank Delaney. With his devious, seductive writing he keeps story addicts from their sleep.'   *OK!*

'Frank Delaney's *A Stranger in Their Midst* is excellent.'
Woman and Home

'A powerful story vividly told.'   *Choice*

'A good old-fashioned tale of simple Irish folk doing battle with the future.'   *Evening Standard*

ISBN: 0 00 649318 1
(Published in paperback in May 1996)